Miriam Berkley

About the Author

The author of eight books for young adults, CINDY DYSON grew up in Alaska. Her work has appeared in *National Geographic*, *Backpacker*, *First for Women*, *Women's World*, and other publications. She now lives in Glacier Park, Montana.

PRAISE FOR
And She Was

"Dyson deftly peels back the layers of Brandy's persona to reveal the woman behind the blonde hair and high-heeled boots while revealing the layers of tradition, suppression, and mystery shrouding Dutch Harbor. As the story shifts back and forth from the present day through 250 years of Aleutian history, the reader becomes immersed in Aleutian culture and the loss of that culture at the hands of Russian traders, early missionaries, social workers, and World War II relocators. . . . Combining her personal memories of slinging drinks in the 'birthplace of the winds' and meticulous research into Aleutian anthropology, she has created an unforgettable first novel. Highly recommended."

—*Library Journal* (starred review)

"Dyson expertly interlaces Brandy's story, set in 1986, with the vibrant history of the Aleuts, hundreds of years earlier. While relishing the smart prose, bawdy humor, and 1980s references, readers will find themselves rooting for the hard-as-nails blonde as she wrestles her demons and begins to redirect her fate. Dyson delivers an original and provocative first novel."   —*Publishers Weekly*

"Brandy—a natural blonde who likes to believe she was named after liquor—is an emotional cowboy. As the offspring of the ill-fated match between a failed scholar father and a roving femme fatale mother, she's used to being a wanderer. After years of following men from town to town, she knows that she is a drifter, but when she follows her latest fling to a fishing village in the Aleutian Islands, she's reached a whole new level of rootlessness. . . . It might all be too clichéd if Brandy weren't so likable and wild and her surroundings so oddly compelling."   —*Kirkus Reviews*

"An impressive first novel that echoes Kingston's *Woman Warrior* and Proulx's *Shipping News*. . . . Dyson's talent is overwhelmingly evident in her nimble balancing of tribal perspectives and those of her canny, questing protagonist." —*Booklist*

"Dyson packages thought-provoking content in a wonderfully readable form. She evokes the island's harsh beauty and unceasing winds. It would be easy, and less effective, to allow her central characters to become brave and unfortunate stereotypes; hers are real people facing hard dilemmas. Dyson also effectively shares the aboriginal history, neither sidestepping the horrific actions of the island's conquerors or the behavior of the Aleuts, which at times conspires to keep them victims. The resulting novel is far more complex than it first appears, and its impact sneaks up on the reader. What starts out feeling like a light story ends up packing a walloping punch." —*Denver Post*

CINDY DYSON

And She Was

HARPER

NEW YORK • LONDON • TORONTO • SYDNEY

HARPER

Grateful acknowledgment is made to reprint the following:

"And She Was" by David Byrne. Copyright © 1985 Index Music, Inc., and Bleu Disque Music Co., Inc. All rights administered by Warner Bros. Music Corp. All Rights Reserved. Used by permission of Warner Bros. Publications US, Inc., Miami, FL 33014.

"Rodeo Song" by Gaye Delorme. Copyright © 1980. All Rights Reserved. Used by permission of Gaye Delorme, New Westminster, British Columbia, Canada, v311m.

A hardcover edition of this book was published in 2006 by William Morrow, an imprint of HarperCollins Publishers.

First Harper paperback published 2007.

Designed by Jo Anne Metsch

The Library of Congress has catalogued the hardcover edition as follows:

Dyson, Cindy.
    And she was : a novel / Cindy Dyson.—1st ed.
      p. cm.
   ISBN: 978-0-06-059770-2 (acid-free paper)
   ISBN-10: 0-06-059770-4
    1. Women—Alaska—Fiction.   2. Aleutian Islands (Alaska)—Fiction.   3. Aleut women—Fiction. I. Title.

 PS3604.Y75A84   2005
 813'.6—dc22

                                    2005043417

ISBN: 978-0-06-059771-9 (pbk.)
ISBN-10: 0-06-059771-2 (pbk.)

07 08 09 10 11 ❖/RRD 10 9 8 7 6 5 4 3

Dedicated to Mark,

for all the right reasons

Acknowledgments

This book is a conspiracy of sorts. Partly because I wrote it sometimes in the dark of night in a silent house. And partly because I felt clandestine, ashamed to call what I was doing work, because it rarely was. But mostly because I didn't write this book alone. I conspired with others—along phone lines and through e-mails and on my front porch and in bars and on road trips and through the mail. We did it everywhere.

And these are the people, my coconspirators, I wish to thank.

Rick Knecht, Douglas Veltre, and Lydia Black, my archaeology and anthropology experts, for keeping my Aleutian history and prehistory as close as we could make it. And for devoting your work to investigating this fascinating place and people.

Claire Wachtel, my editor, who frustrated and confused me—and who will consider that a compliment—and made me think and write harder than ever.

Marly Rusoff, my agent, my fairy godmother, for liking my stuff enough to say yes.

My critique group—Jake How, Debbie Burke, Marie Martin, Leslie Budewitz, Dixon Rice, Jerry Cunningham, Karen Wills, Todd Cardin, Jeanne Jackson—for your generosity, not just in giving sturdy, difficult critiques but also for velvet gloves and soft voices.

My friends Kim Kozlowski, Keirsten Giles, Kathleen Brown, Jessica Lowell, and Dana Haring for helping me craft not just this book but a wild and rich life. For devoting as much passion and intellectual acumen to a discussion of boots in one minute and a dissection of theology the next. And then in the turn of a cocktail napkin, focusing all that intelligence and compassion on one of us who was wronged or simply defeated.

My sisters, Wendy Shaw and Jana Ozturgut, destined for author-dom themselves, for the culture we created as children and hold dearly as adults. Wendy, for half the good lines. Jana, for nurturing freedom in me.

Jane Dyson, my mom, for setting me on a course that has satisfied my hunger for the unknown, for challenges. Fred Dyson, my dad, for the story with its foggy lakes, and silent canoes, buried gold, and a world of intrigue and possibility. For never checking the price on a book.

Mark, my husband, for the countless nights on the front porch with a bottle of wine and an idea to track or a character to flay. For your mind and your heart. Simon, my son, for bringing to me an under-standing of the power—the vicious, all-consuming power—that is motherhood.

"And She Was"

by Talking Heads, 1986

And she was lying in the grass
And she could hear the highway breathing
And she could see a nearby factory
She's making sure she is not dreaming
See the lights of a neighbor's house
Now she's starting to rise
Take a minute to concentrate
And she opens up her eyes

The world was moving, she was right there with it
  (and she was)

The world was moving she was floating above it (and she was)

And she was drifting through the backyard
And she was taking off her dress
And she was moving very slowly
Rising up above the earth
Moving into the universe
Drifting this way and that
Not touching ground at all
Up above the yard

She was glad about it . . . no doubt about it
She isn't sure where she's gone
No time to think about what to tell them
No time to think about what she's done

And she was looking at herself
And things were looking like a movie
She had a pleasant elevation
She's moving out in all directions

Joining the world of missing persons (and she was)
Missing enough to feel alright (and she was)

world was moving

I felt the edge slip sometimes. When I was there. Nothing obvious, just the disquieting feeling that something had come loose, something had shifted and reassembled itself beneath me. There are places like that. Places that fall apart and re-form right under your boots. Places that can remake you. I think now it's because these places themselves are still undone, still being formed.

The Pacific plate began its slow plunge under the American plate, revealing the red meat of the earth. Along the wound, volcanoes rose like cysts, spewing molten rock into cool water, creating the Aleutian chain seventy million years ago. Strewn like stepping-stones, the 1,400-mile island chain arched from the Alaskan Peninsula to the doorstep of Siberia. And then the winds began, so persistent, so fierce, the islands became the Birthplace of the Wind and the Cradle of Storms. The winds erode from above; the Bering Sea and the Pacific Ocean wear from below.

These islands are at once being born and dying. The battle of fire and water is old and living. Both will keep killing. And keep giving life. This is the edge, the slip. They are, like us, unfinished. People do not possess such places but are possessed by them. I felt it when I was there. I imagine the Aleut people have been feeling it for thousands of years.

And I believe some of them still remember the power that lurks in this land. When I first heard their story, I felt as if the wind were lifting a veil, revealing something I already knew. And some part of my brain stepped back from the edge of extinction and smiled. Their story takes a shape our instincts recognize. The whisper under a shout. And in my mind, I'm standing again on a cliff overlooking that siren ocean, feeling the wind press into my lungs. And I, too, remember.

It blows over the beach below on this sunny, cold afternoon long ago and into the face of Tekuxia as she stands among the rocks and sand. She and thirty others from her village have gathered here at Tumgax's request. Another vision has come to him.

"Something is coming," Tumgax says, leaning forward to peer into each person's eyes. "The wind will bring newcomers from beyond the sea, and everything will change."

Tekuxia shudders when the shaman tells of these visions. Her children whimper with nightmares after such talk. But she listens well.

And she believes.

"Last night I journeyed again to where the spirits talk." Tumgax turns his face to search past the breakers, past the towering rocks guarding the village cove, toward the open ocean. "These newcomers will bring new ways. The People will take up their ideas, their clothing, their lives. Until no one remembers who we were."

Tekuxia shivers under the cold sun. The villagers know there exist people much different from themselves. Twice in her thirty-seven years, parts of a whale-size boat have come to rest on the beach. The bits of iron, holding water-soaked wood together, were quickly stripped and hammered into knives and awls, their blades wearing much better than stone. And she has heard the tales of a people to the west, beyond the last island. But these tales have grown so old that they now sound like myths serving only to warn the young men not to venture too far from home.

"When they come," Tumgax continues, "we will welcome them. We will embrace their God and their *toion* and everything will change."

As the gathering breaks, Tekuxia scoops up her little girl and holds her close, feeling the dark shiny hair under her cheek. Tekuxia does not fear for herself; she feels certain her generation will pass before the change. But Aya. Aya will see it all. She sets the girl down and kneels in front of her.

"Aya, you must remember what I am going to tell you. Say you will."

The girl looks up, surprised by her mother's urgent tone.

"Yes, Mama."

"These hands," Tekuxia says, turning the sand-caked palms upward in her own, "in them you hold your fate, and in no one's hands but your own does your future rest. Do you understand?"

Aya understands only the strange desperation in her mother's voice, only the first notions of fear. But she nods.

"Yes, Mama."

In the years to come, Aya will listen to her mother repeat this strange ceremony, the turning up of her palms and the heavy words. But she will not come to understand them until her mother is long gone and the change has blown down upon her like a williwaw.

Hurl yourself forward 220 years and fly inland to another girl learning at her mother's side. My mother's legacy of wisdom was no less insistent, no less burdened by a maternal instinct to warn her daughter of what she fears.

"Brandy," she says, buttoning up her blouse, but not too far, as I gaze into the depths of her cleavage, "you always want to take up the hem some on a store-bought dress. At least two inches. Got that?"

"Yes, Mama."

Two inches. Two inches.

The water bed sloshes with the rhythm as I repeat the words in a whisper, scared to forget anything even then.

"And," my mother says, bending forward at the waist to invert her blond curls and burden them with spray, "this Aqua Net is the best shit on the market."

Aqua Net. Aqua Net.

She takes my face between her two hands as she passes by me for the door. "Such a pretty girl," she says, and I squint to see past the barriers of black-clumped lashes. I squint to see into the wreck of my mother's eyes. She throws her customary parting over her shoulder as she leaves. "Be bad enough so they call you good." The smell of perfume and hair spray and a protean dampness lingers in the room.

Of course, my mother passes on more of her hard-earned wisdom. I learn about padded bras, and perfume samplers, lying down to zip up tight jeans. And I believed as a five-year-old, as a fifteen-year-old, as a twenty-five-year-old, that a short skirt and the right hair spray are a girl's sword and talisman.

And as a thirty-one-year-old, when the wind blew me into the Aleutians in 1986, that's all I had.

hear the breathing

I am blond, and that's where most of my problems started. Not just the problems of the moment, but yesterday's and last year's and a lifetime's. I had let my hair get away with too much. I saw it now reflected in the dark window, those feathers of light surrounding the oval of my face. I could see the ferry's lounge behind me, striped with orange glow. And I could see right through myself, into the black ocean, rolling like a great wind-billowed tarp. The split worlds met here at my image on thin, cold glass. For a moment, I felt as if that reflection were as real as me.

The ferry had followed a string of islands, simply called the Chain, for three days. I'd rented a cabin, but mostly I'd been sitting here watching. I'd seen the Fourth of July fireworks showering over the water at King Cove when we stopped to unload and reload. I'd seen the piers of Cold Bay, False Pass, Akutan. With each stop the passenger list dwindled, until now it was only me and a group of about twenty guys, heading for the fishing grounds. Tonight we would arrive at the end of the line, Unalaska Island.

Even on such a big boat, heaves of water had made me sick, not enough to embarrass myself by throwing up, but enough to tinge the excitement with greenish-yellow edges. I sipped carefully at a whiskey sour and focused past myself into the blackness.

Dutch Harbor appeared suddenly beyond my reflection as the ferry rounded an invisible point. I watched the lights get closer. All two of them. The ferry terminal was a scrap of light, echoed over the water and hushed everywhere else by mountain black. It looked like a last stand against the night. An outpost of civilization, surrounded but fighting.

At that moment of first seeing, I was afraid of it, this tiny island in the midst of so much nothing. I wanted to stay in this lounge, let the ferry disgorge its last passengers and turn back to the real world with me safely on board. And if I'd had something to go back to, I probably would have done just that. The fear was a premonition, the barest inkling that this place would take something from me, something that would change everything. I was wrong, as it turned out. It wasn't what the *island* would take, but what *I* would take, what I would steal.

I smoothed on fresh lipstick, finger combed my hair, and swallowed hard. I wasn't sure why I'd come. A rush of hazy thinking, involving, of course, a cute guy with curly hair and no long-range goals.

Of course, I was following a man. Women just don't come out here on their own.

Not women like me anyway.

It was near morning when the ferry docked, still dark. I grabbed my duffel bag, zipped up my jacket, and hustled down the gangplank right into his arms. I knew I looked good walking through pools of shadow and light on the dock in my tight jeans, pale suede boots, and jacket. I sucked in the ocean-dock smells of dead fish, wet air, and diesel. Smells near the ocean feel ancient to me, like all earth's history is in that smell. It's entirely right, entirely mysterious. He smelled the same way—his gray-green oilskin coat, his mud-caked boots, his salt-stiff hair.

We kissed. I could feel his desire to make this reunion more than it was, feel him try to make it one of those cinematic kisses you'd expect when two lovers meet by the sea after a long separation.

"I missed you," he said, soulful, honest.

The wind blew, snapping my pant legs against my boots and Thad's oilskin against his legs. I felt flimsy and ill prepared in that wind, the way it rushed at me and over me. But at the same time it carried an undertone, a trailing hint that it shouldn't feel this way, that I wasn't living up to its potential.

A sudden irritation flashed through me. "I can't wait to get you to the hotel room," I murmured, refusing his interpretation of this script, of me.

He smiled and kissed me again.

Thad checked us into the HiTide, which is the upscale hotel on the island. It has its own bar. Room 114 was covered in paneling. Burgundy flowers amid green trees draped the bedspread, and the same print, reversed into a perverse forest of burgundy trees and green flowers, dressed a child-size window. The stiff fabric shuffled rather than flounced in the drafts from the air vent underneath.

He unbuttoned my jeans as he kneeled in front of me, his breath warm and moist against my abdomen as he exhaled, suddenly cool as he inhaled.

"I missed you," he murmured, peeking up at me from between my tits.

He had that way about him of charging his gaze with meaning, taking his time, touching with intention. I laughed and stepped back, erecting a barrier with my eyes. I rocked my hips down through the jeans, slowly, hands caressing my thighs.

"Just watch," I said. I had to be lightly aggressive, formidably coy until his arousal overcame this tendency toward significance. I could not tolerate significance.

"Come here," he said.

I shook my head and pulled off my shirt, letting it drag my hair across my face. Then I slid my hand into my panties, a sigh slipping through my teeth.

As he approached this time, I didn't need to push him away. His eyes closed, hands fumbled, groped for my crotch. I'd won. I'd enforced my rule so well he didn't know there were any. The victory freed a hot melt of arousal. He didn't speak as I pressed his mouth to my nipple, didn't open his eyes as our genitals collided, then mine gave way.

Thad was beautiful and energetic, as always. I faked the second orgasm, just to keep up with him. As I lay in the warm glow, I watched him through pretend-closed eyes until he fell to sleep, cheeks still flushed. I'd just come eight hundred miles over the Bering Sea to be with him, and I didn't know why.

I couldn't relax, lying right next to so much contentment, so I dressed, grabbed my jacket, and walked into the dim corridor. Outside, from the mountains to the east, asterisks of light flared in the valleys, sending streaks of color across the hills. I watched three huskies sitting on protruding bumps of a steep hillside across from the motel. Their ruffs stood up in the breeze. They each looked unwaveringly toward the ocean. I followed their gaze and let the wind smooth over my face until my ears crusted with cold, until the last radiating rings of my orgasm dissipated. Then, prompted by something I couldn't sense, the huskies bounded simultaneously down the hill, silent and smooth. They loped around a curving dirt road out of sight.

The light had spread over the island now, and I turned to survey my new home. The parking lot was half filled with trucks and rust-splotched vans. The HiTide stretched rectangular and flat along a dirt road, its double glass doors smudged with handprints and dog snuffles. Two ashtrays flanked the doors, and the wind dashed a steady stream of butts over their sides. I walked the row of trucks and vans, the little white and brown pilgrims skittering along with me. Below the hotel, water lapped at muddy shores. Tall grasses grew where they could. I could see the blackened stumps of forgotten pilings jutting here and there. The wheelhouse of a submerged fishing boat lay a few feet off-shore. To the north stretched the road I'd traveled earlier, a potholed two-lane flanked by immense canneries, Quonset huts and prefab metal buildings offering prop repair, diving services, welding, web patching. The town seemed to exist outside of time. Nothing—not the utilitarian buildings, the signs, the vehicles—spoke of any certain year. Or any decade for that matter. It was 1986, but I got the disconcerting feeling that this place had looked the same ten years ago and would look the same ten years from now.

Toward the south, the road looped around a bay, crossed water, and disappeared between two hills. Another hill, grass covered with bending fireweed below outcrops of weathered rock, rose in front of the hotel. But everywhere else it was mountains. Deceptively soft with sunrise green at the bases, stretching to fog-streaked rock at the tops. Mountain upon mountain as far as I could see. And eagles. I spotted six right by the HiTide, perched on poles or cliffs or flying low over the water, seagulls scattering from their paths.

The steady wind only intensified the illusion of silence—until the whine of a truck engine separated itself from the rush. I turned to see a pale green, rust-spotted king cab round the bend, spewing arches of gravel behind each tire. It skidded to a stop. The passenger door was flung open.

"Get the fuck out." The driver, a man with his baseball cap pulled low on his forehead, shoved someone out the open door. He floored the gas, making a clumsy start on the loose gravel. The passenger door flopped several times before the truck's momentum slammed it shut.

A lumpy figure emerged from the road dust. She clutched a sacklike purse to her chest, making her short-legged walk even more awkward. "Asshole. Fucker. Pisshead." She muttered a string of names as she crossed the road.

She saw me just before she shuffled into me. Or rather she saw my chest. A good six inches shorter, she had to take a step back to look at my face. "Shit," she said, dropping her purse with a thud between us. "Gimme a cigarette."

I slipped a Marlboro from my pack and handed it to her between two fingers, followed by a cheap lighter. Her face disappeared into the seamless cup of her hands and reappeared in a hefty flow of smoke.

She inhaled a few times, then looked up. "Shit," she said again. "Fuckhead."

She wore new jeans and a tight raspberry T-shirt with an airbrushed unicorn under an open windbreaker. But what I noticed first were her rings. Every finger had at least one. Turquoise, gold nugget, zircon glinted each time she moved her hands. She was five feet tall, with a round body from which her short arms and legs protruded like sprouts on a potato. Her black hair had been meticulously curled several hours earlier. She wore black boots with high heels that she rocked on from side to side. One of the heels kept kicking out, threatening to come loose.

She eyed me long enough to make me feel uneasy. "White girl. Fuckin' blond, white girl." She didn't say it like an insult, just an observation.

"Very white," I said, then added, "very fuckin' white," just to win her over.

She smiled a touch, not with her mouth so much as with her eyes. Her smooth lids curved downward at the outer corners, and when something of a smile snuck up on her, they slid out and up. She had beautiful eyes, Aleut eyes. "Come on," she said, picking up her bag. "I grabbed his stash when he was in the head."

I couldn't remember the last time a woman, and only a woman, had asked me to snort coke with her. Sure, plenty of women were usually around, attached or attachable women. But the drugs were all acquired and doled out by men. I felt off balance, a little wary.

She had already slung her purse over one shoulder and started toward the road. She looked back at me without expression. I glanced at the HiTide, where I knew Thad was sleeping sprawled naked across the bed. I pictured his curly hair on the pillow, the curve of his chest muscles over the steady rise and fall of his sleepy lungs. What the hell. The island had cast its spell, and I was used to going along.

She nodded as I fell in step with her. "Bellie," she said.

"What?"

"Bellie."

"Oh," I said. "Brandy."

"Brandy?"

"Yeah."

My name comes straight from the liquor cabinet. I can picture the scene: Mom and Dad bring home their new baby girl, set her on the couch, coo a bit, adjust the blanket. What should we call her? I don't know. How 'bout Victoria? That's from Dad, of course. What, you want her to grow up to be all snooty? Jane, then, after your mom. A gouging stare. Teresa? Amy? Jan? The possibilities flash between them, threatening regrets, resentments. Nothing comes without baggage. Dad gets up, yanks open the liquor cabinet. He pours amber liquid into a glass. Get me one, she says. He brings glasses and the bottle over, sets them on the coffee table. I'm not quite asleep and Mom runs the back of her hand along my cheek. Dad holds the bottle over her glass and is pouring. Brandy. She says it all breathless with wonder. Brandy. Dad turns the bottle, assesses the label. Brandy. Then they smile, clink their glasses, down a dose each. Can't turn out bad with a name like that. I fall to sleep, the crisis of the name melting into a warm bubble of boozy domesticity.

Bellie led me off to the right, onto a narrower, rockier road. It curved along the side of one of the hills, where the wind eased. My back released the cold-stiff I didn't notice until it left. Discarded rotting tangles of net sunk into the mud along the road. Obsolete hunks of machinery tilted out of the grass. We walked maybe half a mile before the trailer came into view, a single wide, white with a dark brown skirt. A porch clung to the south side. A forgotten dory rotted into the shallow soil. She climbed three steps to the porch and gave the door a brutish shove. It gave, caught on something, then swung wide open.

"This is my place," she said, tossing her purse on the floor.

I stepped through the door and into Bellie's world. Around the open living room window a rainbow of pastel skipped in the breeze. A pink afghan stretched tight across a green plaid sofa. Pillows with purple, pink, and yellow ruffles covered what little plaid the afghan neglected. And everywhere perched collector's plates decorated with garden cottages and white churches, and rigid figurines of sweet-faced children and painted birds. Above the couch hung a wicker birdcage stuffed with a menace of plastic flowers. The kitchen was immaculate. And all geese. The curtains were flocks of geese, likewise pot holders, dishtowels. A line of white geese, dainty blue ribbons around their necks, walked around a wallpaper border. A goosey cloth flowed down a round dining table, topped with a goose-painted empty vase.

Bellie waved her jeweled hand toward the kitchen table and disappeared into the narrow hall behind the living room. I sat in one of two folding chairs. She returned with a book-size mirror, etched with a prancing unicorn, dumped a little mountain of coke over the unicorn's horns, and quickly laid out four narrow lines.

Bellie sat back. "Who you here with?"

"Fisherman I met up with. Thad Rouke." She offered me a short pink straw, and I held my hair back with one hand while I sniffed.

"Thad's not bad. Just get in on the ferry?"

"Yeah."

Bellie reached for the straw and did her lines. "You won't like it here."

"How do you know?" I smudged my ring finger through the blurry residue.

"I can tell." She laughed, covering her mouth, and started a pot of coffee.

I didn't know what to say to that. And it pissed me off. So I laid out two more lines to buy some time. I've never really liked coke. But I liked doing it. The feel of razor against glass, the chopping and sliding and the perfect lines drawn together. At least in the company I kept, snorting coke was communal and ritual, the prelude to seemingly meaningful conversation, secrets revealed.

"The thing is," Bellie said above the sputtering Mr. Coffee, "it's not the kind of place you should come to by accident. And you," she said, eyes taking in everything from my boots to my hair, "look like an accident."

I sipped at the coffee she offered in a goose-spotted cup, wondering if she was right. Is this what I'd been feeling before the ferry docked? The disgrace of coming so far from everything by accident. I looked up at her, raised my eyebrows, and smiled. "Fuck you."

She snickered again, behind her jeweled hand, and sat down to snort her line. I watched her. The left hand, the one not holding the straw, moved to her forehead, fingers moving over the line between hair and skin. And I saw the mark. A birthmark white as the cocaine, bright as a spotlight against her brown skin, peeking through that curtain of black hair.

At 7 A.M. I was heading back down Bellie's rocky road toward the Hi-Tide. The coke was wearing off, leaving that edgy, needy stain behind. Not that I wanted more blow. I wanted something necessary to do. I looked toward the ocean: 800 miles to Anchorage, 1,100 to Seattle, 2,000 to Russia. I kept thinking about the words scrawled on ancient maps to warn sailors when they neared the boundaries of the known world—Beyond here be monsters. Bellie was right; I'd missed the warning, floated across and landed on terra incognita.

Of course, I was used to missing the warning signs. I'm blond. I miss things. I neglect things. I ignore things.

When I say I'm blond, I mean that I'm really blond, that the color is real and that it's very blond. The color of loose women and trailer trash. It's the kind of hair that demands a sleazy respect. I didn't realize how much I'd let my hair control me, define me, until I came to Dutch Harbor. Until I met them. The Aleutians were made for people with black hair. Straight, shiny black. They were a dark background that revealed my image slowly, then all at once, like staring at a Magic

Eye poster. And when I got it, when the squiggles shifted into form, it wasn't pretty.

"I could show you the Elbow Room," Thad said two hours later while we shoved eggs Benedict into our mouths at the HiTide dining room.

"Sure."

"You're going to love it here." Thad's grin was all boyish yet tinged with sexual promise. I swept my hair away from my face and grinned back. Thad had that kind of infectious smile. He lived in a sunny world. It made sense and treated him well. This is not to say he was Pollyannaish, just that the place he occupied liked having him around and never tossed up anything too ugly. He was the kind of man people wanted to please. He handed out nicknames that stuck and were accepted with secretive pride. It felt good to be among his circle. You sensed that by sticking close, he'd draw you along even if neither of you knew where you were headed.

Thad laid down a ten-dollar tip for our twenty-dollar meal and followed me out the door. I felt his eyes on my ass. I have a great ass. I was wearing another pair of tight jeans, stone-washed to a nice marbled pattern with little front pockets stitched in arrows pointing toward my crotch.

Thad had borrowed the boat's truck for the first few days of my arrival. We climbed from the gravel parking lot into the new '85 Dodge. The windshield had only one neat, thumb-size nick.

I'd barely swung both legs in, when Thad's hand followed the arrows. His fingers tightened around my pubis bone, and I arched toward his hand and ran my fingers across my tits.

"Damn, I missed you," he said, switching hands to slide his Ray-Bans on, then turn the ignition.

We drove past beaches littered with rusty metal, old wood, slabs of shoved-over concrete, and across the short Bridge-to-the-Other-Side. Dutch Harbor is really two towns, on two islands. Dutch, on Amaknak Island, is the harbor town, with the big boats, the docks, the canneries, the HiTide. A tiny channel of Captain's Bay separates this small island from the large one—Unalaska, where the second half of town lies and is formally called, of course, Unalaska. This is the old town with the longtime residents, the church, and the Elbow Room. Thad pulled up and parked beside a battered blue building, nearly flush with the beach at high tide. Around the bar stood the village center, a series of similarly battered frame houses, all small, most with additions of one sort or another projecting from them. Dirt paths scattered across the stiff grass laced with buttercups, a map of who visited who and how often. And many of them led straight to the Elbow Room.

I'd heard a lot about the Elbow Room in the last few months. Simplified, it was a bar. But, as is often the case in small towns, the bar is the community center, the concert hall, the therapist's office, the job service. But the Elbow Room wasn't just an any-town bar, or maybe it was the best and worst of all the any-town bars roughed up, scrunched down, and stuffed into a vintage World War II shack.

I'd heard about the brawls, the knife fights, the drunks freezing in snowbanks steps from the door. I was expecting more. But at 2 P.M. on a weekday, the Elbow Room felt safe and familiar. The essentials were all there—the bar topped with some variation of Formica, backed by a dazzle of mirror-backed booze bottles; red vinyl booths pushed against paneled walls in the back and along the dance floor; a tiny room in the corner with a booth that overlooked the bay; a plywood platform in the corner of the dance floor; and bathrooms squared off across the long axis. Two classic barroom icons decorated the place. The spread of photos tacked on the wall flanking the bar, chronicling patrons' stages of inebriation. And the lady painting—this one a black-haired beauty stretched among apricot chiffon on some kind of settee. The bar, like the town, seemed timeless. Only by flipping through the jukebox could you find yourself on the time line—the Eagles, Billy Idol, Fleetwood Mac, AC/DC. Notably missing were Madonna, Duran Duran, Cyndi Lauper.

"Hey, Thad. What do you want?" The woman behind the bar leaned toward us.

"Two beers."

She pulled the tap and knocked two glasses down.

"What's going on?" Thad said. We scootched up onto bar stools.

"Not much."

"This is my girlfriend, Brandy. Marge."

I smiled at the woman. She was in her fifties, burly, and well made up with gray-white hair piled and pinned a good four inches above her head. Dangling gold earrings, heavy lipstick, eye shadow. "I've heard a lot about this place," I said.

"Worst bar in the country. *Playboy* wrote us up as the roughest anywhere." I'd hear the boast regularly in the following months. Whenever newcomers struck up conversations at the Elbow Room, they were sure to hear just how illustrious a place they had wandered into. Hallowed ground. A few times I would even meet someone who had dropped in because they'd heard the stories and wanted to see for themselves. Actually, I would later read, the Elbow Room was never labeled the worst bar in the country. Just the "most despicable." Of course, it didn't look too tough that afternoon. There were four of us— me, Thad, Marge, and a hulking, bearded man two stools down.

Marge followed my gaze. "It's different at night," she said, going on the defense. "You'll see."

You may not be familiar with the kind of places where rough bars are considered attractions. Where the best place to be, the only place, is the worst place. But I understood. There isn't much danger in most of our lives, and some of us feel its absence like a kick to the stomach. People seek edges—mountains, thrill rides, painful men. The Elbow Room on some nights had that edge.

"I had to take a gun away from an asshole just two nights ago," Marge added, on the offense now.

"Who?" Thad asked.

"Some drunk Russian. Off one of the boats."

"You keep his gun?"

"No, he came back for it the next morning. Nice guy really. He gave me a box of them god-awful Russian cigarettes. I gave them to Carl."

"Shit." It was more of a grunt than a word, coming from the hulk down the bar. "Weren't cigarettes. Cardboard around strings of tobacco." Carl slid a flat rectangular box down to me.

I slipped the pack open and pulled out a poorly wrapped gray cigarette. The paper end crackled when I lit it. Thad introduced me to Carl while I inhaled a ball of unfiltered tobacco. They were bad, ragged on the throat. Carl was ragged, too. No, that's too strong. He was unkempt. Carl was six foot three and well fed. The kind of man with hard fat, like retired football players. He wore a dusty blanket poncho, giving him something of a Mexican bandito look. And he had all the hair possible. Curly brown hair on top, full beard, furry arms. A long scar trailed, just visible behind his beard, from his ear to his collar. I liked him.

"You got any more of those *baidarkas*?" Thad asked him.

Carl waved his hand toward Marge. "Gave 'em to her."

Marge lifted a jar filled with dark floating globs and set it on the bar. I peered through the dim pickling juice. "Try one," Marge said. She fished out forks and stabbed inside the jar until she speared one of the slippery shellfish.

"What are they?"

"Baidarkas," Marge said, handing me the loaded fork. "That's Russian for *kayak,* which they're supposed to look like."

I pride myself on being someone who can eat anything. So I did. They tasted, of course, like anything pickled does—like pickles. Texture is what counts, and these resembled really tough, large shrimp. Nothing you could just pass through your mouth and swallow. You had to chew these guys—and chew, and chew.

We sat with our beers and pickled kayaks for the next two hours. Thad and Carl talked about people I didn't know and boats I'd never seen.

Thad and I were used to sitting in bars together. We both came easy to bar-stool intimacy. Having a boyfriend who is equally matched when it comes to mingling is essential for spending long afternoons at the bar. One time we settled into a Sea Galley bar, I think it was Medford. We were waiting for a money wire to move on north. We waited from late morning 'til probably 6 P.M. I got adventurous and traded my Bloody Marys for T&Ts then mai tais. We struck up a conversation with a businessman away from home. Named Jay Jay, I think. "What I wouldn't give to be doing what you two are doing," he said, slouching over a melting vodka on the rocks. "No one giving you orders, no place you have to be." He ordered us another round. I liked seeing Thad and myself through Jay Jay's eyes. We were wild and pretty, Bob Dylan free. Staying poolside in cheap motels, drinking in dim bars all afternoon, and heading north in a silver Camaro. An entirely wonderful thing, to swap drink tabs with someone who looks at you with envy. Gifts of perception offered freely and often. I borrowed Jay Jay's image of me, believing it, reveling in it, holding on to its residue until I coaxed a replacement from someone new. Moving from gift to gift. Empty hands outstretched.

At the Elbow Room with Carl and Marge, Thad had already seduced the denizens. I didn't have the part I liked to play. I'd plopped myself into a town filled with people as free as me. I felt like a warm-up band—eclipsed. There was a certain nostalgia to the feeling. It was the same one I'd had those first few years going out to bars with my mom, after Dad left.

She favored lakeside marinas and golf course watering holes, any-place that had the aura of a step up, of better quality men. Although quality, of course, was relative. Those first couple of years, before I'd learned, before I'd watched and measured her gestures and clothing and words, she was everything. She'd walk into a place, a den of men, and instantly the mood would change. A woman had arrived. A real woman, with a dress on and perfume and sprayed hair and that certain assurance of curves and heat. She worked hard at her game, never coming on too strong, waiting for them. I'd sit beside her, about as noticed as the purse she hung over her chair, and watch. We always had a new one interested within a few minutes. I could feel the jockeying that went on behind us. The rush of attention, followed by the hush of calculation as some ancient hierarchy was established. And one would approach, a sortie, as the others watched. Drinks would be bought. A story told. And sometimes a new man with his own boat or his own family and only a few stolen weekends. Sometimes he'd move in. Sometimes he'd stay a few months.

I had watched and I had learned. I was probably better than her by the time I hit seventeen. But this was different. This was no golf course watering hole, no marina lounge. This was a bar.

Here there were the locals like Marge and Carl, but fully half the people in town at any moment had come just for the money, the novelty, the escape. I was just another girlfriend, following another fisher-man, following another trail of money.

"I've got to visit the head," I told Thad, trying out the fishing lingo. He smiled widely, his eyes twinkly with four Rainiers.

I slid off the stool and took six paces to the women's bathroom. It was a tiny thing—one sink, two stalls. I picked the far one and pulled down my jeans. It takes a long time to pee when you're drinking, like your kidneys are processing as it comes. I waited and surveyed the stall walls. As usual there was plenty to see.

I've collected bathroom wall writing ever since visiting a bathroom in Florence, Oregon. Someone had written in ballpoint "The problem with this fucking world is apathy."

Someone else had scratched an arrow pointing at the word *apathy* and scrawled "What's that?"

Another addition, this time in black marker, responded "Who the fuck cares?"

The exchange got me thinking. Maybe there was something to be learned from the messages we leave for each other to pass the time while waiting to excrete. Latrinealia, or the art of bathroom writing, goes all the way back to the Roman Empire. It's part of the human urge to be creative when the body is, well, predominately at rest. I've collected some great stuff over the years and filled two half-size ledger books with messages from bathroom writers across the country. Never once had I written anything myself. This hobby was pure voyeurism.

The Elbow Room had the usual. A few messages about guys who were bastards. A few names and dates. The expletives that stand alone, those little words—*Fuck, Asshole, Dickhead*—summing up all a writer needed to say. One line about a death-trap boat: "Keep off the *North-wind,* it's a hole waiting to flood." Nothing of special interest.

I finished up, reached for the toilet paper, and began to pull. I don't get drunk easily, and watching toilet paper unroll has always been my way of discerning just how far gone I am. If I get kind of mesmerized by the process, if the paper takes on an odd ribbonish quality, I'm drunk. This time, however, the toilet paper acted like toilet paper.

But because I was staring so intently at the toilet paper holder, I saw another bit of writing peeking out from underneath the roll. It was actually scrawled on the metal holder itself. I leaned down till my head sunk below my knees. I still couldn't see enough to make it out. I know it seems idiotic, but I'm really into this latrinealia thing. I had to read this. It could be a real gem. And the curiosity of it. Why would anyone take the trouble to remove a toilet paper roll bar just to write something like "Fuck You," where no one would read it?

I don't think there's a locked toilet paper holder in all of Dutch. I simply slipped the roll and bar off the holder.

Killing hands.

I touched the words, just barely, but the metal sent a signal through my finger and up my arm. Not like electricity or heat exactly. More like the sudden sense that the metal was touching me. I jerked back, causing the toilet seat to slip against the rim, nearly dethroning me. I ducked to look at the message again. Scrawled words in felt-tip pen. *Killing hands.* Just words. I took in a slow breath. Odd, but not particularly insightful. I slipped the roll back on, finished up, and headed to my bar stool.

Marge examined me from under creamy blue eye shadow when I'd situated myself back at the bar. "You need a job. Thad says you've cocktailed before, and we haven't had a drink girl for a few weeks now. Last one upped and got a cooking job on a boat. Me and Les get slammed."

"What's the money like?"

"Eleven an hour. Tips usually come in over two hundred a night. We need ya between ten and three. Thursday through Saturday."

"How bad are the guys?"

"Oh, you know, most of them are teddy bears. When something breaks out, you just yell 'fight.' Les and me'll handle it."

this way and that

I never said I'd take the job, but I did. I had nothing better planned. I can't say what I had imagined myself doing when I took the three-day ferry ride from Homer to Unalaska. I just knew I'd be with a man and out of the roommate problem.

A few weeks before, in Anchorage, Thad had introduced me to two other women-in-waiting whose men were fishing. He'd left me with his Camaro, $3,000, and the company of women. We had an executive apartment, the kind that's set up for traveling light and fast. It came with a supply of all the basics, two pot holders, a dish set, pots, corkscrew, bedding. I unpacked my couple of boxes, and presto, a home. I didn't even have to buy towels. The three of us hit it off okay, at first. Then Kathy hooked up with a hard-drinking guy who hung out at The Hub. It didn't take a week before he was smacking her around. I listened to Nan try the roommate-girlfriend talk. "You've got to lose that guy. Have more respect for yourself." Silly words, useless words.

One afternoon I came home from a successful Nordstrom shopping trip to find Nan, car keys in hand, rushing off to the hospital. Kathy hadn't faired well after the last argument. She had a dislocated shoulder and a brain hemorrhage. Nan, ever hopeful, thought we should both be there when Kathy woke up.

"You go ahead," I said, lifting a new angora sweater from a shopping bag.

Nan stared at me. "She doesn't have any family here. We're all she's got. Come on."

I held the sweater against my chest, feeling the tickle of it along my neck. "You go ahead. You know her better anyway," I said. I knew even then I was shirking my foundling girlfriend role. Living with women had set me on edge. I didn't know what to expect from them or what they expected from me. Men were just so much more reliable. Besides, I couldn't pretend it mattered to Kathy if I showed up.

I was pulling the pale suede jacket from another bag so I couldn't see Nan's glare before she turned and slammed the door on her way out, but I felt it smash against me and rummaged around for the matching boots.

Three-inch heels. Mom would be proud. "Never wear flats outside your own house," she'd say. The floor of her closet was a wreck of strappy sandals and high leather boots. "You wear flats, people will think you don't have any pride in your stride. Got that?"

No flats. No flats.

Kathy was released the next day. Nan brought her home and tucked her in bed before she told me to leave. I knew I could still salvage the situation, but I didn't want to. I needed out.

I packed up my two boxes of stuff and my Nordstrom's loot and moved to Super 8. I got through to Thad the next day on the ship-to-shore radio.

"I ran into some trouble here. I need to move on."

"Move on?"

I'd chosen the wrong words. Words that telegraphed too much. I lay back on the motel bed and stared at the ceiling. "It's just not working out for me right now. Nothing to do with you."

He paused, and I listened to the static across the curving surface of ocean between us. "Why don't you come out to Dutch?"

When I didn't respond, he continued. "Brandy, it's the most beautiful place I've ever seen. It will blow you away, I promise."

"That's not what you said before. I remember you calling it the rainiest, windiest hellhole on earth."

"Well that's true too. But I'll be coming in every few weeks."

Perhaps he understood me better than I knew. What I needed was him, any him, just someone to steady myself in. I thought about the alternative, finding a cocktail waitressing job, waiting. I knew if I said yes, I would cross some threshold. I'd been following men a good deal of my life. I'd followed one to college for a couple years in Seattle. I'd followed another to Austin, Texas, for five months, another to Redwood City, California, and, of course, Thad to Anchorage. I tried to count the number of times I'd gone somewhere simply because I wanted to. The answer— zero. But until now, I'd never considered following a man someplace so remote, so far from what I knew. It clarified my situation; I had no place, no plan, no pride. I'd drifted so long, I was willing to drift anywhere.

"Will there be anything for me to do?"

"You can see me," Thad said. "We'll be coming in pretty soon, taking a week break."

I sat up, planted my feet on the beige carpet, and said it. "I'll be on the next ferry."

I left on July 2. Three days later, I was in Dutch.

The next day I was the Elbow Room's one and only cocktail waitress.

The Elbow Room began in the 1940s as a military bar, the Blue Fox Cocktail Lounge. Unalaska was buried in military buildings at the time, as American forces beefed up defenses along the strategic swoop of the Aleutians during World War II. The bar was all but forgotten in 1966 when two guys bought it for six hundred dollars and renamed it the Elbow Room. They had to haul crates of burlap sandbags, camouflage netting, and C ration cans to the dump, but soon Unalaska's three hundred residents had a sit-down place to drink. By the mid-seventies, the crabbing boom hit Dutch and transformed the Elbow Room. It was big money, loads of drugs, and hot tempers. It entered legend. Nearly every book or article about king crab fishing mentioned the Elbow Room. That notoriety was holding strong in 1986 when I stepped inside and became part of its infamy.

A reckless, shameless place. Even before my shift began, I knew this job would be different.

Most bars don't allow employees to drink. This is a standard, hard-

and-fast rule that is secretly, unilaterally ignored. The reason is simple—the absolute worst place to be is sober when everyone else is drunk. Cocktail waitresses the world over know this and practice seditious acts to avoid it. There is a system. Bartenders slip rum into the Coke you sip on by the waitress station. They slip shots of tequila into your hand at thigh level as you come behind the bar. You turn your back, pretending to look for a clean tray or more straws in the corner, and gulp it down.

At the Elbow Room subterfuge didn't exist.

"What do you want?" Marge asked, knocking an empty shot glass on the bar the minute I stepped into the place.

"Schnapps."

She poured; I drank. She poured another.

"Where's Thad?"

"He had to run some gear out to the boat."

She nodded. "It's gonna be busy," she said. "This is Les."

A slim, stunning man at the cash register fluttered his fingers in an over-the-shoulder wave.

"He's a fruit," Marge said. "Half-Aleut, half-white, all fruit." She handed me a tiny cash box. "You got a two-hundred-dollar bank for making change. If someone gets out of line, let us handle it." She turned away.

The tables and stools were full, and about ten men clumped in standing groups. Three dogs lay near their owners' bar stools, occasionally yelping when someone stepped on a tail. Swirling patterns of muddy sand had already formed across the painted wood floor. I worked the tables first. I noticed the Aleut guys seemed to prefer them, sitting shoulder to shoulder, while the white guys like to hold the center, standing in armored clumps. Not that the place was segregated. A few white locals squished in at the tables with their Aleut buddies. And a few Aleut guys mingled with the standing white hordes. And they all drank the same stuff—beer, rum-and-Cokes, screwdrivers, and dirty-mothers.

I knew within five minutes that I'd overdressed. Dressing is performance art for a cocktail waitress, and your audience can sour on you fast. I'd worn tight jeans and a tightish black T-shirt with crocheted lace around a V-neck. I'd left my hair down and done a medium makeup job, which meant everything but eyeliner, brow, and contouring pencils. The object is to look sexy enough to bring in the tips but not enough to bring on the hassles. In Dutch, I could have rolled an old piece of carpet around myself and been too sexy. The mistake had been made, and all I could do now was make the most of it. I snaked through the crowd without meeting eyes. I took orders and delivered drinks without small talk.

The tips were astounding. I've worked in lucrative bars before, but the Elbow Room was like nothing else. Five-dollar tips were average and a ten common. Once that night a guy threw a fifty on my tray.

Les was good. By ten-thirty he had lines three deep around the bar, but the second he saw my cork and plastic tray waving above the crowd, he was there. "What do you need?" And he was fast, he could fill my entire tray in two minutes. I noticed a gold earring dangling from his right ear and wondered if it gave him any trouble. I didn't imagine this was a progressive crowd.

By midnight, the Elbow Room had become a mass of men and very few women drinking and swaying to a jukebox that played mostly George Thorogood, Fleetwood Mac, and Judas Priest. I don't know how Marge and Les kept all those guys drinking. I've never seen bartenders as fast.

Thad came in a little after midnight. He kissed me and slid his hands up my lower back and into my hair.

"Having any trouble?"

"Not much."

"I'll sit right here," he said, nodding at an occupied stool next to the spot I wiggled into to order drinks.

I set my tray on the bar and shouted a lengthy drink order at Les. Thad turned to the man on the stool he wanted.

"You're in my seat."

I couldn't see their faces, but neither moved for maybe five seconds. Then the man grabbed his drink and left. Thad lifted his oilskin and sat. Les slid a beer in front of Thad and leaned toward him, cupping his cheek in his palm and bending his elbows on the bar so that he was looking up. I couldn't hear what he was saying, but I left the two in earnest conversation to make another round.

The price I paid for misjudging my audience came each time I snaked through that crowd between the bar and tables. I'd hoist my tray over my head and search for openings. I pressed my hand lightly on one back, another forearm. Sometimes one of the guys would see me coming and make a show of helping me out, shoving his buddies aside, yelling, "Blondie coming through. Get out of the fucking way."

I could never tell who was doing the groping. I'd feel a hand squeeze a chunk of my ass, and no matter how quickly I turned or how closely I scrutinized the mass around me, I couldn't finger the culprit. Not that I wasn't used to it. Cocktail waitresses handle groping in one of two ways. We either play the oh-I-can't-believe-you're-so-naughty part, giggling innocently and pretending we haven't been pinched a dozen times in the last hour. Or we play the get-a-life part, acting a touch disdainful and pretending to be beyond caring. I do both well. But at the Elbow Room, the attention was so persistent, so frenzied and exuberant, I had trouble keeping in either character. Out of necessity, I stooped to ignoring it and tried to vary my route each trip. All I did was present my ass to a wider spectrum of gropers.

Bellie came in a little after one o'clock. She slid into a booth with three guys in the back.

"Hey white girl, you're still here."

I shrugged. "Looks that way."

"Sex on the beach and a tequila." Her sparkling fingers played with dark loosening curls.

The guys ordered shots and beers.

I returned with their order and felt the table rock on uneven legs when I tried to set the drinks down. I clustered them all in the center to avoid a spill.

"Found a place to live yet?" Bellie asked, picking up her shot glass first.

"No."

"Tell Thad to meet me tomorrow sometime. My aunt has a place." She set the empty glass down, and the table tipped toward her.

At quarter after two, we had a minirush. Apparently, the other bar on the island, the HiTide, closed at two o'clock, and several determined drinkers, along with the cocktail waitresses who had been serving them, swept into the Elbow Room.

My counterparts at the HiTide were also blond. That made five of us. They seemed to know a good number of the men and immediately fell in with a loud group in the center of the room. These women had definitely overdressed. Two had short black skirts and nylons; one wore black tights topped with a sweater that descended to the bottom of her butt cheeks. The other actually wore a dress, striped with a wide sailor collar.

Marge flicked the lights twice. Last call. I made one more pass of the tables and kept my eye on the cocktail waitresses. Blond hair gets attention. Something about the light in dark spaces makes it hard to focus on anything else. Even fellow blondes fall victim. I've noticed it when watching a Marilyn Monroe movie; your eyes just keep straying to her, even when you make a point of watching another actor. Anyway, one of the cocktail waitresses was cradling some man's ass with both hands. He lifted her up, yelling something unintelligible. They had big, throaty, head-back, too-many-cigarettes laughs. I decided not to like them. Partly because they had brought their flash into my bar and were upstaging me, stripping me of the attention I'd been arrogantly ignoring. Partly because I just have a policy of not liking bleached blondes. And even in bar light, I could see the signs—orangish, stiff, the kind of hair that must be curled, sprayed, and untouched to look good, and good is too generous. To look like hair. Anyway, no one pinched my ass for the rest of the night, which wasn't long.

Marge turned up the lights and yelled "Bar's closed" four or five times. That's when the chant started.

"Rodeo Song! Rodeo Song!"

Someone in back started, and by "fuck" the entire bar was singing.

> Well it's forty below and I don't give a fuck
> I got a heater in my truck and I'm off to the rodeo
> And it's alaman left and alaman right
> Come on you fucking dummies get your right step right
> Get off the stage you Goddamn goof you know
> You piss me off, you fucking jerk
> You get on my nerves.
>
> Well here comes Johnny with his pecker in his hand
> He's a one ball man and he's off to the rodeo

And it's alaman left and alaman right
Come on you fucking dummies get your right step right
Get off the stage you Goddamn goof you know
You piss me off, you fucking jerk
You get on my nerves.

It's a catchy song, and we sang it maybe five times. And no, I don't know what *alaman* means. There's something about singing in a dark bar at the end of the night. There's a warmth, a nostalgia in scores of untrained voices. It puts you in a mood. Even the HiTide cocktail waitresses sang with enthusiasm. I don't know how the "Rodeo Song" became the national bar anthem, but I liked it. I've heard bartenders say it leads to fights, but I've never seen anything but a sense of drunken camaraderie. And it helps clear the bar. Men drifted out the door, still singing as they careened down the dirt road toward town or piled into van taxis waiting outside.

I was supposed to stand by the door and make sure no one left with any booze. This should have been easy. But some of these guys had become quite attached to the half-finished drinks in their hands. I let the beer bottles go and focused on getting the glasses back.

My first night at the Elbow Room ended with $250 in tips, a rosy ass, and another two shots. Les handed me the second shot and swished over to the register to cash me out.

"Where's Thad?"

"He gave someone a ride home," he said, knocking back a shot of his own. "I think there's a present for you in the head."

"What?"

"Just go look."

I made for the bathroom, knowing it couldn't be good. My "present" was Little Liz. Marge had told me a bit about her. She was short but not little girthwise. She was a regular in the worst sense. By early evening she was always planted at the same bar stool, where she would remain until she had to hit the bathroom. Most of the time, she never made it out.

I'd seen her that night, but she'd been in the Blue Room, a little partially walled-off corner with a wide window overlooking the bay, sitting at the bar, so I hadn't served her. In the nights to come, however, I would learn that Liz was my special burden. She would wear the same outfit night after night, or maybe she had several identical suits she swapped out. And suit is the right word—brilliant pink polyester slacks and blazer, the kind you sometimes see at Salvation Army stores. You know it had been neatly folded and boxed twenty years ago until its owner died and her heirs sorted through the basement, squabbled over the good stuff, and placed this suit in the box labeled DONATE.

Polyester is not forgiving, and each ring of fat bulged through that cocoon of petroleum-derived fabric. On her lapel drooped a fake red carnation.

I would never see Liz speak to anyone, although plenty of locals journeyed to her corner to say hi. I sensed a sort of homage in these greetings. Liz would always turn her shoulders, smile to expose her questionable dental habits, then turn and go back to drinking, even if the pilgrim was still talking.

In Anchorage, Little Liz would have been one of the scores of drunken natives staggering down Fourth Avenue, sometimes freezing on cold winter nights, lost to anything more than the next bar, the next drink. But here I got the idea that Little Liz was somebody, or had been.

I smelled the piss the moment I opened the bathroom door. She was slumped against the brown paneling sloppily singing a song I didn't know.

"Come on. Time to go," I said, squatting to grab her arm.

She looked at me, still singing. I didn't even see the hand come up. She slapped me hard across the cheek. The accuracy of her aim surprised me.

"Leave me," she spat.

I stood up, touching my cheek.

The last time I'd been slapped, I'd expected it, provoked it even. Four years ago I'd visited my mom to help celebrate the death of her fourth marriage. She's on her way out the door, dressed trashy as usual, but worse now that she's in her late forties. I'm camping out on her couch but get up to help her find her purse. "How do I look?" she asks as I hand her a sequined denim clutch. "Like a tramp," I say. "Watch your mouth," she says. When I explain that I am just trying to help her out, help her see herself, help her see us, from other people's eyes, she slaps me. I smiled at her and held the door open.

This slap, however, caught me off guard—a stinging reminder that helping a pathetic tramp or a sloppy drunk is a thankless job.

"Stay here then, you fucking drunk," I said.

Les and Marge laughed at me as I stomped out of the bathroom.

"She slap you?" Marge asked.

"Yes."

"She'll do that if she's not totally passed out. You gotta grab both hands before you even get close. Come on, I'll show you." Marge came around the bar.

I was in no mood to learn how to stuff a slap-happy, piss-soaked, polyestered drunk into a cab. "Fuck that," I said and stomped back to a bar stool to wait for Thad.

Marge shot me a look. "I'll do it this time. This time. Got that?"

"Whatever," I said.

Marge made for the bathroom.

Les giggled and poured me another shot.

"You know, I'm in love with your boyfriend," he said.

I had absolutely nothing to say to that.

"I was making progress until your fucking creamy ass showed up." He smiled but flicked his cigarette aggressively. I wasn't sure which gesture to give more weight to.

"My ass is far from creamy at the moment. Feels black and blue."

"I'll bet." He looked me up and down, at least as far down as he could with the bar hitting me right below my tits. Handy height, most bars, you can often rest them right there.

Marge slammed back through the bathroom door, yanked the taxi phone from the hook by the door. "Yeah," she said. "It's Little Liz." Pause. "Don't tell me that, you little peckerhead. Get your ass over here."

Les turned back to me. "Guess the competition's too stiff. I'll have to find another honey of a fisherman to woo."

Marge harrumphed into the phone and clomped back to the bathroom. Les and I watched through our jets of smoke as she half carried, half dragged Liz from the bathroom to the wall beside the door, where she let her slide down to the floor. Neither of us moved.

Les half turned toward Marge as she came around the bar and started counting out the till. "Hey, Marge, who do you think would like a dark-eyed beauty like me?"

"Shut the fuck up, Les."

He rolled his eyes and leaned across the bar toward me. "I figure her for a dyke who doesn't know it," he whispered.

"Shut the fuck up, Les. Where's that fuckin' taxi?"

The door banged open, and Thad walked in, the wind whipping his coat around his legs. Les straightened and smiled. "Can I get you something, Thad?"

I winked at Les and slid off the stool before Thad could answer. "I think I'll take care of him." I hooked a leg around his and pulled his oil-skin open.

"Get out," Les said.

I wasn't sure if I'd made a friend or an enemy.

We almost made it to the truck.

"Hey, Thad, wait a minute." Marge was shouting out the door. "That fuckin' taxi didn't show. You gotta take Liz home for me."

I laughed aloud, my head leaning back against Thad's shoulder, because of course he would just keep walking, laughing too.

Except he didn't.

He was walking back to the bar. He was wrapping his arms around that puddle of a woman. He was, gulp, sliding her into the truck.

"Thanks," Marge shouted, and I could hear Les laughing before the bar door banged shut behind her.

I held my breath and climbed into the truck. Liz had drooped over to the driver's side, and Thad lifted her a bit to get in. He let her slide back to rest her head on his shoulder. I rolled down the window quick as I could and stuck my head out. Her place was only a few blocks down, by the creek. Thad pulled in, set the emergency brake, and helped Liz to her door. The headlights shining a path for them.

The amazing thing was that by the time she got to the door, she seemed to be walking on her own. I watched her kiss my boyfriend on the cheek and whisper something in his ear.

Thad pounced back into the truck. "She said to tell you she was sorry," he said, throwing the truck in reverse.

"No she didn't," I said and jerked my head to look back at her as the headlights pulled away. She was still standing there. And she was looking at me and her eyes were wide and her head was up and she was looking at me and her lips were moving and she was shouting something and it wasn't in English. "No she didn't," I said again.

Famine

The people of Unalaska Island called themselves Unangan, The Real People. They were part of a larger group who called themselves Unanga or The People. They have lived on these water-soaked volcanic pinnacles for more than eight thousand years. Always near the ocean, from the ocean, and with the ocean. They live in a rich and fearsome place, where nature whips the sea into towering waves, sends rivers of lava over the beaches, and hides its creatures, leaving bellies empty for weeks. It is a place held lightly by men, who know that magic and taboo are the breakers between themselves and death.

The Russians found them first. In 1741, Vitus Bering spotted the fog-shrouded coast known in legend as The Great Land. Although Bering died on the journey home, his crew returned to Russia with a cargo of furs. The conquest of the Chain had begun. The Russian men who followed committed brutal acts against the Aleuts—murder, rape, kidnapping.

In 1763 the Aleuts of the eastern Aleutians stopped raiding and enslaving one another and formed a rare alliance to fight back. They attacked the crews of four ships wintering on Umnak, Unalaska, and Unimak islands. Of the two hundred men aboard, only twelve survived.

Commander Ivan Solov'iev vowed retribution. He systematically gathered information on Aleut strength, then attacked. Aleut warriors failed to stop him. Solov'iev rampaged, destroying a people's means of *survival—their boats, weapons, and hope. Solov'iev entered The People's folklore as Solov'iev the Destroyer.*

Ayagax-Agaluun was seventeen as the summer ended. A full woman, with a husband, and a baby at her breast. She moved to another dying patch of crowberries, wrinkled with loss of juice. She wove her fingers through the scratchy twigs to find every last one. These three baskets of berries would be the last harvest. With those drying in the village, they would have enough to last maybe four months, five if they didn't feed the older ones. She was getting used to the feeling of doom now. She felt it in muscles that always held themselves ready. She felt it in her belly, which she was careful never to fill. She felt it when she climbed to the rock lookout that her people had once used to watch for enemy raiders and that she now used to search the ocean for returning warriors.

Little Anshigis woke hungry as usual. She wailed and kicked. Aya left the berry patch and sat in the low grass beside her baby. She lifted the little one and slid her under her kamleika. The baby's dark eyes held on her mother's as she sucked, smiling around the nipple in her mouth.

As always when her body was at rest, Aya's mind turned to calculations. Thirteen had been left, and two more joined after escaping the Russians at Illiuliuk. She numbered the caches of fish and berries, still unable to stretch the supplies past five months. And with little seal oil left, the winter's cold would take its own toll. Her husband along with the other warriors had set out four months ago now. The year before, the Destroyer had attacked villages across the island, killing and pillaging weapons and food caches. Aya's village had been spared, simply because it was so small and remote. But they had heard the stories. In villages that resisted, people were slaughtered; villages that didn't fight were stripped of their weapons, food stores, and dignity. Many starved. The men of Aya's village had met with the remaining men in other villages across the near islands. They had all known it was a battle they could well lose. And they had gone, vowing to avenge their lost wives, mothers, fathers, sons, and daughters. Although no one spoke it, Aya knew most of them were already dead. Even him; he would have fought too bravely, too foolishly, she thought. Perhaps a few would return, when they were able.

The ones left behind had been old, young, or women. The *kalgas* had fled back to their own villages on other island groups as soon as there were no men to enforce their slavery. Of those left, only Aya and four others were strong. Most were children still learning to climb for eggs and wait near snares. The two old men had been brave. When they understood that the men were not returning this season, they had paddled out to lose themselves in the sea.

Aya pulled the baby from her breast and took up her baskets. She had walked several miles in search of berries, and it would be nearly dark before she reached the village. A stiff wind pushed against her, coming off the water and floundering through the mountains, sometimes at her face, sometimes her side. Anshigis cried when the wind turned to the south and stung her eyes. Aya stopped to pull the sealskin over the baby's head.

Aya's face was not plain. She had been decorated since late childhood. First the pierced circle of ivory beads that rimmed her ears. Next her aunt had punctured her face with a fine needle rubbed over black stone until two parallel curving tracks ran from her hairline near her ear to the curve of her nostril. When these had healed, she had a broad band of five lines tattooed from the lower curve of her lip to her chin. Later she had added labrets, bone carved like barbed hooks inserted below the corners of her mouth. Her bangs were cut straight and high across her forehead. Before the trouble began she had worn her hair knotted in back. But now she often forgot or didn't have the energy to wind and fix it.

The sun had left the sky when Aya reached her village, situated on a headland between two bays so that if enemies invaded from one direction, the villagers could escape from the other. The waters were high and growing. The wind pushed waves farther up the beach. Perhaps they will bring us a whale, Aya thought. She had held such hopes many times, even wandered far along the beach after such onshore winds, looking for a gift. So far, the sea had not given one.

She descended the notched driftwood log into the calm air of her *ulax* and quickly placed her baskets of berries in a storage pit, covering them with a stone slab then a grass mat. Slukax stirred an egg and net-tle mix over a stone hearth while her two small boys fought over a drift-wood stick they had tried to carve into a throwing lance.

"Alidax!" she said. "Take your brother outside. You two will poison the dinner with your fighting."

When the boys, still shoving and tussling, climbed outside, Slukax lifted her face to Aya. "When the winds leave, we will walk the beach. The sea knows we won't live without a gift. Perhaps he will leave one for us tonight."

Aya nodded.

But the morning brought nothing. The two women traveled six cragged miles along the east coast the first day and four along the west the next. The second day, they had to wait out the tide and stopped to eat dried salmon and berries beside the sea lion rookeries, deserted now as fall came.

"We should have come with seal clubs months ago, when the men first left," Slukax said. "My mouth waters thinking of seal meat."

Aya's eyes darted to the older woman's face. She saw no sign Slukax was teasing. A flash of fear ignited in her chest followed by a lingering hope. Twice in the last weeks, Aya had peeked at the spears, throwing boards, and clubs stored in underground pits. The men had taken the best weapons, but a few remained, some broken, some forgotten. She had been afraid, even though she'd been careful to make certain no one was watching. But the spirits, she knew, were always watching. A woman's power did not mingle well with the power of a man's hunting weapons. A woman's power, her mother had explained, was too wild, too uncontrolled for the fragile precision of a spear or a throwing board. To touch them, even talk about or gaze at them, could provoke a spirit of the hunt. And soon the ocean was hiding its creatures from the hunter or cursing him with impossible seas. And then people were dying.

She had never touched one of these magically crafted things. But Aya knew what each did, how each was used. She'd been with her own brother, now gone with the others, as he'd practiced launching his spear into kelp bulbs staked to the beach.

He felt her envy and teased her often. "Too bad you'll be a woman," he taunted as he pulled his lance from its target. "I will hunt great sea creatures, while you hack up their stinking blubber on the beach."

When her mother learned Aya had been watching her brother practice, she had taken her outside. "Aya," she said, "do not take your brother's hunting power from him by looking too long. He will need it, and more." Then she had taken Aya's hands, turning them palm up, and recited the same strange words Aya had heard since she was a child. "In your hands you hold your fate, and in no one's hands but your own does your future rest." She squeezed Aya's hands. "Do you understand?"

Aya nodded. "Yes, Mama."

Her mother pressed a bead into Aya's hand. "For your necklace," she said. Her mother looked away toward the water as Aya strung the bead with others around her neck. "If you watch, watch in secret," she said, turning to go back inside.

Aya had expected worse for testing this taboo, and her mother's leniency had frightened her more than a threat of shunning or even banishment would have.

Aya's fingers went to those beads now as she thought about how to answer Slukax. Slukax had taken a fearsome risk even speaking of sea lion clubs. Aya turned the pierced bead as she listened to how her next words would sound. She spoke them with care.

"The sea lions are feeding in the kelp." She said it without inflection. Slukax could take this many ways.

Neither spoke for several minutes. Aya felt the wind on her face and the openness of the sea before her. When the baby on her back cried, relief cracked her stiff shoulders. She unbundled the little one and nursed, grateful for a reason not to meet Slukax's eyes. The moment had passed.

Aya felt Slukax's eyes on her back many times in the next weeks. A tension between them rattled like ryegrass in an uneasy wind. Aya could not discern what Slukax was watching for. She'd look up while mending a parka to see Slukax's eyes skitter away from her. She'd feel them on her when she turned her back to climb outside, slowing her movements, making her conscious of even the most ordinary tasks. Perhaps Slukax had seen her gazing at the weapons cache weeks before and had spoken of the clubs to trap her. Or perhaps Slukax felt she had betrayed her own evil thoughts and now watched out of fear that Aya would denounce her before the others. Perhaps they were both too afraid of what spirits may have been listening to their hearts. Aya's wariness grew, but her understanding of her own desires grew as well. Her certainty rose in proportion to the shrinking supply of eggs, berries, seeds, and seal oil. It grew in proportion to the emptiness that had ceased being hunger and consumed her doubts. When Slukax had first spoken, Aya hadn't known if what she heard were the first calls of evil or the dawning of hope. Now she did. She wanted to hunt, to touch the forbidden weapons, pierce through skin to muscle, and suck the fat from a once-living creature.

She wanted to eat.

The first to die were the two nieces of Slukax. Their mother held on three more days. When bellies were empty and muscles shivered in the cold, even a small sickness could bring death. Slukax insisted they be laid within her own house.

"More pits will need digging in the walls soon," Slukax said the evening after the women and girls had been buried in compartments off the main room. "Unless"— Slukax looked up from her mending to meet Aya's eyes—"someone is willing to do more."

"A person may be willing," Aya said quietly. The risk was great, but Aya's fear was greater. Her milk didn't flow as it had, and the baby was not yet old enough to eat.

"What would such a person do to begin this fearsome task?"

"Such a person would need to inspect the kayaks and weapons. But such a person would need the help of other persons."

"Would another person be at the weapon stash tomorrow morning when the others are collecting driftwood?"

"Such a person may."

Aya let the dense silence of the last few weeks fall around them again. If Slukax was laying a trap, it was one Aya must walk into. She saw no other way.

When Aya approached the weapons cache, Slukax was waiting, crouched on the balls of her feet.

"So," Slukax said, rising to her feet with a smile, "we have decided to trust each other."

The relief spread over Aya's face. She smiled and bent to throw off the skins covering the pits.

The women pulled two kayaks from their hiding places in the brush, their skin covers still intact. After rewrapping spear fastenings, they lay them in the boats alongside the throwing boards they'd found, and stashed the gear in a field of stiff heath beyond the curve of the beach. The next morning as they practiced in early light, they also found another hunter.

Aya and Slukax dropped their weapons as they watched Tugakax approach.

Tugakax was new to the village. She and her grandfather had come three months before from another village, just south of Illiuliuk, where the Russians had first landed. Tugakax had not said much at first. But as the weeks passed, Aya learned that Tugakax's village had been invaded early on, that several of the people had been killed. That Tugakax herself was barely living. She had survived only because she'd been young and beautiful. A Russian officer had held her for three seasons, leaving her with a half-white baby and a deadness in her eyes. When the Destroyer came, he had killed most of the men and some of the women. The rest had been left to starve. Only Tugakax, her child, and her grandfather had survived until summer, when they could travel the old inland trails.

Tugakax looked at Aya and Slukax now with a ferocity Aya had never seen in her. "I know what you do. I will help."

"No, don't bring any more misery to the village," Slukax said. "We do this because we must. But the spirits will not care. Aya and I are willing, and that is enough."

But Tugakax stood before Slukax and spoke with her head up and her eyes still. "I have seen men lined up back to back to test how far a Russian bullet would travel into flesh. I have seen babies bashed against rocks until dead. And I have seen women bat their eyes to save their own lives. I have seen so much my eyes have closed. Now I will help."

Slukax hadn't argued. Neither she nor Aya had heard Tugakax speak before about her time with the Russians. They had seen an old man and a woman, carrying a small child, coming down from the hills just before sunset. The old man had approached the women, who went to meet them, Slukax in the lead. He explained that they had traveled for three weeks across the mountains seeking a new village to join. He had gestured toward the woman.

"Tugakax, my granddaughter," he said, "makes fine kamleikas and mats. She will work hard."

Slukax looked at the woman, who had not once glanced up from the ground. She could see the lighter and rounder eyes of the child in the woman's arms. They must have suffered much and been in great danger to risk traveling inland. "We do not have much," Slukax said. She led the newcomers to an *ulax* and gave them enough food for two days.

The old man had remained only long enough to see Tugakax and her child settled into village life. Then he had disappeared into the ocean with the other old man. Aya had tried to make Tugakax welcome. She invited the new woman to come with her to collect shellfish at low tide and was careful never to mention her child's mixed face. Gradually Tugakax had begun to smile, to let other women watch her child. But she had never spoken of her life before.

As Aya looked at Tugakax now, she understood that for this woman suffering soaked through to her soul, and that angering the spirits could add nothing to her pain.

Slukax nodded. "Three hunters are better than two."

After several days of kayak practice, Slukax decided they were ready to throw.

Aya had watched her brother and other hunters use the throwing board before and thought it easy enough. But as she practiced, she discovered how ignorant she had been. The throwing boards had been made to fit each hunter's arm, the length of the throwing handle equaling the length between the hunter's middle fingertip and elbow. These weapons did not fit her body. And the women had no one to explain or demonstrate. Only the chance strike taught them the series of movements, the correct angles, the perfect moment of release.

Slukax pretended to know more.

"No! No! Aya, you are twisting your wrist too much. Straighten the angle."

"No! No! You both are turning the shoulders too much."

But they knew Slukax's lectures were without meaning. She knew no more than Aya or Tugakax. Her throws hit with no more regularity.

In the weeks that followed, the sun grew more cautious, traveling ever closer to the horizon. As the women snuck from the village on foraging trips from which little food resulted, three more died. The old woman and two more children. Nine were left, and the snows would come any day. Practice had become a luxury.

Late fall, the women knew, was not good hunting. They gathered before dawn in the cove to the east of the village where they had hidden the kayaks and weapons. They mixed charcoal with water and painted dark lines under their eyes to cut the ocean's glare. Aya and Tugakax lifted the one-hole kayak and carried it to the water for Slukax, then the two-hole kayak for themselves.

Childlike waves tickled Aya's ankles as she strapped her weapons to the bow of her boat. She watched Tugakax and Slukax do the same. Aya's fingers trembled as she tested the weapon straps. The air clung to her like damp hands. They had dressed in warm parkas, then waterproof seal-gut kamleikas. Aya's eyes traveled across the endless gray hunting fields. The ocean had always meant life, comfort, and safety. As the sun rose that day, she knew it as an enemy, intent on taking her body below for its own purposes. She understood the fear she had seen the men cover with elaborate ceremony, costume, and words. She felt awash in ignorance. The sea spread to the end of the world, and its creatures knew it like a lover. It would protect them with everything it had, and Aya had little skill with which to steal a piece for her dying village.

The three women paddled their kayaks out past the reef rocks to the east. They paddled around the next cove, keeping their boats angled slightly out to sea to oppose the tide that pressed them back to shore. They paddled for two hours until they reached the kelp beds. The seals had been here two days before when Tugakax scouted them. A few would likely remain until the snows.

Before the men left, seal meat had comprised half of the village's diet. Their kamleikas were made from the watertight throats; their kayaks from the hides. With these creatures, Aya and her people felt a dependence as strong as a family bond. Aya's mouth watered just observing the dark brown heads undulating in the waves.

Slukax raised her hand, and Tugakax held her paddle in place under water, slowing the kayak behind Slukax's. The women watched the dark brown bodies, each as fat as two boats and as long as one, seeking fish among the kelp near shore. They remained until their fingers ached and legs cramped, quietly paddling backward to keep their boats stationary. Aya felt her breasts swell with milk, then leak inside her kamleika. She had heard the men's stories of finding prey then waiting often nearly a tide until the right moment. But neither she nor the other women knew what they were waiting for, how to tell if the time was right. They waited until they felt the tide shifting under them.

Slukax looked at Aya. She motioned toward a seal feeding closest to shore. Nothing would make them more able or ready. The women dug their paddles into the water like shovels. The kayaks shot forward.

Aya fastened her eyes on the beast as the boat skimmed across the tops of the kelp. Several animals rolled aside as the boats cut toward the target.

When they were fifty feet away, Aya slid her paddle across the bow into the paddle holders and reached for her throwing board. She hadn't realized how cold her fingers had become and fumbled with the skin loops that secured her weapons. Tugakax held her paddle to the side at the top of the water to stabilize the boat for Aya's throw.

Aya glanced at the seal, now less than thirty feet away.

Slukax yelled, "Aya, now!" Slukax had positioned herself on the ocean side and fumbled with her own throwing board.

Aya slid the board free and ran the dart, tipped with a barbed harpoon point, through its groove. She glanced at the careful loop of sinew coiled on the kayak's bow that connected the dart to an inflated seal bladder. She hoped they would whip away from the boat as they should. She raised the throwing stick above her shoulder, pinned her eyes on the fatty neck, and threw.

She felt every rise and fall of the boat and the pull of the tide as she watched her dart speed toward the seal, then wobble as it lost momentum. She could see Slukax's dart skim across the water and sink, its inflated bladder bobbing uselessly at the surface.

Aya watched her harpoon point scrape through a layer of gray-white fat on the seal's shoulder and tilting uselessly into the water. Although the seal had only been grazed, it lifted its head with a great fountain of water. A silver fish flopped in its mouth as the animal turned toward the boats. It rolled underwater, somersaulting its silver-brown body to point toward the ocean, churning a wave that rolled outward toward Aya and Tugakax.

Slukax let loose another dart, heaving it forward so hard her kayak rocked to the lip of its hole. But the seal was moving now, and the spear sliced into the ocean harmlessly. The animal dove and resurfaced to the offshore side of Slukax's kayak. The seal peered behind her at the would-be hunters with her soft brown eyes. Aya's eyes locked on the animal's. She knows, Aya thought. She knows we are women. Then the seal rolled down again. The deep cleave of her tail disappeared into the gray sea.

Suddenly the women were alone. They had failed, and that failure stretched to the end of the world. The other seals had blown out air and descended to the sea floor to escape. They were well beyond range now. Tugakax paddled furiously to keep the kayak in motion so that the water, churned into a dozen patterns, didn't roll them.

When the water calmed, they paddled toward one another and lashed their kayaks together for stability. Aya felt she needed to explain but had no words. For once, Slukax didn't harangue her for aim or form. Her miss was not hers alone, and the other women knew they could have done no better. Slukax unlashed the kayak cover and reached inside for a small bag of dried berries and clams. The women passed the bits of food among themselves without speaking and watched the shore recede with the tide.

Twice more the women tried to spear a seal in the weeks that followed. The sea mammals, trusting their bulk and eager to feed before winter's scarcity, didn't grow more wary. But the women's aim didn't grow more sure either.

Their efforts led to death nonetheless.

Aya returned to the warmth of her *ulax* late after their third failure. Although the weather was turning, the *ulax*, dug five feet below-ground, remained warm. Rafters of whalebone and driftwood held up the dense sod roof. The sleeping quarters, separated by woven grass mats, lined the side walls. Piled with mats and hides, only a small oil lamp or two were needed to keep warm. The *ulax,* twenty feet wide and thirty feet long, was too big for their needs, now that the men were gone.

She took her baby from the thin arms of the woman who had been watching her and put the infant to her breast. Anshigis sucked eagerly with the strength of her hunger. Aya leaned against the wall. She had been thinking of her husband much of the day. She had known him all her life, but as a husband only a year before he'd gone to fight. He was a good husband, able, gentle. She had never known how much she needed him, his bravery in the kayak, his warm hands at night. When he'd courted her, she'd known only that he made her laugh and that people said he would bring her many fine skins to sew. If he did live, if he was in hiding on another island, somewhere far inland, if he did return, would he want her now? Would he know what she had done?

Behind her thoughts a panic began to form. Aya looked down at her baby, still sucking eagerly. She had not felt the tingling release of milk. She shifted Anshigis to her other breast and waited, trying to relax her shoulders, think of something else. Anshigis became frustrated and fussed through her increasingly frantic sucking.

Slukax descended the ladder just as Anshigis gave up and set to wailing, flailing her fists against her mother's dry breasts. Aya's eyes met Slukax's. Slukax turned around on the ladder and departed. Aya slid her finger into her baby's tiny, wailing mouth, but the baby soon found nothing flowing and returned to her wail.

When Slukax returned, she had a small bundle of berries in her hand. She didn't look at Aya or Anshigis but sat against the opposite wall and began to mash the berries in a carved bowl. To the mash she added water and poured the pale pink mixture into a tube of seal intestine, tying off one end and squeezing the other tight with her fingers. She handed it to Aya.

Anshigis did not like the feel of intestine in her mouth, and she did not like the sharp taste of berry. She cried and fought as Aya pried her gums apart and let drops of the mixture fall into the baby's mouth. She force-fed half the mixture, then tied the open end and set it next to her. Anshigis slept for a few minutes, fitfully, then came full awake. She arched her back and opened her mouth wide to let a stream of pink juice flow out. To Aya it seemed the fluid of life. She let it stain the baby's wrap and seep into the floor.

"Try again in a while," Slukax said.

Aya tried for the next two days, coaxing and forcing fluid into Anshigis. Sometimes the baby's body accepted it, most of the time it did not. Aya mixed her ration of stored eggs with water or fat; she made soups of nettle and edible leaves. Slukax gave part of her own ration to Aya, trying to coax milk from her body again.

The third day Aya woke up with Anshigis curled at her chest. She knew. The tiny body was still warm, but life was gone. Aya brought her knees up and wrapped her arms around the baby's body. She felt the punishment of her failure to throw the spear, and beyond that the punishment of God. She had made herself unclean, touching weapons, lifting the kayaks, breaking taboos.

A groan, deep and empty, rose from Aya, the sound of mothers across time and place, who understand that their children have suffered and died for their sins. Allowances are made for no sound worse than this; the vibrations would rip the universe apart.

Slukax left her alone there, visiting her boys in another home. She brought food to Aya that went untouched and spoke words that went unheard. Nothing moved in Aya's mind those first days.

She was vaguely aware when Tugakax and Slukax descended the ladder and quietly sat by her side. She felt Slukax lift her sleeping skins and her hands. Slukax pulled the baby into her own arms and leaned back. She closed her eyes and let a low moan through her lips. Then she began to rock, forward and back, a rhythmic moan pressed out with each forward motion. She rocked Anshigis's body like this for an hour or more then passed the body to Tugakax, who did the same. When another hour had passed, Tugakax gently pushed Aya into a sitting position and handed her the baby.

Aya looked at the two women, rocking and moaning for her baby. She held Anshigis to her chest and rocked with them. The moan that grew from her own mouth rose to a wail for a time then dropped to nearly a whisper, a cycle that lasted through the night.

When dawn came, the women began to dig. They removed the skin floor from Aya's sleeping place and dug a small, deep pit underneath. Aya wrapped Anshigis in skins and lay her down. She was not able to replace the dirt over her only daughter, and Tugakax took over. When the burial was complete, Aya curled up on her daughter's grave and let her rocking moan carry her into sleep.

Tugakax and Slukax let Aya mourn. They told the other women about the death. Mothers held their children and forced them to be still, to conserve energy. Mothers who had lost babies already, dreamed of their wombs and wondered if they would ever be full again. They longed for their men, for a whale, for children with happy, full bellies. The wind did not blow that day, nor the night that followed. The women cast quick glances at the sky, the mountains, the ocean, looking for movement in the clouds or grass or waves that would signal the wind's return. They saw no movement and shuddered.

The next afternoon Tugakax and Slukax returned to Aya.

"Get up," Slukax said, trying to sound stern. She pushed Aya with her foot, then took hold of her shoulders and sat her upright. "Tugakax and I have a proposal."

Tugakax knelt beside Aya and touched her cheek. "Aya, my daughter is shrinking as I watch. I feed her everything I find, but still her face becomes more hollow and her legs and arms like reeds. Everything I have done, I've done for her. I fled the Russian because I would not have her growing up seeing me as his *kalga*. Even though she is half Russian, she is mine. She is the future for me. I will do anything so that she can live. Even go to the caves."

Aya listened without hearing. The weight of her sorrow pinned her to a void into which she kept falling inch by inch. She didn't understand what Slukax and Tugakax were saying until the words thudded into her consciousness—dead-man's fat. She opened her eyes.

"I know these caves," Slukax was saying. "It would be a simple thing."

Aya felt the weight shift, felt hope slither between it and her body. She reached for it.

"Aya," Slukax said, "we will die one way or another. We may as well die as crazy women than as starving women."

The meaning of Slukax's words dropped like mist around them. They seeped into Aya with a permanence that would last all her long years. An age-old bargain with nature, with God. Take my will, my clear thoughts, and give me life. Aya knew that afternoon, sitting over her baby's cold body, that the trade-off always lurked nearby, and that it always demanded someone to bow to it. She had gone this far, already contaminated herself. She had no more children to sacrifice. Aya knew then that this was the moment for which her mother had prepared her with those strange words and urgent voice. Perhaps it was the knowledge of a mother with a dead baby, perhaps the knowledge of lasting hunger, but Aya sensed the weight and curve toward darkness that her own next word would bring. Yet she would not let her destiny be controlled by something other than her own hand.

"Yes."

That next morning the three women dressed in warm kamleikas and set out for the hills. They trekked down a long valley that gradually rose into the saddle of two mountains, a shortcut to a deep bay to the west. The first snow came gentle as the hands of a child. Aya felt it flutter over her eyelashes and caress the back of her neck, where it melted and trickled under her kamleika to form parallel rivulets flanking her spine. She arched her back away from her clothing to let them run.

When the women reached the ridge, they stopped to drink from their seal bladders. They topped the saddle and traversed across the western hill on a narrow path beaten into the ryegrass until the trail reached the sea then turned south to parallel the ocean. Slukax led them past several rough caves that darted into black lichen-covered rocks thrusting through the grass and tundra. At midafternoon she stopped before the broken face of a rock outcropping that leaned out over the sea. The gap, just wide enough to allow a body, faced away from the sun, and the women could see nothing but black inside.

When Slukax tried to move inside, Aya stopped her. "I will be the one," she said. It was what she wanted. To touch the dead now, linger with them.

She closed her eyes and saw Anshigis's smooth cheeks and sleep-damp hair as she withdrew her tinder of birds' down, sprinkled it with powdered sulfur, and struck her spark rocks together. She heard An-shigis's nursing murmur as she poured a shallow pool of precious seal oil in the hallow of her stone lamp and floated the burning tinder on it.

Aya moved past the other two women. She slid one leg and the arm holding the lamp inside, poking her head in to see what lay before her. The cave opened wide just inside, and the lamp's light didn't reach the walls. Turning her head back outside, she breathed deep from the fresh air. She refused to let her eyes find Slukax and Tugakax, standing a few feet away. Pulling her body inside the cave, she gave herself several minutes to stop trembling; she could not drop the lamp. She stepped farther in and held the lamp first to the right then to the left. The light illuminated the dim face of rock to the left, and she moved toward it. She held the lamp as far away from her body as possible.

The bodies didn't frighten her. And she understood all at once the change that had replaced the girl she'd been with the woman she'd become. Some part of her mourned for that girl, with a life of children, sewing, cooking, loving before her. But the larger part looked into the future, saw a woman who would never forget the cold, small body against her chest or the feel of a spear in her hand, or the taste of a dead man on her tongue.

She reached for the exposed hand of a man, lain along the wall. She could see this hand had been tasted before. Only two fingers remained. She was grateful the cave wall had sloughed, hiding his face in earth. She would never know who he was, although from the feel of his flesh, not yet dried hard and black from the warm vented cave, he had been dead no more than a few years.

Aya set her lamp on the uneven floor. The light sprang up and made the low ceiling dance with the shadows of dead limbs. She could see at least six bodies, laid on driftwood platforms along the wall. She held her breath, reached for her slate knife, and placed it at a slight angle to the dead man's second finger joint. She steadied the blade and carved through the joining bones, placing each piece of finger into a skin pouch.

The bodies held the power these men had gained in life. And if the living were willing, that power would flow to them. Although the only sanctioned use of these corpses was for power to hunt whales, Aya and her people knew the power itself was not so narrow.

As she turned back toward the cave opening, Aya heard the first moan of the returning wind. She wrapped her hand around her bead necklace and let go of the breath she had held too long.

When she squeezed from the cave into the open again, Slukax and Tugakax stood with their faces into the new wind. They would hardly meet her gaze. She could tell that they tried, as if by a connection of the eyes they could share her doom. But they were unable. Tugakax at last broke through the barrier and slung the pouch of dead-man's fat from Aya's shoulder.

"I will carry it," she said, offering herself as well to the forces that now marked Aya.

The three women started the long walk back to their village. Slukax hung back, and Aya could feel the press of her indecision rolling like waves against her back. She wondered if the flesh she had touched brought such easy awareness. At the saddle the women again rested as the moon glowed after the setting sun. Tugakax had set the pouch near her on the ground, and when they rose again, Slukax lifted it onto her own shoulder and wordlessly began walking down the mountain.

A wind whipped across the beach and toward the sea the next morning as Aya, Slukax, and Tugakax stood ankle deep in the water and washed. They scrubbed sand across their faces and hands, giving their woman-scent to the ocean in return for the smell of sea. Aya opened the pouch and pulled out three joints. Although the rituals, performed by men since ancient times, were the secret ways of hunters, a man could not lie beside a woman, share her life without passing something. Knowledge came in pieces, a whisper, a stolen glance, but the women knew enough to begin. They smeared the fat-layered skin, now warm and viscous, across their cheeks and palms as they had seen men do. The smell reminded Aya of whale and seal and her hunger. She bit off part of the meat, as did Slukax and Tugakax. The fat melted on Aya's tongue and pooled beside her back teeth. She closed her eyes and swallowed, letting the skin glide down her fat-slick throat, unchewed.

The three women pushed their kayak into the waves, laced the skin covering tight under their arms, and paddled straight into the sea.

Aya had felt her new power all night. She heard the breaths of Slukax and her boys even through her sleep. She knew when a child awoke in another house. She felt the wind shift and begin rolling off the island. And her dreams had come in waves of color that mocked the gray sky. So she was not surprised when she felt the presence behind her.

They had paddled far along the coast, searching kelp beds for a lingering sea lion. Now in more open water, they skirted reefs uncovered by the outgoing tide. Aya laid her paddle across the boat. Slukax and Tugakax stopped paddling as well and waited for her gesture. Aya nodded behind her, and Tugakax and Slukax dipped their paddles into the water to let the waves turn the kayaks.

The whale breached as their bows pointed straight at it. None of the women had envisioned a whale. This one was small, a gray whale, and young.

Aya reached into the kayak for the small pouch of monkshood oil. She held it upright as she slid the tip of her spear inside, coating it with poison. She unfastened her throwing stick and slotted the spear. The whale remained at the surface, within range. She circled her tongue against the entirety of her mouth, tasting for remnants of the deadman's fat.

And threw.

Slukax shouldered her own weapon, waiting to see which way the whale would break. The spear shot forward in a low arch; it landed with a popping noise to the rear of the fluke. Aya had not known to aim for this vulnerable spot, where the poison could readily enter the beast's bloodstream and work its slow death, but her arm had been directed there nonetheless. The whale immediately dove straight down. Slukax had no time to throw.

Aya watched the spear disappear with the whale. The waves from its plunging descent splashed at the kayak's bow. She dropped her weight low and waited. When she looked up nothing remained to show she had speared a whale. The water calmed like a pond, and fog sunk across it.

Aya felt her legs cramping under the skin skirt. Her mouth grew dry. She could no longer see Slukax. They found each other with their voices and began the journey back to shore. Aya began a song, and Tugakax and Slukax joined. They sang a wedding song and a birthing song and a song to the birds and, at last, a song to the whale.

For three days, Aya sequestered herself in the isolated whale-hunters *ulax*. Slukax and Tugakax, she knew, would find a story to tell the others. Although women did not enter this *ulax,* they knew what the men did there. They grieved so that the whale's suffering spirit would be drawn toward theirs. Aya neither ate nor drank. When she found herself thinking of things other than the whale, she let a mournful sigh into the silent walls. With her mind, she told the whale how it should die. She promised it she felt its pain as her own. She wondered if her husband had felt the whale the way she did. Twice since their marriage, he had hidden himself away in this same *ulax,* willing his own whales to die. Did all hunters feel this connection? Or had the Dry One given her something more?

Aya tore at her kamleika; she pulled her hair from her scalp. She ripped the beads from her neck and let them fall to the ground, an offering to the land itself for what she had taken. As her mouth dried and her stomach ached, she told the whale how she suffered with it. She felt it slow in the gray water. An ache stretches along its body. It can no longer sound as deep and must keep returning to the surface for breath. And each time, its eye takes in the rough shores of the island. Aya told it to let her pain draw it further toward death, toward land.

On the morning of the fourth day, Aya climbed outside to find Slukax and Tugakax waiting for her. Aya led them along the beach. An image of the whale, belly bumping against the rocky shore, had formed. She led them toward the place she saw in her mind. When they drew close, Aya saw it was true. Her whale had followed her through hunger, thirst, and pain, and died for her.

As she came close, a thrill she'd never felt coursed through her. They would live. She felt the power of life and hope.

"Cut here," Slukax said, directing Aya's knife around the spearhead, still embedded in the whale's flesh. "Now here, and here." Slukax traced a jagged line around the wound in what they hoped would be mistaken for the bite of a killer whale. Tugakax returned to the village to tell the people that the sea had given them a gift at last.

Aya heard the excited shouts and saw three boys round the bend first. The entire village came running, knives held high, pulling skids behind their skipping feet. She was wet from feet to waist, having waded in beside the whale to slash away at the skin and blubber around the spear puncture.

The boys yelled as they spotted the gray beached form. Slukax's boy Alidax ran hard into the water to jump up on a flipper, trying to spring to the whale's back. He slipped and crashed into the waves. His two friends laughed at him and jumped to the flipper, then boosted each other up. They were shouting and jumping, slipping and laughing when the village women reached the whale.

Tugakax's little girl placed her hands on the whale's cheek and raised to her tiptoes to gaze into its open eye. "Look, Mama," she said, pulling Tugakax over, "I am in the whale's eye."

Tugakax clutched the girl to her chest, closed her eyes, and hid her tears in her daughter's hair.

Aya didn't need to worry about the mark of her spear on the whale. With skill and relish, the women fell on the carcass, marking squares of blubber with their short knifes. This was women's work, and they did it well. Slukax shouted needless instructions. Two women took the whale's back, ripping regular squares of rubbery skin and yellow fat, which they handed down to two other women, who placed it on skids and harnessed themselves to drag it back to the village food pits. Others carved the sides and finally rolled the carcass to expose the belly. Children smeared fat in one another's hair and licked their fingers clean. Women smiled and talked in hushed, brief sentences.

"Such a gift. Such a gift." Slukax repeated the phrase often through the afternoon, giving the village women a safe word to remember.

They worked until nightfall, leaving the bones and innards for the next day. The village women and children walked together back to their homes, full with meat and the knowledge that they would live for another winter.

Aya watched them leave. She heard the questions they buried under the taste of fat meat. Some knew this whale had not drifted onto the beach. But Aya also knew that suspicion had been driven under hope, and the village women would ask no questions. She knew these things through her new awareness, a dark awareness she could touch only lightly.

She stood near the whale much of the night. The wind skidded across the beach, making its way toward the ocean. Her black hair lifted like fingers telling tales across her face. It stuck to the whale blubber smeared on her chin and in the moisture brought from her eyes by the wind. She didn't lift her hand to brush it away until the dark straight mask covered her face, until she could no longer see.

making sure

Darlene Panov unlocked a heavy padlock on the grayed plank door. It swung into a narrow arctic entry, bare and dry. Thad and I followed her through another door into the cabana. She gave us exactly twenty seconds to look around, which was really more than we needed. I loved it.

"You want it, two hundred fifty a month." Pricey for a place with no water, no electricity, no telephone wires.

Thad flicked several fifty-dollar bills from a roll.

I don't know if it was the view, the smell of old sea-soaked wood, or the way Thad handled rolls of cash, but blood fell immediately to my crotch, and I wanted nothing more than a good, slow fuck on the hardened floorboards. I pressed myself against Thad, conscious of making hip contact. Darlene left without a word.

I had my doubts about whether Darlene actually owned the cabana. More likely she owned the padlock. The feel of smooth dry wood under my shoulder blades and Thad's tense weight on me mingled with the smells of grass and ocean brought in through the open door.

Five replicas of our cabana dotted the hill below, and I could see the rotting remains of dozens more sinking into the scrub all around. The military had built these cabanas scattered in the hills after their typical barracks housing system proved, well, deadly. Up until June 1942, most of the soldiers stationed on Unalaska were housed in long barracks, an efficient plan no doubt. But when Japanese Zeros bombed the base on two consecutive days in June, these sprawling buildings were obvious targets. Seventeen boys newly arrived from Arkansas heard the air raid siren, figured it was a call to fall out for inspection, dutifully lined up outside their barracks, and were promptly bombed. The military realized their mistake and quickly switched housing plans, scattering small cabanas all over the place.

Now these cabanas on Ski Bowl Hill were part of Unalaska's coolest housing stock. Here, only these five had held up. I could see the rooftops above the low bush and tall grass, the smoke curling from two. Looking west, I could see the bay and the road leading to town. About half a mile from the valley floor, a track sunk off downhill, where the residents parked and a network of paths trickled off to each cabana. Thin grasses poked up from the thigh-scratching heath and rippled like wheat in the wind.

The soldiers built these retreats from rough boards carried by boat from southeast Alaska. Trees do not grow in the Aleutians, and the few that struggle near town were either planted by Russians two hundred years ago or by homesick soldiers during World War II. The tiny forests can't propagate well and are slowly dying.

I thought sometimes of these soldiers, snatched from their cheery farmhouses and busy cities and stationed at one of the most battered, remote, and dreary bases of the war. The only assignments worse were the bases farther along the Chain. These soldiers did not choose to come here. Most of them were drafted before they'd had time to decide just what it was they were fit to do with their lives. The military offered a purpose, something large to do—fight for your country, fight for freedom. What they really fought was the weather. More planes were lost, more men died at the hands of the wind and the fog than any Japanese gun or bomb. When the war ended, these men had discovered one goal, at least—to get off this shit-hole of an island.

The cabana was a fifteen-by-thirty-foot rectangle of open space. A rung ladder dropped between the kitchen-dining area and the living area, above which a king-size loft tucked under the roof peak. Mural-like windows faced the valley. A hillside of moving grass and shrubs slammed into a small back window. Because the building had been dug into the hill, the front deck gained height toward the edge. It was broad and solid, without railing or adornment. The view astounding. The wind whipped across it, shifting from behind to straight-on, as cool mountain air rushed down at night and up in the morning, tangling with the steady ocean wind.

The bathroom stood thirty feet behind the cabana and was built of the same grayed plank. The decorating attempts of a dozen residents lined the interior walls. Someone had stapled greeting cards, their flaps openable, on the right-hand wall. A stack of gray-ancient *Geographic*s mildewed on the board seat. The hide of a fox sagged against the back wall above the hole. Several enterprising sitters had carved a few words into the old wood. My favorite: *If you got to take a shit, there's no better place to sit.* Nothing as odd as the lone message on the toilet paper holder. On the door hung a curling poster of Billy Idol, lips sneering, leather pants pulling tight at the crotch. The seat faced the same view as the porch. I preferred the view to Billy Idol's stare and never closed the door.

I'd been in Dutch exactly two days and I had a job and a place to live. In two more days, Thad would be gone fishing and I'd be alone. Only two days left to learn how to operate a generator, refill propane tanks, start pilot lights, and ride a motorcycle. Thad bought me an old 500 to get around on the island. I would rent a truck every couple of weeks to carry in propane, gas, and groceries.

At least water wasn't a problem. The little neighborhood had a rain-catching tank uphill with pipes flowing into each cabana. Dutch got so much rain we never worried about running dry.

The next morning we headed to town for supplies. Rudger's Store had most everything, although few choices. You could get a white down blanket or a yellowish velour. You could browse the dish aisle and decide between the thin white plastic with little yellow daisies or a supply of paper plates. The cabana had come somewhat furnished with two worn recliners, a built-in bench under the living room window, and a Formica table with chairs. I would have stuck to the basics—bedding, pots and pans, dishes, candles, flashlights, food, liquor, boom box, music, and pot. But Thad had a hearth-and-home bug up his ass. He picked up a couple of braided rugs, throw pillows, a set of polished wooden vases, and two framed Aleutian prints that he asked me to hold on my lap for the jarring ride home.

"Why did you get all this crap?" I asked as he hammered nails into the wall to hang the pictures. He'd already picked wildflowers to fill the vases and arranged the rugs and pillows.

He smiled. "I've been wanting a few of these prints since I first came here. Never had a place to hang them until now. Looks homey, doesn't it?"

He set a sketch of a tattooed and bone-pierced Aleut woman down and circled his arms around me, swaying and singing along with a Bad Company tape we'd just bought. "Baby, when I think about you, I think about looove."

I socked him in the gut and ducked under his arm.

When he left, I had gobs of canned food, four bottles of Baileys, three Baggies of pot, and a small notebook half full of instructions. How to mix gas and oil for the minigenerator that ran the lights and stereo. How to disconnect and reconnect propane tanks. Where the pilots for the propane stove, refrigerator, and heater were.

The motorcycle was the toughest. First of all, it was black with dingy chrome, and if you squinted it looked like a mutant spider, its gas tank a bulging abdomen. The fuel gauge was missing. Thad showed me how to whack my knuckles against the tank and listen for a minutely different tone. It all sounded the same to me. Second, it required amazing feats of foot strength to shift gears. Whenever I tried to knock the shifter with my foot, I'd lose what balance I had and wobble. I blamed the road. It had been built, like all the roads stretching into the hills, by soldiers who had big trucks and didn't give a shit. They didn't bother with gravel. These roads were rock—most the size of a fist, many the size of a head.

The bike was probably too big for me, and keeping it upright while rolling over fist-and-head-size rocks required more speed than I liked. In the end, I just had to forget shifting and get down the mountain onto dirt roads, where it all became relatively easy. The worst part of using a motorcycle for your main transportation is the idiotic invention of a kick starter. I learned to throw my body onto the starter rather than just my leg weight. I learned to keep jumping on the damn thing long after it made sense. And I learned that it would often start if you said the right things in the right order.

It became an incantation. At first you talk nicely, maybe explain to the machine that the two of you are going on a nice little ride. When that fails, as it usually does if the motor hasn't run in the last hour, you start in with the threats. Gentle at first. You remind it that you're still shaky with the gears and may have to run it in first past 30 mph. You stomp harder. About a quarter of the time, the machine is still reticent. So you start cussing. You *must* be original and firm. Piece of junk doesn't cut it. You must mention scrap yards, private parts, hell, heaven, sin, and fornication. Also you must slip and fall into the bushes at least once. The machine expects and waits for this. If you've wrestled with kick-start and pull-start engines, you know these tricks. If you haven't, remember. Someday, somewhere, you will find that your only hope is an outboard, a snowmobile, a motorcycle, or a chain saw.

I did come to an understanding with my first motorcycle, generator, and propane appliances. But that was, of course, long after Thad was hundreds of miles away at sea. I'd been so busy jotting instructions in my notebook, I hadn't thought much about what it would be like when he was gone, when I was alone. I'd been alone in the past, but always a temporary solitude busy with the quest of finding someone new. This time I would just be waiting.

The sun slipped into the water as we approached the dock out on the spit, where his 110-foot trawler, the *Seawind,* was tied. Thad pulled off onto the shoulder alongside a dock flanking the spit for hundreds of feet. An ocean wind, laced with spray, hit my face full-on as soon as the bike stopped.

I could see across the navy blue bay to Unalaska Village, and up the shadowed green valley to where our cabana was. Diesel fuel mixed with the ocean smells, and the sounds of work broke into the hard wind, metal striking metal, men yelling. A row of fishing boats lined the dock, sulking a good ten feet below on a low tide. Men on the back decks lined up gear, numbered buoys, leaned against rust-stained railings and smoked.

"The *Seawind*'s out there," Thad said, pointing to a series of steel rods jutting high above the dock. His hand cupped my waist and pulled me into his kiss, dry and deep. "Come on." He slid his hand down to take mine.

I followed Thad past a series of boats, past a series of "Hey, Thad," and "Hey, Thad, who you got there?" Thad's oilskin spread wide behind him in the wind. His heavy boots landed solidly with each step farther out. The clouds had thickened, and now rain came in fidgeting spits.

I saw him off beside his boat. He held my face and kissed me. "Will you miss me?" he asked, brushing wind-licked hair from my eyes.

"Of course. I can't stand being alone," I said, grasping his neck to pull him close for another kiss.

"You didn't answer my question," he said when I let him go. "Will you miss *me*?"

"I said I would."

"Missing me is different from not wanting to be alone."

"What are you talking about?"

He looked at me oddly, like I had spittle in the corner of my mouth, then kissed me again, quick and hard.

I stood in the wind watching until his boat churned a wake into the open ocean as the drizzle became a rain.

On my way home, I dropped in at the museum-bookstore across from the Elbow Room. A wood-burned sign above the door announced OLD VOYAGERS. The two-room shack was baking warm, which felt good after the good soak I'd had riding over. The walls displayed reprinted Aleutian drawings by early explorers. Women with bone-studded faces. Families gathered in half-underground homes. Men trading with sailors under towering ships. The typical renderings of a vanquished people. Memorials to the victims. We feel pity for a split second and move on for ice cream. I recognized the two prints Thad had put up to domesticate our place. The store was empty except for the fiftyish Aleut woman who ran it.

"I'm looking for a book about the island," I said.

Without speaking, she handed me an oversize book called simply *The Aleutians*. One of an Alaska Geographic series, full of great pictures and geared toward giving the reader an overview.

"You got anything more?"

She had already begun filling out my receipt. "More?"

"Yeah."

She eyed me from over the top of wire-rim glasses. Her black hair was pulled back into a tight knot at the base of her skull, which descended into the fitted crew neck of her sage L.L. Bean pullover. I could hear the plop of soft-soled shoes tapping the wooden floor behind the counter. All in all she looked like a cross between a graduate student and a librarian. "Read that, then I may have *more* for you."

I handed her twenty dollars with the distinct feel that she neither expected nor wanted me to come back. I tucked my one new book inside my coat to protect it from the rain.

As I stepped out on the tiny porch, I bumped into Marge, whose body hovered protectively over a cardboard box in her arms.

"Watch it," she said, mounting the porch as I jumped down.

"What are you doing?"

"Basket weaving class."

"Basket weaving class?"

"Yeah, Anna holds them in back every week."

"Oh," I said. I watched her trudge into the shop as the cold rain sucked my jeans to my legs again.

I had only one visitor that first week. Thad had left me in the care of Carl, who was to look out for me, check up on me, and generally come to my aid. This meant Carl stopped by twice in the first week to make sure I hadn't blown up anything. Otherwise I was perfectly alone.

Mornings, I'd sit on the edge of my porch, the wind pressing my back, encouraging me to fly. Dangling my legs off the edge, because a deck chair just didn't seem appropriate, I'd sip my coffee and watch the cloud shadows sweep the mountains and the ocean curling itself against the shore. I hiked up into the mountains behind the cabana a couple of times. I wasn't a hiker sort, but all that soft summer green looked so inviting, beckoning really. At the saddle, all I could see was more of them, cresting into the distance. I thought about going on to the next one. But where would it end? You've got to watch out for those inklings to see what's next. Usually it's just more of the same.

I loved coming home to my empty cabana at night after running that gauntlet of groping fishermen and cramming Little Liz into a cab half the nights. At least she hadn't slapped me or shouted at me in Aleut again. My cabana was a sanctuary—at first. I'd check the heater, propane levels, turn off the generator, and revel in that fleeting feeling of self-sufficiency. But once all the tasks were done, the emptiness and the silence would begin their patient work. Like water that drip by drip hollows out a cave, the solitude eroded my pretense of adequacy. Reading helped. It gave me another mind to lose myself inside. I'd nestle in comforters while the wind skated over the roof, flick on my battery-powered book light, and listen to the voices on the page. I was smack in the middle of Stephen King's *It,* which had just come out, but I kept putting it down and picking up the Aleutian book.

The Aleutians are the world's longest archipelago, a thousand miles of volcanoes, pushing the detritus of two warring tectonic plates out from fissures in the crust, the final dumping ground for Pacific geological garbage. Two thousand years ago, at about the same time Vesuvius turned Pompeii into a treasure of relics, one of the world's largest calderas, Okmok, just west of Unalaska, exploded, smothering the land in ash and lava. Eruptions upon eruptions, century upon century. And underneath these volcanoes, the earth quakes, giving birth to tsunamis. On April Fool's Day in 1946, a 7.4 quake hit southwest of Unimak. A hundred-foot wave swept over the Scotch Cap lighthouse, killing five. The wave sped down the Pacific at more than five hundred miles an hour. In five hours it hit Hawaii, killing 159 people, then raced on to Chile, where thirteen hours later it struck, rebounded, and returned to hit the other side of Hawaii.

These are the seams of the world, geologist Juergen Kienle wrote, *and it's never going to calm down. That's where things are happening.*

The Aleuts didn't want to come here. They were the last of three waves of migrations from Asia over Beringia at the end of the last big ice age. The interior Indians had already taken the best land; then the Eskimos took the coastal land. The Aleuts, when they finally made it across, had no choice. They were pushed farther south, farther west, until they settled at this violent edge of the world nine thousand years ago.

At least that's the popular theory. It's the theory I believed at the time.

But they did okay. By five thousand years ago the Aleuts had developed a marine culture elegantly adapted to their environment. They were the finest small boatsmen in the world, exploiting one of the most desolate, unforgiving, beautiful, and biologically abundant places on earth. Then the Russians found them.

Within a hundred years, they were nearly extinct, suffering the longest and most brutal conquest history of any Alaskan people. I felt sorry for them as I read about what happened in those early years. The men who were lined up and shot just to see how many bodies a Russian bullet could penetrate. The young girls taken by a crew of Russians to an offshore island to pick berries and never seen again. The village women speared for sport. The men and women who watched their culture dying before them.

I climbed down from the loft to look at the prints Thad had hung. A Louis Choris 1816 drawing of Unalaska takes in a sweep of boiling sky, hinting at an infinite ocean beyond pinnacle mountains. A soft green horseshoe of land rings a pale gray ocean. From the grass rise the square boxes of the first Russian houses. Among them mound the soft lumps of Aleut homes, low and easily overlooked. In the foreground, a group of tiny Aleuts stand or lounge on what appears as manicured lawn.

I stepped to the left, to the second print, and read the caption. "Woman of Ounalashka. Drawn by John Webber, official artist for Capt. Cook's Third Voyage on July 2, 1778." She's a young woman. Little round beads outline her left ear. Two tracks of dark tattoos curve from the lobe, across her cheeks to the flare of her nostrils. A pyramid of tattoos rises from her chin to her lower lip. And from the center of her nose hangs a loop of oblong beads. Her hair is cut blunt across her forehead and twisted at the back. I stared into her eyes. They peer slightly to her left through whatever lay before her. From her eyes, you'd believe she is worried, a little sad. Thirty-eight years passed between when she sat for this portrait and when another sketch artist drew a nearby village. And everything has changed. On her mouth plays something of a smile, something of a frown. It's the expression of a victim, measuring her actions, even the cast of her eyes, in hopes that she'll survive. She's lying down and pretending to enjoy it.

The wind scraped the branches of a salmonberry bush against the back window. I stared out at the roving brush shadows. When I turned back, I wasn't so sure. I looked closer, blocking one feature then another. Something is off. Her lips don't belong to her eyes.

An Aleut Mona Lisa. I stepped back, taking in the whole sketch again. My hand dropped suddenly when I realized I'm touching my own lips, tracing their expression.

We're alone here, she and I, sharing a cabana, separated only by time. The men are gone—dead, fighting, fishing, fleeing. And we're alone; we're left to exist, victims of all the propane appliances and the solitude and the Russian brutes and a world undone.

a neighbor's house

I fell to sleep in the loft with my cheek pressed against a picture of several Aleut kayaks approaching a Russian sailing ship. It must have been a couple hours before dawn, the darkest part of the night, when I awoke with a jolt of fear that shot to my toes. I heard the high, cracked ending of an eagle's scream. And something else. Someone was pounding on the door. I flung myself down the ladder, grabbed an ax by the stove, and slid into the arctic entry, stepping over the perpetual oily spot by the generator.

"Who is it?"

A small voice carried through the planks, just barely. Enough to know it was a woman. I unlatched the door.

She was Aleut, nearly naked, and badly beaten.

I opened the door wide and led her to a kitchen chair. She sat down. The question-and-answer part of my brain backed off, leaving room for the basics like getting light, warmth, and tea made. I cranked the generator to get the lights on, turned up the heater, and started a pot of water on the stove.

Both of us were inhabiting that shut-down space, aware that it was temporary, that more would be coming, but that right now, certain steps had to be taken.

She wore only socks and pants. I pulled down a comforter from the loft, and she wrapped it around her shoulders. Her left eye had closed. A jagged rip tore across her cheekbone. Crisp blood ringed her nostrils. A doorknob-size bump pushed through the bangs on her forehead. She had bitten nearly through her lip. From the way she hunched, I guessed her solar plexus was bruised, and she cradled several fingers on her right hand as if they were broken.

I gave her a mug of tea, which she held in her left hand and sipped, wincing as the cup touched her lip. She drank in silence for several minutes.

"I'm your neighbor." The woman stared into her tea. "Nick . . . Nicholas, my husband, just got back."

It was one of those comments that tells it all. In those few words, a series of days and years revealed, a relationship sketched and understood. I wondered what I should do with her. Normally, I would have picked up the telephone and called someone more equipped. But, of course, there wasn't a telephone or anyone more equipped nearby. She needed to get to the clinic, but I had no car. I tried to think of a way to get out of this. Then I realized a part of her story was missing. A vital part.

"Where is he now?"

She shrugged. "He was gone when I came to."

A steel arrow sliced down my spine. I had been around these kind of men before. My former roommate Kathy had only been one in a succession of women I'd known who'd gone in for fists-of-fury men. I've never understood this dynamic in women, never wanted to understand it. It was enough to know that I was not susceptible. That I wasn't weak. I did understand the dynamic for men a bit though. They were just feeling ineffectual, helpless, and therefore angry. And a hopeless, angry man is astoundingly predictable.

I picked up a flashlight, went to the front door, and slid the locking latch closed. I shone the light along the door frame. The lock screws were maybe a quarter-inch long; I could rip them out myself with a few good shoves. The interior door didn't have a latch, let alone a lock.

She looked up at me as I came back in. Panic bounced between us. I turned to refill her tea in an effort to stop the cycle. I brought out a bag of peas from the freezer for the swelling and dug out a long-sleeve T-shirt, sweater, and a pair of rubber boots that slipped off her feet if she didn't keep them pressed to the floor. I pulled on a pair of jeans. The actions helped me stay in the false calm of emergency mode.

"I'm Brandy," I said when we'd dressed.

She looked at me from under the peas. "Mary Sivtsov."

The wind rattled the outer door. We both jumped.

"Will he look here?"

She shrugged.

"We should get you to the clinic."

"I'm okay."

"I think your fingers are broken."

She tucked her swelling hand into her lap.

I peered out the window. "Which place is yours?"

"Right below you. I saw you the day you moved in."

I looked through the window at her cabana, a dark outline on the hill below. Another jolt of fear shot to my toes. I jumped up and turned off the lights. I wanted to panic. Nothing is worse than knowing you can't because somebody else is even less able to figure out what the hell to do than you. Not three minutes later I saw light brighten the window below us. He had probably been on the path when I'd turned off the lights. I had two options. I could kick Mary out of the house, leaving her to deal with him on her own, or I could try to get her on my bike and into town. The first option looked good—end of problem. But this time there was no Nan to pick up my slack; no choice that didn't leave me culpable for the consequences. And something about having hauled propane tanks, started generators, and ridden a stubborn motorcycle conspired to make me feel more, well, surly and capable. I didn't want to be such a pansy right then. She had come to my house. And we were alone.

"Shit," I said. "Come on. We're leaving."

Another shrug. "I'm not going to the clinic."

"I don't give a fuck, but I'm not waiting for him to figure out where you went."

I don't like being depended upon. I don't like helping people. Don't confuse my actions with anything heroic. I was scared. Guys who hit their wives don't like other women to interfere, and the distinction between wife and interferer isn't always clear to them. They'll smack any-one who gets in the way. Besides, I couldn't sit still with all this panic breaking loose in my body.

The path was straight enough to follow in the dark. Mary moved slow but kept coming. I wanted to run and fought to keep pace with her, consciously controlling my muscles. I thought about the bike as we walked. It was loud, and if it didn't start quickly, Nicholas would have plenty of time. I talked to it by telepathy, trying to get to stage two at least before we reached it.

It didn't work. I had to go through the entire process—the soft en-couragement, the serious threats, the swearing, and the falling. A green truck was parked at the pullout. Mary sat down on a tuft of grass. I tried to swear quietly, but the machine would have none of it. When I saw a beam of light shining toward us from Mary's place, I gave up.

"Mother-fuckin, ass-licking, crap-taking, slimy, sadist crap," I screamed as I stomped on the starter, scraping my calf on something sharp and metal. The engine caught. I grabbed for the gas grip, missed, and lost my chance. The beam of light swung toward us. It was too far to illuminate, but it began to move.

"Shit!" I glanced at Mary. She was up and staring at the light. I nod-ded toward the truck. "Do you have keys?"

"Fucking bitch. I know that's you." The wind caught Nicholas's voice and brought it directly at us. I glanced toward him. He was far-ther away than he seemed.

Mary shook her head.

"Shit!" I stomped on the starter again. It caught. I massaged the gas grip. A rough idle took hold. "Get on!"

Mary grimaced as she raised her leg to straddle the gas-abdomen and slide behind me. I had never attempted to ride with a passenger. I had no idea how it was done. Mary's left hand clutched my shirt, and her right elbow crooked around my chest. Her damaged fingers couldn't grip.

"Fucking bitch. I'm gonna kill you."

I saw the flashlight bobbing wildly. He was running now, he'd be at the road in seconds.

I pulled the clutch tight to the handlebar, flicked the gear with my toes, and goosed the gas. It was too much. With the extra weight in back, I popped the front wheel. We both lurched forward to stay on just as a flashlight hit my shoulder. He'd made it within throwing distance, but not soon enough. I went faster than I ever had before—in the dark, with a passenger who couldn't hold on, let alone cling. I expected to see headlights behind us any second, but he didn't follow.

She wouldn't let me take her to the clinic, which was dark and deserted anyway. We settled for her sister's place. I parked the bike under an eave on the side of the house. It would be hard to see until the sun rose. Mary's sister came to the door wearing a robe but wide awake. She took a look at Mary and yelled for someone inside. She guided Mary to a chair.

"I don't know what got into him. He had a hard time fishing. They didn't catch much. I think he forgot about getting the kids back. If it weren't for those social workers, he wouldn't be like this." Mary's barrage of explanation all pointed one way—toward excusing her man.

Her sister had heard it before. "You're crazy. If you left him, you'd get the kids back. You know that."

"The kids are his. They have no right . . ."

Mary's words stopped. The oldest woman I have ever seen moved from the darkened back hall. She wore a flannel housecoat and beaded leather slippers. She walked with the gait of a tired bull rider. Her face was a puzzle of folded skin, too deep to be called wrinkles. She sat in a chair next to Mary and lifted the great burden of her lids to meet Mary's eyes.

Mary crumpled. She fell onto her knees, her head finding the old woman's lap. "I'm sorry," she moaned between sobs. Hands, as gnarled and dry as driftwood, moved across Mary's tangled hair, sweeping again and again. And then the old woman began to moan. A low, quiet moan I'd never heard before. It filled the small house with an ageless sadness, burdened the air with mourning.

I moved backward to the door, leaving them there. I could feel the rhythmic moan as I started my bike. The engine seemed to pulse with it, the air seemed to hold it. The sun was creeping up below the horizon, and I had no place to go where I wouldn't be alone.

Except Bellie's. Even the thought of sleeping on her couch with that horrid cage of flowers dangling over me was better than being alone tonight. Sure, I was a little worried about Nicholas, but he'd be more angry with Mary than with me, once he sobered up. I was more afraid of myself, of this sudden blunder of a rescue I'd actually accomplished. I needed someone who was chatty and had coke.

take a minute

I stayed with Bellie a couple days, until Marge told me Nicholas was back out fishing. After Bellie's riot of a house, my little gray home on a hill felt more lonely than ever. Thad wouldn't be back for a couple more weeks at least, and I had no one to ease myself around, no one to gauge myself by, no one to be anything for. My defenses were down, and I got reflective. Not just about the past, but the kind of reflection that flings the past forward to clash with the present. And battle for a future.

I would think a lot about the last time I'd seen my dad.

I had been cocktail waitressing in Redwood City. The man I'd been shacked up with had just decided to go back to his wife and kids. He left me with an apartment I couldn't afford and a red Fiat with low-profile tires. I packed up everything I wanted to keep, which barely filled the backseat, and left. I can't say why I wanted to see Dad one more time. I did not love my father. I had no hope that we'd ever be close again. It may have been a need to know that at least I'd seen him once near the end.

Grandma Jane had given me the address of Yolanda and Phil Caracus at Ever-New Wrecking and Salvage just south of Bakersfield, outside a town aptly called Weed Patch. She also said he was sick. "Oh, honey," her voice crackling with age, "he'd just love to see you again." I knew she sent money now and then. That she'd given up visiting. That he had become one of the invisible: ties dissolving, eyes averted, and waiting to die.

The temperature had climbed into the nineties, even though it was mid-April. And no, I didn't have air-conditioning in the Fiat. I kept the windows down and a towel between my legs to keep them from sticking together. I found Ever-New right on Highway 56, a two-lane several miles from Weed Patch. The dust made a ball of haze around the car when I stopped. It was close to what I expected—a low-slung, half-metal, half-wood building, the front obscured by crap—an old lawn mower, dissolving cardboard boxes overflowing with small engine parts. A collection of wind chimes and twirlers buried the front door. Nothing moved.

A dangle of humongous bells banged against the glass as I pushed the door open. Inside more junk, once loosely organized, now given way to entropy. To the left a long, fleshy-colored Formica counter stretched under a burden of boxes, grime, and four ashtrays. A man's head rose from below the counter. His hand felt toward a cigarette burning in one of the ashtrays.

"What can I do for you?"

A small man, thin and made of bundled wires, he seemed both stiff and coiled.

"I heard you know where my dad is. I'm Brandy."

He looked at me with bargain-hunter eyes, appraising, figuring. "You're the daughter. He talks about you sometimes." He crushed out his cigarette. "Let me get Yolanda. She'll take you out to see him."

He disappeared through a door behind him. A minute later Yolanda appeared, all tight jeans, sprayed hair, and sharp boots. She came around the counter and stepped right up to me, cupping my face in her lacquer-nailed hands.

"Oh, you sweet thing," she said, shaking her head slowly. "You poor thing. It's good you're here. He could use a reason to keep going."

"Ah, leave the poor girl alone, Yolanda," Phil said.

Yolanda's honey-mother expression broke into a sour-wife expression as she turned, still clutching my face, to Phil. "What do you know about it?"

Phil shrugged.

Yolanda turned back to me, honey-mother expression firmly in place again. "He hasn't seen his own kids in thirty years," she said. "He doesn't know diddley." She released my face to capture my hand. "Come on. I'll take you to your dad."

She led me back out the front door and along the side of the building. I felt like a toddler being dragged behind her mother toward something I was damn suspicious of. It was probably good that Yolanda had me tightly by the hand. Although I'd just driven five sweaty hours to see him, it wouldn't have been uncharacteristic of me to run at the last minute when something ugly or weighty reared up in front of me. Enough of my father in me to make running the best-looking option a good deal of the time.

I realized Yolanda was talking as we rounded a five-car-high pile of squashed metal. "You know a lotta folks say Phil and me are loony for taking them in like this. But you know I always say 'When God gives you a solid foundation, you gotta share it.' With my career going along so well—I'm a Mary Kay consultant, you know—I just feel that I need to give something back. They aren't bad men, most of them. Oh, sure, we lose a few dollars from the till now and then. But most of them are like family. We let 'em fix up one of the bigger cars to live in, which don't cost us nothing and keeps 'em off the street. I'm the mother hen. Your dad, now, he's not one to take advantage. He ain't never been mean, even when he's drunk. That's when he gets weepy. Starts talking about his smart little girl."

Yolanda squeezed, and I could feel the slick sweat between our hands. It would be so easy to slide out of her grasp. We wound through rows of smashed cars, the sun bouncing off crumpled metal and forming force fields of rippling heat that looked so substantial you'd be afraid to walk into them.

He was bent over a chocolate brown Pinto, prying off the inner door panel with a crowbar. The ugliest dog I'd ever seen lay, head resting on too-big puppy paws, in a patch of dusty earth shaded by the front bumper.

"Henry," Yolanda shouted. "I got your daughter here."

When he turned, I had one of those slow-motion moments that in a movie would have blurred at the edges and been accompanied by haunting, spare notes on a cello. Was it shame I saw in his face? Disgust? Pain? Whatever it was, it was not the face I remembered. He was no longer tall. His frame stood, resolute with habit, but his flesh twisted and shrunk around it. He lifted his hand to shield his eyes from the sun. His tan face glistened with sweat trails running from his hairline. He still had his hair, still sandy blond and thick at fifty-two. I saw the tremble in his hand, and he must have seen me see. He quickly lowered it. A smile came tentatively. And he stepped over a bent door frame lying in the weeds. The dog jumped up, came with him, nose even with his thigh.

Panic swirled in the space between us when he got close enough to reach. We bobbed uncertainly toward each other, then retreated. I would like to say I threw my arms around him. But I was afraid of him. This was the first time I'd seen him as an honest bum—a drunk. That last time, five or six years ago, he was still pretending, still keeping an apartment, finding jobs now and then. Back then we had still been able to make believe. Standing in this heat with my father an arm's length away, I was suddenly aware of the power shift. For years I'd been daddy's girl, pleasing him with grades and a passion for hot rods; then, when he left, I'd followed my mom's lead and hated him by turning against everything he'd wanted for me and toward everything he disdained about her. For the last ten years, we'd been in a no-man's-land, rarely seeing each other but aware that we could negotiate a truce, a slow compromise—if we had the time. And that's what hit me now, that we had no more time. That he'd robbed me of the time and would leave me with a lifetime of regret. He was going to die and take away my chance to have my father back. At that moment, I hated him for it, and I pitied us both. I wanted to leave him there with a parting hateful remark and never let myself need him again. And I wanted to rush him to rehab and force vitamins into his mouth, and put him to bed on clean sheets and make him recover. Either action would have been better than what I did. Once again, I let him decide.

"I was just passing by and heard you were staying near here," I said, offering a neutral choice that left all the others open.

He nodded. "Glad you did."

We remained three feet apart, our feet light, uncertain.

"Oh, for the love of mud," Yolanda said with a sigh. She shook her head and stepped over to my father. "Give your daughter a hug, Henry." She shoved him toward me.

One of his arms came around my shoulders, and we stood maybe six inches apart as he patted my shoulder half a dozen times. "Good to see you. Good to see you." We remained in this awkward half hug, half standoff for maybe four seconds, then he backed up a couple steps.

Yolanda, hands on her hips, rolled her eyes and blew out a disgusted sigh. "No wonder," she muttered as she turned to walk back to the shop, leaving my dad and me alone among the corpses of Lincolns and Oldsmobiles.

Dad watched her until she rounded the corner. The silence lay like a blanket folded so long the creases were permanent lines of dust and shadow. I wanted to hold the silence longer this time, force him to ease us out of this. The dog snuffled, watching me.

"Who's this?" I asked. I couldn't do it, no matter that I'd been on my own so many years, that his weakness shouldn't strand me any longer.

"Cowboy," Dad said, reaching down to scratch the thing's head. Cowboy tilted his massive skull into the scratch. "My sidekick."

I knelt and reached my hand out. Cowboy jumped forward, missed my hand, and crashed into my knees. Of course, my knees were balancing the rest of me, which fell back with a plop into the red-dry dust. The dog's head pushed into my hair, and I had to shove him back to stand up again.

Dad slapped his thigh, and Cowboy leaped across the few feet separating us. "He's one of the pups Phil's guard dog had after a wayward weekend. This one seemed to have been born with an affinity for me. Phil let me keep him. Drowned the rest of the litter."

I couldn't help but think this was for the best. One of these atrocities in the world was enough. He was massive. Although still a pup, Cowboy's head came most of the way up my thigh. His body was one coiled muscle, and his head flattened with a low forehead and squared-off jaw. His hair was slick and short and gray-brown brindled, ideal camouflage for a junkyard. His tail was a thick cord of whipping muscle.

"What is he?"

"Mother's a rottweiler. Think the sire was a big wolfhound that kept sniffing around."

"He's a monster."

Dad nodded. "Hardly fits in the Lincoln anymore, and he snores. But we've negotiated an arrangement. He sleeps in the front seat; I get the back."

Cowboy came toward me again, still too exuberant. But I was firmly planted on both feet. He rubbed against my leg, and I stroked his flat head. He panted and looked up at me.

"He likes you."

Suddenly I was thankful for this monstrosity of a dog. He had given Dad and me a way to talk. A link that passed between us without the weight of our past. I knelt and hugged the big puppy, who smelled of heat and dust.

"You want to get something to eat?" I asked.

"Sounds good. I'll be done here in a couple hours. Place not too far down that sells good burgers." He paused. "Don't know if Phil's paying today. May have to owe you."

"I got it."

Dad walked me to my car, Cowboy flopping his big paws in the dust between us, occasionally stopping like his tail was on fire to dig his teeth into the hair on top of his rump. Fleas.

Dad opened the driver's door for me just as the sound hit us. One of the garage doors on Ever-New swept upward as an ignition echoed inside. Through the haze of exhaust, we watched a long, purplish Cadillac slowly, carefully back out. It turned, cleared the garage, swung left, then eased forward until it rolled to a stop beside my Fiat.

Yolanda stepped out.

She had on an unbelievably tight pantsuit. Her hair was pinned up in a scaffolding of curls, her face an American bimbo version of a geisha. How she had accomplished the transformation from western hoochie mamma to bimbo businesswoman in ten minutes still befuddles me.

"Are you guys off somewhere?" she shouted above the Caddie's throaty engine.

Dad didn't say speak.

"No, I'm going to get a room. We're going to dinner later."

"Well," she said, waving her hand over the car, grinning, posing, "what do you think?"

The Cadillac's fan turned on, already overcome by the heat. Across the back, in metallic gold were foot-tall letters that spelled out MARY KAY LADY. Now Mary Kay pink is not a pretty color to begin with. Its paleness has an organ quality. Yolanda's obviously self-made Mary Kay Caddie was off a bit. Too much purple. Too much shine. And the letters. Mary Kay letters are small, gold, and in a cursive script. Yolanda's were block letters so large they stretched all the way across the wide car. They had been spray painted with stencils, and the paint had leaked through, blurring the letters at the bottom.

"Isn't it just gorgeous?" Yolanda ran her long-nailed hand over the hood. "Phil did it for me. After my gooney sponsor messed up and didn't count all my orders. I had a car coming. Anyway Phil says, 'Babe, I'll fix you up with a better Mary Kay car than any of those makeup sissies.' Didn't he just do a delicious job?"

Yolanda turned to rub a smudge off the hood. Dad and I grinned at each other behind her back. I saw the smirk twitching at his mouth. It broke loose, and he coughed to cover it. My dad is one big mess of problems, but one thing he's never lacked is a sense of the humor and the irony that stings everyday moments.

I stroked the car's hood. "Wow," I said.

Yolanda smiled wide. "You know, hon, you could use a facial treatment. How 'bout I give you one. I'm all set up for a facial party in a couple hours, so everything's all ready. I was just heading into town to make a delivery, but it can wait. I can squeeze you right in." The smooth back of her nails traced my eyebrows. "Even give you my discount for anything you wanna buy."

She stuck her torso into the car, switched off the engine, and manhandled two large, rectangular pink cases from the passenger seat.

Now, I've always thought Mary Kay looked like corpse makeup, so thick you couldn't properly move your face underneath. But Yolanda was so sincere, so sure. "Sounds fun," I said, figuring I had little choice at this point. And I had an inkling even then that a makeover was exactly what I needed. I just had no idea what sort of remake I should go for, and a pretty good idea that neither I, nor Yolanda, were up to the task.

"That okay with you, Henry?" The Caddie's door moaned as she shoved it closed. "I'll have her back to you by the time you're done."

Dad nodded.

"Okay, then." Yolanda balanced a case on each hip. "Give me five minutes?"

We watched her hobble toward the garage, Dad and I side by side. Our eyes took in the custom Mary Kay job still ticking in the heat.

And we laughed aloud this time. Cowboy sat between us, looked from one to the other, then tilted his head up and howled. Not a husky howl, all lonesome and eerie. But a broken puppy howl, tentative and willing.

I fought down the bubble of hope-need that rose in my throat.

Yolanda and Phil lived in an apartment attached to their shop. The front door opened up to the store counter, the back door to the junk-yard proper. Yolanda ushered me to her dining table, a typical '80s glass and brass thing. I sat in a brass and faux wicker chair and looked out at a living room of emerald green carpet, berry couches with emer-ald accent pillows. A poufy flowered valance over the sliding doors to the back.

Yolanda had it all set up—probably not regulation Mary Kay setup, with incense burning, a Kenny Rogers tape playing, and the bottle of bourbon on a pink tablecloth. I could see the flip charts and the cos-metic mirrors and the pencil and order forms all lined up. It was all so clean and smelled of air freshener, the kind you put in your car.

Yolanda poured us both a tumbler of bourbon. "You want ice?" She had to yell over Kenny's singing.

I nodded. She went to the fridge and pulled out a tray. The bourbon splashed as the ice hit. I took a sip. I'd been to a Mary Kay party or two in my life, and this was the first time I'd been served booze or listened to speaker-perforating Kenny Rogers. "Is this normal?" I shouted. "Bourbon and makeovers?"

"It's one of the tricks I picked up. They won't tell you all the tricks at the sales seminars." She lifted a steaming washcloth from a boiling pot on the stove with tongs and let it drip before pressing the water out. She set it on the table in front of me.

"First thing," she said, taking a swig from her tumbler, "is cleansing. And you're going to talk. I got to know some things about your dad—

and you. Get all that old stuff off your face so we can see what we got to work with." I heard her refill my glass as I scrubbed away at myself. "So tell me," she said, "about your dad."

I set the smeared washcloth to the side. "Aren't you supposed to start with the Mary Kay story?"

"Dang, I forgot the flip chart." She propped an oversize flip chart on the table beside her. "Okay, this is the Mary Kay story."

"What?" I yelled.

"The Mary Kay story," she said, exaggerating her lip movements for my benefit. "This is Mary Kay. She's going on seventy in this shot. This is what really sold me on the products. Just look at her." Yolanda and I both swallowed more bourbon. She lit a cigarette and flipped to the second page—a young woman chatting on the front porch with another woman. Yolanda squinted at the caption. "This is what Mary Kay is all about, making friends, changing women's lives." She laid the flip chart down. "Thing is, before I can figure out what kind of change you need, I got to know how you started out."

I stared at her. "Aren't you supposed to go all the way through the chart? There's a lot more pages there; I can see them."

"Yeah, well." Yolanda flicked her ash tip into the ashtray. "I like to improvise. Mary Kay doesn't want robot makeup saleswomen, you know. Besides, that picture of Mary Kay really says it all."

She set a trio of toner, face and eye moisturizer in front of me. "Go ahead and put all that on," she yelled. "So here's what I know already. Your dad's a smart guy, from a good family, some money from construction. He goes to college but can't cut it, gets kicked out. He meets your mom. She's the best-looking piece of cake he's ever seen. They get married, have you. How am I doing?"

"No, you got it wrong. He met her before he got kicked out. He was almost done with his degree in Russian history. And it wasn't his fault. She was keeping him up all the damn time and he had to cheat to get a midterm done. And I don't really want to talk about it, okay?"

She stared at me a moment, then yelled, "I think this music is too loud. We can't really talk with it this loud." She got up and turned it down.

"That's better. You want to put the creamer stuff around your sensitive eye area. Yeah, that's better." She took hold of my face and turned it to each side. "Just what I thought, you're a winter. Most blondes are a summer, but if you're really light, you slide toward winter." She rummaged in a large plastic pink case. "I get it now. You blame her."

I stopped dabbing at the creamer. "No, I didn't say that. But he got caught. He bought a paper from some guy, and maybe the paper was too good. It didn't help that the guy had sold the same fucking paper to another guy in the class. And it wasn't construction. Dental moldings."

Yolanda squeezed a dollop of pink-tinged beige on my cosmetic tray. "Here. Try this foundation. Use upward strokes first to really get it in, then down to smooth it."

I smeared the foundation on my cheeks.

"No, not like that. Don't you listen. Blend." She pushed aside the cosmetic mirror, turned my chair to face her, and refilled both our glasses. "I'm just going to do it. You're gonna muck it up."

She started in with the contour; I lit a cigarette and kept talking. I didn't want her to have it wrong, to have the wrong impression of how Dad had ended up here.

"She gets pregnant, with me. He gets a job driving a truck around town, delivering beer and stuff. His folks are pissed and probably embarrassed for him. They don't like her one bit. He gets pissed right back, marries her, and cuts them off. Ta-da, a family is born."

It only got worse from there. Yolanda moved on to blush, eye shadow, mascara. I didn't tell her that my mom ground my dad into the dirt daily for loving her. In the early years, he'd sit at the table, reading the latest analysis of Russia's ambitions, arguing out loud with the author, explaining how the author didn't understand the nature of the Russian people, which undergirded everything that went wrong. He writes editorials for a couple history magazines and the newspaper. I am so proud of his name on the page, and when he reads his words to me, I think he's a giant among men.

And I remember her screaming at him, waving the paper. "You're embarrassing me with this shit. You're an embarrassment."

By the time I am eight, he isn't reading much history anymore, and she's done with him. She's going out a lot. We both know there are other men. She's got jewelry and clothes he didn't buy. She gets a job selling real estate and shows too many houses late at night. And Dad knows. He's drinking more. He's drunk even in the afternoons. He drapes his love on her every time she comes home—I love you, hon; anything you want, hon. And she hates it. He's weak and he's pathetic; I see it in her eyes. We have a loser for a husband-father, a "spineless prick," she calls him. She's going to win; he'll leave and I'll be at her mercy.

I picked up the mirror and looked at how the makeover was going. The purple eyes and all that creamy cakey foundation stared back at me. Mom favored purple eyes. Once I had the fuchsia lipstick on, I'd look just like her.

Yolanda returned and stood in front of me, surveying her work. "You look great. Right shade of lipstick is all you need.

"I look like a middle-aged whore."

"Don't be silly. It's the light in here. It's not flattering. You'll look great. When we're done, I'll light a candle and turn off the lights. You'll look great in the candlelight."

"Everyone looks great in candlelight. Maybe we should just turn off all the lights. Bet I look great in the dark."

"You know what's going on here," Yolanda said, digging in her case for a lip color. "You're pretending to hate your mother so as you don't got to blame your dad for anything. You can blame a person without betraying 'em. He wasn't a helpless victim, you know."

I stared at her as she stretched my lips out under the pressure of a waxy mango lipstick. "Ya don't know da hurst huckin ting aout it. Hu do ya tink ya er?" It didn't come out right, not just because I couldn't move my lips, but because I was kind of stunned and couldn't get my thoughts in place.

"Shhh. Let me turn off these lights." She did and lit a candle. "Tell me, what was so bad about your mother you've got to run so far behind her to kick her in the fanny."

"Okay, how about this one. I'm sixteen in my senior year and I start screwing my English teacher. Mom's real proud of me and all, makes sure the house is empty for us whenever we have plans. Then she finds this new guy, the owner of one of the bars we hang at, and she starts wanting the house for herself. He's married, of course. So she rents this cabin for me and Mr. English Teacher. It's an hour out of town on a mud puddle of a lake. I spend the whole summer after graduation screwing my teacher in this little cabin. No one ever finds out. We are so discreet. Mom is so fucking proud of her little girl, who can bag a teacher before she's out of high school and keep her reputation up all at once."

I stared Yolanda down, and she dropped her eyes. "You want more? Because I've got more. You want to know about the boyfriends I had that she fucked? Or the ones she had that I fucked? You want to know how we laughed at Dad? What we called him?"

Yolanda pushed the cosmetic mirror in front of me. She was silent for a minute. "Okay," she said, "you win. Your mom was a cruel heartless hussy and your dad was holy and blameless. You win."

She packed up the flip chart and all the tubes and compacts. I could not believe this junkyard therapist crap. I stared at myself in the mirror, in the candlelight. I couldn't breath, move.

"I'll put together a box of the products we liked on you," she said. When I still didn't respond, she added, "Hey, you know what, I'm not even gonna charge you wholesale. It'll be a gift. I want you to go out into the world with your new face and knock 'em dead."

Yolanda was right. I did look better in bad light. I looked like my mom.

When I stepped back into the evening light, I felt like something raw and wounded. But well layered with cosmetic protection. Dad, Phil, and two other guys were sitting on the front porch talking. Cowboy's front paws drooped over the edge, his massive head resting on Dad's thigh. The other two guys were bums like my dad. I watched from the car as Phil handed each of them a few bills. My dad stuffed them deep in his jeans and headed toward me. Cowboy leaped off the porch and fell in beside him. The other two men melted off toward the yard.

He stopped a few feet from the car. I knew what he saw. He saw her. I shrugged.

"I had no choice."

Dad grunted and reached for the door handle. Cowboy leaped past him as he opened the door, falling over the emergency brake and ending up with one pair of legs on each seat.

"Back," Dad yelled, and Cowboy jumped and wiggled between the seats. He immediately turned to face the front, his huge jaws protruding between us. And that's the way we rode to the diner. Father and daughter together again after so many years, gratefully unable to look at each other through the gray-brown-striped head of the world's ugliest dog.

I noticed right away how the other customers watched my dad as we found a seat at Joe's Good Food and Drink ten minutes later. They were all stares, followed by glances that stretched the eye muscles, refusing to let the neck turn. Even those sidewinder looks could pick up the evidence. I used to feel so proud being with him. As a little girl, I remember watching the faces of the people he talked to, registering the effects of his big words and sure pronouncements. I used to think that everyone believed my dad was the smartest, most knowledgeable dad in town. Now I watched those faces registering a bum, a drunk. He was way too thin, his rear end disappearing behind pockets of red-dust jeans. Broken blood vessels marbled his face under a sunburn that flaked bits of skin across his nose and cheeks. His eyes had that vague cast that goes with final stages. But most of it was in his attitude. He had a subservience about him, like he'd be just puppy-happy if you smiled and treated him like half a man. He thanked the waitress five or six times for seating us.

"How's your mom?" he asked while picking at an egg. We'd gone with breakfast even though it was past five.

"Same. She's got a new husband. He's about seventy. Has money. She's talking about starting a dance studio for disadvantaged girls." I rolled my eyes to let him know I didn't think much of Mom's ever-changing plans.

He chuckled. "She always did have big ideas."

"Or not big enough." I looked at him across the table, his meal still mostly intact. "She's still a mess."

I figured her latest man would last all of two years. I'd called Mom a few weeks back to congratulate her on the wedding, which I'd neglected to attend, even though it would have been only a three-hour drive. I just couldn't handle the thought of meeting yet another soon-to-be ex-stepfather.

"How long you going to stay with this one?" I had asked.

"Oh, sugar, you got to be like that? He's a good one. You'll like him."

"How long, Mom?"

She sighed, a tribulations-of-motherhood sigh. "This hostility is not attractive, Brandy. Lighten up."

But Dad didn't really want to hear about Mom. Just that she was okay, proof his leaving hadn't left a permanent mark. We talked about the weather, about Grandma, renewed an old discussion about what kind of car would be best to drive in a demolition derby. Then he got all serious.

"So you got anywhere on becoming a historian?"

"No."

"I heard you were enrolled up at Seattle."

"That was four years ago."

"Never finished?"

"No."

"No plans to get back to it?"

I shrugged.

"Still plenty of time."

"What are you, my career counselor?" It suddenly pissed me off, him doing this father act. Trying to help me get a plan for my life.

He lowered his eyes to his plate and pushed toast through puddles of egg yolk. "It's just you had the grades. You coulda gone to any school you wanted."

He had to get in one more lick. Part of me wanted to let him have it. I had the grades because that had been the one thing we shared, because I'd loved it and been good at it and knew, even then, that if I were smart enough and studious enough I could save him, prove to him that I wasn't her. I had the grades because I longed for that moment when he would ignore her and turn to me and my neat little row of A's. The thing was I could never be sure if it was for him or for me, or if it was the same thing anyway.

I remembered her standing at the door in a short dress with sleeves that ruffled over her hands. She must have been about thirty-three or -four, old enough to have honed this script. Dad and I are at the kitchen table, going over my report card. He's opened the special notebook he keeps to record my school achievements. She watches Dad and me for a minute. "It's sick, Henry," she says. "You know that? She should be going out with friends her age, having fun. She's too pretty to stay locked up studying."

"She's fourteen," Dad says, his tone flat.

"I'm so fuckin' sick of this, I can't stand to watch it." She smells of Chantilly and Kools as she pulls the door shut behind her.

I watch him watch her leave and watch him watch the door another minute, expecting the improbable. When he turns back to me, I waited for the smile, for his eyes to really see me. He picks up the stiff blue card, nodding seriously.

"You're gonna do anything you want with those kind of marks," he says. "You're gonna conquer the world, baby," he says and squeezes my shoulder.

The notebook is a sacred totem on the table between us. He clicks it open and tucks the report card into a protective cover, adding to the growing pages of certificates, achievements, and winning essays.

He gives me two bucks. "Go get yourself an ice cream or something." The swell of pride is an invincible bubble around me. Not pride in the grades so much as in knowing I'd taken him from my mother. And even then I must have sensed that I was giving something to him too, that as long as I was studious and skipping grades now and again, he could pour his hopes into a mold of my future and forget his.

I get back with my triple dip. Dad has the Wild Turkey on the table now. He talks about my "promising" future. I present my attention tied up with a bow and absorb. He talks about his days at U of W.

I get up to pee and come back to see Dad passed out draped over the table. His arm has knocked the Wild Turkey over, and the brown liquid spreads over the pages of the notebook, pooling on the vinyl protectors. At the top edges, where the vinyl opens, the booze has softened and stained the report. I watch the stain creep deeper inside, the paper soaking up the liquid like thirsty dirt.

It is the last entry in the notebook, the last report card that will ever make it home, the last time I will care.

"Why don't I take you out for a drink?" Dad was smiling now, with a few bites of egg and dry toast in his stomach. "There's a place just down the road."

Maybe it's wrong to drink with a drunk. Enabling and all that crap. But I wasn't here to rescue him; I knew that now. And he wasn't going to rescue me; I knew that too. He was just a man who had failed in so many ways. And I was just his daughter who could be his drinking buddy if he wanted. We had time for that at least.

"Sure," I said, and suddenly I understood why I was here—simply to be with him in this dirty, dying place.

Cowboy, Dad, and I drove to the Last Chance Saloon as the sun set. Cowboy was all big head, blocking my view. When I turned into the parking lot, he fell forward, conking his wide forehead on the dash. I left the window rolled halfway down and followed Dad up the gray wood steps into the bar.

We ordered rum and Cokes. He settled into his stool, boots looping the low rung, elbows poised on the bar. This was his domain. I had never been out with him before. I had seen him after the drinking was done, stumbling home, passing out. I can't explain how weird it was sitting at a bar with my father, knowing I was going to watch him get dead drunk.

Nothing happened to turn him into a drunk. Nothing happened. He had always drunk some, everyone did. But nothing kept happening. He kept driving a truck, coming home to a woman who was just going out. I could not have marked a day or year when so much nothing had happened that he let go. I'm sure he couldn't either. He slid and kept sliding. He never made a decision to drink more; he never made a decision to become a drunk, or a decision to become a bum. It was all in what didn't happen, or get said, or done. Just like proving a negative, looking back at nothing to see where it went wrong is impossible. What can you go back and fix? Nothing.

After the first drink, Dad came alive in a sense. He lost that beaten, subservient air. He talked about the plans he had. He'd met this guy who inherited a little printing business. But this guy wanted more than business card print runs and mailing labels. This guy was brilliant, wanted to start an alternative press, something to give a voice to provocative ideas. This guy liked what my dad had to say about Gorbachev and Russia's technological slide. He kept asking Dad to get something written up so they could get it out there, shake up the discussion. Dad had been jotting down some thoughts. He'd been picking up books at the library. Thought he'd have enough for an essay or two pretty quick.

When he got up to use the john, I looked around the room. It was filling up now. Six other men had bellied up to the bar. A group of three women, all in jeans, had grabbed a table. Several booths along the wall were crammed with couples or foursomes. I caught the eye of a man down the bar. He smiled and raised his glass. I returned the smile, instinctively. He was too old, too fat, too average, and seemed to be sitting more on his backbone than his ass. I scanned the counter behind the bar and saw the half-full jar of AA sobriety medallions, a sign hanging around its throat, FIRST DRINK FREE FOR YOUR FIRST YEAR COIN.

Dad returned, and my concentration narrowed to his face. Drink four was straight rum, a double. And he turned. I felt it coming in the silence that preceded it. He looked at me, eyes beginning to glisten. "You're a good daughter." He nodded as if tamping that notion into his brain for keeps. "I know I haven't been the father you should have had. I didn't make enough of myself. I didn't deserve you or your mother. But that's all gonna change. Soon as I get these books going, I'm going to need a researcher. Someone who really knows her way in the library. Probably have to send you to Washington, do some specialized research. Things are breaking loose in Russia. Ripe for a guy who understood the Russian mind-set, the people. Gonna shock some folks. You don't believe me, do you? Well, I will. I know I don't always do what I say. But this is for real. Six months, a year, I'll have that first book done. I'll get you working for me. Good place to start. We'll make sure you finish up that degree. Probably need to at least get your master's. You're going to do something in this world. Not like me. You got advantages. You got a brain, and you're young. Still young enough. You got the world by the tail, hon. Once I get this line of books going, I'm gonna make sure you get back in school. You can count on that. I know you don't have a good reason to believe me. But it's true.

"What have you been doing for work lately? No? You can do better. Yeah, much better. You always were good in school. And you got the looks. You got your mother's looks. She was a beautiful woman. She taught you a thing or two, huh? You'll do better. You got plenty of time yet. What are you now, twenty-eight? Thirty-one! Well, you don't look it. You got to get yourself married, have some kids before long. Lot easier to find a good man when you're young. I know I wasn't the best father. But I did the best I could. Leaving was the best I could do. Better for you. Your mom could find a better man that way. And she did, didn't she? Whole string of better men."

He was crying now. "I know I wasn't the best father. You turned out okay though. You sure did. You're going to make something of yourself. Not like your old dad. They say I'm not going to make it too much longer. You know, I sure am glad you came out here. Sure am."

"Come on, Dad. We better go."

He hadn't tipped the bartender all night. I put a five on the bar and followed him out to the parking lot. Cowboy sprang up when our feet crunched on the gravel. On the road, we passed a package store, and Dad called out for me to stop. I did a U-turn and pulled close to the doors in the empty parking lot. The lights at Party Time shot up into a dark, starry sky. "Just got to get a little something," Dad said. He was back with a brown paper sack, twisted around a bottle.

We pulled into Ever-New's parking lot. I asked Dad where his car was parked. He motioned toward the back. "Do you want me to help you?" He shook his head. Cowboy leaped from the passenger side, following Dad. I backed up. I saw Dad twisting the cap off the hidden bottle, Cowboy slam dancing at his side. I watched him for a minute. It was still him I wanted to please, even the way he was now. Even though at fourteen I'd turned my back on him and his hopes—and his hopes for me.

I got out of the car, left it running. Because I knew it was starting—that kind of crying that betrays you, because you want to just be angry and the sadness keeps leaking out, tainting the purity. I was pissed that he was dying, and I could see it in the way he walked, not shuffling, not stumbling, but so functionally getting to where he needed to be, no effort to waste. I was angry because I guess after all these years I still somehow believed that he held the secret password, that he had within him a word and a look that could resurrect the person I'd started out as.

"Dad!" I shouted as he disappeared behind the building. "Dad." And I ran, through the dusty parking lot and around the corner of the building. He had stopped there in the building's denser dark. Cowboy's ears pricked at me as he stood by Dad's side. "Dad," I said again, more quietly in the sudden gloom.

"You need something?"

I took a step forward, tried to think of something to say that was short enough to cover the tightness in my throat and the fluttery shakiness.

"No, not really."

"Night."

He walked away from me, and I let him. I let him, again.

"Coward." I whispered it—just to hear myself was enough. I guess it was that moment, watching him walk into the shadows of piled, rusting junk cars, that I really gave up. If he did have the password, he wasn't talking. And I was the fool.

I felt more alone at that moment than I ever had. Shit, was this really all up to me? I walked back to the Fiat. It was all I had. A red Fiat, a few bags of clothes, a couple notebooks. It didn't look like much. It didn't look like enough.

I found a room for eighteen dollars and unloaded my stuff from the backseat. I showered off all the sweat, turned on the ceiling fan, and lay on the orange-flowered spread until early morning.

I was in a strange motel room, in a strange town. I was burning through men faster than Yolanda could change expressions. And I had no idea where I was going next, what I was going to do, or who I was going to do it with. I was thirty-one, the daughter of a bum and a slut, saddled with a liquor name.

I stayed two more days. I left with a cardboard box full of Mary Kay makeup, a dozen promises from Dad to write, and a crust of dog slobber on my forearms and neck. Cowboy had whined at me after the awkward good-byes. He stayed by Dad's leg as I walked away but kept standing, then sitting, looking at me intently and whining. The superstitious part of me wondered if he was trying to tell me something. Looking back, I know he was. That he'd take care of Dad the best he could. That he'd be my emissary when the time came. That we'd meet again.

I drove west until I hit I-5, then south. I kept the car at eighty, the radio blasting, slept at a rest stop. I knew speed couldn't wipe out the feelings that seeped under the deadness, that first harmless trickle before the breach. But it blurred the cracks. You have to be alert at eighty and keep a good part of your mind on driving. Still, thoughts about Dad nagged. I wondered about the imprint left by happy childhoods. I imagined who I'd be if mine had been different. I couldn't get a clear picture. I was helpless in my connection to the past. I wiped four tears from the tip of my nose and decided to forget Dad. I'd remember the dog instead, his ugly head on Dad's thigh, protective, proprietary.

The car died in L.A., or rather a section of L.A. called Santa Anita. I got out. A monolith of a racetrack, big and old, swelled up from across the road. It would have a bar, and it would need a cocktail waitress.

Thad showed up two weeks later. He'd been hanging out with fishing buddies in San Diego between seasons. A silver Camaro on a used car lot had caught his eye, and he'd decided to drive the coast all the way north. He walked into a shady offtrack bar called Trader Santeros, where I'd discovered they served free mini-chimichangas. For the price of a margarita, I could stuff myself. He was cute, thirty-three, and willing. I was really the only attractive woman in the place, so naturally we hit it off. I could tell right away he was safe. He didn't talk about the future, or goals. Or the past. He liked to start drinking early in the day and couldn't keep his hands off me. He was the kind of man I needed—just like me. A few days later, my bare feet were sticking out the window of his Camaro as we cruised I-5 north.

Two months later I found myself alone in this cabana overlooking a strange world of ocean and ryegrass and wind and memories.

touching ground

When I showed up for work on Thursday, Marge had a letter for me. I'd finally written to Dad, mostly about this odd place I'd landed. I sent a map along with the letter, circling Unalaska Island, to give him an idea of just how close to the edge of nothing I was. I sketched the basics of how I got here and asked about Cowboy.

Yolanda wrote back. Dad was hanging in there, still scheming. She made sure he took his pills. Cowboy had grown into his paws. The weather was hot enough to kill a crow. She'd included a compact of Mary Kay eye shadow in a trio of lavender, mauve, and pink. The teensy mirror had cracked, in the mail I assumed. I read while sipping my prework drink then folded the letter into my pocket. I handed the eye shadow to Marge.

The Elbow Room felt more cramped than ever. A boatload of Russian fishermen was in town, and they seemed to have turned up the energy a notch for everyone.

In the first hour alone, someone rang the bell hanging over the bar three times, which meant I had to hustle around to supply free drinks to everyone. My wrists were cramping up under the weight of the loaded tray.

The first fight broke out before midnight. I was setting drinks down at a table in the back when I got rammed from behind so hard I fell forward across the table, knocking drinks over with my chest. I turned to see two guys shoving at each other. The one who'd knocked me over pushed the other guy against the wall and started whaling on him.

"Fight!" I yelled.

The lights came up, and Marge rammed her way through the crowd, holding a rubberized bat in her right hand. She planted her feet and swung. The bat connected with the man's upper arm. By the time he turned toward her, she held the bat like she was waiting a pitch.

"Take it outside before I decide to aim."

Something about a burly, oldish woman with piled-up hair and blue eye shadow holding a bat takes the fight right out of most men. I'd see it again and again. Marge was a grandmother with combat training and meaty shoulders.

Several guys shoved the bruiser toward the door.

"You too," Marge said, pointing her bat at the guy who'd been up against the wall. "Out."

A group of about fifteen men followed the combatants. Moments later I heard the shouts that signaled the fight had resumed in the parking lot.

"You just going to let them go at it out there?" I asked Marge. "Aren't you going to call the police?"

She looked at me blankly and shrugged. "Police station's across the channel. The boys will make sure no one gets hurt too bad."

"But don't you think . . ."

Marge stepped toward me. "We like to take care of things ourselves. Keeps everyone happy. Got that?"

In the years that have past since by brief stay in Dutch, I've often wondered why bars tend to use big, burly guys as bouncers. I think a woman, who looks like someone's grandmother but knows how to swing a bat, is far more effective. It's hard to hit your grandma.

Within three minutes the lights were back down, the music blaring. Oh, outside two guys were beating the shit out of each other, but here in the circle of flowing booze, all was well.

Taking it outside is not a new bar management technique. It started about the time bars started. As with most of low culture, we can thank ancient Rome. While people have been drinking communally since the first guy tasted some rotting fruit, stumbled back to the village, and persuaded his buddies to come along, Rome turned it into a business. After all, you can't have people having so much fun and losing so much inhibition without a payoff.

I'm something of an accidental expert in the debaucher of ancient Rome. It was 1981; I was twenty-six, had dropped out of college for the second time but still lived with a college guy. After six years in the University of Washington's history doctoral program, Ned had finally produced a mess of notes that were somehow supposed to morph into a dissertation. He believed a few shots of Bushmills gave him better insight, but usually passed that fleeting window so fast he didn't have time for more than shuffling his notes around. At night, I worked at an underground punk bar, the kind that flashes black lights and serves drinks in plastic cups. But during the day I found myself in our basement apartment with nothing to do but watch *Donahue* and *General Hospital*. In desperation, I started reading Ned's notes during commercials. Pretty soon, not even Luke and Laura's battles could distract me. For some reason the Res Romana just grabbed me. The ferocity with which those people believed in Rome, in the idea of Rome, felt so large, so encompassing. When I read, I almost believed with them. I almost believed in causes, and purposes, and meaning. It was the almost that kept me going. At first it was just Ned's notes. But then I had to check his sources and read a few more. I ended up writing the whole damn thing. Ned's title, "Roman Roots of Social Degradation" became "Conquest of Sin: Roman Organization of Drinking, Prostitution, and Debauchery." I never knew if Ned's dissertation passed in defense or if he even used it. I left the morning I finished the manuscript. I placed it on the kitchen table and left with two suitcases, a box of tapes, a whole lot of knowledge about Rome's seamy side, and a smattering of a dead language from a dead empire.

I'm not sure if it was a preemptive retreat, knowing he'd kick me out once he understood that my gift had stripped him of his illusions, or if I just sensed I'd used up the best of Ned. Or maybe I'd scared myself. Those few months had brought my two sides into sharp contrast. They begged the question I'd pushed aside for years. Was I like my mother? My father? Or something else entirely?

Basically, Rome had two kinds of drinking dens. The bar was just that, a big, usually marble, counter that opened onto the sidewalk. Patrons simply pulled up a stool for refreshment during their errands. The tavern, on the other hand, had a door and separate rooms for eating, drinking, and, of course, fucking. Because Rome hadn't invented neon or etched glass, they decorated with murals instructing patrons in bar protocol. One painting excavated in Pompeii shows two gamblers arguing over who won a game. The owner pushes them toward the door, and a caption announces, "Go on outside to do your fighting."

Those bars in ancient Rome must have felt much like bars today. The high-flying and the sullen sitting side by side, feeding whatever inklings lurk inside, afraid to come out in dry spells. And, if any of those lurking inklings do come out, they must go outside. If they don't go peacefully, Marge will hit them with a baseball bat.

About three minutes after Marge ousted the men, I peeked outside. I'd always assumed that a mob of men surrounding a fight were there to egg it on, see blood. I'm sure that's part of it, but that's not what I saw. Several men peeled the winner off the loser. Two other men helped the loser into a cab. The rest filed back into the bar. I held the door open for them, my assumptions rearranged.

The rest of the night I worked with a drink-soaked shirt. A screwdriver had stained my shirt orange across the tits, which made for an evening of delightful commentary. The bell rang at least six more times, and my wrists creaked each time I straightened them after emptying my tray. When the HiTide babes showed up, their heels slipping in the muddy goo of the floor, I was relieved to know it was almost over.

Just before closing, I made my way to the table in the Blue Room to see a girl from one of the canneries stripping while she danced on the table surrounded by cheering men. I could see Little Liz ducking and craning from her bar stool, trying to get a peek through the bodies.

"Hey," I shouted. "Hey. Get her off there."

One of the guys stepped in front of me when I tried to grab the woman's wrist.

"Just a little fun," he yelled into my ear. "Here." He yanked a Baggie of weed from his pocket and threw it on my tray.

I looked at the pot, shrugged, and left her there, down to her panties.

She was a chunky redhead with run-together freckles and would probably remember this swarm of adulation for the rest of her life. Liz laughed at me through her missing teeth as I left the Blue Room to its vices.

Bellie had been guffawing most of the night with a table of fishermen in the back as usual. I'd come to understand that, in the purest of ways, Bellie was as much an Elbow employee as me. She was just more of an independent contractor. In general the guys she hooked up with were nice, smelly sometimes, and a bit vulgar, but not vicious. I guessed she liked their company almost as much as their coke.

I was standing at the door at closing time, trying to collect as many glasses as I could while Marge pushed the stragglers out. Two tall fishermen, held together on each side by Bellie's short arms, lurched as one through the door.

Bellie leaned across a midriff. "Come over to my place tomorrow."

One of the guys bent to whisper in her ear, and she covered her mouth to laugh. "Not too early," she shouted over her shoulder as the threesome made for a truck in the parking lot.

"Maybe I can't just pop over anytime you want," I shouted back. "Maybe I have plans."

"Yeah, right," she yelled from a truck window as the driver cranked over the engine.

By the time the bar cleared I needed my shot of schnapps more than usual. While Les poured, I scrounged in the storeroom for something to prop up the wobbly table's pedestal. I found a block of wood and crawled across ridges of drying mud to wedge it into place.

I checked the bathroom and thanked God Liz had made it out under her own power.

I got to Bellie's sometime after noon. She had become my only friend. It wasn't my fault. I don't really make friends. Bellie just assumed our friendship, and I went along. We did have some things in common: at twenty-eight, she was close to my age, and we both worked in the Elbow Room serving men. Beyond that I didn't see any reason for our friendship. We did coke together when she had it. She worked the Elbow Room most nights and would tell me to stop by if she'd scored. I came to realize she was what we called a coke whore. And she wasn't the only one. The HiTide fake blondes were too, or so I was told, and chose to believe.

Coke whores are a bit different from your street walks and call girls. They retain control of their relations a tad longer because their men are never quite sure how the gift exchange goes down. Such relations can appear like a date, or at least a party, for a while.

Bellie had acquired two new things since last night, a truck and an eight-ball of coke. She was in fine form, really flouncing around her place, playing tapes, dancing, cleaning her fridge. And talking fast. Apparently she was taking me somewhere. One of her cohorts had left a truck in her care while he fished.

She laid out and snorted a couple lines in between scrubbing the vegetable bins.

"Maybe we'll find something. Maybe not. You never know. You've never seen the pillboxes or the middens. I made a lunch."

She continued chatting while she packed the truck. Last, but most important, she tossed in a small mirror and her doubled-Baggied stash of coke. Ten minutes later we were cutting off the main road, following an even rougher road along the northern coast. She drove fast, still talking. I don't know how to impress on you how odd it is for an Aleut woman to chatter. I believe it can only be done under the influence of an amphetamine. Aleuts aren't gabby folks. In fact, if there were any people who could keep a secret for a long time, it would be Aleuts. Even when they do talk, it's a circuitous language. Oh, they may be speaking English, but it's different enough to be called foreign. Rarely are they talking about what the sparse nouns and verbs would make you think. It's all about nuance and pattern and timing. And the meaning is buried. You have to listen and dig and likely as not, you'll misunderstand. Coke, however, made Bellie speak plain English, if a sped-up version.

As I look back now, I think Bellie was really two people—the coked-up fun gal with lots to say, and the other Bellie, the one I had only a few glimpses of until the end. With a few lines up her nose, Bellie was like a barrel rolling right toward you. You got the sense something with momentum was on the way. You almost felt relieved when it didn't crush you, when it stopped and said something. Bellie was always funny, sometimes wise. She could laugh until the curls unwound from her hair. And she was adventurous. At least that was Bellie on coke.

The unpowdered Bellie was quiet, stoic, sad. I rarely saw her this way, something I now think she was careful to engineer.

". . . eight thousand years. That's what they say. It's actually a lot longer. To the beginning of time, if you believe the stories. Which I don't. But it is longer. And that land bridge stuff is shit. We didn't walk over from Siberia. Shit, would you walk if you had a kayak?"

We hit a Buick-size hole in the road going forty, which jarred Bellie out of her history spasm. She slammed on the brakes, stretching her leg from the hip and slipping so far down the seat she could barely see. "Shit, I think we passed it." She grabbed the shifter with both hands and shoved it into reverse. The rear tires bumped back into the enormous hole, tipping the cab so I had to grab the suicide handle to keep from landing in her lap. She slammed into first, and the truck's rear wheels hurled rocks behind us as we lurched over the lip of the hole again.

"There it is." Bellie pointed inland at a faint two-tire track heading up between hills. A creek flowed in one of the ruts. She turned the wheel hard and floored the gas to make it over the line of rocks that edged the road. I had to hold on tight with one hand while grabbing stuff spilling from side to side and front to back in the cab. The CB mike, bolted to the ceiling, came loose and whacked me in the eye. Bellie kept talking and driving fast. If the truck stopped, it probably wouldn't be able to get going again, and there was no way to turn around. About half a mile up, the track curved inland behind a hill for a stretch then climbed again toward the coast. Dark open holes edged by the rusty arches of metal supports sank into the hillsides—old underground military installations, tunnel entrances. Half-fallen wooden structures, concrete rubble, the ghosts of telegraph poles. Unalaska was littered with the evidence, with the history of what it had seen and been. We stopped about five yards from the edge of a cliff that fell away to the sea.

"Made it," Bellie said. Wind battered the truck, lifting it in gusts and rattling the doors and fenders. Bellie reached for the mirror, which had remained intact on the floorboards. She killed the engine and began laying out lines. A sharp trickle of coke stung my throat as I took in the view. The mountains looked like the soft bodies of women lying side by side. But gentle curves had been sliced away at the sea, the rock exposed like grayed bones. Sliced bodies surrounded by a voracious ocean.

A low hexagonal concrete structure bumped out of the bare rock at the top of the hill, close to the edge of the cliff. Its roof had accumulated enough dirt to support a tuff of lichen-moss hair.

"It's a bunker," Bellie said, pointing with her pink straw. "Come on."

I could hardly shut the truck door against the wind and had to slam it with my body. We walked to the bunker across a carpet of black and silver lichen and crawled through the low entry. The floor was gravel. Inside the wind whistled through three slits that opened out on the bay. They were just big enough for a spotting scope and a pair of eyes. I ran my fingers along the lower frame and felt the grooves worn by countless soldiers as they slid their scopes in and out of the opening. I wondered who had been up here when the bombs fell and what he had done. The Zeros had probably been too quick for him to call out coordinates to the guys manning the big guns. Did he try anyway, needing to do something? Had he been paralyzed by fear, by indecision, and done nothing? Did he watch while others died?

I scooted to the side of the lookout to get out of the wind and lit a cigarette. Bellie bummed one. While she often had decent coke, she rarely had cigarettes. The smoke rushed out the door on a path of wind that shot straight from the gunnery slots to the entry.

"My mother was here for part of the war," Bellie said. "They moved her and everyone else to a camp in southeast after the bombing. She didn't come back for years. Said the soldiers had trashed everything. I wasn't even born here."

We talked for maybe another half hour, about her family, about men, about the island. As the coke wore off, Bellie became quieter. I crawled to the spotting slits and stared out through the wind. When I turned around, Bellie was crying. No shoulder shakes or sounds. Just her small palms covering a wet face.

"What's wrong?"

She shook her head.

I crawled across the gravel on my knees. "Bellie," I said, lifting one of her hands from her forehead. The brilliant birthmark, smeared with tears, seemed to shimmer in the dim wetness. It wasn't like me to try this hard, but something was shifting in me, a need was growing, nurtured by these unpredictable surroundings and the way they kept me off balance. And frankly, I felt sorry for her. After reading what those women suffered at the beginning, when the Russians came, I had a general sympathy-pity thing going for all the Aleut women. Especially Bellie, with her pudgy middle and her ducky kitchen and unicorn mirrors. I knew just enough to see them all as victims, even 250 years removed.

"Tell me," I said.

She looked at me then, dropping one hand and pressing the other over the mark. Her eyes drifted past me out the gun sights and across the waves. "I didn't know," she said less to me than to herself.

"Didn't know what?"

She was silent, but her fingers twitched, rhythmically pressing and smoothing the white mark of her forehead.

Sometimes when a friend cries, then refuses to tell you why, it's because she wants you to work at it a bit. She wants to talk, but wants to pretend she doesn't. I didn't get that from Bellie. I let it go.

A few minutes later, her eyes were dry. "Come on," she said. "We'll walk down to the middens."

I crawled after her. We started down a zigzagged trail that leaned inside lichen-encrusted outcroppings and patches of dark mossberries down to a narrow valley, emptying to the sea. We walked carefully and silently for twenty minutes. At the base I could see a mound of gravel and sand. Bellie jumped the last three feet of the trail and landed squarely on the sand. I jumped after her.

"We're really not supposed to dig around here. It's an archaeological site. Once in a while a couple of guys from some university come and poke around." She lifted a silver chain from her shirt and held it up to me. At the end were three small beads. "I found these here. They're bone beads."

She sat down cross-legged and began running ringed fingers through the sand. I sat down nearby, pulled the Baggie tip from last night out of my jacket, and loaded my stubby pipe. We passed it back and forth for a couple minutes. It was good stuff. When I felt the change, I knew this was perfect.

I've paid attention to what drugs are good for what activities. Mushrooms are great for watching really odd movies and northern lights. Opium is just right on a summer night at the top of a mountain overlooking the lights of a city. Coke for parties and late-night conversations. And let me tell you, pot is perfect for sitting on a wind-sheltered sand midden thousands of years old and running your fingers lightly under the surface, feeling. The grains flowed over the thinly covered bones of my hands in a sensual tickle. Rivulets of sand ran off the sides of my fingers, scattering veils of dust as they fell. I listened to the waves breaking on rocks at the end of the valley. My hands knew more than me. They slithered through the sand; my body scooted to follow. Bellie and I grew farther apart then back together as we chased our hands through the sand. I found an arrowhead, broken or never finished at the tip. Then my fingers pinched around something tiny and hard. I lifted it out of the sand and held it up. A tiny white bead, its center unevenly carved.

"It's a calcite bead," Bellie said, taking it in her hand. "A gift from the sea. They aren't that common." She stroked it smooth of sand. "It's a woman's bead."

I watched her fingers clamp over it and her eyes shut.

"Well?" I said. "Are you going to give it back?"

She held her hand over mine. "Thanks for what you did for Mary," she said and let the bead drop in my palm.

"No problem." I shoved the bead deep into my jeans pocket and lay down on the sand while Bellie continued to search. I couldn't imagine finding anything better.

Pestilence

Early explorers estimated *fifteen thousand Aleuts had lived on the islands before the Russians came. A hundred and fifty years later, the famed John Muir expedition found only 2,369. Tuberculosis, venereal disease, alcohol, forced labor, and malnutrition had obliterated as much as 90 percent of the Aleut people.*

The atrocities of conquest had also taken a toll. In 1796, Hieromonk Makarity, the first Russian priest to visit Unalaska, learned from Aleut toions that Russian fur traders were stripping village food supplies and abducting men and women—forcing the men to hunt sea mammals and the women to become companions. Makarity gathered six predominant Aleut men and journeyed across the ocean and Siberia to bring their complaints to the Russian emperor. He did nothing. Makarity and the Aleut men, who had spent years on the journey, died on the return trip when their ship sank not far from Unalaska.

When a smallpox epidemic swept the Aleutians in 1838, the Aleuts were already an endangered people. The Russian government ordered vaccinations, and local priests administered the shots. But far from the Russian strongholds, in remote coves and guarded bays of Unalaska, there remained villages that had not succumbed entirely to the new ways. They had been baptized by traveling Russian priests, but their lives were little changed. Strong shamans remained true to older paths. Vaccinations

failed to reach several of these villages, and the epidemic raged, taking en-
tire families, leaving villages empty to the wind and the rain and the fog.

Sometimes an idea is born and threads itself through the generations
of a group set apart. It grows slowly, taking sustenance from fresh
atrocities that feed its central tenet. Not many can hold such a young
idea. It needs a legend, a womb of knowing people, and darkness.
Aya's mind was such a place. Inside the folds of its memories, an idea
lived. It preyed on her like a parasite, feeding on what she saw.

People said Aya lived so long because her mind had been taken out
to sea, keeping her body from knowing when to die. Her great-
granddaughter believed them. She also believed the sea had given
Aya something back, a sign of respect for the old woman to wield on
dry land.

Even as a child, Agripina had sensed that her great-grandmother was
different. She had felt the old woman watching her, measuring her from
the beginning. People told stories about Aya. Agripina used to watch her
great-grandmother's shriveled face, trying to look inside her eyes and
see if they were true. Now at nineteen, Agripina believed everything.

Aya had never married, although she had taken many lovers, some
married, some nearly boys. She had many children. Three girl babies
had died as children. Six strong sons grew old and died in this village.
One son, Algemalinag, had become *toion* of a village to the east. He
had perished with the priest and other men forty years before. Aya had
warned him not to go, that no Russian *toion* would care that the Aleut
women were being taken as captive Russian concubines, or that Aleut
hunters were forced from their villages to faraway islands to hunt fur
seals. But Algemalinag had believed the priest, he'd believed that
words could make a difference. When Algemalinag didn't return, his
wife and children along with the others had abandoned their village
and joined Aya's.

Agripina sat at her brother's side in their family *ulax,* fanning him
with a grass mat. His fever was peaking, and Agripina knew he would
die. Already her emotions were pulling back, like a snail's foot retreating into the protection of its shell. Agripina had seen too much death,
and the numbness that follows tragedy had already invaded her heart.

The children had gone first. Six new graves mounded under the waving grass above the village. Now even adults were falling. The Russians called it smallpox, but the Aleuts had no name for this strange disease that killed in days.

Agripina held a bowl of thickened tea to her brother's lips. When he had first fallen ill, she had nursed him with devotion, telling him stories of their adventures together. She reminded him of the time, as seven- and eight-year-olds, they had packed food and determined to journey into the interior to find the village of the Outside Men, that mythic clan on whom her people blamed the small calamities— broken weapons, missing food. "Did we even make it past the second peak?" Agripina had asked. "Then the clouds came and the rain. Remember how I cried and you held my hand?" She reminded him of the bird nests they had raided and the driftwood houses they had built. At first, he'd listened, laughed even. But that was days ago. Agripina had seen no sign in the last two days that he even knew she was there. And her heart had closed itself as his awareness sunk beyond her grasp. He would die.

He turned his head, trying to avoid the stink even now. She forced the liquid in. The shaman, Usilax, had told her to make him drink every few hours. Her brother moaned and turned his head from side to side. Agripina had not seen Usilax's herbs work on any of the sick.

Usilax had always been a creeping sort of man. Agripina and her friends called him Crabman, but only when he couldn't hear. Not just the way he walked, scuttling on bent knees, but also the way he scavenged from people's minds, pinching bits of gossip and reading unguarded faces. He'd refused baptism and a Christian name, hiding inland when the priest came. As the death toll grew, Usilax had begun to speak of evil spirits, punishment for unseen deeds. The village *toion*, along with many of the strongest men, had been taken several years ago to hunt for the Russians off distant islands. Without leadership, Usilax had stepped in. The people watched one another. Accusations began. Agripina knew if the sickness didn't end soon, they would begin betraying one another in hopes of finding out who was to blame. The newcomers were watched especially close. Four more had come last spring after abandoning their dead village. Agripina had seen three such waves of remnants absorbed into her village. Although no one counted, she knew what it meant. The Aleuts were dying. And now Usilax meant to discover who was bringing this death upon them.

Was it her? Agripina wondered, for sometimes she felt a blackness in her, like a dark cliff exposed only when the tide fell.

As she set aside the remaining tea, the door blew inward, whipping a snarl of snow inside. Aya shuffled through, struggling to close the door, then squinted into the dim room. She wore her hair cut blunt across her forehead and knotted at the back, refusing to let her bangs grow long as so many of the women did now. Her face creased into angled planes, shielding her thoughts with age.

"Agripina," she said roughly. "I want to speak with you."

"Grandmother, come in. Sit down."

"Not here. In my house I will talk."

"He must not be left alone."

Aya looked at her fevered great-grandson. "You nurse a dead man. It does not matter. Come with me." Aya turned and pulled the door open again. She did not bother to shut it.

Agripina jumped up and ran to the door. She saw Aya's back disappearing into the blowing snow. The old woman rarely spoke, and something about Aya's demand left Agripina feeling honored. She shut the door and leaned against it. Should she follow? She went to her brother and wiped the sweat from his cheeks. But Aya was right, he would not live.

After filling an oil lamp to keep her brother warm, Agripina slipped on her kamleika and stepped into the storm. The walk to Aya's house was difficult against the wind-driven snow. Aya lived at the edge of the village, in what Agripina sometimes thought of as self-exile. Her *ulax* was the old style with the entrance on the roof. Agripina climbed up and lifted the hatch, descending the ladder into the warmth of her great-grandmother's home.

Agripina was startled to see two other women sitting near Aya. She knew both well. Teresa and Kristinia had played with Agripina as a child, like older sisters. Kristinia had lost two of her three children to smallpox. Teresa had lost her grandfather.

Aya didn't look up as Agripina entered. She sat on the floor, shredding a piece of grass into whisper-thin strands on the back of her long, hardened thumbnail.

"Sit here beside me," Aya said.

Agripina looked at Teresa and Kristinia with a question.

Both women shook their heads.

"Of course none of you know why I have called you here," Aya said. "Silly girls. What would your great-grandmothers think, watching you now?" Her eyes pinned each woman.

The old woman's perception always startled Agripina. She saw things without looking. She knew things without being told. To Agripina, her great-grandmother's awareness felt not so much a violation of her thoughts and feelings but a comfort. Her great-grandmother knew her and yet granted a rare approval.

"I will tell you the secret. The birth of the stories you have heard about me, about others. I will tell you everything." Her voice was hard like waves rolling boulders under water.

A ripple of excitement passed through Agripina's chest. At last, she thought, I will know. Aya is trusting me with the truth.

"Don't be pleased with yourself," Aya spat at Agripina. She pointed the end of her stiff weaving grass at one woman then the next. "You will never be the women you once were after you know what you are to do. Your great-grandmothers knew. This is no honor. It is duty and comes with a price higher than you can imagine."

She didn't speak for a few minutes. The women waited in silence, frightened, wary, excited. Then Aya seemed to soften. "It was your great-grandmother, Kristinia, who came to me with the idea." Aya set aside her pile of split ryegrass and smiled. "She spoke about seal clubs, and I thought the worst of her. That she meant to trap me. For I had been thinking of hunting too."

Aya told the young women everything. She spoke of the corpse slowly turning to a mummy, of the fat they had tasted. The change she felt and the first whale. She told of the other hunts, the seals they killed the next spring at the rookeries, the fat sea lions. She talked of the strength her arms found and Tugakax's sharp aim.

"When a few of the men who escaped returned the next year, we put aside our weapons and kayaks. We met with other villages, and the young women found new husbands. Many hunters took more than one wife even though they would not have been judged able to support them in other times. None would take me. None would take your great-grandmothers." Aya bent forward, her hair like a shield guarding her face. "Your great-grandmothers and I had broken the band of sinews that had kept us safe since our people came to these islands. We had broken it with our teeth and tasted it with our tongues. There was no way to spit it out; it soaked into us like water into sand. It soaked into our wombs and waited for daughters to be born."

Aya's story thrilled Agripina in a way she hadn't expected. Taboos against women hunting were strict, and Agripina had been taught since she was a child to avoid handling her father's and brothers' throwing boards and spears. She believed that women were made wrong for hunting. Yet, her great-grandmother's story flicked at the edges of a question that had formed a scab inside her. Underneath lay a shiny pink wound called resistance, defiance. Now she knew she had been born with it, the legacy of her great-grandmother's sin.

"These stories you hear. They are just stories told by people to explain what they do not understand. We were supposed to die, to starve as so many others. But we refused. Your grandmothers and I, we took our fate from God's hand. The spirits have hunted us since that day. And they will hunt you."

Aya stopped and stared at each woman in turn. "You must kill Usilax."

Agripina held her breath, willing her eyes to remain on the hands in her lap.

"The Russian doctors have medicine that can stop people from getting sick," Aya said. "In Illiuliuk the children are well. It is only in villages with arrogant shaman like Usilax that people still die. I have heard mothers talk, saying they would like to get this medicine. Usilax shouts that they are causing the sickness by their failure to believe. He is killing our people with his cowardice. Once he is gone, the mothers will be heard.

"You must do this thing. Your great-grandmothers and I have decided."

Silence invaded the underground room, curving thick around the women's bodies.

"Our grandmothers are dead," Teresa said finally. She stared at Aya.

Aya's dry laughter puffed from her lips. "Ah, foolish girl. Your great-grandmother knew better than the rest of us what it meant to live in suffering times. She gladly took the task upon herself, and gave it to you, the daughter of so much pain. She sits behind you even now. It is the dead who make all the difficult decisions." Aya continued to laugh, the sound settling like dust. "Go now. I do not want to hear your protests."

The three women rose and climbed the ladder, eager to get away from Aya's madness. As they reached for the hatch, Aya spoke once more. "This is your place," she said. "You are our daughters, and we chose this for you long ago."

Agripina let the hatch fall and descended to the ground. The three women stood for several minutes, showing their hooded backs to the angled snow. Teresa stomped her small feet and crossed her arms. "Your grandmother is crazy, Agripina," she said, her face, telling of her mixed blood, hidden by her kamleika hood.

"This is true," Agripina answered.

"I will not speak of this again," Teresa said and turned to find her way home.

Agripina glanced at Kristinia. Did she see something shining in her friend's eyes, under the red scarf she always draped over her head? If any of them should be willing to kill, it was Kristinia.

Kristinia had returned to the village just one year before. A Russian crew had taken her husband along with other men several years ago, and Kristinia had gone with one of the Russians just after her baptism. For many seasons, she lived with her white husband, receiving colorful scarves and glass beads, and food for her betrayal. At first she had stayed for the sake of her two children, her fully Aleut children. Without the Russian's supplies, the children would not have lived, she may not have lived. Her own husband had not been able to stop the Russians, but at least this white one protected her from the others. She'd seen enough unattached women raped and whipped and speared to understand the trade-off. But as the seasons passed, she stayed because she had grown used to him and knew she enjoyed a luxury many others didn't. And they had had children. Two baby boys and a girl.

Then one sunny spring he told her he was returning to Russia, that very day, and that the boys were coming with him.

"In Russia, they will be educated, learn to read and write," he said, shoving her away as she tried to clutch at the boys only three and four, crying now, small brown hands clenched in fists. "Stop making a scene. I will bring them back someday. They will be translators or company managers."

"Then I will go with you," Kristinia said, rising from the dirt floor of their yurt. "We will go to Russia with you. I will keep your house clean, give you more beautiful babies."

He threw his head back and laughed. "My wife would not take you in. The children, yes. Not you. Not your Aleut children."

She'd followed him across the beach, pleading as he made toward the skiff that would take him to the ship in the harbor. "How can you do this? I have given you everything." She dropped to her knees in the sand, tearing at her clothing, her hair.

He did not turn. Even when the oldest boy slipped his grasp and tried to run back to her, he simply reached behind to grab the child.

As he lifted the boys into the skiff, she saw a woman rush the boat, grasping for another child. She saw a man raise a musket and fire. She saw the woman fall back into the water. She listened to the cries of her boys grow faint, then lost under the sound of waves.

It was only then that she heard it. Voices. Like hers. Circling the beach, lifting from the sand and over the ocean toward their sons. She turned toward the beach and saw the bodies of other women, collapsed on the sand. Hers were not the only children moving away from the island.

The scarves she still wore and the glittery beads around her ankles reminded her that her children were in a rich land, where such clothing and decorations were cheap enough to buy an Aleut woman.

Agripina watched her brother die in the early morning hours. His tongue grew black and swollen. Pustules rose, broke, and rose again across his face and neck. Agripina's uncles, aunts, and mother took turns wiping his face and forcing the medicinal tea into his swollen lips. But he died with a last faint breath.

Agripina's uncle, Aleksey, flung the wooden bowl holding the remaining portion of tea against the wall. Aleksey had been like a father to the young man. He had taught him to guide a kayak, to throw a spear, to carve a throwing board, and to tell a heroic hunting tale.

"Usilax says evil spirits are punishing us," Aleksey said, his loss and anger swirling together and filling the small house. "The ones who have brought this on us, they must be found."

Aleksey pulled on his kamleika and threw open the door. Agripina knew he went to meet with Usilax and the other men who followed him. A sudden murky fear pooled in Agripina's chest. Whom would they accuse? Aya maybe. She had left herself a target for many years with her strange ways. Or maybe one of the mothers who had been whispering about the good of the Russian medicine?

She watched her mother stroke the hair back from her son's face. "What will they do?"

"We will see," her mother answered, pouring more oil into her cooking lamp.

"Do you think the medicine could help?"

Her mother turned to her. "Agripina, God will decide. No medicines can interfere with his right to take people when he wishes. Such foolish talk. Have I taught you no better?"

"Aya says . . ."

Her mother shook her head. "Your great-grandmother's mind was lost long ago. Even your grandfather knew this and did not listen to her strange talk. Do what I tell you and leave Aya to her nightmares."

A week passed before Usilax called the village together. They met on the beach, still streaked with snow that lay like fingers reaching to drag the land into the sea. The wind had stopped, leaving the grasses and clouds motionless around them.

"Where is Aya?" Usilax demanded when he had surveyed the people and found her missing.

No one spoke.

"Go find her," Usilax said, pointing at Aleksey.

Aleksey turned his short legs toward Aya's house.

"Two more children have been taken and Aleksey's nephew, like a son," Usilax said. "The men have met many times, and I have been seeking knowledge of who has angered the spirits to punish us this way."

He stopped speaking, his gaze ringing the circle of forty people. "Even the wind has left us."

Agripina felt the same pool of fear, growing deeper now, reaching into her belly and hips. She tried to catch Kristinia's eyes, but the woman kept her head bent and shielded by her hood. Teresa, however, was looking up and out to sea, her hood back. Agripina watched Teresa like a hunter, waiting. Teresa could denounce Aya now, let the village know what her grandmother had commanded. It was the time to do such a thing. Agripina's breaths shallowed as she waited.

Usilax was speaking of death and his journey to converse with the spirits when Teresa's eyes suddenly swiveled to Agripina. The women stared at each other a long moment. Agripina saw nothing in Teresa's face. Like her great-grandmother decades before, it was the waiting that shifted the sands of indecision in Agripina's heart. Now as she stared at Teresa, she knew she wanted to kill. Agripina could not have said that she believed Usilax's death would allow her people to live. Of such things she had no knowledge. Her desire was darker. She wanted to be part of what Aya had begun. She wanted to look into Usilax's eyes and know she would kill him with her hands. She wanted the power Aya had found and taken for her own. She did not measure the distance between killing a whale and killing a man. The results were as close as the pebbles that nestled to form the beach—she would hold the power her great-grandmother had taken. And her people would live.

Teresa's eyes broke away when Aleksey, clutching Aya by the meat of her arm, neared. Aya did not come willingly. Aleksey dragged her to the circle.

"Aya," Usilax yelled at the old woman. "You are the cause of the death that eats at us." He approached Aya, holding his hand in front of him as he neared her. "You will be like the dead."

As he spoke the words of banishment, Aya crouched suddenly on the wet sand and lunged for Usilax's legs. Her old arms circled his knees and sent him thudding to the sand on his back.

She was on him like a beast.

Aya's gray-black hair fell around their faces as her few remaining teeth sank into his cheek, tearing.

Usilax screamed and shoved Aya to the side.

She rolled facedown on the beach, thrashing and biting into the sand. When two men lifted her by each arm, Agripina could see her face. Sand caked her lips, mixing with Usilax's blood. Her eyes were no longer eyes, but dark slits. She screamed and writhed under the men's hands as they dragged her from the circle.

Agripina listened to the screams grow distant as Aya was dragged from the village. Even when the waves overpowered her great-grandmother's voice, she knew Aya still screamed. A part of Agripina had expected this. But she imagined her great-grandmother serene, proud, accepting her fate and perhaps uttering a few wise, strange words. Now, the grotesqueness of Aya's insanity dug into her like a clam into the sand. Aya may have been wise, Agripina thought, but she was also quite crazy. Perhaps the insanity would make death easier. Agripina imagined Aya sitting on a hillside overlooking the ocean. She imagined the long hair clinging inside deep wrinkles. The snow and cold settling over her great-grandmother as she waited for death. No one would offer food or shelter to Aya. No one would speak to her or even look into her eyes. She was dead to the villagers and would not live long on her own.

As the people hurried back to their homes, Agripina watched for a sign that Teresa or Kristinia desired to speak. But neither looked at her nor lingered on the beach. Agripina ran to catch up to her own family. She fell in beside her mother, who trudged with her head tucked despite the calm air.

"Mother?" Agripina said gently. She knew her mother had not been close to her husband's grandmother, but still she imagined grief and loss within her mother's silence. When her mother didn't raise her head, Agripina tried again. "Mother?"

The family reached their home, and her mother shouldered past Agripina through the door without looking up. She filled an oil lamp and squatted over it, tucking her arms inside her kamleika. The rest of the family remained silent as well. Agripina watched them, rage and pity slamming her like waves. Did they feel nothing?

Her family did not speak of Aya. They would never speak of her again, as if she had never been. Agripina could hardly eat the seal her mother prepared. She listened to her uncles slopping the juices and watched them cut the meat at their mouths with their short knives.

Her stomach turned when she tried to chew, and she spit the meat on the floor. Agripina let her bowl fall and left, pulling her kamleika on before slamming the door as she stepped into the windless twilight.

She wandered across the village first, walking near the water. The tide was rising, and Agripina noticed the few pieces of driftwood pushing onshore. Without conscious thought, she marked where they would land. She walked past the *ulaxes* and farther around the eastern cliffs. She could not go far. The tide would cut off her path soon.

The thin light was almost gone when Agripina noticed the dark form of a person walking toward her. She wanted to turn back to avoid contact but realized how obvious her action would be. Instead she walked faster.

As she drew close, she recognized Teresa, slightly taller than the other women, her face not as round or as dark. The women stopped a few feet from each other. A blue-tinged moon brightened above the ocean as the darkness came. Agripina didn't trust herself to speak. She watched the moon's light trembling over waves, rising and falling like breaths, and waited.

At last Teresa spoke. "God created such beauty," she said, turning to Agripina. She spoke her next words hesitantly. "People should not die under such a moon."

"No," Agripina said. "They should not."

"Perhaps Kristinia would walk with us under this moon?"

"She may." Agripina felt the air stir and turned her face into the returning wind.

Kristinia had come. She had lost two children to a Russian man and two to a Russian disease; she would not lose another.

"I will take the knife to Usilax's throat for my children," Kristinia said as the three women walked late into the night. "It is my right."

Kristinia's willingness, eagerness to kill Usilax surprised Agripina. She would not understand for many years what it was that crept into Kristinia's mind, into her body as she watched her children taken, then watched them die, as she held the one that remained against her body, wrestling against a world that refused her will. She would not understand the full vicious rage of motherhood until she looked into the face of her own first infant years later. But she would remember the bite of Kristinia's words and the look on her face. That night,

Agripina only thought that perhaps what Aya said was true. Perhaps their great-grandmothers' acts had marked them before they were born.

The next day they hiked to the cave. Although only one had to enter, they each wanted to, drawn by a desire to cut through the bodies and release the power. Agripina wondered as she held her oil lamp to the walls, from which of these men Aya had eaten.

Agripina was surprised she felt no fear here in the cave filled with the warm, dry breath of mummies. She placed several bits of dry flesh into a sealskin pouch. An arrow of light sliced through the cave opening. It faded before reaching the back wall. Agripina walked around the jagged oval. She counted the bodies stacked on wooden frames, some partly obscured by rock sloughing from the walls. She guessed at least twenty men lay here waiting. Probably even older bodies lay behind these, buried by earthquakes and time.

Agripina exited last. She and the other two women stood outside the entrance, looking down at the waves licking the rocks below. Each had a small bag weighted with a bit of the flesh from a Dry One. Agripina longed to speak about what they had done, about what they would do, but as she looked at her friends, she recognized her own feelings in their faces. Like her, they did this because they were meant to, because their lives now followed the line of more distant choice.

She saw the short-handled ulu as she was about to start down the back side of the cliff. It lay on a shelf an arm's reach below. Kristinia and Teresa followed Agripina's gaze. The rounded blade with its carved wooden handle had not been worn by the weather.

Agripina knelt to reach for it. Her fingers slid over the handle. She held the ulu before her.

Teresa and Kristinia studied the blade. It was a woman's knife, designed to carve tough blocks of blubber and skin.

"It's Aya's," Agripina said.

Seeing the ulu, holding it, Agripina sensed the substance of the act of killing for the first time. This edge would slice into living skin, find the lines of blood and cut their paths. She drew its serrated edge across her palm, from the base of her little finger to the base of her thumb. Her blood rushed from the cut, ran over her wrist and dripped, bright red and eager down the face of the cliff, a stain on the gray rock. She looked into Teresa's and Kristinia's faces and knew their minds held the same images and the same mingling of revulsion and desire.

The women did not have to speak what they knew, that Aya had placed her ulu here for them to find. That she had smoothed their path in doing so.

Kristinia reached for the knife, which Agripina let slide away from her bloody hand. Kristinia tucked it inside her kamleika and turned toward the backside of the cliff and the path down to the beach. Agripina and Teresa followed.

They had to work quickly if they were to use the gift Aya had given. Aya could not live long alone, and although the villagers might believe her spirit would kill, they would even more quickly blame her living body.

The killers met in the early hours before dawn, around the eastern cliffs at low tide. They peeled back their hoods and faced one another. The bits of corpse were no longer filled with the fat of life as the corpses of their great-grandmothers' time had been. No one had placed the honored whale hunters in this cave for many years, and old bodies were mummy dry. Agripina mixed the dry, black flesh with seal oil until a thick grease formed, as Aya had instructed. The women washed their hands, rubbing wet sand in broad strokes until the skin broke. They rubbed fat into the lines of their palms and onto the smooth skin of their foreheads and broad cheeks.

They didn't speak. They felt nothing but were acutely aware of the void. Like the nothingness itself swelled with profound emotion. These killers would come to know this feeling well, until other emotions became foreboding intruders.

When they had completed the ritual and the dead-man's fat was only a sticky residue in their throats, the women moved together toward the village. Toward Usilax.

Usilax did not live alone. His daughter and her husband slept in the same *ulax*. The children, Usilax's nephew and niece, had died several weeks before. The women had not spoken about how they would handle the others, who were sure to wake up when the disturbance began. They did not want to speak of it.

The women undressed, leaving their clothing outside the *ulax*. Agripina descended the ladder, naked and quiet as a spirit. The awareness came to her as her foot touched the dirt floor. She heard Usilax's breath and felt his body lying in a dugout to the right. Sounds of lovemaking came from the larger dugout on the left. She stepped aside to allow Teresa and Kristinia to descend. A man's soft grunting and the shuffling of bare skin against hides gave rhythm to their work.

Kristinia pulled the ulu from a strap around her waist. She tipped her shoulders to slide past Agripina without stepping on the collection of lamps and bowls in the center of the house. Agripina followed, ducking to avoid the hanging idol she could not see but felt in the darkness. Kristinia pushed aside the grass mat that separated Usilax's sleeping quarters and crawled inside. Agripina and Teresa followed, creeping on all fours. Only one other person could fit inside, but the women pulled themselves close, holding the flap to the side and crouching at the entrance.

Kristinia bit the ulu between her teeth so she could use both hands to feel the wall and floor as she slid alongside Usilax's sleeping form. When she had reached his head, she balanced on the balls of her feet, knees bent, torso hanging over the rise and fall of his sleeping skins.

Agripina watched the opposite dugout, listening to the man's heavy breathing and now a woman's softer ones. They were close to finishing. She felt the man's tension coming like arrows and the woman's rising up from the ground. She turned back to Kristinia and Usilax when the connection of blade touching skin whispered to her.

Kristinia sliced deep as if into the tough hide of a sea lion. She knew this motion well. Aya's ulu separated most of Usilax's head, leaving only his spinal column untouched. Usilax never made a sound. He died in a dream he had every night. He is paddling, leading them all to an invisible island, untouched grasses swaying against soft swelling ocean, eagle chicks chirping above. Behind his people's smiling faces fog swirls in, covering their tracks.

Agripina felt the mist of the dream fading from the *ulax* as Kristinia dropped the ulu and stepped over the body. Teresa and Agripina rose from their crouches and moved to the ladder, climbing to the lovers' final moans.

When dawn came and Agripina heard her mother and uncles rising, she stretched and pulled aside her sleeping skins. She had not slept that night but had lain awake, listening with the new ears given her. She heard the slight change in the sound of waves that marked the changing tide, and listened to the breathing of the village, the sleep words spoken in another *ulax*.

The family was still eating their breakfast of dried fish and berries when the news reached them. Usilax's son-in-law pulled open their door. "Usilax has been killed in his sleep," he said. "A meeting is called on the beach."

He left to alert others before anyone could respond.

Agripina's uncles scraped up the last of their breakfast. They were out the door before Agripina and her mother had collected the scraps and thrown the bones outside.

No one spoke as they assembled on the beach, strafed with offshore wind. Agripina heard scattered thoughts as if they were spoken. Some were afraid, others curious. But the thoughts she heard most clearly came from the ones in which hope was growing. Usilax would not be mourned by these. She listened carefully. One man began packing his kayak for the long journey to Dutch Harbor. She listened to him plan how to ask the priest for the inoculations.

Usilax's son-in-law stepped forward. "It will not be difficult to discover the monster who has done this terrible thing." He held up the ulu. "This was beside Usilax. His blood still clings to its blade." He moved around the circle, holding the ulu for each person to inspect.

Teresa and Kristinia came first in the circle. Both women studied the ulu without speaking until he moved to the next person. When the knife passed before Agripina's mother, she gasped and turned her head.

"This ulu is known to you?" Usilax's son-in-law asked.

Agripina's mother kept silent, her head bowed.

"If you know, speak."

Agripina's mother didn't look up as she spoke. "It is Aya's."

* * *

A search was begun for Aya. But through days of effort, she could not be found. At last the villagers gave up. Aya was likely dead by now, her strength lasting just long enough for this one act of revenge. Already the ancient cave burial customs were fading from the people's memories. So much had changed too fast, and so many had died too young. Only the three women found her body, sitting in the warm, dry air of a cave opening at the sea cliffs, its power dwelling in the dark with others, waiting.

Years later, when Agripina had entered into the stream of motherhood with four children of her own, including a girl just becoming a woman, Agripina went to her great-grandmother to ask the question that had gnawed at her since the day she had killed. Aya had hunted, killed a beast to bring her village back to life. Agripina had murdered, killed a man to stop more death.

"Great-grandmother?" Agripina crouched by Aya's blackened body and touched her shriveled fingers. "Was it wrong?"

Agripina heard nothing but wind skidding through the cave's mouth and felt nothing but the insistent shadow she had come to know so well. It was the shadow of Aya's sacrifice, elongating now as it moved toward the next generation.

open up her eyes

I found her slumped in the far stall at closing time. A puddle of urine seeped from her pink pantsuit. Her chin crusted with vomit, which had flowed, unwiped, until it trickled through the papery petals of her corsage.

"Liz?" I stood a safe distance from her and nudged her with my boot toe. "Liz, wake up."

She grunted, and her head rolled forward.

"Marge! Liz's passed out."

"Get her out. I'll call a cab."

I looked down at the pink form, an unfamiliar sense of compassion buzzing like a pesky horsefly. Shit, I was going to have to touch her. Somebody loved Liz. Didn't they? Somebody cared. Even Dad had Yolanda. Yolanda wouldn't leave my father lying in the bathroom of some bar. If Yolanda could do it, so could I. I studied the angle of Liz, how her legs were splayed, the distance to the stall door, trying to figure out how to drag her out without touching either the wet suit bottoms or the crusted top. If I squatted by her shoulder, I could hook my arm around from behind, gripping under her pit.

I knelt beside her and slid my arm along her back. I turned my head from the smell on her lapels, which were now right under my nose. I got her halfway up and had to adjust my feet to finish the lift.

Unfortunately, I stepped right in the largest accumulation of urine and slipped. Liz slid back down the wall with a damp plop, coming to rest in exactly the same position she had occupied. I, however, came down hard, my head hitting the protruding metal of the toilet paper holder right on the edge. My legs skidded out the stall door. The holder snapped. Blood gushed from just above my temple.

I slumped to the floor beside Liz, scooting my rear across the urine-puddled floor until my back rested against the wall too. When I touched my head, my fingers came away stamped with blood. I glanced at Liz to make sure I hadn't crippled her.

Her eyes were wide open and staring right at mine.

She grinned, her gums wet and naked. Her hand reached for my hair, a light touch, then came down to clench my knee, and she began to laugh. Her breath came at me in waves of booze and vomit. Maybe I should have been indignant, but I was sitting next to a pink-polyestered drunk in a pool of pee beside a well-used toilet in a tiny bathroom in a remote fishing town on the Bering Sea. I laughed too. I laughed while blood trickled off my eyelashes. I laughed while Marge's head appeared in the stall doorway.

"What the fuck?" she said. "Get up. Shit."

But I couldn't stop laughing. I laughed until Liz threw up again. It didn't stop her, however. I grabbed onto the broken paper holder and hauled myself up. That's when I saw the second message.

Another.

Written in blue marker, the word stood alone, no trace of that first odd message, *Killing hands,* underneath. I must have stared at it too long because Marge growled at me, "Gimme some fuckin' help."

Marge was trying to get her shoulder under Liz's arm. I grabbed hold of her other arm. We had to turn ourselves sideways to squeeze out of the stall. I moved carefully, partly because I felt a bit woozy and partly because I didn't want to slip again. As we pulled Liz through the door, I turned back, taking a last look at the carnage. I saw the imprint of Liz's polyester butt on the floor as a sort-of dry spot. I saw where her urine and my blood had mixed and formed an orangish pool. And I saw the blue marker, lying at the rim of the floor behind where Liz had passed out. Marge had Little Liz in a good grip. I risked letting go to lean down and grab the marker. I slipped it into my jeans pocket.

"Hey, what're you doin'?"

"Nothing."

I couldn't sleep for a long time that night. I lay under my white down comforter and listened to the wind harass a loose plank on the roof. I'd washed the bloody patch of hair at my kitchen sink, but the gouge still felt moist, not so much bleeding as leaking. I forced myself to quit touching it. Instead my fingers toyed with the bead, which I'd hung on a thin chain around my neck. Just because there'd been a blue marker under Little Liz's butt and a new blue message on the toilet paper holder didn't mean Liz had written the message. She could just as likely have plopped her pink behind on a marker someone else had dropped. The marker didn't even necessarily have to be the same one that had written the message. But the coincidences gathered in my mind, and I decided to believe Liz was my mysterious toilet-paper-holder graffitist.

I woke up early, made coffee, and sat on the edge of my deck. I hadn't been laid for going on three weeks and was feeling edgy. And all this time alone. It was taking a toll. Every day I had hours to get through, hours with no one watching, no one nudging with smiles and innuendoes and possibilities. That's why I'd become so interested in the bathroom scrawls. I was bored. I'd been here for almost a month. I'd saved two thousand dollars already, carefully counted, rolled, and stuffed into a Crown Royal bag I had stashed behind a row of books. While groceries and fuel were expensive, there wasn't much else to spend money on. Thad wouldn't be in for a few days, and then he'd leave again. You take out shopping, sex, and all of your obvious amusements like movies, road trips, club hopping, and you're left with a pile of time and a brain desperate for stimulation.

At half past nine I headed down the path to my bike. It took the requisite five minutes of yelling and stomping, but I got the damn thing going and made it to the Elbow Room before it opened at ten.

Carl was leaning against the building, waiting for Marge to open up. He was wearing that same grungy bandito poncho. He grunted in my direction when I pulled the bike alongside the porch step. The motor died the second I took my hand off the gas. I pushed the kickstand into the sandy ground and hopped off. I was still pulling the underwear out of my ass when the bike began slowly tilting toward the left as the kickstand sank under its weight. I made no attempt to grab for it. The bike eked its way to a forty-five-degree angle, then gave way to gravity and fell with a thud. Taking a wide stance, I grabbed hold of the upper handlebar and pulled with my arms, back, and legs. I managed to get it up about six inches.

Carl pushed himself off the wall and stood next to me. We stared at the bike. It didn't move. Carl reached over, yanked the bike up, grunted again, and shoved it against the wall.

"Might be better off with something smaller," he said. We heard Marge unlocking the door from inside, and Carl turned with another grunt and pulled the Elbow Room door open.

I followed.

"Marge," Carl said as he pulled out a stool, "see if Norm still has that one-fifty Yamaha. Brandy needs it."

By the time I'd finished my first Bloody Mary, Marge had found me a new bike and sold my old one.

"Norm'll come down sometime today with the bike," she said, hanging up the phone. "You can take a look."

"Thanks," I said, snubbing out a cigarette. "How's your basket class coming?"

She lit a cigarette and leaned her elbows on the bar. "Working on the lid now. That top knot is tricky. But it's really the key to the whole basket. Now, I can't say my grasses are as good as they should be. Anna keeps telling me I'm too lazy, not looking hard enough for the delicate strands she wants. But shit, look at my fingers." She held out her right index finger and thumb. I could see healing, vertical gashes on each. "Anna says I'm supposed to split on top of my thumbnail. But I can't get the hang of that. Let me tell you—"

The phone rang before she finished talking.

"Elbow. How many? Who? Yeah. Shit. I knew something like this was coming."

Marge set the phone down and sloshed a stream of tequila into a glass. She stared out the Blue Room window, then turned to Carl and me. "The *Northwind* went down," she said. "They rescued one. Five others dead. Alex Ocheredin dead. So's Ian."

I'd met both men briefly in the bar. They were brothers, born and raised in Dutch. The night before they'd left for fishing, they'd been in with their skipper, a guy from Seattle, drinking seven-and-sevens. The skipper had been so drunk, Ian and Alex had had to prop him up to get him out of the bar.

"I warned those boys," Marge said, lighting a cigarette. "That boat nearly sunk twice before. And that skipper. He had 'em load a case of hard stuff plus all the beer."

"Haven't had one this bad for four, five years," Carl said, pushing his glass toward Marge. I noticed a series of scars across the knuckles of his right hand.

"Last one we lost was Hal Noise. 'Member that, Carl?"

"Two years ago this winter."

"Who was Hal?" I asked.

Marge leaned against the back bar and crossed one leg in front of the other. "It was just plain weird the way he went." She blew out a jet of smoke that nearly made it across the bar before spreading into a cloud. "He was this big Swede, came out here from the Lower Forty-eight. Married a local girl, Alice. He got himself elected to the council, got in tight with some of the businessmen peckerheads at the Ounalashka Corp. Pretty soon he's leasing out O.C. land to canneries and boat businesses, the bigwigs in town. Some of the old folks didn't like a white guy handling so much of the Aleut land deals. Then he up and dies."

Carl nodded, twisting his beer glass.

"Right in the middle of a council meeting," Marge said, lighting another cigarette. "He's clutching his stomach, falls outta his chair, and hits the floor, dead. They sent someone out from Kodiak to investigate. But then the body turns up missing. Nobody ever did know what happened. Didn't stop the rumors from flying."

"He was up to something," Carl said.

"That's what I always thought," Marge said. "Nothing ever got proved though."

Carl mumbled something that turned into a grunt.

Marge poured herself another shot. "Shit. I can't believe Alex and Ian are gone. Wish it had been that prick Nick instead. Did you see what he did to Mary?" Marge didn't wait for an answer. "Shit. Worse for her is not having them kids. She don't even get to see them hardly. Shit, you'd think they could find a foster home closer than Kodiak." Marge shoved a rag along the bar. "Martha says she's gonna die without them kids. I believe it. She's no good at picking men, but she sure was good with them kids. Member that time the little one broke his arm over at the day camp?"

Carl mumbled something I didn't hear because the door banged open and several guys came in.

"Marge, turn on the marine radio," one of them shouted. "Coast Guard's talking about the *Northwind*."

A steady stream of people came into the Elbow Room that afternoon. They listened to the radio, shared what they knew. Talked about Ian and Alex. As the place filled up with locals, mostly Aleuts, I felt the shift. I'd become the minority. I felt too big and bright. An interloper. As a member of the conquering tribe, you're supposed to feel confident and powerful among the natives. But when the numbers work against you, all that disappears, and you become aware of the color difference, aware of the shameful past. I would have left, but I wanted that new bike.

People told stories about the two men, crammed bills into a collection jar for the families—an impromptu wake. Part of me wished I'd known these men, could consort with the sorrow in the room, and part of me was glad that I didn't and didn't have to try.

I sat and drank, feeling like a trespasser, and waited for my bike to show up. I was starting to wonder if it ever would, when the door opened again and I saw the ancient woman from Mary's sister's place come in. She scanned the crowd, then made her way to the bathroom. I'd never seen her in the Elbow Room. The bathroom door closed behind her. Less than a minute later, it opened and she emerged. She scanned the bar again and saw me staring at her. She held my gaze; I felt as if I were being pulled under all that loose skin and into those eyes. Then she turned to the door and was gone.

Something in the way she looked at me made me feel like I'd been measured and weighed. I slurped up the last inch of my watery Bloody Mary and slid off the stool. I hesitated. What did I expect? I had no idea, but that battered bathroom door drew me.

The room was still fairly clean this early in the day. I opened the far stall door and slid the toilet paper roll off. Liz's, or whoever's, message was gone. The metal had been scrubbed clean. I touched the bar— still damp.

I had only started to wonder why the old woman had cleaned up Liz's scrawls when my new bike arrived. Norm, a slim, middle-aged man, had a 150 Yamaha Enduro in Day-Glo green he was willing to sell. Knowing nothing about motorcycles, I proceeded to the only test that mattered. I walked around the bike, noted that the plastic front fender was only slightly askew, that it had a gas gauge. Then I lifted my right foot and gave it a hefty kick. It fell over onto the sand parking lot. I reached for the handlebar, pulled hard, and righted it.

"I'll take it."

I traded the 500 plus two hundred dollars and didn't care if I'd made a good deal.

Les pulled up in his Subaru Brat as I threw my leg over to straddle my new bike. He ran his hand along the seat. "Nothing like something big between your legs, uh?"

I rolled my eyes at him.

"Heard from Thad lately?"

"I'm not talking to you about Thad."

"No need to worry," he said, his lips mimicking a pout. "Actually, I got a new honey."

I raised my eyebrows.

"New guy. Doesn't know any better." He laughed and patted my ass. "'Course, I'm keeping my options open, so don't go getting careless with our boy."

As usual I didn't know what to say to Les. I slammed my weight on the starter and eased the gas. The bike started the first time. I waved over my shoulder and took off down the beach road.

I swung right, drawn to the old woman's house. The yellow-checked curtains were closed. I turned toward the road that ran east and north along the beach and out of town. I popped the bike into second then third. The difference was astounding. I hit potholes and bounced out the other side. I gunned the gas over gravel patches. I even practiced a couple of sliding-turn stops. I kept going until the road turned into a two-track trail. I stopped at a five-foot berm piled at the end of the road to block traffic. From here a four-wheeler or a bike could make it fine. I thought about going on but decided not to press my luck.

Looking out over a field of heather, its lantern blossoms tipping like tiny bells in the wind amid lacquer-shiny leaves, feeling close to pure in the lash of cold wind, I almost felt glad I'd come. For just one moment, the view, the bike, my sense of competence mingled, and I felt lucky to be me and to be here. I lifted the front wheel and turned the bike around.

The motor whined as I worked through the gears and got up to forty-five. With no windshield the wind stung my eyes, and I was afraid I wouldn't be able to see if I went any faster, although I could tell the bike wanted to.

Before I headed home, I stopped back by the Old Voyagers. Because of my new bike, I was feeling cocky and willing to risk Anna's derision.

She was wearing another L.L. Bean ensemble, pleated khaki trousers and a crisp pink oxford, completed with leather dock shoes and argyle socks. I didn't know if she was a Bean groupie or just didn't have any other catalogs to shop from.

"So, you finished the first book."

I glanced up at my Aleut Mona Lisa. "Yes," I lied.

Anna followed my gaze and her face softened as she looked at the print. She bent to heft a box from the floor to the counter. "All for you." She shoved the box to my side of the counter. Her eyes locked on mine. A challenge.

I peered inside. Four books stared up at me, and judging from their height and the depth of the box, at least three books lay under each. And these were not casual books. These were the kind of books that could only be called tomes. I hefted the top one. *Notes on the Islands of the Unalaska District* by Ivan Veniaminov. I lifted another. *A History of the Russian-American Company* by P. A. Tikhmenev.

I looked up at Anna, a book in each hand. "You ordered these for me?" Now I was feeling extracocky. I was actually winning her over.

She smiled, a true and gleeful smile. "I have given you *more*," she said, and the smile stretched.

I smiled back, just as wide, swelling actually like I'd been knighted by the queen. "Great. How much?"

"Normally, two hundred eighty dollars, but I'll let you have them for two-seventy."

"Amazing generosity," I said and pulled $300 in fives, tens, and twenties from my wallet, which was stuffed.

"You read all these and I may let you join my basket weaving class." I heard her shoe soles tapping the floor as she filled out a receipt.

"Yeah, soon as I've finished my knitting class."

Her face turned then and her smile arched up to reveal perfect teeth and allow a laugh. "Yes. First learn to knit, then I'll teach you to weave."

I could still hear her chuckling as I lugged the box out the door.

I had no problem with the road up to my cabana this time, despite the extra hundred pounds of paper in my saddlebags. When I switched off the motor, I gave the bike a pat on its politely sized gas tank. We were friends.

I unpacked the books, read the table of contents pages, and organized them into piles on the kitchen table. One stack for the slimmer books that I'd read first, another for those fatter ones with pictures on the cover that I'd get to later; and a third for those really fat ones with no pictures on the cover and university press stamps inside. I picked up a few dirty clothes on the floor and looked around at the bright room, not really lived in, just scattered with the trappings of habitation. The bookshelves were, for the most part, gaping holes. Two sets of dishes couldn't even fill one cabinet. I'd never refilled Thad's flower vases. I touched one of the little wildflowers now wilted over the side, shriveled and stuck to the wooden vase. Two slim dark petals broke and fell to the table. That's when I felt my first flaking. I hadn't noticed myself wilting or seen myself go brown, but standing there looming over those little dead petals, I knew decay had been working at me for a while now. Like a painted Roman statue, too long in the sun and rain and wind, the surface weakens, a flake breaks loose, floats to the ground, and lies helpless on the pedestal. Then another. The form underneath begins to show, something less glitzy, less radiant emerges. As I stood there, I could feel the flakes falling. I didn't know what to do, what expressions to wear, how to laugh or tilt my head or sit or stand. All these things usually came to me from someone else. Little hints that this tone or that look would work just right. But no one was here to give them to me. No one had been here for days, weeks. And that feeling from the bar lingered, whispering, "interloper, outsider, intruder." Another flake fell. How many would it take before I was unrecognizable? And what was underneath? I needed Thad back before this went too far.

I scrambled for an observer, a safer perspective. I imagined myself in a movie, being watched, judged. The surface of my skin hardened and held. I measured paces to the kitchen table, wrapped a rubber band around my hair, and shoved aside a sweater to uncover the first Aleutian book, still not finished. Clutching it to my chest, I went to the window and read.

I imagined the half-underground homes that once slung low behind the beach. I could picture those first encounters with Russian sailors, the initial excitement to trade for rare metal. In the beginning the Aleuts hunted sea otters for the Russians willingly enough, although hostages were taken to ensure the islanders didn't attack the outnumbered newcomers. But within a couple of decades, the Russians had virtually enslaved the Aleut hunters, forcing them to relocate to seal-breeding, seal-slaughtering islands. Meanwhile many of the Russians took up with the wives left behind. The czars did make decrees that the Aleuts be treated well. But as the Russians said, "We are here, and Mother Russia is far away." Murder, rape, kidnapping often went unpunished.

To think about these things while living at the place they happened brought their histories close. I wondered what happened to the mind of a woman whose husband had been taken by force to hunt, who was made to cook, clean, and bed his enslaver during the months he was away. Did she seek revenge in small ways, spitting into dinner stews? Wetting sleeping blankets? Did she ever try to run? To kill? Or maybe she went the other way. It's not as heroic but probably far more practical. Did she accept him as the new alpha male, stronger than her last, more able to protect and provide? The book didn't say; I could only imagine the thoughts of a woman in another time.

I leafed through books stacked on the table. Would any of them have the answers? Probably not. I'd read enough history to know that nobody had asked the women who lived through these things. The few priests and botanists and ethnographer types who accompanied the explorations in those first hundred years asked questions. They observed rituals, sketched homes and faces and tools, collected legends. But they didn't ask the women. It's not that they hadn't wanted to know; it's just that trying to figure out what a woman sees and thinks and feels is kind of messy and maybe scary. And besides, what's a woman gonna do. She's down for the count.

Darkness slowly invaded the hill. I stopped reading when I couldn't make out the words anymore and stared out at the few lights below. I kept thinking about Little Liz and the blue marker and the old woman's clean-up job. I had to pee, so I found a flashlight and trudged up the hill to the outhouse. The half-open door creaked softly on its hinges. I shone the light on Billy's leather pants as I waited for my bladder to overcome the shocking cold on my ass. Because I kept leaving the door open, poor Billy had begun to fade and wilt with the dampness. The entire top of the poster had curled downward, and only the top middle staple remained. The effect was not good. Billy's only redeeming physical characteristic is his sneer. Now all you could see was one of his skinny arms and his leather pants stretched in lines across his crotch. I leaned forward and ripped the poster down.

My flashlight caught the faded words underneath immediately. I shone the light across each line.

She took 19. Sent them away to white [here the words had faded too much] *tree houses. She would have taken more. We did it like our mother's mothers said, with dead-man's fat* [another few faded words]. *No one knew I let the gas on and lit the candle. I saw* [unreadable] *before I shut the door. I thought we would save some. 1968—one year past.*

I read the words several times, studying those faded parts carefully. Obviously this was not your classic outhouse graffiti. This was more like a diary entry recounting an event. But whose event? The "mother's mothers" line pointed to a woman. And what event? Although the words didn't say, I thought they pointed to a murder. The writer and someone else, or elses, had killed a woman because she took something. They had done it by setting up a propane leak. This had happened in 1967.

Sitting with my pants around my knees, pee threatening never to descend, shining a thin beam of light on an eighteen-year-old message, I took it as the honest writing of a woman who had killed another woman. For some reason, she had been compelled to write these few lines about it a year later. The victim had taken something so precious this woman had killed for it. A chill ran through me, which didn't help my attempt to pee.

I concentrated hard and managed. As I finished up, I saw the lights go on in Mary's cabana below. Just what I needed—the solidity of another person. I closed the outhouse door for once. I didn't want to expose the words to the weather. I'd study them more closely in daylight.

As I made my way to Mary's place, a skittish rain began, shy as a first recital. The first uncertain drop fell on my eyelid, then another on the back of my neck. It ran down my spine, and I shrugged my shoulders to stop its flow. I knocked on the door softly.

"Who is it?"

"Me, Brandy."

She swung the door open.

"I saw your lights. I'm bored."

"Come in. I'll put on some tea."

I followed her into a replica cabana, except she had added furniture, curtains, carpet. She had made a home. "I like what you've done with the place."

Mary shrugged. "Thanks. Nick's gone a lot. I get bored. Catalogs keep me busy."

She had good taste, if a bit on the country-decor side. I noticed the shelves of collector teddy bears and the too-well-matched rug-curtain sets. I guessed her outhouse would have a matching toilet seat cover and rug set too. And everywhere were pictures of two cute-as-a-button Aleut kids. She had floor-to-ceiling bookshelves covering one wall and not a book in them. They sagged with toys, Legos, and stuffed animals, laser guns, and Barbie furniture. A watermelon-colored buoy hung by a rope from the rafters, the traditional Dutch swing.

"You look better," I said. Only a couple of yellowish spots showed where her bruises had been. Two of her fingers were still in homemade splints.

"Yeah," she gazed down at her hand. "Sorry about that. Nick's not so bad. He's messed up about the kids being gone. He's had it pretty rough. Sorry I woke you up." She lifted her head to meet my eyes. "Thanks for what you did."

I nodded, feeling awkward. "Who was that old woman at your sister's?"

She put a kettle of water on the stove. She kept rubbing the scab on her lower lip with her upper lip. I thought she wasn't going to answer. But, as I was learning, white folks are too impatient.

"Ida," she said.

"How old is she?"

"No one knows. But I think she's in her eighties. Looks a lot older though."

She moved to the window and leaned against the frame while looking out at the dark valley. "She was old when I was just a kid. My brother and I used to watch her out in the bay. I think she had the last skin kayak left. She used to paddle out and around the island." Mary smiled. "I remember her two sons kept trying to talk her out of it. They even had the elders come to her house one day to tell her she wasn't allowed to go out alone anymore. It was too dangerous for an old woman."

Mary covered her mouth as she giggled. "They say she laughed at all those old men and spat at them. I would have loved to have seen that. She must have been in her late sixties then."

Mary was silent for a minute. When she spoke again her words were quiet and measured. "She didn't listen. I think those old men were afraid of her. I never saw them try to stop her again. Not until her youngest son, he was only forty or so, drowned. She stopped then."

I had one more question. I couldn't come up with a good segue so I just asked.

"Do you know who used to live in my place? Like back in the sixties."

"We moved in maybe ten years back. There've been four people since. The last were two young guys, white. Darlene Panov lived there a while. Before that I think Liz had the place. Ida said she moved into town in the late sixties, early seventies. Couldn't get up the hill anymore once she started drinking so heavy."

Liz. Of course, Liz. I must have gasped or something because Mary was looking at me funny.

"What?"

"Nothing. I just didn't know it was Liz."

"What was Liz?"

"Who had lived there."

Mary turned back to the counter to measure out tea leaves. I studied the delicate white tea pot on the counter beside her. Yellow and purple flowers intertwined with green ribbon around the rim; another circle of flowers on the side.

"Anyway," Mary said, pouring hot water into the pot, "thanks a lot for what you did."

"Sure," I said, inhaling the smell of spicy Russian tea. "You think you'd get the kids back if you left him?" It was my attempt to remind her of the connection, the trade-off. I suppose I could say that I just didn't want her banging on my door in the middle of the night again. But that wasn't really it. I felt responsible for her.

"That's what the social worker says. But I don't trust her. And I don't know how we'd get by without him. I only work part-time at the grocery store."

"Maybe they'd put you on full-time."

"Maybe." Mary's eyes traveled to a picture of her and the kids, all dressed in navy with a professional background of fall leaves. The two boys looked to be school age, eight and nine, I guessed; the girl younger, maybe five. "I got to get them back. But I'm all he's got. I love him."

"How? How could you love someone who does that to you?"

I knew even as the words left my mouth that I'd gone too far. I had

neither the wisdom nor the experience to go with this responsible feeling. And Mary knew it too.

She turned on me. "You don't even know me, and you want to tell
me anything. Nobody asked you."

Mary got up to pull two teacups from a dish drainer on the counter.
I waited, caught in a kind of no-man's-land of my own making. No
wonder I usually stayed out of this kind of thing. Mary placed one cup
carefully on the table in front of me. She held the other cup and
stroked its smooth surface with the back of her index finger. When she
spoke again, her voice was calm, instructive even.

"You think I don't know about you? Haven't been watching you?
You're no different from me. I see you waiting for him to come back,
needing him. But you'll wait for him to leave too. Won't you? You're
no different from me. You just don't love him is all. You haven't even
got that."

I felt my lower lip tremble and saliva pool in my mouth. How could
my motivating role have turned so quickly? How could a woman like
Mary have so much clarity when it came to men? How could I have so
little?

I gulped down my tea, burning my tongue and throat. "I better go."

Mary stood up too. "I didn't mean it to sound like that."

"Yes, you did."

I pushed against the gray planks of my door and stepped into a cabana
that wasn't as empty as I'd left it. It seemed weighted with the past,
with Liz's presence. I lit the kitchen propane light and watched the
shadows form along the walls. I poured an eight-ounce glass of Baileys
and sat down at the table. She'd sat here. She'd stared out these windows. She'd been that other woman then. I could almost see her, moving about the cabana, straightening, making dinner. She has all her
teeth; her hair is sleek, she wears something light colored and wool
and cotton. She hums as she works. Maybe she's preparing for a visitor. But she stops now and then. She puts down her broom or her
spoon and walks to the windows. She looks out over the valley, and the
smile leaves her lips. Something heavy is already growing in her, some-

thing that will soon submerge Liz beneath a torrent of guilt. And then a flood of booze.

As I climbed the ladder up to my loft, I thought about her hands clutching these same rungs, like me, head spinning from a night of drinking. I lay in my feathered loft, feeling the empty space beside me.

taking off her dress

Bellie and I were sitting at her kitchen table, inhaling the leftovers from a three-day relationship with a fisherman called Reek. I leaned back and inhaled sharply through my nose. I could feel tiny bits of powder clinging to the cilia.

"That bitch from the HiTide made a play for him," Bellie said, getting up to pour herself an orange juice. "He goes, 'I want an Alaskan woman.' And I say, 'Of course you do. You're not stupid.'"

Bellie had been raging about the thin work ethics among the women who worked the men in Dutch. It seemed the HiTide whores weren't playing by Bellie's rules, which were quite simple—if she had targeted a man, everyone else had better back off.

She dumped another little mound of coke on the mirror. "Besides," she said, "I've got other things to deal with. I can't have my life messed up right now. You know?"

"No. What things?"

She looked at me then, tearing her eyes off the lines she'd been slicing. "Nothing. Or everything. Nothing." Her focus returned to the mirror and razor work. "I mean, there's so many guys. You don't have to get like that. I could knock her head off. You know what I mean? All those fuckin' blondes are bitches."

She looked at me with a startled expression. "Except you."

"I'm not that kind of blond. Mine's real."

"What's the fucking difference?"

I pinched one nostril shut and sniffed. "There's a big fucking difference." I began to explain my blondness theories to Bellie. I've come up with a fairly well constructed paradigm.

The first known fake blondes were these Roman highbrow women. They were all pissed because their husbands had the hots for the fair-haired, buxom German captives they kept bringing home from the campaigns. Now, these chicks were slaves, plain and simple. But they didn't act like slaves, the way I imagine it. They held their conquered blond heads high in that sea of dark hair and sparkled. They were the outsiders, the other, and yet something about them, about their hair at least, captivated their conquerors. Soon the Roman women were mixing stuff like pigeon dung, vinegar sediment, goat fat, beachwood ash, crocus flower, leaving it on their hair overnight and waking up bleached. Sometimes the German women would sell their long golden locks to wig makers, who stuck them on well-to-do Roman heads. Even the men went blond sometimes. I'm not sure why rich, world-conquering Romans would clamor to emulate their own captives, but that's what happened.

The pure and true-hearted Romans, however, knew it wasn't good. They knew that if you let the vanquished people set the trends, you'd basically relinquished the power of your conquest. All that blood and beheading and so forth for naught.

Tertullian, one of the early Roman Christian proselytizers, was not the first to complain about this egregious capitulation, but he was enthusiastic. "I see some women dye their hair blond by using saffron," he wrote. "They are even ashamed of their country, sorry that they were not born in Germany or in Gaul! Thus, as far as their hair is concerned, they give up their country."

Did those newly blond Romans feel guilt for their bloody conquests? Did they go blond like we hang dream catchers in our windows or turquoise bracelets on our arms, to identify with the victims? Mingle ourselves with them and shed some culpability?

Or do people just instinctively need to change their appearance from time to time? The epic quest for a new look.

Either way, it started with insecurity and stuck there.

I noticed Bellie was no longer in the kitchen. "Where did you go?" I yelled.

She didn't answer, but I heard the drier down the hall start to rumble. She returned to the kitchen with an armload of laundry and dumped it on the counter.

"I was just saying it's about insecurity."

"Um-humm," she said, folding now.

I could feel the coke zinging along my limbs and circling my brain. I couldn't stop now.

Frankly, fake blondes give us real blondes a bad rep. The truth is that most women with iffy morals attempt to go blond. Check out any corner where the hookers hang out. Count the blondes. You'll see. It was the same way in Rome, where blond hair quickly became the trademark of the working-girl set. But even your ordinary bleached blondes are little better. They may not be true hookers, but they sure know that by going blond, they're advertising. Bleaching is a signal that screams—I'm easy. I'm insecure. Just give me a man, and I'll be okay.

Then we come to the dumb blonde phenomenon. The crux of the issue is that it's true. Blondes are dumber. Here's how it works. A blond girl starts getting attention. Even if she's butt ugly, she'll get it from the rear. She's walking down the sidewalk. A carload of boys cruises up behind. They see that cascade of hair swaying and start to hoot and honk. Her hair gets all that attention before the boys pull alongside and notice she's got three eyes or something. If she's reasonably symmetrical, the hoots and hollers continue. So our blond teen grows up with the feel of being singled out by boys and men. She finds out her looks can get her in, take her up, squeak her by. So naturally when it's her looks that conquer, she doesn't have to concentrate as much on, say, learning the dialectic or figuring out which way is north, or all that complex birth control stuff. A bubblehead in the making.

Of course, it's not just men who create the blond psyche. Women do it to each other too. We have a sense of the blonde's sexual power. So maybe we don't expect as much. Our brains are so impressionable this feeds on itself, and soon what was once a blonde's tendency to use her sexual power more than her intellectual power is just who she is. She's dumb but blond.

I know all you blondes are sputtering, "But I'm blond and I'm smart."

But think how much smarter you'd be if you weren't blond. I took a rinky-dink IQ test once. I was one point away from a genius score. That one point is my hair. And my mother's obsession with it.

I can trace the beginning to that one night—the night my father passed out and fouled my report card. I'm still sitting there, watching it, watching him when she comes home.

She cradles my head against her chest, and I can remember the sweaty smell and the smooth glassiness of the dress. "Oh, Brandy," she says, pulling my hair back from the sticky tears on my cheeks. "I told you not to listen to him. I tried to warn you, honey. He's weak. He's not like us."

She holds me like this for a minute or two, then she turns me around to face her. "There's something I've been saving for you." She's all soft smile and humble victor. "I was going to give it to you for your birthday. But now's as good a time as any." She takes my hand and leads me to her bedroom.

It's a makeup kit—Maybelline, in a three-tiered travel case in swirls of brown and green. I count the eye shadows—twenty-four. The blushers—five. The lip creams—sixteen. And there are pencils and pluckers and sharpeners and brushes and three tiny bottles of perfume. I run my fingers over the mirror sewn into the case lid and over the clean rows of colors and instruments. And I know I'm crying because I can't see any of it.

She sits next to me on the water bed and squeezes me. She leans in to my ear and whispers as if there was someone to keep a secret from. "I knew you'd love it."

A month later, he left for good. I hadn't been good enough, smart enough, studious enough. But, as Mom said, I was pretty enough. And I was blond enough.

For those who aren't—the fake blondes—it's worse. These chicks are often not that smart to begin with. They know, somewhere under that mouse brown hair, that they aren't cutting it in the brain power world. But, they think, I could gain the upper hand in the looks department, because let's face it, sexual power is power immense. So they take the cheap, easy route and go blond. Hence a great many blondes, both real and fake, are tipping the scale toward dumb.

"So that's the just of it," I said, turning to Bellie.

Her ass was sticking out of the fridge, her head buried deep inside as she sprayed and swiped.

"Bellie?" I said louder.

She pulled her head out. "What?"

"Do you get it now? Do you see what I mean?"

She sat down across from me and drew her straw through a less than perfectly straight line. She pinched one nostril shut and snorted deeply.

"Shit," she said, looking at me like I'd been masturbating in front of her. "All you blondes got some kind of stick up your ass about it?"

"No, just pisses me off, is all."

"You definitely got a stick up your ass."

"I'm trying to say, there are different categories here."

"Yeah, but you're blond."

I changed the subject.

I admit I did have a stick up my ass about it. And that stick was beginning to chafe. I'd always been able to place myself into a superior category to the other blond, loose, directionless women I'd known. But, out here, with so few of us and so many of them, I'd been less able to keep my delineations distinct. I was slipping, or perhaps just understanding I didn't have any height to slip from.

So you can imagine my reaction when one of the HiTide babes invited me to a party. Her name was Honey, and she had a bad bleach job. The kind with that chalky, crispy texture that gives way to a spreading dark part that seems to be cleaving the head in half. Even more than usual I needed to separate myself from the desperate fake blondes that came my way. But I was also bored, sick of being alone, and not given to rejecting party invites.

"It's going be a blast," Honey said, the next afternoon when I was sitting with Carl at the bar. Sitting with Carl was just that. It does not imply conversation, just sitting. We'd been trading Russian cigarettes again. I don't know why this became such a hobby in Dutch. The cigarettes were bad, every single brand. But we traded them anyway.

"Me and Jill can give you a ride out," Honey was saying. "These guys from a trawler are throwing it. Shit, they've flown in a case of tequila and fuck knows how much beer." Honey leaned toward me and whispered in my ear, "They've got some connection in Sand Point with fantastic blow. These guys made like forty-thou each."

She stuck her cigarette firmly between her lips to free her hands so she could reach down to adjust a wayward boob. She blinked her purple-smudged eyes several times to clear the smoke that drifted into them. "Anyway, there's like seven of these guys and only four of us. So they asked us to get some more girls for the party. We thought of you."

And there it was. I'd been lumped into the blond coke-whore set by the blond coke-whores themselves. These fake blondes had so little self-awareness they couldn't see the distinction between themselves and other blond cocktail waitresses who wear tight jeans and padded bras. A moment of panic set in. Who else was oblivious? I wondered if the distinction was all that distinct. I looked at Honey's short denim skirt and stiff, sprayed hair and felt immediately better. I would never wear a skirt at the Elbow Room, let alone one that rode up to my crotch when I sat on a bar stool.

"Oooo! I want to come. I want to come," Les piped in, giving a stiff-legged hop and clapping his hands.

"They want girls, not queers."

"Actually, I can be very girlish." Les leaned across the bar toward Honey and rested his cheek in his hand. He pushed his full lips out in a kiss and made an exaggerated smacking noise. When Honey didn't seem convinced, Les straightened and turned his back on the bar to fiddle with booze bottles. "Brandy can't come without me," he said over his shoulder.

Honey looked at me.

I shrugged. "I'm merely a pawn in Les's game."

"Whatever," Honey said, crushing out her cigarette. "We'll pick you up around three o'clock." She pushed her short skirt off the stool, swooshed a large leather bag over her shoulder, and headed for the door. Turning as she swung the door open, she tugged the hem of her skirt down over the back of her ass and left.

As soon as the door closed, Les did a backward moonwalk. "Going to a party and we're going to get laid. Going to a party of love," he sang to the tune of "Going to the Chapel."

"Les," I said, "what do you think you're doing? If these guys asked for girls, the chance they're going to switch over for your skinny ass is less than remote."

He didn't answer, kept singing.

"Les," I said again, "why do you even stay here? I mean the queer scene here is, well, limited."

"You don't got a clue," he said, moonwalking toward me now. "There are strange things done in the midnight sun by the men who moil. . . ."

He stopped moving and leaned in to me so close I felt his breath moving my hair. "Why are you here? I mean the white girl scene here isn't, well, that happening."

When I didn't answer, he turned to Carl, two stools down. "Whadda you think, Carl?"

Carl grunted and reached for the jar of beet-colored pickled eggs.

"What the fuck's he doing here?" Jill, the driver, leaned across Honey's thighs, packaged in black leggings, to shout out the passenger door.

Honey lifted one leg over the gearshift to slide toward the driver. She shook her head and rolled her eyes. "Who knows."

Les started to climb into the truck.

"No room," Jill said. "Get in the back."

Les grabbed my hand and boosted me into the truck bed.

"Hey, she can ride up here," Jill yelled, craning her neck backward out the driver's window.

"Drop dead," Les said.

"Dipshit," Jill said and ground into first.

Les and I scootched our butts against the rear of the cab.

I had worn tight Levi's tucked into my suede boots. On top I'd put on a short lilac Benetton sweater that would ride up over my belly button when I reached up or took a deep breath or moved. I'd put the front third of my hair into a ponytail, which hung down over the loose hair in back. I had on Mary Kay mascara, powder, and lipstick.

Les was wearing what Les always wore. Jeans, of some nonlabeled brand, and a T-shirt with a jeans jacket over the top.

"Look at them," Les said, pointing behind us into the cab. Jill and Honey were passing a bottle of tequila between them. Les rapped on the window. When they turned, he made a swigging-the-bottle motion.

Jill rolled her eyes and passed the bottle to Honey, who struggled to open the rear slide window. It was rusted shut. She rolled down the passenger window and squeezed herself through up to the waist, reaching out with the bottle. I leaned out over the truck bed and made a grab for it. The truck lurched through several potholes, and we fumbled, like relay racers fucking up the baton transfer, but eventually made the handoff.

I took a swig then passed to Les. He took several swallows then handed back to me. When Jill rapped on the rear window, Les had the bottle firmly planted between his thighs. He lifted it to his lips and returned it to his crotch. Honey rapped again. I turned to see her morgue-purple lips yelling and her fuchsia nails gesturing. Les took another drink and nestled the bottle back between his legs. He gazed straight ahead at the gulls soaring over the road between the ocean and the cliffs.

"The thing is," he said, talking more to the water and rocks than to me, "I can be *the fag* in Dutch or *the Indian* somewhere else. I'm where I belong."

I stared at him, maybe a little too long. "Okay," I said and settled back against the rattling cab and watched too. A rare beautiful day made the shadows deepen along the cliffs and turned the waves nearly translucent green at the crests. When Jill and Honey gave up their window rapping, Les shared the tequila again. We passed it back and forth in silence and watched the gulls careening in our dust and the waves sharing themselves with tidal pools.

The party was being held at Humpy Cove, a perfect curve of sand about thirty minutes east of town. It was a rough trip. I think Jill tried to hit every pothole she could, knowing Les and I would get the worst of it. She pulled off at a wide spot in the road. Two trucks were already parked there, two wheels off the road. I stood up slowly, kicking my legs in turn to get the kinks out and hopped over the truck side. Several men, each holding a can of beer, stood around a good-size fire. Two others were rolling a big driftwood log close to the blaze. The other two HiTide babes were already there, beers in hand. A stack of liquor lay on the sand.

My plan for this party was to keep from getting drunk. I wasn't really sure what was expected of me and figured I'd better be somewhat firm of mind. Whenever you get invited to a party to balance the number of guys and gals, it's kind of ambiguous. With me along, there were five girls and seven men, which left two guys out. I wasn't sure how I should calculate the Les factor.

Jill and Honey didn't wait for us. They slammed the truck doors and headed for the party, waving and shouting hellos. Les and I followed more slowly, picking our way through a stretch of beach grass littered with driftwood. He still had the tequila, which he used to balance himself. I noticed immediately that I was a bit tipsy. My boots slipped from the tops of the logs I attempted to walk on and sank into grassy sand, which made for an awkward journey. I usually don't notice my impairment level when I'm sitting down. And while watching toilet paper unroll is a fair test, walking driftwood logs is even better. I'd have to switch to plan B, not getting any more drunk.

As I cleared the grass-log field, I saw that two of the HiTide chicks had already chosen their guys. Lots of body draping, laughing, and beer sharing. The other coke-whores were still choosing. Four of the guys were paying very good attention to everything they said. One poor guy was still off trying to wrestle driftwood logs. At a certain stage of intoxication you can pick up on all sorts of dynamics between people that usually go unnoticed.

"Hey," Honey said, pulling herself away from an engrossing conversation with two of the fishermen, "this is Brandy."

"Hi," I said.

"I'm Les," Les said because no one else would.

"She's over at the Elbow," Honey said, ignoring Les. "But we're trying to get her on at the HiTide."

The two paired-up guys raised a Bud in my direction and bent back to their fake blondes.

Of course, this was news to me. It was bad enough that the HiTide babes and I shared a hair color and a certain slutty sensibility. I didn't need to share their bar.

I dug through the ice chest and came up with a Bartles & Jaymes Very Berry wine cooler. I tossed the cap into the fire. Out on the beach, the wind blew more aggressively than in town. I tipped my head back to take a long drink then reached up to slide the rubber band out of my hair. It streamed back as I stared out at the sun-skimmed water and let the wind into my eyes.

"Hey," Honey said, suddenly beside me. "So what do you think? Looks like Jill's leaving, and we'll need someone."

"I like the Elbow just fine." I wanted her to hear my dismissive tone, but she wasn't adept at picking up subtlety.

"It's better at the HiTide. The guys aren't as hammered. The hotel gives us free rooms." Honey downed the last of her beer. "And, do we know how to party."

I smoothed an arch in the sand with my right foot.

She leaned toward me, her voice lower. "It's just classier at the Hi-Tide. You probably didn't know, but the Elbow usually has a native girl working the floor. You know, someone local. You'd fit in better over with us."

Fit in. I looked at the scattered party participants and realized that for the first time in weeks I was with an all-white crowd, that I *fit in* with this gaggle of blondes. I thought about the Elbow; it was true. It was a native place. Sure there were lots of white fishermen, but always an Aleut backdrop. Always that undertone feeling of trespass. At the Elbow I was the blonde, however uncomfortable. At the HiTide I'd be one of the blondes; I'd lose my backdrop.

"I don't want to fit in," I said.

This time Honey picked up on what I'd hoped was a haughty tone. "Fine. Whatever." She swayed back to the two fishermen she'd left.

I walked away from the fire toward the ocean across smooth sand. I hated the part of me that wanted to join them, be one of the pack. I'd never had a sister, hadn't even had a best girlfriend since grade school. As soon as the boys arrived on the scene, I'd been too busy. I turned my back to the wind to watch them for a minute—hanging on their men, but still together, shouting conversation, laughing. I'd read about myself once in a women's studies course. The definition had jumped off the page. Male identified—a woman whose self-esteem, self-worth is achieved only through relation with men, often shunning female companionship. I'd quickly listed several women I knew and decided I didn't fit the definition. And even if I did, I was nowhere close to overcoming my diagnosis by attempting to female identify with these chicks.

The wine cooler went down easy, and as I drained it, the driftwood-rolling guy was there with another bottle.

"Tom," he said, handing it over.

Tom was a nice-looking guy—sandy brown hair, longish and thick. He was about five nine with a broad chest and a round, hard ass. He was definitely the kind of male with whom I liked to identify.

"Aqua Vitae," I said, clinking my bottle against his Corona. "Brandy."

Tom shoved one hand into his pocket. "Do you live here?"

"Sort of."

"Where you from?"

"A little of a lot of places. I spent time in California and Seattle."

"San Luis Obispo. I surf."

"You mean like for a living?"

"Nah. I wish. Been coming up here every season so I can surf the rest of the year."

"How's that working?"

"Choice." Tom gave me a grin that closed the area around us. He dug a half-smashed joint from his pocket and lit it. After taking a toke, he handed it to me. "What do you do?"

I sucked in the smoke and held on to it. This wasn't the usual stuff I'd had around Dutch. This was straight from Kona.

"I'm a cocktail waitress."

"You mean like for a living?"

I took another toke, passed the joint back, and refused to answer.

Honey and one of the guys stumbled past us, arms winding around each other as they made their way down the beach. Honey giggled and winked at me, which pissed me off. I gave her a hard, I'm-not-your-buddy look and turned back to Tom.

He threw his drained beer bottle and pulled another from his coat pocket. "You ever surfed?"

"I'll surf the day they put sharks on the endangered species list."

Tom laughed. We walked along the beach. He pointed out the various stages of the waves, how to look for patterns that belied underwater topography. This same knowledge made it easier for him to pick up his second favorite hobby, sea kayaking.

"You know right here is where they invented kayaking. Well maybe not invented. But the Aleuts were the most radical kayakers in the world. They would outdistance the big sailing ships. They'd scope out a big swell, then go for it, riding for miles. I mean, they were basically surfing."

As the sun reached for the horizon, turning everything lustrous and gold, the wind stopped. After so much unseen force pushing on my body, fiddling with my hair, playing with my clothes, the sudden calm felt odd. Like I'd stepped indoors into the largest room imaginable. I was also quite drunk. As Tom and I picked our way back to the fire, he took my arm now and then to keep us both upright.

At the fire, someone was roasting *baidarkas* on a stick. Two of the coke-whores were making out with two of the fishermen. Les, straddling a driftwood log, was deep in conversation with one of the unpaired guys. A pot of clams in seawater boiled away on a rock at the fire's edge.

When the clams opened, one of the guys poured out the foamy water. We all grabbed a couple, unhinging their shells and peeling up the small bodies. After the clams, a joint made its way around the fire.

That's when the jokes began.

Tom told of a ship's crew who spot a pirate gang fast approaching. "The captain says, 'Quick bring my red shirt.' The captain slips it on. They all kick ass and win. The next day, two pirate ships attack. The captain says, 'Get my red shirt.' It's bloody, but they kick ass. Stoked from their triumph, the crew asks the captain why he always wears a red shirt for battle. 'Well,' says the captain. 'If I get cut up in battle, the red will hide the blood, keep morale up.' The next day, they spot ten pirate ships coming on. The crew is freaking. But the first mate says, 'Captain, should I get your red shirt?' 'No,' the captain says, 'bring my brown pants.'"

The joke fit the Aleutian-beach-party mood. Several more jokes, most involving a priest, a rabbi, and something else, made the rounds. Les told one about a priest, a rabbi, and a fag.

Perfect timing. Everyone laughed. So he got adventurous.

"Three guys in a bar are arguing about who's got the biggest dick. The bartender gets sick of listening to them, so he says, 'All right, pull 'em out and lay 'em on the bar. I'll decide.' So the guys whip their dicks out on the bar. Just then a queer comes up. 'What'll it be?' the bartender asks. 'Well,' the queer says, 'I was going to order a sex on the beach, but on second thought, I'll take the buffet.'"

Les didn't notice the not-quite polite chuckles that whispered "enough." He was standing up now, hands on his hips.

"What's the nicest thing one guy can say to another guy at the bar?"

Shrugs all around. Silence.

"Let me push in your stool." Les laughed alone, oblivious to the shift. "Okay, so after a blow job—"

The fisherman with Jill stood up. "Who the fuck brought the fag?"

The dying-sunset feel, so sensuous and cozy moments before, turned ominous. I looked at Les's face, just going slack as he realized his error. As he realized he was no longer among friends.

I didn't admit I brought the fag. But I did launch into the only jokes I knew. The best rescue I had in me, stoned and drunk as I was.

"So," I said, standing up and rolling my shoulders back so my sweater rode up. "Mary Jane was walking down the alley one night when four boys grabbed her and started ripping off her clothes." I said it with the required sweet southern voice. "But Mary Jane just laughed. She knew her clothes wouldn't fit those boys."

It was a hit, and Mary Janes were the only jokes I could ever remember, so I told another.

"Mary Jane went to the movies one night all by herself. This man came and sat right beside her. Well, he started reaching his hand down her bra. But Mary Jane just laughed. She knew she put her money in her shoe."

"That chick's a moron," one of the fishermen said.

A few more rounds of jokes eased the tension and kept everyone together for a time. Then pairs began dispersing into the night. By the time I noticed, all four of the HiTide chicks had taken off with their chosen guy. Tom slid his arm around me.

"You want to take a walk?"

I looked at Les, now left with the two unattached guys, still trying to think up more jokes. He wasn't going to get laid, but it didn't look like he was going to get the shit beat out of him either.

"Why not."

Tom and I started toward the road because everyone else had gone toward the water, and it was probably getting crowded that way.

We managed the grassy strip with only one fall and were soon over the road and climbing the soft rounded hills behind. The sky capped the island with a slow-turning spangle of stars. We climbed a narrow path shadowed under a half-moon to the top of the first mountain and didn't even pause as we descended again and climbed the next.

Hiking when you're drunk is not a graceful thing. But hiking stoned is like floating sometimes. I was both, but the pot seemed to push to the front as my boots found the path passing between hillocks of rye-grass, mounding from the rocky earth like moguls. Coming down I couldn't help but skip now and then, giving way to the push of gravity. I forgot about Tom as I hopped from one tuft to the next. With each launch, I felt for a moment at the apex that I might not come down. That I could hop three or five or a hundred at once. I think I may have flapped my arms a couple of times. You never can tell. There may be minute gaps in gravity that only those lucky enough to be springing across tufts of grass would discover.

Of course I fell. It was the boots, poorly made for tuft jumping. Tom reached down to help me up, forcing me to remember he was there and that I wasn't sure what I was going to do with him. We climbed the next soft mountain and found a pillbox at the top. The perfect concrete hexagonal throne. I listened to the waves and watched the sparkling ridges that are an ocean under moonlight.

He put his arm around me and drew me in for a kiss. I kissed back. Then started the requisite speech about how I had a boyfriend, how much I liked him, always making sure I didn't seem too sure, because I wasn't. Thad was a million miles away, and Tom was close. Very close. The two were unlikely to meet up anytime soon.

We started kissing again. Tom pulled my sweater over my head, and the wind licked at my black-brassiered chest, leaving streaks of cool that Tom's hands smoothed warm with each caress. I lay back on the concrete, the rough cold contrasting with Tom's smooth heat. He murmured in my ear, words that quieted indecision. I was beautiful, sexy, hot. I relaxed into the comfort of a man's hands stroking, gripping. Tom unbuttoned my jeans, and I gave up deciding how far I'd let this go.

As he moved faster, I closed my eyes and concentrated on getting to my orgasm, which can be tough when you're as drunk as I was.

He was still inside me when I heard the whine of a motor. The teensy orgasm I'd been working on melted. I tilted my head away from Tom's thick breath and listened. It grew louder. Maybe I thought that if I didn't come, I wouldn't have to think of myself as such a slut, so much like them. Maybe I was just tired of working so hard for what would undoubtedly be a less than earth-shattering orgasm. The minute Tom stopped shuddering, I slid from under him and sat up. I turned toward the sound coming up the gravel road from Dutch.

"Doesn't sound like a truck," I said.

Tom pulled up his jeans, which had only made it down to his hips. He listened. "Three wheelers. Two, I think."

How do men know these things? I've heard countless men rattle off not only the model of an airplane flying overhead or a vehicle approaching but the engine size and year. I suspect men's ears are specially made to pick up infinitesimal variations in sound vibrations that can quickly be transferred into certainty that this particular motor is a Blah-Blah 1500 with a turbine blah-blah. Or that there are two three-wheelers headed our way.

I hopped off the pillbox and stepped into my jeans just as the first gust of a new wind hit.

"Where ya going?"

"To see."

Tom shrugged and dug rolling papers and weed from his pocket.

I walked downhill to a line of taller shrubs and looked back to see white paper swirling under his fingers in the moonlight.

The whine grew louder until it neared the pull-off for the beach. I still couldn't see anything, but then the motors wound high, and I saw the headlights of two three-wheelers bouncing along a trail below me. I followed their progress around the curve of the mountain.

The three-wheelers stopped where the path between the hills turned back toward the sea. I moved down the slope to get closer. Don't ask me why. I suppose it made for a convenient diversion. The engines cut out, and I could make out four figures climbing off. One of the passengers needed a hand. The passenger moved to the front of the machine and used the headlight to look into a bag. I was only about fifty yards away now. I could see her face. It was the old Aleut woman. She turned on a flashlight, and one of the others cut the headlight. Before the lights went out, I saw two other faces I knew, Anna and Little Liz, whose face looked almost menacing now in its sobriety. I didn't get a look at the fourth.

I crouched, mostly to get out of the wind, which numbed my bare arms and stomach. I slipped, just a shuffle's worth of noise.

Ida straightened.

I watched her shoulders, then her face turn toward me. She raised the flashlight. And although I knew she could not see me, in the dark, crouched among brush, high above her, I felt she did. I felt an arching slice of fear as the flashlight moved across the brush shielding my pale skin.

And then they were gone. The single point of light moved slowly off to the east, following the backs of the mountains.

What were these old women doing riding three-wheelers around at night? Let alone taking off into the mountains by themselves with a flashlight? Something about the place, the stars, my unrealized orgasm, and my bare skin skating with wind made it all surreal. And I guess, looking back without the benefit of booze and weed, I can say that it was.

I hopped the rest of the way down to their three-wheelers, wishing I had grabbed my sweater first. I didn't have a light, but I ran my hands over the three-wheelers. I thought about following the old women, but my faith in the uniformity of gravity had returned. I climbed back up and found my sweater and Tom. We shared a joint; he whispered fishing stories. But the women didn't return in the next hour.

We eventually picked our way back down to the beach, where we found everyone in confusion. Apparently, Jill had had a fight with her guy and stumbled off in a huff to drive back to town. That left twelve of us with two pickup trucks.

The mood had definitely changed. The sweet swaying intoxication had dissolved into a staccato of logistics, fringed with disappointment. All wasn't right with the world; we just hadn't noticed for a time. Someone doused the fire. Someone piled booze into a truck bed. No one picked up the trash.

Les, Tom, and I ended up in the back of one truck together. Tom made a valiant effort to neck a bit more as we headed back to Dutch. But this was a teeth-knocking, head-butting experience that did nothing for my disappointed nether regions. And I couldn't stop thinking about those women.

I guess the best way to describe how I felt that night is haunted. These old Aleut women had settled into my life without provocation or invitation. They kept appearing, doing odd things right in front of me. Ida was giving me the eye. Anna was testing me with reading material. The ghost of a younger Liz was walking around my cabana late at night. I really didn't believe that they were watching me, but that's how it felt, like I'd come to their attention and had better figure out just what that meant. As we bounced along the beach road under a sheer cast of moonlight, I decided to go on the offensive—I decided to start stalking them.

drifting through

'd woken up several times during the night, sure that Liz was in the cabana. I thought I heard her washing the dishes I'd left in the sink. I heard her light a candle on the table. I felt her leaning against the window, staring out at the dark valley. When morning finally came, I shook off the comforter and peeked over the loft edge. The dishes were still in the sink, an unlit candle on the table. I had to figure out what those women were up to before I lost my mind.

I studied what I had come to think of as Little Liz's outhouse confession when I took my morning hike behind the cabana. The daylight didn't help me decipher anything more. I'd only frequented two bathrooms in Dutch—the Elbow and my outhouse—and Liz had written in both. Odds were on that she'd left evidence elsewhere. If I could find it, I'd get closer to the truth, closer to ransoming back my sanity. And, of course, I'd prowled through public restrooms before without even this much rationale.

I had the next three days off. So at 10 A.M. I stuffed my latest graffiti notebook and a pen into my saddlebag and set out to recon Dutch's public bathrooms.

Oddly enough, Romans instigated the whole graffiti craze, as well as the bleached blonde phenomena, and the bar thing. We know this largely because of Pompeii's ashy fate.

One of Pompeii's brothels, a line of spare cells along a corridor, had drawings on the wall beside each woman's place of business. The paintings showed variations of the sex act. Next to them, customers would scribble their comments, advertising their virility along with their companion's skill set. These must have been similar to what you can see in any raunchy men's room today. *Nancy gives head right here in the head. For an easy lay call Debbie.*

Rome was dripping with graffiti. On building walls people scribbled everything from political endorsements to boasts about how many steps it took to walk the length of their patios. One political candidate had so many graffiti endorsements that some punks began making fun of him with graffiti messages that declared support from groups like the Sleepyheads en masse and the Drunken Stay-Out-Lates en masse. Graffiti was so common Romans started writing graffiti about graffiti: *I marvel you don't collapse, O walls, beneath the burden of so many scrawls.*

I didn't need to hit the Elbow Room. I'd been checking that bathroom three nights a week when I did my Little Liz closing-up chores. I decided to start with the grocery store. Dutch had only one. Anywhere else it would just be a well-stocked convenience store; here it was the superstore. I found mostly kid-writing. Plenty of *Todd is soooo cute* and *Puffins Rule*. A girl with a sense of justice had scribbled the name of her nemesis with instructions to call her for a blow job.

I bought two cans of sardines, Ritz crackers, and a block of cheddar, stuffed them into my bike bag and headed over the bridge, along a road flanked with towers of crab pots and to the docks. The dock lounge had a rec room with vending machines, arcade games, laundry, and showers. I think you're supposed to have a boat tied up to use the place, but nobody cared. The women's bathrooms here were rarely used and thus rarely cleaned. I checked the toilet paper rolls. Nothing. On the walls most of the messages warned about boats and their crews.

Cooks on the Brigadier *work on their backs.*

Watch out for Joe Finkle.

And my favorite, *Smell my ass!* I imagined some woman sitting on the can here and pulling a pen from her pocket. Um, she thinks, what should I write? Then it comes to her, "Smell my ass." But something is missing, that period on the end doesn't capture her passion. I added *Smell my ass!* to the notebook.

The HiTide was next on my list, but I wasn't eager to drop by simply because I didn't want to run into anyone from last night—especially Tom, who I knew was staying there. The bar, however, was strangely empty. Only Jill and the fixings for the Bloody Mary I was craving.

"Hey," Jill said when I leaned up to the bar.

"Bloody Mary, make it strong," I ordered. "I've got to use the head."

"Got it."

I checked under the toilet paper rolls first. Nothing but screws spreading rusty rings around themselves. The walls had been painted over the same gray several times. The heavy markers bled through at least one coat, sometimes two. You've seen it all before.

I was here but now I'm gone. Left my shit to carry on.

Harold Kattov has VD.

The white rabbit fell down the hole.

Screw my husband again and I'll cut your head off—Taylor.

Class of '85 Rules. On this one someone had scratched out '85 and written '87, from which someone else had drawn an arrow and written, *Punks!*

I jotted down the rabbit one, just because.

Jill was just plopping a pickled bean into my drink when I scootched up on a bar stool. I pulled it out and sucked the tomato gruel off the end. I preferred celery, but a bean was better than some of the garnish variations that can accompany a Bloody Mary—peppers, lemons. I've even been handed a drink with a pickle in it.

"So what did you think of the party?"

"I drank too much."

"Looked like you hit if off with Tom pretty well."

I downed half my drink. "Why'd you take off?"

Jill turned her head quickly and started rearranging the perfectly ordered booze bottles. She was crying. Shit. I slurped hard, trying to finish up and escape before something intimate happened. But Jill was too quick. As a professional server, she must have heard me sucking bottom and had another Bloody Mary in front of me before I'd uncrossed my legs. Jill had spent way too much time with her makeup and hair this morning. Her face and hair looked mannequin-hard, sharp edged and thick.

"That fucking asshole." Jill's tears started again with her words. "I really liked him. I mean, I thought he was different. He'd been talking shit about me going back to Seattle with him. He has this seven-year-old daughter and was saying how much she'd like me. He has a house. . . ."

Jill poured herself a drink.

"I'm like making plans to go. I packed up my shit. Then last night he says he doesn't know. This is after I balled him, you know. God, he's not even that good. He never gets me off. He says his ex is all tweaked about him having other women around his kid. He says he better talk to her before I come down. He didn't even stop by before catching the morning plane out. The prick." Jill wiped her cheeks. "I turned thirty last week." She tilted the last of her drink back. "Shit."

Jill's admission hit me like a jab in the throat. I had assumed she was older than me, thirty-three at least. Could she really be a year younger?

I wish I could say that I comforted Jill, commiserated at least about the shitty men in the world. Told her she was still young and attractive and there were plenty of fish in the sea. But I didn't. I guess I couldn't. Saying I didn't know how to find the words isn't true; I didn't want to find the words. Words have too much power, especially if you listen to your own. All I could come up with were the few lame phrases I'd heard my mom say again and again: get while the getting's good; never stay long enough to say you're sorry; never leave empty-handed. Seemed our wisdom only covered the leaving; not the being left. None of these seemed appropriate. I felt a panic surging like vomit in my throat. And the thought repeated with the rhythm of wet shoes in a drier—*she's younger than me; she's younger than me*.

Ka-thunk. Ka-thunk.

I needed distance between myself and Jill the Younger. Slapping a ten on the bar, I made a lame show of having somewhere to be, and ran.

By the time I got the bike started, my quest had fizzled. What was I doing? Riding around Dutch, checking bathroom wall writing. Taking a notebook with gems like *the white rabbit fell down the hole* in it. All

because an old Aleut woman was writing nonsense mess
bathroom. I was really too old for this crap.

I had to get my act together.

I stood there straddling my bike for a minute or two, not knowing
where to go now that all the fog of importance had drifted away from
my plans. I did the only sensible thing—headed for the Elbow Room.

I had a message waiting. Thad was coming in. The boat had caught its
limit and would be in for a three-day break. He'd be at the docks in
four hours.

Saved. I wouldn't have to figure out what to do with myself for the
next few days. I wouldn't have to think about myself, or them. Thad,
my hero who rarely showed, had come through.

"Better get your rear in gear," Marge said, winking in slow motion
with the weight of her eye shadow.

And that's what I did. I rode like crazy up to the cabana and cleaned
like crazy. I didn't have time to wash all the bedding and figured it
would be smarter to leave it until after Thad's visit. In two hours, I was
back on my bike, roaring down the hill toward the high school. I'd discovered the high school shortly after Thad left. You paid $3.50 for a
swim and could use the clean, well-lit shower room all you wanted.
They even supplied towels. I loved to swim, but this time I didn't even
splash around in the pool after paying the young lifeguard. I went
straight to the locker room. There was absolutely no writing on the
walls here. What was wrong with these high school girls? Did they really have so much school pride that they reserved their graffiti urges for
the grocery store?

In an hour, I was showered, blow dried, made up, and dressed casual but sexy in Levi's and one of Thad's work shirts, barely buttoned.
One hour to go. I stopped by the grocery store and filled my saddlebags with more cheese and crackers, apples, and two bottles of not-so-
bad wine.

I made it to the docks to see the *Seawind* bucking the choppy waves
of a wide tide rip that streaked its foamy, garbage-strewn back across
the bay. The boat settled back into calm water. Thad stood on the bow,
a thick line in one hand, his other stuffed in a pocket. The boat rocked

with the waves; he let his knees find the tempo. He waved, his curly hair blowing back in the boat's wind. I watched him jump on the dock. He landed squarely and wrapped the line around a body-size cleat once, then leaned against the rope, pulling the slack past the cleat. I stepped close and watched Thad wind the line in a figure eight around the cleat and double one end back. He rose from his knees and straight into my arms. We held each other and kissed for a long, long time.

I felt the wind blowing against us, his oilskin folding itself around my body, his arms bold, his lips warm.

"Take me home," I murmured into his ear.

He pushed me away to look at me. "You mind if we hang here for a while? Steve's buddy is moored across the dock, and they invited us all over for some steaks."

I pressed close to him again. "Actually, I'd rather have you to myself."

"I really want you to meet the guys I work with," he said, slipping his hand down to take mine. "They're important to me, like family. Spend more time with them than I ever did my brothers."

"That is exactly why I don't want to meet them." I kept a playful tone, but I was dead serious. I did not want to meet Thad's folks; I did not want to meet his brothers; I did not want to meet his best buds.

He tugged me toward the boat. "Come on. We have plenty of time."

The skipper was just hopping off. "I'll be back tomorrow," he said, striding past Thad and me. "Make sure you get all that crap cleaned up."

The *Seawind* was big and beautiful in a diesel-machine sort of way. I hopped across a void of gray ocean to the deck and immediately felt the rumbling engine beneath my boots. It pulsed with power that exhilarated. Power that could take you safely to places that are far from safe.

I met Bill first. From an open hatch, his thick arm protruded, attached to a meaty hand holding a wrench. His head and shoulders followed. He boosted himself topside as the engine wound down. He wore sweatpants in grease-streaked red. Sweat slathered his bare chest.

"This is Brandy. Bill," Thad said.

Bill drained a Rainier he'd left by the open hatch and stuck his hand toward me. "Eeeow!" he yelled, throwing his head back. He reached inside a case of beer and threw us each a Rainier. I tapped the can top and pulled it open, leaning back against the boat rail before taking a

good swig. The deck was tidy. A crane boom ran down its length,
six feet up. In the rear lay a gargantuan pile of thick yellow web
braided with orange seams. The long tube of a net dragged along the
Bering Sea floor, scooping up bottom fish by the tons. Parts were ar-
rayed near the engine hatch; a couple of orangey pink buoys lined the
rail; and a waist-high stack of Rainier cases squatted beside the cabin
door. The bow of the boat rose into a two-story cabin. Along each side
narrow welded ladders led to the upper deck.

"Come on," Thad said, taking my hand again, "I'll show you around."

And so he did. The captain's quarters on the second deck, the three
staterooms, the galley. They dined at a horseshoe booth. A large-screen
TV and VCR were bolted to the ceiling at an angle to the table. A
built-in stacked washer and dryer led away from the kitchen toward a
tiny head, completely watertight so that the room itself was the
shower.

I met the second crew member, Steve, while I was still marveling at
the shower setup. He was a giant of a man with a long torso and short
legs, who liked to talk about two things—his half-Aleut, half-Russian
heritage and Holly. Steve and Holly had just gotten married in Seattle.
Holly didn't like him fishing. He'd promised her this would be his last
trip, although it wouldn't be. Holly was scouring Washington and Oregon for their new home. They dreamed of a quaint farmhouse surrounded by at least twenty acres of pasture. Nothing too near the
ocean. She wanted to raise horses. He wanted to make her happy. The
$200,000 they'd saved plus what he'd make this time out would give
them a good start.

After ten minutes with Steve, I was shell-shocked. Thad had mean-
dered off to check on a part for Bill after informing me that we all had
a dinner engagement with the crew on the boat tied behind us. So I
was all alone—with Steve's dreams and the assurance that this evening
was going to go on and on. I was blinking spasmodically and could feel
my smile muscles tiring. Nothing worse than listening to someone go
on about a future he is actually sure of and working toward.

"Don't know if the Aleut half of me can stand living inland," Steve
was saying, "but Holly says we'll find a place close enough to drive to
the ocean. It's so cool you came out here. Thad really missed you. I

wish Holly would have come up and seen this place. But she didn't want anything to do with fishing. Too dangerous."

I lifted my slacking smile muscles. Blinked.

"More deaths commercial fishing than any other occupation in the U.S. Alaska fisheries are the worst. It's the water. Go overboard in this stuff, and you've got like five minutes before you can't move and fifteen before you're dead.

"We're pretty careful though. You don't have to worry about Thad. Hey you guys should come down and visit us after the season ends. Holly would love you. Maybe we'll have our spread by then. You guys could stay awhile."

I was beginning to see that Steve, thanks to Holly, was one of those men with a true blue sense of romance and an unflinching belief that it could be nurtured and nudged into love. Such people are dangerous.

"Well, Thad and I haven't really made plans yet," I said. Thad and I. Made plans. Using both phrases in one sentence sent my lids into another spasm. But that's what people did, right? They paired off; they made plans. Together. An image of Thad and me at Steve and Holly's farm flashed, all green hills and red barns, through my head. We'd be holding hands, of course, walking through thigh-high hay, smiling without tiring our facial muscles. I'd know how his brother had hit him with a snowball when he was six and left that little dent in his forehead. How his mother had instilled the lifelong belief that glassware always belonged in the cabinet to the right of the sink. I'd know what his fourth grade teacher's name was and that she'd been his first crush. I held on to the image for all of ten seconds. About as long as I'd held on to the image of me as a history professor with a worn wooden podium under my palms and a coliseum of eager faces in front of me. Or me as a new mother, lifting the corner of a yellow blanket to play peek-a-boo with my baby.

"I'll have to think about that," I told Steve and let my smile go slack.

"Hey. What's going on?" a guy yelled from the deck as we jumped down onto another boat. His name was Loren.

"Not much," Thad and Steve said in unison.

Loren's wife, Amanda, and another deckhand stepped out of the cabin. "Come on in," Amanda called. "I got dinner ready." She had curly brown hair down to her shoulders, seemed in her late thirties, and thin as the tip from a table of schoolteachers.

She took my hand and squeezed as we stepped into the galley. "Damn, it's good to see another woman. I've been listening to these peckerheads for seven weeks straight. Promise me you won't talk about boats or fishing or your cousin's hunting cabin, please."

I raised my right hand. "Promise."

Amanda had piled seven steaks on a platter in the center of the galley table. A big bowl of mashed potatoes, straight from the box, steamed next to them.

We barely squeezed in around the horseshoe table. Thad's thigh lay along the length of mine. His arm slid around my back as he pulled my upper body close as well. I caught myself wanting to jerk away, from his arm, from his pride in me and this cozy little scene. Who was he trying to impress? I stiffened, and his arm dropped.

Amanda and Loren lived in Renton, which is Seattle if you're not from the area. The other guy was called Smoker. We all smoked, but Smoker had a habit of lighting cigarettes, forgetting about them, and lighting more. During the course of the night, he would have as many as four burning at once.

"How much you get this trip?" Thad asked Loren.

"Slow at first, maybe hundred thousand tons the first month. Then we headed up off the Pribilofs and took in another hundred in a week."

"We did pretty good up there too," Steve said.

Amanda shot me a rolled-eye look.

I returned a such-is-life look.

The steaks were tough, the potatoes runny, the beer cold. In fifteen minutes, we'd scarfed up all we could. Smoker stabbed his first afterdinner cigarette into his remaining potatoes. It stuck there like a little soldier mired in quicksand. Soon an entire regiment struggled in the goo.

Squeezing herself from the table, Amanda grabbed his plate and slammed an ashtray in front of him. She piled the rest of the dishes into the sink. Thad's arm snaked around me again, and I shrugged it off to get up and help with the cleanup.

"How'd you end up out here?" Amanda asked as she scrubbed dried grease from the steak pan.

"I hooked up with Thad a few months ago," I said, settling the pan into a flimsy plastic drying rack. "When he headed out here, I thought it would be fun to see what it was like at the end of the world. How about you?"

"End of the world. Ha. Loren's been fishing the last ten years. I started cooking three years ago. Loren said he didn't like leaving me back home, spending money and flirting with his brothers."

"What's cooking like?"

"Most the time it's not bad. But shit, when the waves start slapping you around, try flipping hotcakes while the deck is rolling and you're barfing in the sink. I lose twenty pounds every trip."

"The Barfing Sea Diet."

She laughed.

Loren got up and came back with the coke, and Amanda and I returned to the table. The conversation finally left fishing and found its way to the best driving roads.

"Highway 101 in a Camaro," Thad said. "Cliffs on both sides, second-gear turns. That's a road."

"You don't have to drop below third in a Jag," I said.

"When did you drive a Jag?" Thad asked.

"Guy I knew had one. He let me drive from San Francisco to Crescent City. Took four hours."

Thad looked at me a long minute. I'd made a mistake. Never let on that a previous boyfriend had a hotter car. "The car was hot; the guy was not," I said to restore myself.

"Yeah, 101's nice, except for all the damn RVs," Loren said.

"I drove this two-lane through the Ozarks down in Arkansas in a Spitfire my brother had," Steve said. "Holly was screaming the whole way, 'Oh, my God, you're going to kill us.' That was cool."

"Anybody ever driven the Haul Road up to Prudhoe Bay?" Bill asked. "I hear you got to carry your own fuckin' gas. Shit, it's like five hundred miles of nothing."

Amanda handed me a coke-laced cigarette and turned her shoulders toward me to create a conversation alcove. "Your hair's so natural-looking. I've tried going blond a few times. Loren says I look like I've got Rice Krispies pasted on my head. Do you get it done professionally?"

"It's natural."

"Uh-huh."

"It is. I don't do anything." I felt the lifting rush of the coke hit my bloodstream. This is what I liked about coke—I get gabby and can keep up with the extroverts.

"Fine, be that way. I just wondered what shade that's called. I used to have really white hair when I was a kid. It was like your color. I think if I found that same color, it would look natural."

Ah, the tired when-I-was-a-child line. I think brown-haired women who once long ago were blond children feel they aren't so much dyeing their hair as reclaiming its true state of nature. Perfectly justified. Even my mother, true blond until her late thirties, had succumbed as she watched her platinum blond shade to gold then honey; then she'd gone on the offensive.

I remember her inspecting my hair, mashing a handful of it between her fingers. "Same color mine used to be," she said, turning to her vanity mirror, reflecting our blondness back to us. "Now, Brandy, listen. I may not be around when you need this advice. Everyone wants hair like we've got, and you've got to keep it that way, know what I mean? I'm still all blonde and nothing but a blonde, but at a certain age, you'll need to help it along some. I don't think of it as bleaching so much as brightening something that's going dull."

Brighten. Brighten.

So far I hadn't detected any dullness and could still claim bleach virginity so I bent my head toward Amanda and separated my hair at the top. "See. No dark roots."

"You probably just got it done."

"Out here? I haven't seen a salon within five hundred miles."

Amanda blew a jet of smoke into my unsullied-by-dark-roots blondness. "Only one way to prove it. Dare to bare the bush."

The male conversation stopped as it will when certain words filter into their consciousness. Amanda had given them three—*dare, bare,* and *bush.*

This was not much of a dare. I had uncovered the evidence to larger groups than this. I took another drag of the laced cigarette and handed it to Amanda. Bill started banging his palms on the table in some rendition of a drumroll.

I stood up, popped the row of buttons on my 501s with one yank, and nudged my purple panties down far enough to reveal a line of peaking blond hairs.

When the hoots subsided and my jeans were well buttoned again, I glanced at Thad. He wasn't smiling; he wasn't recovering from a hooting spree. He was simply looking at me, not with desire but the blankness of confusion. I shot him a what-the-fuck look.

Amanda leaned toward me. "How do I know you didn't dye that too?"

I lit a cigarette. "Sometimes we just have to live with uncertainty."

Amanda laughed. Real blonde or fake, at least I was willing to talk about something other than boats, cars, and fishing.

Thad, however, wouldn't look at me.

Two hours later, all the coke had been snorted and smoked. The conversation faltered. Someone said he knew someone who had some more. Loren's boat had just bought a used truck with two jump seats, so it was decided, I'm not sure how, that everyone would go.

How many times had this same scenario played out? You're with a bunch of people, doing coke, drinking, thinking you're having great conversation, when someone announces you have to make a coke run. Now logic would have it that one or two of you slip out to hunt down a connection. But this rarely happens. Instead, exactly three people more than will fit in the available vehicle must go. The first connection is never home, so the quest continues. You may have to try several possibilities, all the time crammed in a truck or an El Camino with a bunch of people who are quickly losing their buzz.

Bill and Steve took the jump seats. Loren, Smoker, and Thad sandwiched thigh by thigh on the front bench seat. Amanda and I took the laps. Riding on a lap in a truck cab at night over Dutch roads is an awkward thing. You have to keep your head scrunched down, hang on to the dash with at least one hand, and try to keep your ass mostly on your own boyfriend's lap, especially after you've shown everyone your pubic hair.

Thad's hands remained on the sides of my thighs. Even when I slid one of them front and center, pressing my crotch into his palm, he didn't respond. He waited until I let go, then moved his hand back to the outside of my thigh. He wasn't going to be easy, and the challenge excited me. These were the kind of skirmishes I knew how to win.

No one was home at the first house. But Smoker knew someone else, so our search party continued through puddled streets. I never wanted more coke once the first batch ran dry, but I was often in the company of people who did. There are two kinds of drug users—those who take it when it's offered, smoke it, snort it, forget it, and those who seek it, long for it, sell for it. I felt very much apart and superior as my ass bounced on Thad's knees.

We pulled up to a house and Amanda and I climbed out to free everybody else. That's when I noticed the dog. A black lab-cross stood on the wheel well in the bed, leaning most of his body over the side. He panted happily and gave an eager body shake when I stroked his smooth head.

"Whose dog?"

Loren stretched himself out of the truck. "Guy we bought the truck from. We try to drive off, and this dog jumps in the back like he's coming along. So the guy pulls him out. Next morning, I go to make a town run, and this dog's in the truck again. He just keeps coming back."

I scratched the dog behind the ear. I would later learn this was the way it worked in Dutch. The dogs took a liking not so much to their owners but their owners' trucks. If a truck changed hands, the dog did too. Half the trucks in Dutch had an ugly mutt in the back, stretching his nose into the wind. And with this truck he bonded for life.

Rubbing the dog under the chin, I wondered if Cowboy felt this way about Dad's car. It wasn't a truck, but it did have a missing rear window he could lean out. Cowboy would be over a year old now. He'd probably grown into those tremendous paws. He'd rest his head on Dad's leg at night, keep him from being alone.

Smoker came back from the house. "The guy's at the HiTide."

We piled back into the cab for the trip back over the channel and parked next to another truck with another dog in the back.

Our dog barked once—What's going on?

He cocked his ears at the other dog's reply—Not much.

The exchange of dogs taking a ride on an island so small they clearly aren't going anywhere they haven't been before.

At the HiTide, Smoker scored, and we returned to the boat with enough coke to finish off the night. The dog whined softly and curled up in the truck bed when the motor shut down.

"What happened to the bike?" Thad asked when he saw my phosphorescent 150 in the parking lot late that night.

"I traded it in for something I could pick up. It also starts."

Thad threw his leg over the seat and kicked the starter down. Sure enough it started. It looked ridiculously small under him with his oilskin obscuring most of it.

"I feel funny on it," he said.

I hurled myself behind him and pressed my chest against his back. "Who gives a shit. Get me to the cabana."

So he did. We rode straight over the Bridge-to-the-Other-Side, down the valley, and up the hillside in the dark. The feel of his body against my chest, the vibrating machine between my legs, all worked. When he pushed open the cabana door, I forgot the odd way Thad had been acting that evening, the tension between us. We did it without foreplay the first time and lots the second. We started on the living room floor and ended in our nest of a bed, where we stayed, until all the Ritz crackers were gone and I'd had one extravagant orgasm and two of the general variety. With him beside me in bed, I didn't hear Liz puttering around the cabana or feel the guilt she'd stockpiled in the outhouse.

"So how you been doing here without me?" It was early morning and we were sitting on the deck, sipping cold coffee, wrapped up in our down comforter. Even in midsummer, the mornings were cold enough to take the steam off a mug within minutes.

"Okay." I wondered if I wanted to tell him about Mary and her late-night visit, about the three old Aleut women hiking in the night. After my deflating bathroom wall excursion, it all seemed horrendously stupid. I sure didn't want to tell him about Tom. "I'm making good money at the bar. Getting to know some people."

"Yeah? Like who?"

"Well, like Les. We went to a beach party together day before yesterday."

"I guess he's safe."

"You know, he has a crush on you."

"Yeah, he tells me every time I see him."

"I told him to back off before I kick his ass. That's something I don't get. How come no one gives him a hard time? I mean he's so flaming, and he comes on to half the fishermen in the bar. You'd think he'd get the shit kicked out of him with regularity."

Thad took a gulp of coffee and pulled the comforter around us tighter. "I guess it's like Les is not just any fag. He's our fag, so he's okay."

I watched his face as he spoke. "That's kind of what Les said."

Thad stared over the valley, swaying wildflowers and grasses in an easy wind. He took a last swig of coffee and set the mug on the gray planks. "So what do you think of going down to visit Steve and Holly when the season ends?"

I laughed. "Not on the top of my list."

He didn't look at me. I waited.

"What's going on with us, Brandy?"

I knew what was coming, felt it like a sudden freeze in my gut. I dropped my hand to his thigh, sliding it upward, an instinctual reaction.

"Stop it." He pushed my hand away. "All you ever want to do is screw. We need to talk."

"Okay. Okay." But I smiled—in that way.

Thad stood up. "What the fuck's wrong with you?" he said, looking down at me. He turned away and went inside.

I sat out there for an hour, trying to figure out where I'd gone wrong, how I'd missed the signs. Thad wanted to love me. It seemed so clear now, but a few hours ago I would have laughed at the idea. All I knew was that I couldn't fix this for him or for me. When I came inside he was just sitting on the couch. I sat beside him. "I guess I didn't know you felt that way," I said.

He turned to me. "Why did you think I asked you to come out here? Why did you think I got this place all set up? What did you think I wanted, just something to fuck when I came into town?"

His face was so raw and open. His curls, lying against smooth skin like a child's, set off the maleness of his body, the sweep of his shoulders and the arches of his biceps. I wanted to cradle him in my arms and cry for him. I wanted to protect him from me.

"I don't know what I thought." It was the only truth I could offer. "I guess that it didn't matter that much to you."

"It does."

"Can we just leave it for now? Can we just enjoy each other for the next few days? Okay?"

When he turned to look at me finally, I knew he was about to lie and I knew I wanted him to. "Yeah," he said. "Okay."

For the next three days, I pretended. I reveled in the old Thad, the one I thought I'd known. I reveled in knowing who to be and how to feel. He borrowed a bigger bike from a friend, and we followed the valley road back until it became a trail and swung behind the mountains and around others. We watched swathes of lupine bending together in the wind. I picked a bouquet and forgot it inside a pillbox where we made love. We lay naked on a flat rock at the top of a hill overlooking the sea. We found the wreck of an old ship below the cliffs, and poked our heads into the wheelhouse, and ate lunch on the rotting deck. We got drunk together at the Elbow Room and walked along the beach afterward. He bought us matching SPAWN TILL YOU DIE T-shirts at the airport gift shop. Black, with a white skull and crossbones, bordered by sharp-nosed salmon, these Ray Troll T-shirts were all the rage. SPAWN TILL YOU DIE was the most popular, but HUMPIES FROM HELL, with its colorful bared-teeth fish, was all over the place too. I slipped mine on and almost felt like I belonged here. Thad skimmed my box of books and kept trying to start Aleutian history conversations. I kept changing the subject. I wanted to just be me again, the comfortable, fearless me I felt in his company. The me that wasn't obsessed with old Aleut women and their dismal history, the me that wasn't alone and scared shitless. I had to separate those two me's by keeping Thad out of it.

All too soon and not soon enough it was over. Steve tracked us down at the cabana. The boat was leaving that night. I saw Thad off under a half moon on the long dock.

I stood for a long time on the oil-soaked planks that reached out over the water, letting the wind beat at my face. He hadn't asked if I'd miss him this time. I hadn't had to lie.

I turned my back to the wind and headed back to land. It was Thursday night, and the Elbow Room would be crowded with drunks and money.

Chaos

The United States had purchased Alaska from Russia for $7.2 million in 1867. And while most of Alaska remained lightly populated and unexplored by its new owner, Dutch in 1904 was a surprisingly cosmopolitan town. The spring headquarters for the Bering whaling fleet and a supply stop for gold stampeders headed to the Klondike and Nome, Dutch overflowed with bars, dance halls, and men. Jack London is thought to have stayed in one of the town's fancy hotels and to have dreamed up the novel The Sea Wolf before its grand fireplace. Dutch was a wild town of fast talk, wicked schemes, daring last chances.

To this town came the remnants of remote villages, ravaged by disease and starvation. Many Aleuts had been well educated under Russian rule, speaking both Aleut and Russian. Now their languages were outlawed and their schools closing. Although Russian Orthodoxy would remain the dominant religion, Christian missionaries came to take up the slack. A Methodist school and orphanage, the Jesse Lee Home, had opened in 1890 and endeavored to educate and shelter orphaned girls. But the home's directors believed Aleut orphans were better off being adopted by white families than by their Aleut relatives, and many were shipped outside the islands. The Aleuts finally would petition against the home in 1910, charging that children were often adopted over the protests of close family.

With otter, seal, and seal lion populations dwindling, new people

streaming through, and a new nation to which they owed allegiance, the
Aleuts were confounded by yet more changes. Two hundred years before,
they had been Unangan; sixty years before they had been Russians; now
they were Americans.

To fall in love. To fall. Love. Fenia believed in it. She believed in it
when she spread her thighs and closed her eyes. She believed even
more fiercely when the man's breaths came quick and her body rocked
with his thrusting. She believed when she smiled, pulled down her
dress, and folded his money into her palm.

With each new man, and they were usually new, she'd watch him
closely. She smiled at him shyly. She loved each one. Sometimes she
walked to the harbor and watched the boats coming in. Whom would
she find to love on each of these? She most loved the Revenue Service
men, with their government checks and their heroic stories. She loved
the adventure tourists with their sketched maps and chests of liquor.
She loved the gold seekers with their eager walk and new wool coats.
She would wait. She was young. She pulled the scarf from her head,
letting her pink ribbons lift back with her long dark hair, and her full
skirt flattened against her legs.

A red-bearded man approached across the jutting pier. "Are you
waiting for someone?"

She looked up at his blue eyes, eager and sure. "Maybe for you."

He smiled and took her hand. She led him through the narrow
streets of Dutch: past the grand hotel, where white women chatted on
the porch, past the gambling houses, and bars. She led him up the gray
wood stairs to her tiny room. She didn't speak but cast quick glances at
his face. Red hair. She liked that.

He unbuttoned his pants. She untied her pantaloons. She lay back
on her bed. He moved on top of her.

"Never had an Aleut," he said, pushing into her.

She smiled and closed her eyes.

When he couldn't pay, saying he was sorry he'd spent everything he
had on his grub stake, she touched the stiff red hairs on his arm and
reassured him. She knew he wished he could.

"When you come back from Nome, you can pay me then," she said.

"In pure gold." He kissed her lips and waved as he stepped onto the landing, still buttoning his pants.

"I love you," she whispered as he left. And she did.

Fenia washed herself and stepped into her pantaloons, drawing the string tight around her waist. She looped the ends into a bow and straightened her ribbons.

"Fenia," came a whisper, followed by a soft knock.

"Come in."

A thin woman cracked the door and slid through.

"It's started again."

Fenia concentrated on swinging her arms in two perfectly even arcs as she followed Olga down the creaking corridor and into another identical room. On the bed lay the body of a woman, naked. Throat slit.

Fenia knew her well. Sophia had been one of the first girls at the Jesse Lee home to befriend Fenia when she arrived shortly after her mother's death. Sophia had taught her how to survive, showing her in secret how to make the Russian letters and, in public, how to fold her napkin in her lap. Together they had practiced flirting with the white strangers, and later, Sophia had taught her how to take their money.

Arranging her skirt as she sat tenderly on the blood-soaked bed, Fenia stroked the dark hair, loosening the strands sticking in blood. She pulled each one, reverently, until hair lay in rays on the pillow. Fenia gazed up at the Holy Mother icon Sophia had hung over her bed. The Mother's hand lifted toward the viewer, offering herself. Fenia pulled a cover over Sophia's body and began to sing.

Looking at her you would have thought her intimacy with the dead body strange. She never cried, never closed her eyes. She touched the body as if it were alive, as if Sophia could feel the hands on her face and hear the song. You would have known something was wrong with Fenia. It showed.

Olga couldn't watch this time. It had been only a year since the last spring influx of stampeders, when the girls started dying. That time, two had been beaten to death before Olga, Fenia, and Katherine had found and killed him. Would men like this come every spring, Olga wondered, waiting for news the Bering ice pack had broken, waiting to board their flimsy boats and continue the adventure?

She went to the window and gazed at the street a floor below. A group of men in woolen trousers and woolen vests, their coats draped over arms or shoulders, went arm in arm toward the point. They sang something sad as they went. Two women, white and dressed in full pale blue skirts, almost matching, bent to talk to each other as they walked. Olga saw them cross the hard-packed dirt street when they neared the singing men. Still the men watched. But these were white women, and the men kept their thoughts and bodies to their own side of the street. For her, she knew, they would have crossed over. They knew Aleut women were less fuss when it came to chastity, monogamy. It was easy to be a whore. But Olga did not find it easy to be a killer. She didn't think she could continue without losing herself. And she knew Fenia was already lost.

"We better do it now," Olga said, watching the singing men disappear behind a hotel. "There's little sense in waiting for more to die."

Fenia picked up Sophia's limp hand, cradling it to her breast as her quiet love song gave way to a sweet high moan. "Yes," she said. "He loves the blood. She is prettier with it on." Fenia remembered Sophia's dreams of marrying a whaling captain and traveling to California, where she heard the sun shone every day. Sophia had told Fenia about waters warm enough to swim in and houses with windows as wide as her arms stretched. Fenia closed her eyes and let the images come; she danced in a yellow gown across polished floors, holding the rough hand of a man she loved. She waited patiently for another to pull out a chair at the candlelit dining room at the hotel. She unbuttoned the shirt of another, slowly tracing her fingers over revelations of chest, abdomen. Then she danced again, head tilted back, eyes closed as his strong arm held her.

She smiled, opening her eyes and finding Olga in the dim room. "She must have loved him," she said.

Olga nodded, still looking out the window to keep from having to look at Fenia. "I'll ask around."

It wasn't hard to find a killer here. Not if you knew the town, who's who and what's what. The whaling fleet, scores of makeshift boats, and barges wintered at Dutch, bringing their tired, sickened crews. Steamers from Seattle and San Francisco stopped to pasture hungry horses and restock supplies. They disgorged streams of eager, hopeful men bent on the gold in Nome and the Klondike. Hungry men they were, waiting to move north, waiting for news the Bering ice pack had broken up. The town, only a few years before an enclave of Aleuts and Creoles—speaking Russian, drinking Russian tea, draping Russian scarves about their heads—ran white with outsiders. Wood-frame hotels, bars, dance halls, a giant whale-rendering plant spread over the sand and ryegrass. Dirt paths gave way to mud roads then to planked boardwalks. The world was steaming into Dutch Harbor.

Fenia was picking lupine above town when Olga found her that evening. The purple spires, reaching to her thighs, rippled across the hillside in a light wind, reminding Fenia of hands passing along piano keys.

"I found who he was," Olga said. "He's at one of the taverns."

Fenia pressed her face into the flowers. "Won't these be pretty on my dresser?" She inhaled and closed her eyes.

Olga nodded. "I'll get Katherine."

"Yes, I'll pick a bouquet for Katherine too."

Olga touched Fenia's cheek, and she tilted her head into the touch. "It will be okay," Olga said. "We'll take care of you."

Fenia smiled. "I know."

Fenia watched Olga hike back down the hill and smiled to think of what the night would bring.

Katherine wasn't a whore. She had married a Creole, half-Russian, half-Aleut. A middle manager in the fish-packing plant. She supplemented the family's seasonal income by making baskets, which sold to the whites who visited. Already Aleut baskets were gaining fame because of the fineness of the Aleutian grasses and the skill of women like Katherine.

The three women walked, first on the sand, then taking a faint trail into the hills. They were silent until they reached the backside of the first hill. Except Fenia, who hummed softly as she walked behind the others.

"Are you sure you found the right man?" Katherine asked.

Olga nodded.

"I suppose it would be wrong to wait to see if he does it again. See if he's the right one."

Olga nodded. "It would be wrong."

Katherine glanced back at Fenia. "She is getting worse."

"I know."

"I worry sometimes that she'll start doing it without us."

Olga walked without speaking for a time. "We will take care of her."

The three women returned to the cave and carved out their power from the dead bodies. They were not frightened. They were the daughters of daughters of daughters, and the power had rooted with each generation. As before, Fenia stood within longer. She filled her lungs with the warm dryness until her mind reeled into the pink-spotted darkness of too much air.

"And these are the generations of Fenia." She touched each body, whispering the words she'd been taught never to forget. "Aya begot Aggixia who begot Agripina. Agripina lived sixty-three years. These are the daughters of Agripina, Emily and Mary. Of these daughters, only Emily was marked. And Emily's time was sixty-five years and saw much hardship and the vanishing of her mother's village. Emily begot two daughters who lived, Rita and Patricia. And Patricia was marked and begot daughters, but only Fenia survived."

Fenia finished the recital as she completed the circle of bodies. At the last man, black with age, she touched his stretched and screaming lips. "It's good to remind you of the living," she said.

Born simple and happy, perhaps Fenia would have remained a slow, pretty girl if it had not been for the weight of her place, revealed to her when she was only thirteen. Her mother, dying of tuberculosis, told Fenia the story before she was ready. Sometimes only those least able are willing to carry such a burden.

Fenia could remember only through a mist the first time she had loved a man through death. Her mother had explained, and she had obeyed, not just her mother's voice, spoken with the voices of her ancestors, but her own voice and vision, which saw more clearly when it killed. Fenia knew her mind was not whole, but when she killed, she felt it growing, almost large enough to understand. With sweet duty, she had held the body of the last man as he died. She felt his weight in her arms now and smiled with the memory. Only the gentle waves of time had carried him from her. And she missed him. Now, she would get him back, for a while.

The maternal ancestors of Olga and Katherine had likewise drawn a circle of duty around their daughters. Katherine's and Olga's mothers had moved them to Dutch as the sea otters vanished and starvation and disease cast whole villages to the wind. The girls grew up with looming whalers stalking the harbor, white men hurrying, the rustle of fine dresses in their ears. And they grew up knowing their duty was to kill. They weren't girls anymore and had learned to be somber, to turn their faces from blood. Katherine and Olga would not have chosen Fenia as a comrade in this duty. It was the way she loved doing it that unsettled them, and the permission her elation gave them to grow flush with excitement, with purpose when they killed. When they watched Fenia, saliva pooled thick in their mouths, defined their swallows. And they found it hard to deny the power and how good it felt.

Fenia found him still at Blokes. She fanned her hair and ribbons across her shoulders and stepped up to him. He turned to see her young face smiling shyly.

"Can I get you a drink?"

She sipped at the shot of whiskey he handed her. She slid her hand down to take his. "Come with me," she whispered.

They walked hand in hand along the dark beach. Fenia leaned against him now and then, thinking of his wind-sheltering body. Each time she looked up at him, her chest grew heavy. She loved his long legs and rough hands. He stopped to press her against himself and feel her small breasts. She sighed and felt the warmth of her desire spreading into her arms and legs. When they rounded the soft mounds of grass mingling with the beach, Fenia stepped away from him.

She heard him think how beautiful she looks here in the sand with starlight at her back. The short wooden oar rocked his head forward. Olga swung again before he could turn, and he went down. Fenia cocked her head to the left and watched him fall, watched Olga raise the oar again and again until stillness. Fenia knelt beside him. Her hands smoothed his blood-smeared hair and stroked his cheeks.

"Oh, my love. My sweet, sweet love," she crooned as his body trembled, then convulsed. She bent and kissed his lips. "I love you. I love you. I love you," she song-chanted as he took a last struggling breath.

She looked up at Olga and Katherine, at the still glistening streaks of dead-man's fat on their cheeks. They were watching her, and she could feel their disgust, and she could feel their faithfulness. She felt their arms around her even as they trembled at what they had done. Tears left her face, fell to the sand, forever part of the moving grayness of the island. She looked past her friends at the stars, shedding light like falling feathers. "The world," she said, "is growing thick."

no time to think

It was even worse than I expected. As Thad's boat left, many others had arrived. The bar was packed with guys I didn't know. Guys from all over the country, there to make fast money and leave. Guys without families, untethered, unrestrained.

I pushed my way through the mob and behind the bar to get my bank and tray.

"You're late," Marge yelled while pouring a line of four whiskey shots without lifting the bottle.

The Elbow Room had flown in something of a real band from Anchorage for a week-long stint. Two guitarists and a drummer stood on a plywood platform, butted against the wall. In front of them, a mass of people writhed, most not even partnered up. I figured there were exactly ten women in the whole place, counting me and Marge and Les. Through the bodies, I caught a glimpse of Bellie dancing. As usual, she jacked her body about in some version of the twist.

Someone rang the bell.

I tried to get to the tables along the side of the dance floor, but after losing a tray of drinks to a floppy-armed-Grateful-Dead dancer, I gave up. I kept to the six tables in the rear. They were drinking fast enough, and it was taking long enough to get through that crowd of men controlling the floor like the center of a chessboard. I skipped the table laid with thin white lines of coke to give them time to finish up. The block of wood I'd set under the tippy table had been knocked out, and I lost an entire load of drinks to a slow slide.

"Three screwdrivers, six Corona, nine tequila," I yelled at Les, who had leaned toward me while pulling a tap to signal I could order. He nodded and slid beers to two guys who had pushed up to the bar.

Neither he nor Marge were smiling. They were in mad-dash mode. When Les had my drinks ready and leaned over my station to fill my tray, I shouted, "What's going on tonight?"

He shook his head and rolled his eyes. "It gets like this sometimes," he yelled.

The bell rang again.

I hefted my tray over my head and took a deep breath before plunging in. The gropers were in fine form. I was averaging three ass grabs a trip, which I ignored because there's not much you can do with a tray full of drinks and a press of bodies around you. As I dodged through like a boxer seeking openings in his opponent's guard, I remembered how Juvenal had described the mob-choked first cities of Rome. "The crowd is so dense the people behind jam against my back and sides. Someone rams me with his elbow . . . this fellow cracks my head with a two-by-four, that one with a ten-gallon jug, my shins are thick with muck, now I'm being rammed by somebody's big feet—and there goes a soldier's hobnail in my toe!"

It helped, connecting to another mind across the centuries. Except instead of rams with elbows, I was dealing with the unintentional and intentional gropes that were impossible to sort out.

I was maybe two-thirds of the way through, bobbing and weaving, when a bearded blond guy reached his hand around my ass and held on to a cheek. He didn't even try to be sly about it. This was intentional, and I felt like this soldier was using his hobnail with tremendous joy.

"Get your fucking hand off me," I yelled and tried to step through another group of men. The guy moved with me and this time reached up for a handful of tit. He was laughing and having a good time with it. So there I was with twenty pounds of drinks balanced on my fingertips over the heads of scores of drunk fishermen with some guy's hand squeezing my tit.

And he was laughing.

I snapped. In one almost fluid motion, I grabbed a beer bottle off the tray, chucked the tray behind me into the crowd, and smashed the bottle into the side of his head.

He would have gone down if not for the crowd. He knocked into someone and keeled over at the waist, clutching his ear.

"Fuck! Fuckin' bitch." He straightened.

I felt the beer bottle still in my hand. I had imagined its end broken into a viciously jagged edge. But as I raised it again, I saw it was still very intact, very blunt. But an image of gouging his face with broken glass had bloomed in my head. I went with it. I lunged. I still can't believe I went for his eye like that. But that's just where I aimed. Someone grabbed me around the waist, and the bottle only bumped a hapless bystander in the neck.

I was pissed. I gripped the bottle, watching for another opening. Beard Guy cussed and lunged for me. Several men grabbed onto him too. By then the ruckus had reached the bar. The lights went up. Marge shoved her way through the mess.

"What the fuck?" Marge said when she reached the scene. She saw the bottle still in my hand and the blood running down the side of the guy's head. "Shit."

Most of the men were laughing. A chant started. "Let her at him. Let her at him."

Marge grabbed my arm. "Get him outta here," she ordered the two men holding Beard Guy. The crowd backed off as she pulled me behind the bar.

"What happened?" Les asked as Marge sat me down on a stool in the corner by the fridge.

"Some jerk was feeling me up."

"Why do you get all the fun?" Les said.

"Shut the fuck up, Les." Marge handed me a shot of schnapps. "You can help us back here. It's crazy tonight."

Les dimmed the lights. The band started in with "She's Got Legs."

I saw a hand reach out to ring the bell again.

I sat on a stool, tucked into a corner, and tipped back my shot with a shaking hand. My lipstick smeared the glass rim, a broken smile. I stared at the cracked pink curve and touched my bare lips, felt them tremble. He'd laughed at me. He had grabbed my tit and laughed at me. And I'd fallen apart.

You walk into a room, dressed to perfection, confident shoes, feeling your body all poised and cool. Then you hear it—a snicker across the sudden quiet. And everything crumbles. You see the jeans and flannel shirts, the sensible shoes. And you know yourself in the contrasts. Your dress is too red, too tight. Your feet too big for those little shoes. Your poise vulgar. All that power you had just moments before, the power of a red dress and willing body, tossed on the ground and squashed by a snicker, remote and deadly. That's how I felt—undone.

A Latin phrase kept pacing through my head. *Etiam capillus unus habet umbrau.* Even one hair has a shadow. I had approximately one hundred thousand hairs casting one determined shadow. It was the one revelation I had, sitting on that stool, watching the mob move. I'd been living in the shade of my hair, completely satisfied to hold all my power in tits, ass, and fluff, never acknowledging the consequences. And then he'd laughed at me. Forced me to grope myself, fumbling for alternative assets. All I'd come up with was a beer bottle. Violence is the last refuge of the powerless. If nothing else works, kick their ass.

"Hey." Marge shot me a dirty look from down the bar. "Get off your ass. The sink's filling up."

I downed another quick shot. Two or three more, I figured, and I'd be in the clear. I wouldn't have to think about my humiliation. About myself.

Mostly I was in the way. Les and Marge had a system—skimming past each other, mixing drinks six or eight at a time, slamming the cash drawer with turning elbows. I kept my eye on the sink and washed out the glasses when it got full. Mostly I drank. I'd dart between the two fast-moving bodies, grab a couple of booze bottles, and mix whatever I'd come up with. Sitting on my out-of-the-way stool, I watched Les and Marge in motion.

What surprised me most was how much action Les was getting. He had learned to flirt on the fly. I'd say with about a third of the guys he served, Les found some way to advertise his availability. Now it was fairly obvious even to a room full of drunks that Les was gay. He had the earring, not a stud, but a nice dangly gold thing. He used his hips more than most women and had a nice floppy-hand dangle. Occasionally, I'd see him lean in to talk to a customer. He'd use it all. His shoulders would move back and forth and up and down with his words. His eyes would get all direct and meaningful. He'd twist his earring with his thumb and index finger. Most often the customer would laugh, wait for Les to serve someone else, then slip away into the crowd. But once in a while, one would linger.

When two-thirty finally came, Marge flashed the lights and yelled for last call. After another round and the "Rodeo Song," this time led by the band, we started hustling everyone out. Little Liz hadn't showed, so close-up went fast. Marge was a bit worried about her, since she hadn't been in for a couple of days. I was just glad for the reprieve, not just from having to sidestep urine and steel myself for the smell, but from not having to think about who she had been, what had brought her down.

I found two fifty-dollar bills underneath a table while sweeping up broken glass, some of which was probably from my tray pitch. I also found a spectacular coke vial, slim, silver and studded with turquoise. It was empty. I shoved it in my pocket. Marge and Les had really raked it in, and each gave me a hundred-dollar bill. So even though I'd done very little drink slinging, I came out okay.

We could hear a bunch of guys still partying in the parking lot, so Marge, Les, and I had a couple drinks to give them time to clear out. When three-thirty came and we could still hear the laughter and shouts, we gave up.

They were waiting for Les. Five guys came up behind him when his back was turned to lock up the bar. Marge was already heaving herself into her truck, and I was about to give the starter a kick.

"You mother-fucking fag," one of them said, calm as a poet.

Les turned, the key still in his hand. "Actually, a fag, by definition, doesn't fuck mothers."

He said it with his feet firmly planted, his hands open by his sides. I could see his pretty face, the way he looked right at them, accepting what he knew was coming. I heard waves hitting the beach and an eagle scream over the water, felt scraps of fog drift over me. And I ached for him in that moment, before the fists and boots and blood. Because what I saw was noble. And because it wouldn't matter.

Les's sensible argument was lost on these guys. One of them socked him in the gut, and Les buckled at the door, his face disappearing into the fold of his body.

"Hey, you fuckers," Marge shouted, barreling toward them. Her piled-up hair had slipped backward through the long night, and she looked like a deranged Quaker lady, except for the makeup. But these guys were too far gone to cave to the natural male instinct to obey a grandmotherly, Quakerish-looking woman. She tried to grab the shoulder of the guy who was now whaling at Les's face. One of the others shoved her off the step. She went down hard in the wet sand.

All this happened pretty fast. I had gotten off my bike and halfway to the door, without any clue what I was going to do. Marge saw me coming.

"Go get the boys," she yelled. "Stormy's."

Stormy's was a pizza joint that often opened when the bar closed to rake in what the guys hadn't guzzled away. Marge was pushing herself off the ground. I couldn't see Les's face behind the guys beating on him. One of them was holding him up, which wasn't good.

I ran. Stormy's was only across the street, but I stumbled through a couple of potholes on the way. I fell once. The skin on my palms ground off on the jagged rocks. I burst through the door. At least twenty guys sat around munching on floppy triangles of pizza.

"Les is getting the crap beat out of him," I yelled between gasps for air.

The response was amazing. Pizza slices dropped like wet rags. Carl overturned a table when he rose. He shoved it out of his way as he sprinted, with the rest of them—Aleut and white—toward the door. I dodged to the side to get out of their way. I was amazed at how a bunch of guys, who are half-drunk, laughing, and eating, can in an instant be on their feet, fairly coordinated, and deadly serious. By the time I got back out the door, the dark mass had reached the Elbow's parking lot. I ran after them.

Three of the guys had tried to run. They'd been caught on the beach road. The other two were still in the parking lot, on the ground. Punches had given way to kicks. Marge had Les around the waist. He looked bad even in the dark. But he could still walk with help. I ran to his other side, and we slid him into Marge's truck. He moaned and folded forward, clutching his stomach.

I looked back. Six guys on the beach road kicked at the bodies on the ground. A larger huddle took turns kicking at two forms in the parking lot. It's one thing to beat someone up. But keeping at it after he can't even stand is sickening. I felt the night air wrapping around me in this clutching, digging way, like it wanted to pull out strands of my guts and let them fly loose on the wind.

"That's enough," I yelled at the backs facing me. No one stopped. I walked closer, shaking. I saw Carl straddling a man, the fringe of his poncho caked with mud. I saw his fist rise and fall, heard the sickening thud over and over. "Enough! Enough!"

Carl ignored me. They all ignored me. I'd become invisible, inconsequential to these men, who a few minutes ago would have hung on my every word. Whatever power I'd wielded had been revoked. I was screaming at deaf men.

Someone grabbed my shoulder and whirled around. Marge's large face loomed. "Come on. We gotta get Les to the clinic."

"They're gonna kill those guys. We need to call the police."

"Get in the fuckin' truck."

The clinic was, of course, dark and empty. Marge used the phone on the porch to call in the nurse who ran the place in between visiting-doctor stints. He got there in ten minutes. I stayed with Les for the two hours it took to check him over, bandage him up, and give him a good shot of something that put him to sleep.

His face, soft swollen and split, came out okay. Nothing broken. Two cracked ribs, a broken finger. He'd have to come in for blood tests every couple of days to make sure his liver was pulling through. "Not as bad as it could have been," the nurse said. "Must have kept his vitals covered pretty well." I nodded, listened to the instructions, and smiled at Les. But the entire time, I saw the parking lot and the circle of boots, sinking into bodies soft with pain on the wet sand.

And I saw myself, doing nothing to stop it. Nothing but yelling and running.

Light came in thin lines, as if it wasn't sure it wanted to come at all. It shot through brief holes in the clouds. Holes that closed when they felt the heat, leaving the light to seek another opening. Five men nearly died there by the beach. They were awaiting a MediVac to Kodiak. Two days later, one of them would die—the one Carl had beaten past unconscious on the parking lot sand. Victims were falling all around me—Kathy, Mary, Les, these five assholes.

The police were there when Marge and I drove back to the Elbow. We told our stories, largely the truth, except we couldn't remember names and faces. I hadn't seen Carl's hammerlike fist hit again and again. It had been too fast, too dark. Marge was arguing with one of the cops, who wanted to go question Les at the clinic, when I left.

The rain began as I turned off the valley road onto my hill. It splattered at first, big spot drops, then came driving at me, stinging my cheeks and pelting my scalp. After cutting the engine, I had to pry my fingers off the handlebars. They were crinkled into half circles and creaked open. I trudged home, peeled off wet jeans, and climbed into my nest, listening to the rain beat its driving rhythm above me.

In the chaos, no one found the other victim that night. Later the police would say that the body had probably bobbed unseen under docks, then drifted from the harbor. Currents kept it near shore where the next high tide swept it alongside the wrecked *Dauntless*. It thumped against the rusting hull for hours before the tide changed, and in the confusing moments when the incoming tide pulls away again, it brushed along the wood and landed on the beach.

what she's done

Three days later, someone found his body, folded around the bow point and half buried in sand. The police came, took it to Anchorage for an autopsy, asked questions. Nobody knew anything about how Nicholas had died. Mary said she'd been expecting him for several days. He'd radioed he was coming in soon, and that's the last she'd heard. They found his boat, tied securely to the dock. All shipshape. Nothing amiss. The harbormaster said he'd come in early Friday morning and hadn't been seen since.

I was just grateful. Mary would get her kids back. I wouldn't have to worry about another late-night rescue. End of story. End of my responsibility. People aren't inclined to be suspicious of good luck, and I was no exception.

The hoopla of the beatings waned and only the plod of investigation remained. August was in full swing, and the weather was as nice as it got. I found myself wanting to get out of town, away from the bar. I pulled on my SPAWN TILL YOU DIE T-shirt and a pair of 501s and started riding the beach road east of town. It was a half-and-half day. Big burly clouds muscled into passive blue sky, only to lose the fight and move on. The sun was betting on the blue.

I find it hard to describe this place. Bob Hope visited the Aleutians during the war days. He got close. It's the only place on earth, he said, where a man could "walk in mud up to his knees bucking a snowstorm that blew sand in his face, while being pelted in the rear on a sunny day." No matter how you try to describe it, one thing is constant: the Aleutians just won't obey ordinary rules. And this rebellion leads to extraordinary things.

As I rode that morning with eagles swooping from cliffs down to the ocean, and waves coiling along the rocks, and hard dirt gliding under my bike, I was aware of this place like I'd never been aware of a place before.

The Aleutians have been described as a necklace of islands, arching through the most desolate expanse of ocean on the planet. They are wind and fog and volcanoes and tidal waves.

The cold Bering Sea pounds from the north; the warm Pacific swirls from the south. The Aleutians are the breakers between. If it weren't for these islands, who knows how the oceans would get along. One of the early Russian priests assigned to the Aleutian Islands called them the Cradle of Storms and the Birthplace of the Wind. It's a middlin world. Not a place you can be too sure of. Not a place of black and white. It's gray through and through.

The Aleuts say, "This is the land that we belong to, not the land that belongs to us." The Aleuts and the Aleutians are one thing. This is hard for me to get hold of. Maybe some of us get it, farmers perhaps feel some identity with the land they work. But I doubt they *are* the land like the Aleuts. And being here, you get a hint of how this land not only possesses people, but makes them one with it. It's not like regular land. It's got a personality, more complex and actualized than most people. I've heard people talk about New York or Paris this way. But those are places created by people. They aren't places on their own. Manhattan would not be Manhattan without the people and their constructs. But the Aleutians—the Aleutians are the Aleutians no matter who's there. Observation, participation not required.

I turned the bike off the road onto a slender path between two hills. I stopped where the three-wheelers had just a week earlier. I realized as I killed the engine that I was still stalking the old Aleut women, regardless of their failure to leave bathroom messages all over town. I almost didn't go. In the hard silence after shutting off the motor, I was suddenly scared and I couldn't say why. But I also felt that if I didn't go, I would always wonder, always regret.

I'd only seen them head off in a general direction, and it took a few minutes to pick up the faint trail that cut through the low brush, giving way to the springy tundra as it climbed. I didn't know what I was looking for, but the sun was mostly out and I felt expectant and full of purpose.

I walked for maybe two hours. The trail, more of a slight depression in the tundra, wound along the back sides of mountains that fronted the ocean. Sometimes it curved along near the top, and I would cut off to get a view. Often a pillbox overlooked the curling ocean, a lonely concrete cap slightly lighter than the rocks. Other times the trail stayed lower, traversing the middle. I must have rounded five such mountains when the path remained straight rather than rolling down again.

I wound around the east side until it gave way to a cliff, stained dark from the ocean's spray. These mountains were more half-mountains, their back sides rounded, their fronts a wall of stone. But here, at the trail, a narrow shelf continued around the face of the cliff. I stopped to decide just how determined I was. How could four women, one of them older than rock, have managed this shelf in the dark? I was quite sure they hadn't come this way at all, that they'd cut off somewhere to another destination. Hell, maybe they didn't even have a destination. Maybe they were just some wacky hiking club that liked the night.

But I couldn't stop following the trail just because it turned into a few inches of horizontal on a vertical cliff. I checked to see if my sneakers were tied and stepped onto the shelf. For the first few yards, it was narrow. I have big feet, and if I placed my back to the cliff, my toes hit the shelf edge exactly. And that's how I took that first stretch, sliding my back along the cliff face, shuffling my feet sideways like a toddler on a balance beam.

Waves crashed beneath me, and I could feel the mist they tossed into the air. I was probably terrified, but I was too busy carefully shuffling my large feet to notice. After a few minutes, the shelf widened to three, then four feet. I started walking normally again. Another few minutes and the shelf widened again into the cliff-face equivalent of a cul-de-sac, a tiny one. Along the cliff wall a jagged crevice opened. It was a cave, but not the nice semicircular opening you think of with caves. This looked like a gigantic zipper opening up the rock.

I ran my hand along the edges. Shit, I thought, I'm going to have to go in there. I delayed with a cigarette, sitting cross-legged on the shelf and watching the waves smash the rocks that knelt at the foot of the cliff below. Although the view was, of course, spectacular, I kept looking behind me at the cave opening. I had this eerie feeling that something was in there, waiting. I puffed like mad because a Marlboro dangling from my lips always makes me feel tougher. Then I had another one because I needed a double dose to battle that creepy feeling. Why the hell was I even doing this?

I knew the answer, at least the first part of it, even then. Something was happening. I could feel it. The way you can feel a storm coming just by the way the air seems to drop around you and the first belches of wind scatter whatever isn't fastened down. The way dogs bark and open doors suck inward with a bang. Something is coming.

I could feel something new in myself, something that wanted out.

Do you think you can change who you are by changing where you are? You're supposed to say, "No, of course not. Everyone knows that." The clichés abound.

You can't run away from yourself.

Wherever you go, there you are.

If you want to find yourself, go home; you'll turn up eventually.

Caelam, non animum, mutant qui transmore current. Those who cross the sea change their place, not themselves.

It's a lie, perpetuated to keep you looking like you, feeling like you, thinking like you. There are places. And you can find them. Like the gaps in gravity when you're stoned, these are gaps in conventional wisdom. This knowledge hasn't been lost. You can still hear the echoes in tales of El Dorado, the Fountain of Youth, Atlantis, Eden. Some part of us still knows there are places that can remake you. You just have to find the right place. And there aren't many left. They are sinking into vague legend like the river somewhere north of Rome that's said to turn one's hair blond if crossed. If there's a place where brunettes emerge as blondes, you can bet there's another crossing where a blonde can emerge as something else. This was it.

Of course, you never recognize these places while you're in them. It's only after you've made it across, made it out, that you can see the change, because it's only in looking back that you can see what you were.

I stuffed the pack of cigarettes back in my jacket and kept the lighter in my hand, adjusting the flame to high. I moved to the crevice. Holding my lighter in front of me, I stretched my arm into the opening and flicked on the light. Thankfully, I had a burly butane with a two-inch flame.

The cave was larger than I had expected from the opening. The light didn't reach any of the walls. I'd have to go in. I slid inside, keeping one hand on the edge of the opening. I still couldn't see anything. I moved farther inside and flicked the lighter again. The flame barely illuminated the left wall, so I moved that way.

As I shuffled closer, I could see the wall wasn't flat. It was rippled with what looked like old roots, dangling from the dirt and rocks.

But Unalaska had no trees.

I reached out to one, and that's when I realized what I was looking at. Bodies.

Or parts of bodies, half buried in the cave walls, reaching out with arms and legs, with the side of a face or a shoulder. The limbs were dry and shriveled but still recognizable. Dried hides wrapped some into tight fetal-like cocoons. Others had broken free, exposing themselves. A scaffold of driftwood supported the bodies like shelves against the sloughing walls of the cave.

The lighter went out when I jerked my arm away. Although I was frantically flicking, it wouldn't light. Maybe it was the wind shifting through, maybe my hands were shaking too much. I stumbled for the brightness of the cave's mouth, almost made it. I tripped over a row of bodies, perhaps three, laid along the left inside wall, close together. I touched a foot or hand, I couldn't tell, as I pushed up and threw myself through the opening.

I was halfway along the shelf when something dry and whispery scattered across my shoulders, inside my collar and down my back.

I ran. Sideways, with my feet threatening to tangle me into the sea. Even as I skittered along, I knew it was probably just loose dirt trickling off from above me, but I did not stop until I was back on the hillside. I must have covered that entire length of cliff shelf in thirty seconds.

As soon as I reached the soft grass, I stopped, gasping for breath and sanity. The chain of my necklace had come undone, the ancient bead dropping into my bra. I fished it out and held it tightly in my hand, feeling the hard node press into my palm. With my other hand, I tapped out a cigarette and smoked, facing the cliff, keeping an eye on the trail, just in case. All drugs have their place, their purpose, and let me tell you, there are many, many drugs that are more suited to dealing with mummified bodies, reaching out from cave walls in a cliff side over the Bering Sea, than nicotine. But that's all I had on me.

No matter how much I smoked that evening I couldn't find normalcy. I kept seeing those powder-dry arms and legs. I kept hearing Liz puttering around inside. I mixed Baileys with my coffee and sat on my porch, wrapped in a big sweater, and tried to make sense of it. I was fairly sure the Aleut women had gone just where I had gone. They had gone to see the bodies. I went through the possibilities: a séance, a visit with dead relatives, a gruesome game of truth or dare.

I went inside and spread the first Aleutian book on the kitchen table. No index. I started flipping through pages beginning where I'd left off. There it was—"Aleut Mummies."

One of the outstanding indigenous achievements of the Aleuts was the preparation and preservation of mummies. Many burial caves and log tombs have been reported from the eastern and central Aleutian Islands. Mummification rested on the belief in a manipulatable power that resides in the human body and a concern for the continuation of the power inherent in the dead, preserved by mummification, rather than a fear of the dead.

The basic objective was the preservation and use of the spiritual power that resided in the human body. This power could be preserved in the body, or let out of the body, but in all cases it had to be regulated and handled with expert care.

I checked the indexes of the other books and found this:

Whale hunters were both respected and feared. A breed apart, they had secret charms and potions they used on their weapons, potions concocted out of the substances of corpses. These charms had powers that in the end destroyed their owners. A whale hunter had to prepare himself through secret rituals and, upon return, to purify himself before it was safe for others to associate with him. Even in death the whale hunters retained their special status: they were buried in caves with elaborate ceremonies, and the next generation sought special, though fleeting, power through contact with their remains.

There was more; half of my books had a paragraph or two on Aleutian mummies. I had to read it all several times to understand, but it was fairly simple. Whale hunters, men set apart by their choice of prey, were believed to die young, or escaping death, to become hopelessly psychotic. The mummy flesh itself, called dead-man's fat, drove these hunters insane eventually. These guys were trying to steal from fate, control the uncontrollable. It worked, but they lost their marbles because of it.

I read more. I read that a few archaeologists did not believe the standard ice age migration theory. That they did not believe the Aleuts were beaten back into these islands by the early arrivals. They did not believe that the Aleuts had come on clumsy feet, plodding after mammoths. No, they had come in boats agile and free, hugging the ice-free shores of that lost land bridge. They had come by choice, pursuing their prey across fog-strewn water to these gray beaches. It was a renegade theory, and I believed it immediately. They had come with intent.

I slammed my index finger inside the book to mark my place and took it with me as I walked to the living room and stood in front of the sketch. My Aleut Mona Lisa. I studied her again. She was hiding something from me; I was sure of it.

"What did you do?" I asked her. "When the Russians came, what did you do?"

Her eyes and her lips shifted for a moment. She looked more sure, more pleading, more beautiful, more dangerous. We stared at each other, exchanging nothing but questions. Until I lost and looked away. "Insane," I muttered, walking back to my books. "Maybe insane."

I'm not much for respecting indigenous religions. Most of them just seem too weird. But I have to admit, as I removed my finger from the book and placed it on the table, this made some sense. The bodies of the dead are a link to whatever lies beyond. There's power there, perhaps power to remake fate. But shit, you've got to watch your back once you've messed with it.

As the sky darkened, I became aware of the light on at Mary's. I definitely needed company. Alone, my head filled with mummies and more mummies, which was better than the flaking, but not by much. I grabbed the bottle of Baileys and walked to her place. Mary was sitting on her porch too, letting the evening melt into night without acknowledging the change.

"You want company?" I asked.

She shrugged. "Does it come with the Baileys?"

"Yes." I sat next to her and filled her empty teacup to the top.

We didn't speak for a long time. Initiating a conversation with a recent widow doesn't come easy. Do you bring up the death right away? Do you try to make her laugh with something else altogether? I didn't know, so I did the best I could and kept my mouth shut.

We watched the first stars peeking through the growing cloud cover. Then we watched the fog roll in. It crept up the hillside, surrounding us in its rich moist blanket. The lights in the valley disappeared along with the stars. I'd drunk enough Baileys now so the horror of the caves, and that feeling that something had followed me back, eased up. Also I'd smoked some weed when I got home, and that had helped. I refilled my mug and lit a cigarette. Mary reached for the pack as I was tucking it back in my pocket. I lit one for her, and she handed the pack back. I set it on the porch boards between us and laid the lighter on top.

"Funeral's tomorrow." She exhaled smoke, which mixed and swirled with the fog until it became part of it. "Everyone's saying I'm lucky he's dead. Maybe I am." The fog created a room around us that echoed strangely with her words.

"Social Services says I can get the kids back soon. They're flying them out from Sitka for a visit next week."

"Can't wait to meet them." I'd never been good with kids. They were too whiny, too needy. "I could watch them for you now and then," I said. I pictured having them over, bringing their Legos and building something tall and awkward. Maybe it wouldn't be so bad.

Mary smiled. "They're good kids. They'll miss him though." She paused. "They loved him."

I looked away from her, hiding the pity.

But she saw it. "I did love him. I just wanted . . ."

Her voice trailed off. It's not something you can explain. The cords that bind people are so much more twisted and knotted than we know. I thought about Thad. I didn't like thinking about him anymore, knowing he wasn't who I'd thought he was, knowing he could love me. Could I keep pretending nothing had changed? And was it fair to keep my life wound with his while I did? Hearing Mary talk of her love for Nicholas, a man whose love could never be wholesome, unearthed in me the knowledge of just how far away I was from anybody, good or bad. I'd managed to make it to age thirty-one without loving anybody. Or anything for that matter. I would not be crushed by unreturned love like my father; I would not confuse excitement and comfort for love like my mother. Unlike them, unlike Mary, I was safe.

The fog eased itself around and between Mary and me.

"What do you think happened to him?" I desperately wanted to know, but actually asking was weird. I probably wouldn't have if it hadn't been for all the Baileys and the strange intimacy created by the fog.

"I think he got killed." She stabbed out her cigarette on the porch and tossed it into the fog.

"Someone murdered him?"

"Maybe not someone, maybe something."

"What are you talking about?"

Mary pulled another cigarette from my pack. She took a deep drag and exhaled. She stared out into the gray. "Do you ever think that pieces of the people who came before stick to a place, to the rocks and wind and water? That a place can kill?" She didn't elaborate.

Finally I asked, "You think rocks and water murdered him?"

Mary shrugged. "Oh, I think they may have had help. But, yes. I think they were behind it."

Suddenly the weed and the liquor were working against me. The way the fog had cut us off, removing us from everyday logic and perception and creating a gray void where things were just more, well, possible. Even weird notions of rocks that directed murder and caves that held bodies offering their power to the living. It was a seductive place; it wanted me to stay, maybe go in a tad deeper. Answers, it whispered. Knowledge.

You know how it is. We back away because we know ignorance is better, far better. And, frankly, we don't believe any of it. Don't want to.

Normally, it's easy. Unless you're sitting by a fire with velvet blackness too close at your back, or you're all alone at home feeling a wind shake the walls, or you're quarantined in an Aleutian fog and you've had too much to drink. I got vulnerable. I'm not sure if I couldn't step back then or that the part of me that didn't want to had opened its eyes.

Anyway, that's how it was. The dangerous, daring, let's-just-see part of me moved further in, not a bold leap, but a tentative step, and another. The real world had stretched thin, and I could see the forms of what lurks beneath. I sat in it for a time. I knew Mary was there. Suffering thins the world too. I can't say there were revelations. No ahhh, so that's what's going on. Just a sense that there is something else. Something of the lives of all the people who had come before—my Aleut Mona Lisa, the young Liz, the bodies in the cave—had been shed here and lay waiting within the gray ocean, dark mountains, and fog. Something deep and gray and moving with intention. That's all I got from letting myself stay.

I felt the wind lift my hair first. It swirled down from the hilltop and into the fog. Within minutes it drove the dense blanket down into the valley and out to sea.

I stood up. "I better go. See you tomorrow."

Mary didn't move. She stared at the retreating bank of fog. I left the Baileys, nearly gone, and the cigarettes, half gone, and climbed back through the brush against the wind.

doubt about it

I t wasn't just the booze I'd left behind that ravaged Mary's face late the next morning. I'd come to the graveyard ceremony because everyone else was going. And, well, I still had that odd sense of responsibility for her. Marge had even closed the Elbow Room, although it would be wide open for the wake that followed.

I tucked myself behind the crowd but had to jockey with two men and a group of teens for the back row. I wasn't the only one who didn't want to feel like part of this rite. We were all standing. Just a wind-blown group, our clothing snapping against our bodies, cluttered on a forlorn hillside of scratchy grass and the sentinels of weathered crosses.

Mary wore a long black skirt and brown jacket. She didn't look up once during the words chanted by the Russian Orthodox priest. Someone had attempted to put makeup on her face. Two stark lines of blush flared across her cheeks. A dab of lipstick dotted the middle of her lower lip.

Standing in the back, I could look around at the crowd. I saw all the locals I knew and many I didn't. Bellie was there, her eyes fastened on her boots. Beside her was a Little Liz I almost didn't recognize in a tan polyester suit with a satin-faced jacket over it. She stood between Ida and Anna. Seeing the three women together again, the women who had led me to the cave and the bodies, scared me, made me want to run.

Ida must have felt my eyes on her, even from across the crowd. She looked up slowly, sliding her eyes into mine. The distance between us squeezed together, like the ground separating us had folded and we were suddenly face-to-face. We weren't, of course, but I could see her eyes narrow, then open wide. The universal expression of suspicion resolving into certainty.

My breath stalled, sputtered, and became a conscious effort. All that breath control reminded me of my lungs. I dug out a cigarette. As I exhaled the first drag, I risked another look at the three women. Liz and Anna were staring too, a puncture-wound of a stare. I dragged my eyes away, but not before I saw the creepy smile stretch Ida's face.

They knew. They knew I'd followed them, been to the cave. The thought flared bright against the inside of my skull, then faded back to reality. There was no way they could know.

The priest, rather youngish and handsome I thought, nodded at a woman I recognized as Mary's sister. She pulled Mary forward and directed her hand to release the anemones she clutched. They fell silently on the coffin. I could see points of blood on Mary's palm where she'd driven her nails into her skin.

Four men looped ropes around the painted plywood coffin, which thudded against the sides of the hole as they lowered it. I looked behind me at the vista Nicholas would have, if I believed in such things. The cemetery straddled the curve of a hill that commanded views of the town, of the bay studded with rocks thrown from cliffs. It filtered the wind over a collection of ornate wooden crosses, two-tiered in the Orthodox style. At the foot of each cross, the unique footbar tilted toward the land and sky, a reminder that Christ had twisted the bar in his agony. Higher up, the grayed, leaning wood of older crosses stood like protectors of the fresher graves below. No one mowed. No one sold plots. Relatives did not come to find solace in manicured shrubs and weedless lawn. This cemetery existed only for the dead.

When the casket settled against the rocky muscle of the hill, the priest nodded to Mary's sister again. Mary was supposed to toss the first handful of dirt over the body that had been her husband. She refused to move. When her sister took her elbow to lead her forward, Mary jerked away.

She muttered something I couldn't hear and covered her face with her hands. Those who had heard Mary's words whispered them to people who hadn't. By the time the words passed back to me, the lack of action had grown uncomfortable.

One of the teenage boys leaned toward me. "She said 'The kids should be here.'" As he spoke, I saw Ida moving from the middle of the crowd. She came alongside the grave and peered down.

The priest seemed relieved someone was following the script. He nodded to Ida.

She shot him a quick grin then kicked a splatter of dirt into the burial hole. She turned without looking up and moved back through the crowd.

The priest scanned the faces in the first row, as if checking for any notice of this break with tradition before announcing the wake would follow at the Elbow Room.

If anybody took offense to Ida's way of sending Nicholas underground, nobody let on. I watched Bellie take Ida's arm as they descended the graveyard path, followed by Little Liz and Anna. They moved as one through the grass. The strength, near grace, in Liz's steps contrasted so with the way I usually saw her, passed out, pissed on. This was the Liz of my cabana, sober, purposeful, and confusing the hell out of me. Liz turned once, finding me instantly in back of the crowd with her eyes. I stopped midstride, fastened. Then she let me go, turning back to the path.

When the trail gave way to relatively flat road, I watched Bellie lean in to Ida, say something, and release her arm. She stepped to the side of the road and waited for me to catch up.

"Gimme a cigarette," she said, falling into step with me. She lit up and slid the half-pack into her own pocket.

"What went on up there?" I asked. "What was that old hag doing?"

"Ida? She's my great-grandma." Bellie held her cigarette up and examined it. "Guess she wasn't that sorry about Nicholas."

Shit, I thought. I have to be more careful. Never know who's related to who on this island. We walked in silence for a minute or two before I found a safer question.

"Tell me about Liz. How did she get like she is?"

Bellie tossed her cigarette to the side of the road and reached for another in her pocket. She generously offered me one. "From what I heard, Ida and Liz used to run this women's group from the church. A long time ago before the fishing started big. They took care of people, found homes for the kids with wasted parents. That kind of thing. Then something went wrong. Bunch of the kids got taken, and the social worker died. Liz just fell apart, started drinking. She never stopped."

Bellie hadn't looked at me during this explanation. But now she did. She stopped in the road, letting the last stragglers pass us. "Liz isn't who you think she is," Bellie said. "Remember that." Then she started walking again, and I let her go.

I didn't go to the wake. I'd attended the funeral out of some warped duty I felt for Mary, but I couldn't see sitting around with a bunch of people, drinking and telling stories about a man I didn't know and didn't want to know. Mary had a gaggle of relatives waving tissues, holding her elbow, and ushering her through. And I needed to think.

I went home and read my outhouse door again. It seemed clear. Liz had blown up the social worker. I closed the lid on the hole and sat there, trying to imagine what had happened back then. I did understand Liz better. She had every reason to souse herself with booze. She couldn't stand herself.

Les was back at work within a week of the attack with only faded bruises and a fragile quality to his movements. Life at the bar got normal—maybe even extranormal. Like we had to put a wallop of effort into everyday gestures and words to tug normalcy back from exile. Marge told Les to "shut the fuck up" even more than usual to make up for the fact that she really didn't want to say it at all. Les flirted fiendishly, his way of showing an indomitable spirit, I suppose. I wore my hair down and put on lots of makeup. We were all working so hard to get back. Even Carl tried.

He invited us all to what he was calling a "Fuck-the-Elbow-Room Party" at his converted bus. Carl lived in the old full-size school bus. It had run when he'd driven it to a nice stretch of rock-strewn sand beside the ocean. But he'd seen no reason to move on, and slowly the tires flattened, the rims rusted and settled into the sand. Carl's bus hadn't moved in years.

Being one of those recluses who likes people but only at arm's length, Carl did not throw parties. That he had invited me, Marge, Les, and Bellie, saying she was the hardest-working employee at the bar, was so out of character that people had been whispering about it for days. As the designated Sunday afternoon drew near, Marge, Les, Bellie, and I all felt this gathering sense of excitement.

Saturday afternoon before the big day, I stopped by the Elbow Room before returning the rental truck I'd used to stock the cabana. I lifted myself onto a stool; Marge set a whiskey sour in front of me. The place felt odd. No Carl.

"Where's Carl?"

"Left early. Says he's got housework to do."

I raised my eyebrows, and Marge shrugged.

"What's with the poncho?" I asked. "Why's he always got that poncho on?"

Marge leaned against the back bar and crossed her legs. "Showing off his Spic heritage, I guess."

"Carl's Hispanic?"

"Shit," she said, crossing her arms, "call 'im a Mexican or a Spic. But you call him a Hispanic and he won't even grunt at you for a week."

I drained my whiskey sour and slid off the stool.

"One more thing," Marge yelled as I opened the door, "you'll wanna eat before."

Sunday afternoon Marge, Les, Bellie, and I all crammed into the cab of Marge's truck and splashed through last night's puddles. We swung around the church, the eagle atop the onion dome, presiding over the well-dressed crowd, mostly Aleuts, pouring out. We passed the boat businesses and the docks out Captain's Bay south of town and kept going. Marge pulled off onto a gravel beach that had been abandoned by the water years ago and drove right up to a long yellow bus.

Carl appeared at the open door with a denim apron tied over the top of his poncho and hanging to his knees. "Beer's in there." He nodded toward a cooler. He turned and heaved himself back up the two steps into the bus.

Les rummaged in the cooler and threw beers at each of us. I stepped into the bus with a sense of wonder. Inside it was very unbus-like. A big foam bed piled with sleeping bags stretched across the back. The middle section had been converted into a genuine living area with two small couches lining the sides and a potbellied stove at the center. The fire blazed through the open firebox door, sweating up the windows and fogging up the view of the beach and ocean. Kitchen and gear filled the front. The windows had been covered over with miscellaneous shelving on which sat dishes, large jars, an assortment of fuel, camp candles, a radio. A small counter complete with tiny sink and a two-burner propane stove lay tucked underneath. On the other side, cabinets and a half-size fridge lined up alongside fishing gear, poles, nets, tackle boxes, buckets.

Carl stood over the stove, flipping something.

"What're you making?" I asked.

"*Alodiks.*"

"Which are?"

"Russian fry bread. Sit down."

When all of us had found a spot by the stove, Carl brought over a plate piled with light brown *alodiks*. We each took one and alternated munching the rounds of crunchy, greasy bread and gulping beer. The bread was actually wonderful, but every few bites you could taste that the grease had gone off a bit. The beer was cold and felt good near the toasty fire.

Although it was only mid-August, the temperature had dropped. A uniform of gray had taken the sky, and the wind held an edge. Summer was closing up shop, and I had mixed feelings about winter. If summer required long pants and a jacket on the best days, what would winter demand?

Carl didn't sit with us. He banged around in the kitchen.

"You got this fixed up real nice," Marge yelled.

Carl harrumphed.

Bellie looked like she needed some blow. Les stared out the windows.

Carl returned with a pot of coffee, five mugs, and a bottle of whiskey. He passed out the mugs, filled them half coffee, half whiskey.

"Fuck the Elbow Room," he said, raising his mug.

We all followed in a chorus. "Fuck the Elbow Room."

Whiskey and coffee is not my idea of a good drink. But apparently we were supposed to drink it like a shot because Carl began refills almost immediately. I quickly downed mine, stuffed more bread in my mouth, and held up my mug.

"Fuck the Elbow Room," Carl said again when the second round was poured.

We repeated the toast again. This happened three times within five minutes. I started to wonder if something had snapped in Carl. He didn't say anything else. Just pour, "Fuck the Elbow Room," drink. Pour, "Fuck the Elbow Room," drink. It was the oddest ceremony I'd participated in. Apparently Marge could only take so much.

"What's your fuckin' problem with the Elbow Room?" She stood up, placing her fists on her hips.

"Nothing," Carl said. "Just fuck it."

"I don't see you saying that when you're sitting there half the day." Marge was getting riled up and suddenly the party was in danger of going sour.

Carl looked her right in the eye. "Fuck the Elbow Room."

Marge shook her head and rolled her eyes. "Shit," she said, sitting back down.

I'm not sure what this exchange was about. Carl was making a point, and I don't know if anyone got it or even tried that hard. I'd had a beer and three whiskey coffees in fifteen minutes, so none of it seemed that important. Just odd.

Lusta broke the threatening mood. Carl brought a Baggie of grayish brown stuff and passed it to Les first. Les opened the bag and stuck his nose in.

"Shit," he said, "that's rank." He grimaced and turned away, passing the bag on to Bellie.

Bellie reached in and broke off a small dried piece and placed it on her tongue. She handed the bag to me.

"What is it?"

"Decayed seal flipper," Les said.

"Just don't smell it. Put it right in your mouth," Bellie advised.

So, of course, I stuck my nose in the bag. I nearly vomited.

They all laughed at me. "Plug your nose," Marge said.

As I've said before, I hate the idea of having some weird food right in front of me and not trying it. I figured people had been eating the stuff for eons, so it wasn't going to do permanent damage. I plugged my nose and fumbled a small piece from the bag. Even plugged, the nose can still get a sense of what's in the mouth. It tasted dry and salty, crisp as a communion wafer, but it definitely smelled inedible. I swallowed quickly.

I'm not going to try to describe it. But you'll get the idea from how it's made, as Marge explained. "They take a bunch of seal flippers, dry them out, salt them up, then bury them along with fish heads and God-knows-what in a barrel. Next spring, they dig 'em out, nice and decayed and tasting like shit."

Not shit, I decided. Much worse.

A wind rattled the bus windows, and I jumped. Dark gray clouds had slipped under the light gray. Something tin and unsecured lifted and flew past the window. Les turned in his seat and raised up to his knees to look out.

"Shit," he said. "It's getting bad."

A tarp blew off and swirled down the beach. Carl stuck another piece of lusta in his mouth and turned for the door. When he opened it, the wind blasted through and lifted loose papers and a plastic plate. I could hear him banging around outside, tying stuff down, weighting tarps. The bus shook again, and the rain started. Not just rain, but rain thrown down at angles that pelted the bus windows, washing the view, which had grown dark as night.

Marge looked out the window. "Carl's a wanted man, you know."

"Wanted for what?" I asked.

"Murder is what I heard, down in Mexico or somewhere. That's why he came way out here. Figures the law won't come looking this far out."

"No, he's not running from the cops," Les said, shifting to recross his legs. "The Hell's Angels put a contract out on him back in the seventies."

"Well, I guess he's running from something anyway," Marge said. "Heard he was a Vietnam vet too. Got messed up."

The door slid open, and we fell silent as Carl came back in, wet and loaded with driftwood. He lit a kerosene lantern and hung it on a hook in the kitchen, then filled up the woodstove. He extricated a gray fold-ing chair from the pile of junk on the driver's seat and crashed it open by the couches. It squeaked as he sagged wetly into it. He dripped. Four reserved puddles formed underneath him.

This was not to be a short burst of a storm that plays out and leaves you to yourself again. This was going to last.

"Did I roll up the truck windows?" Marge asked.

Les shrugged. "Who cares."

Marge shot him an irritated look.

Bellie shifted several times.

Carl kept dripping.

I wasn't sure what to do. "Pass the whiskey," I said. I poured and passed to Bellie. She filled her mug, and the bottle made the rounds.

"Looks like the police gave up on them boys that jumped Les," Marge said, breaking the long silence. "Said they couldn't get no one to say who was involved."

I glanced at Carl. He grunted.

Another silence.

"I know," Les said. "Let's tell ghost stories."

"Shit, Les, I don't know any fuckin' ghost stories," Marge said.

"I'll start," he said.

Les told of the Otter People. Somewhere in Southeast lay an island, uncharted, shrouded in mist. When a group of adventurous prospec-tors stopped there to look around, they were chased by naked crea-tures with the heads of otters and the bodies of men. Only one made it back to tell the story.

It was a good story, and Les had good timing. He looked around at his audience. "Creepy, huh?"

"That ain't nothing," Marge said, apparently inspired. "My sister bought this place on Vashon ten years ago. She's there maybe a week when she starts hearing these funny noises." Marge continued her sis-ter's tale until it ended with a new house, a dead cat, and a lingering mystery.

"I found a dead guy." Carl's tale began, then paused for a swig of whiskey. "I was just out there getting some *baidarkas* when I see some-thing floating in with the tide. I waded out some. It was a dead guy. Been dead a long time."

Carl fell silent. It had been the longest string of words I'd heard from him.

"That's it?" Marge asked. "Who was he? What happened?"

"Don't know. Face wasn't all there."

"Well, what did the police say? When was this?"

"Ten, eleven years ago. Police didn't say nothing. Never knew about it."

"What? You just left him there?" Les asked.

"He didn't seem to mind. Went out with the tide. Never saw 'im again."

"Fuck, Carl," Les said. "You are messed up."

Carl grunted.

"I've got a story." Bellie had been strangely quiet. I knew she didn't have any coke, and that without it she wasn't much of a talker. But even taking cokelessness into account, she'd been withdrawn. She hadn't curled her hair, and it hung in straight slabs over each cheek. She looked so much more deliberate, more native.

"It's an old story. My grandmother told me when I was little." The glow from the stove lit half of Bellie's face a warm orange. The flames reflected in her smooth, dark hair. The bus rattled steadily, with occasional stomach-flipping gusts sending it into a shake. Bellie stared into the fire. I watched her fingers move to the birthmark unconsciously. If you hadn't known about the mark, you would have assumed she had a headache, the way her fingers pressed and smoothed, pressed and smoothed.

"There once was a girl who was born with something living and cold in her body." Bellie's words and cadence were not her own. This was not my Bellie. She spoke with someone else's voice. "People of the village turned away from her even when she smiled. A time came when the people were starving because the Outside Men, living inland, stole food from caches in the night. The thing in the girl grew colder and more alive. She told the village that she would travel into the mountains and take back the food. The people laughed at her, saying, if men stronger than you do not return, how will you do so? She replied, 'I will not be controlled by other than my own hand.'

"The girl went to the caves and took pieces of dead-man's fat, dripping with juice. This was forbidden, for a woman's power was not meant to become ensnared with the darkness of the Dry Ones. But still she grew warmer with pleasure as she smeared the grease on the soles of her feet and the palms of her hands and placed it in her mouth. And with the taste in her mouth, she knew what she must do. She saw the good in it; she saw the evil. And she chose."

All at once, something like iron fell in my stomach. I felt like I was back in the cave, reaching out to touch what I thought were roots but were actually the limbs of long-dead bodies. I must have gasped, because everyone but Bellie looked at me suddenly. When I didn't say anything, they turned back to Bellie.

"She walked until she saw a giant man go to a creek and drink it dry. She watched him beat a drum until he yawned. He put down his drum and stretched out on his back. She threw a stone at him. When he didn't move, she took a rock and pounded into his beating heart. Having killed him, she stretched out his intestines and walked away.

"She reached a village and entered a house filled with people. In the evening, someone came to the hatch asking, 'You do not have a guest, do you?' Another person replied, 'We do have a guest.'

"The first voice said the girl should come to his home to sleep with his son. The man asked the girl if she had seen his brother, a giant man who beat a drum. The girl knew she was to be killed but followed the man to his son's bed anyway. After she and the son had made the bed wet, she lay awake. Hearing someone outside ask if the girl was still in the bed, she lay the sleeping son in her place. Then, using a man's voice, said, 'Yes, she is still here.'

"The man, having come into the sleeping place, struck with a knife and cut off the son's head and sucked the blood. Then the girl told the man he had killed his own son.

"The girl ran back to the house she had first entered. She woke the people sleeping there, and together they made a pit at the foot of the ladder, covering it with grass and piled stones. At daybreak, the man who had killed his son appeared at the hatchway and asked, 'You don't have a guest?'

"The people answered, 'We do have a guest.' The man put his foot on the ladder. The girl noticed his anklet made of the skin of a big seal with pieces added. When he entered, he got stuck by his shoulders, and the girl raised her bow and shot him behind the arm. He dropped into the pit. All the people of the house threw stones at him while the girl shot and killed him.

"Although the girl had become loose in the mind after killing, the people thanked her and loaded her with many things from neck to feet and sent her out, saying, 'In your own hands you hold your fate tight.'

"Thus the girl returned to her village, having killed those who were killing her people, and gone where many did not return from. Her wisdom grew until it touched God's hair, hanging down the sky. This girl never died but passed from woman to woman through the generations, killing when needed. She is out there now, in caves, behind hills, in tidal pools, watching for danger, it is said."

We were all silent after Bellie's story. Something about the battering wind and rain, the crackling stove, drove the story deeper than an old Aleut tale passed down and remembered by a good-natured party girl. I glanced out the streaked windows, almost expecting to see a slim, dark girl darting through the storm. The bead, which I'd restrung, seemed heavy around my neck.

Bellie broke her gaze from the fire and looked at me for the first time since beginning the legend. She leaned toward me, cupping her hands around my ear. "That body he found," she whispered, "she did it. She's always watching you."

Her breath stroked at my ear, and I shivered and shifted away from her.

Les broke the weird feel in the bus. "Shit, those old stories are so lame. Every one of them is about someone killing someone because someone's freaked out about something."

"Yeah?" Marge lit a cigarette. "Well, someone's killing people. Since I been here, four unexplained deaths."

"Oh, come on," Les said. "You got the big bad ocean, man-eating gear, not to mention drink-till-you-fall-down drunks. Surprised more people aren't dropping like flies."

"What's the deal with the caves and the dead-man's fat?" I'd been dying to get their take on it but didn't want to appear eager.

"The mummies," Marge said.

"Mummies?"

"Yeah. The Aleuts used to dry out the really good whale hunters and stack 'em in caves. Some fool wants to hunt whales or take a dangerous trip or kill his big brother, goes up and takes a piece of the body and eats it. Supposed to give him good luck." Marge crushed out her cigarette and lit another.

"They got some scientists out here off and on checking them out. They've only found a few of the caves. Say there's probably dozens more. The bodies are preserved like in Egypt 'cause of the way the Aleuts did it, and the caves are some kind of vents with hot dry air. They got some of them mummies in the Smithsonian."

"So people go up to the caves, get a chunk of mummy to bring them luck?"

"Power," Bellie whispered. "The power a person has in life stays in his body if it's treated right. It stays, waiting for someone living to come and eat from it."

"Bet it tastes like fucking lusta," Les said.

That night, after driving back through the tail of the storm, I could still taste the decayed seal flipper on my tongue—old, salty. Maybe it was those little belches of resurrected lusta that kept Bellie's story nagging at me, eating at me, as I lay in bed. The Outside Man ate his own son's blood. The Aleut girl ate from the bodies of once-glorious whale hunters.

I couldn't help thinking about the taste. I mean, how does a mummified hunter taste? Blood, I knew. We all know blood—old metal, salt. I climbed down from the loft to brush my teeth again. But another lusta belch hit me before I'd retucked the covers around me.

What is it about the eating? Even our very own Eve eats the apple, the ovaries of a tree. The Aleut girl eats for power. Eve eats for knowledge. Knowledge and power—the two loop back on each other as parts of the same whole. I lit a cigarette, hoping the warm raw smoke would cover the lusta belches.

What does power taste like? What is the taste of knowledge? Of good or evil? Like lusta, dry and rank? Or is it sweet?

The nub of my smoked-out cigarette burned my index finger when it hit me—I already knew. That was the point of the story. The taste of power and of knowledge is the only taste we know. We are born and we die with it. It's the taste of a suffering world the Buddhist tries to escape when he meditates. It's the taste of Sartre's existential angst. It's the taste of a dilemma, of responsibility, of culpability. A curse and a gift. It's the taste Eve knew when she opened her eyes and fell.

I knew what the old women had done. They'd gone to take deadman's fat. Which, unless they were just crazy, or maybe because they were plain crazy, meant they had been planning something that required power. The time frame between their visit to the cave and Nicholas's death did not escape me.

I kicked the covers off, suddenly hot, and rolled a joint. I held the smoke deep in my lungs and let it out in a low cloud. What would it be like to care about something or someone enough to eat from a mummy? To decide to take a life? Who was really taking advantage of Eve's gift, the one God didn't take back, the power to know good and evil and direct yourself to whichever you chose?

I, for one, hadn't even been paying attention, let alone choosing anything. I did choose one thing that night under my comforter with the lingering taste of decayed flipper in my mouth—I chose to be wary. I'd accidentally fucked with something that shouldn't be fucked with. And somehow, those old women knew.

War

M ost history books about World War II say that American soil was never occupied by enemy forces. It is only the more obscure books that detail the battles of Attu and Kiska, the bombing of Dutch Harbor. Thousands of American and Japanese soldiers died in the cold, wind, and fog of Aleutian battlefields. At a time when bombers couldn't make it across the Pacific without refueling, both American and Japanese commanders saw the strategic value of the Chain, only 650 miles from Japanese military bases. The Americans built bases, airfields, submarine stations. The Japanese planned their attack.

Although officials had debated evacuating the two thousand or so Aleut citizens along the Chain, so close to the enemy, not a single Aleut had been removed. For the forty-two people on the westernmost island of Attu this indecision meant years in a Japanese prisoner of war camp when enemy soldiers captured and occupied the island. Half died. For the people at Dutch Harbor, it meant watching the bombs fall.

On June 3 and 4, Japanese Zeros strafed the new military bases, killing forty-three soldiers. In the next few weeks, as fears of an invasion mounted, officials scoured the islands lining Alaska's panhandle, looking for places to stow the Aleuts for the duration of the war.

The new homes they found—abandoned canneries and gold mining camps in Southeast Alaska—brought death for many. The water, sewers, *and food were bad. Disease rampaged. When the war ended three years later, only half of the Aleuts returned to their island villages, burned and vandalized by soldiers.*

Ida noticed the trees first. Patches of late-afternoon sun burrowed through their branches, slicing the ground of Etolin Island into misshapen patterns of light and dark. She had seen pictures of these giant plants, but she'd never expected how they would make her feel. They cut her off into a small patch of space, separated from whatever lay beyond, filling her with a dread that would never leave.

Ida wondered what her mother would have thought. Her mother had spoken once of how strange the above-ground houses looked to her when she first moved to Dutch Harbor as a girl, how they seemed to mock the hills. Ida looked at the long, two-story cannery that rose like a red cliff before the green forests. It's better that Katherine died on Unalaska, Ida decided.

She stood on the dock with 121 others, all contemplating their new home. Etolin Island was the most remote of the evacuation camps, forty-five miles by boat to Wrangell, a tiny town itself. They had been the least isolated of the Aleutian Aleuts; now they were virtually quarantined—a situation state and military officials thought wise for Unalaska Aleuts, who were known to drink too much and cause problems.

"Get your stuff from the boat and follow me," yelled one of the Indian Service officials. "Come on. Come on."

Ida followed a line of people, catching their bags as others threw them off. She and her husband had been allowed six, what they and their eldest child could carry. With only a day's notice, Ida had packed and unpacked several times. When she realized that the parkas and clothing alone would fill all their allotted duffels, Ida unpacked, called the children in, and dressed them in layers, topped off with the thick coats despite the July warmth. She told each of the children to select one toy. Five-year-old Dora had picked a sealskin doll. Three-year-old Joseph chose a carved wooden boat. And Ivan, twelve, picked two books. Ida left her Samovar, her sewing machine, her best cooking pots and knives. She packed only a few needles and thread, dried salmon, and tea, which she placed in her grandmother's basket. Marcus and the other men who owned their own fishing boats dragged them on to shore, ferreting out what they hoped would be safe stowage spots in the high grasses near the beach. In those few hours before the officials herded them onto the waiting boat, Ida and Marcus joined others at the church, boxing icons and candlesticks, carefully storing them in the attic. Ida wrapped among her clothing a few of the icons she loved best, one of the Virgin holding the tiny, manlike Christ.

She and Marcus trudged up the beach toward the long building, herding their three gawking children before them. Ida turned to look for her other charge.

"Fenia," Ida yelled, seeing her mother's friend was not following. When Fenia didn't turn but remained looking over the ocean, Ida sighed. She did not want this responsibility. Even as a girl, Ida saw that something was wrong with Fenia. She hadn't approved of her mother's friendship with this woman. At times, after they had been together, Ida watched her mother staring into the mountains, even after a cold wind swept everyone else inside.

Ida stepped out of the line and set her bags down. Her husband touched her arm. "I'll get her," he said.

Ida picked up her bags and continued on with the children. She glanced back to see Marcus standing alongside Fenia, staring out at the ocean that had left them here.

When Ida stepped inside the building, her sense of dread sucked down like a barnacle on rock. She had heard the white officials talking, saying the "duration village" would need repairs, but she had suspected nothing like this. The entire place smelled musty, and rat droppings formed into layers dried black. White mold crusted the floorboards. She could see the green of the forest behind cracks around the high windows. All through the building, drafts rushed about hurrying to find a way out again.

This would be their home. For how long, Ida didn't know. The war could be over in a few months or linger for years.

Ida watched Fenia rise in the darkness and push aside the hanging blanket, separating the family sleeping area from the next.

"Where are you going?"

"Shhh. Sleep again," Fenia whispered and left.

Probably she should stop the old woman. It wasn't safe creeping around in the dark. Loose boards, tree roots. The camp was still falling apart, even after six months of hard work. And there were the drunks.

On Unalaska, their numbers had grown as Fort Mears had grown. The first construction workers had arrived three years before. She'd watched from across Illiuliuk Bay as they tore through the rock and sand of Amaknak Island and lifted buildings from the lumber that came on steamships. Then the rumors that the government would designate Unalaska a naval reserve and order martial law. Ida joined in the campaign to incorporate the village into a town, hoping this would give them some control of their future if the fort kept growing. The soldiers arrived, and squabbles over land, leadership, supplies, grew more intense. Unalaska had become a military town, with flowing money and overflowing liquor. The religious leaders were manipulating land deals, while some Aleut girls were trading themselves for soldiers' money. And everywhere people were drinking. Ida had believed this was a short-term problem. That the war would end soon, the fort would close, the soldiers would go home. Liquor shipments would return to their slow trickle. She had never imagined that it was her family, her people, who would be sent away and that the booze would follow them.

Ida listened to her children's deep breathing, wrapped her leg over Marcus's hips, and lay awake.

When the first sounds of morning broke, Ida rose with relief. She dressed and hurried to the mess hall. Several women were already there, building fires in the cooking stoves. Ida nodded to her friend, Irene, who was poking kindling into a firebox. Irene was the daughter of her mother's other inseparable friend, and the two girls had grown up as close as sisters.

Irene's daughter, Lizzy, sat at one of the long tables, hunched over her scraps of paper. The camp's only schoolteacher had fled after only two months on the island, and now they were awaiting the promised arrival of a new one. In the meantime, the children ran wild in the kitchen or bunkrooms or along the beach. Except Lizzy. Ida watched her dark head bobbing in rhythm with her pen, watched her little feet tangle first in the table's leg, then in the chair supports, then return to the floor only to start the cycle over. Lizzy had always been quiet, but in the last few months, Ida had watched her friend's daughter grow even more shy. And as her mouth slowed her pencil became faster. She scribbled now with such intensity, the lead biting into paper.

"What are you writing, little one?" Ida touched the girl's head and looked over her shoulders at the scavenged pieces of paper she always seemed to be scratching upon. She could see gouges ripped through the paper along with slashes of words, thick and close set.

Lizzy looked up. "Just what I do, what I see," she said.

"You write about your writing? This is all I see you doing." Ida chuckled. "Come, help me fill the water pots at the pump, then you'll have something to write about."

Lizzy folded and tucked the papers into her pocket without a word and followed Ida to the rack of pots.

Ida disliked cooking with other women. She took pride in her custom-mixed teas and the butter-gold flake of her fish pie crust. Now she had to simply pitch in with whatever the supply boats brought every couple months, mostly canned vegetables, macaroni, potatoes, and more macaroni.

Ida handed two pots to the girl and took two for herself. She heard the tin clinking together in Lizzy's hand as she swung the back door open and held the pots to her side so she could see the two narrow steps that descended to the boardwalk. Lying below the last stair was a young man, clearly passed out. Ida ushered Lizzy around him then nudged him with her foot.

"Get up." She didn't expect him to but wanted to feel the quality of his body with her foot to make sure he was alive at least.

He moaned and hunched his shoulder. It wasn't the first time Ida had stepped over a drunk during her early morning routine. For the first couple of months, the unanimous sobriety had seemed strange. No liquor was supplied at the camp. The officials saw to that. When Indian Service or state officials dropped by to check on the Duration Village, Ida often heard them talking to Mr. Walton, the white camp director, about disgustingly drunk Aleuts, about inferior tolerances, childlike need. But liquor found them. Before the third month, the first bottle arrived. At first the officials made a big to-do. Questioning, lecturing on the importance of a dry camp. But these were short-timers. They had given up after a bunch of useless words proved truly useless. It came in waves. One day the drunks were grumpy but sober. The next day bottles would appear all over camp. Some people suspected the government officials were sneaking it in with the boxes of macaroni, making a little extra to compensate for their dismal assignment of keeping tabs on the evacuation camps scattering Southeast Alaska. Others suspected private bootleggers. But with miles of intricate coastline, finding them and stopping them would have been beyond the scope of the tired, underzealous officials.

Irene was presiding over a blazing stove when they returned, and Lizzy ran to her mother's side. Ida set the two full pots on the woodstove then helped Lizzy lift hers.

Irene kissed the top of her daughter's head. "Good, you got her to do some work for once."

Ida smiled.

"Eli didn't come back last night." Irene poured a sack of oats into the boiling pot.

Ida watched the eight-year-old girl quickly look away. She wasn't like other children. She listened too intently to adult conversation, understood too much. Ida had to remember to speak carefully around her.

"Lizzy," Ida said, "you've carried two pots of water. Now you have something to write about." She nodded toward the tables.

Ida kept her eyes on the pot as the little girl moved away. She knew Irene was worried but that she would speak in her own time. Irene's husband was a drunk. One of the worst. During those two dry months, he had become a different man. Ida heard them making love behind their blanket walls. She watched Eli join the other men to build new cabins to relieve the overcrowded bunkhouse. She saw him wrap his arms around Lizzy and heard the girl's shy laughter.

"He's like when he was young," Irene had said one afternoon. "I could love him again if he stays like this."

But it didn't last. When the booze showed up, Eli was the first to find it. Saying he'd found a job working at Wrangell, he'd disappear for days.

"He's probably found a job mending nets or hauling logs," Irene said.

"Probably," Ida replied.

Ida spent the day washing. The camp had no laundry room, so one day a week the women turned the kitchen into an assembly line. They started after breakfast, filling tubs with water. Ida hung the blankets closest to the stoves. With only one per person, they had to be dry by night or run the risk of a cold or worse. The old and the young were falling sick with pneumonia, flu, and tuberculosis. An infant and an old man had already died.

Fenia appeared just before lunch. Ida had forgotten to worry about her during all the work. Fenia picked up a child's coat and hung it near a stove.

"Are you going to want to know where I've been?"

Ida turned back to the pile of wet clothes. "I'm not keeping track of you."

"Maybe you should be." Fenia smiled. She was old but had a girlish way about her. Ida knew Fenia was slow, but sometimes it was more than that. Fenia seemed to live in a world Ida couldn't see. Even now as she stretched wet clothes over lines, she sometimes twirled or walked on tiptoe. Ida found her frivolity in the face of so much work tedious.

"Since you want to tell me, go ahead."

Fenia leaned in close, wrinkles darting into the thin lines of her old lips. "I know where the liquor comes from."

Ida turned, a woolen skirt dripping against her pant leg.

Fenia pretended to be busy picking another damp item from the pile. Ida sighed. Fenia knew she'd gotten her attention and would now make her work for it.

"What are you saying?"

"Last night," Fenia said, her voice sweet as a girl's, "I saw a boat with no lights come in. I saw a boat leave, whispers and dark. People waited on the beach."

Ida's disgust with Fenia did not stop her from believing. Fenia's mind was untrustworthy, but she had special talents. Like knowing what others were thinking about doing and what they had done. She pulled Fenia out the back door.

"Did you see the name of the boat? Did you see who was waiting?"

Fenia toyed with the ends of her gray-streaked hair. "Of course."

"We will tell Mr. Walton."

Fenia laughed. "Yes, dear Mr. Walton." She clapped, then held her hands up to cover her giggles.

Ida grabbed Fenia's arm. "Why are you laughing? Families starve because the men spend what they make on drink. Some of the boys are drinking long before they should. Another generation of drunks born in all this filth and boredom. Your laughter is shame."

"Our lovely Mr. Walton was at the beach as well. He only carried away what he could fit in his pocket. He's such a handsome man. Don't you think?" Fenia closed her eyes and turned her face to the misty sky. "We will have to show him the way. His death will be beautiful, like the others."

Ida grunted in disgust. She refused to listen to Fenia's perverse ramblings yet again. She turned and walked to the church, leaving Fenia alone, face uplifted, smiling slightly.

Within weeks of arriving, Marcus and other men had built the small church named after the one they had left behind, the Church of the Holy Ascension of Christ. Ida touched the treasured icons she had reverently hung on the rough plank walls. She was tired of the old woman's feeble mind. It wasn't the first time Fenia had talked of killing. Sometimes she claimed to have killed ten men when she was young. Other times, three. As a girl Ida had asked her mother about Fenia's stories. Her mother's reply had disturbed her. "Someday I will tell you more. For now, remember Fenia is not right in her mind."

And so Ida believed that because Fenia was unwell, her stories were untrue. She believed this through the next two weeks, until the liquor ran dry again. Until the drunks were snapping at their children, slapping at their wives. She believed this until Irene's husband died.

He must have hidden a bottle or two away. He was the only drunk in the camp that night. He passed out not far from the bunkhouse. The February cold crept into his arms and legs. He'd been asleep when it found his heart and finally his brain.

"He died without pain," Ida said quietly to Irene as a small group left the makeshift graveyard behind the camp. The crowding trees cast shadows over the mounded ground. The people would not have chosen this burial ground far from the sweep of the ocean. Officials had chosen it for them.

Irene looked back at the grave. "He lived with pain; I am thankful he didn't die with it."

Ida noted the careful equilibrium of Irene's face, the neutral poise with which she held her shoulders, her arms, belying her resignation, her determination to meet her widowed future head-on.

"We must talk alone," Ida said. She looked at Lizzy—the serious face, the hunched shoulders. The girl seemed permanently attached to either the loose folds in Irene's skirt or her scraps of paper. She had always been quiet. But Ida could see that the slow degradation of her father had molded the girl into something she never was meant to be. A ghost of a girl, who did not speak with the excited voice of a child, but with the barely heard whispers of a broken heart.

"Go on ahead, Liz," Irene said, gently prying the fingers from her dress. "Go."

The women watched the girl step cautiously along the boardwalk toward the bunkhouse. "Eli was the one who always found paper for her." Irene's voice caught, then she inhaled slowly. "I don't know what to do. She needed a father, even if a drunk one."

Ida let a moment pass before beginning. "Fenia found where the liquor is coming from. I will always feel the shame of not telling you before." Ida met her friend's eyes. "I thought there was more time."

Ida told Irene what Fenia had discovered—where the bootleggers were unloading, Mr. Walton's involvement. They stood together under the giant trees. Leaves on sticks, the children called them. A steady rain plunged straight through the limbs. Although Ida had been living under this rain for months, it unsettled her. On Unalaska the rain never came so brazenly. It skidded, slanted, sneaked its way through the breathing wind. Here the rain hurled itself at her, aimed straight from the sky.

"Of course, Fenia wants to kill Mr. Walton," Ida scoffed. "Old age has not made her any more sensible."

Irene did not laugh. "If Mr. Walton is taking money, he must go before the boat can be stopped."

"Are you as crazy as the old woman?"

"No. No. There are other ways to get rid of him. A letter could be written to Indian Services."

"And what have they done with the letters the women have written about the bad water, the leaking roof, the endless macaroni, the full outhouse, the sick?"

Almost since they'd arrived, she and others had been writing letters. To Indian Services, the governor's office, Congress. Nothing had changed. Many women complained about the unsanitary conditions that bred disease, but Ida's letters raged against the pay-your-own-way system. Although they'd been uprooted and placed in an isolated camp hundreds of miles from home, Indian Services expected the men to find jobs on other islands to support their families. Those who didn't were made to feel like beggars. The system incensed Ida. How dare anyone call her a freeloader after taking everything from her. Now the worthless new schoolteacher was writing letters herself, saying that Ida was a troublemaker and not to pay any attention. It was worse for Marcus. He found jobs now and then in Wrangell, working for a logging outfit or a fish processor, but in between he had little to do but wait. None of them did. In Unalaska, he'd been self-sufficient with his own boat and skill acquired from years plying the gray waters. He'd lived with a modest pride in his ability to provide and to give his surplus to others. Here he had nothing to show for those long years of work, nothing to give his children but stories from the past.

"Well, what should be done then?" Irene asked.

Ida shrugged. She had no answers.

Ida expected Fenia to come to her. That evening when the children were playing hide-and-seek among the blanket walls, Fenia led Ida outside. They stopped at the cabin Irene and her children had been quarantined in after the visiting doctor had diagnosed her son with tuberculosis. Irene left him in the care of three other families, who had also been quarantined.

"Lizzy is acting strangely," Irene said as she and Ida followed Fenia. "I couldn't find her yesterday and looked everywhere. Do you know where she was?"

Ida shook her head.

"In the outhouse. She was sitting there, crossed legs, drawing on the walls with charcoal. The walls were nearly black with bits of writing. I made her wash it off. But this morning I go to do my business, I find another wall covered. I don't know what to do."

"Is this such a bad thing? With all she's been through, maybe writing in the outhouse is not so bad. Maybe she'll learn to write letters better than ours. Letters people will read."

Irene sighed.

Fenia led them through a February evening to a repaired storage shed. High gray sky capped the night in a waiting thickness void of wind. The women settled themselves on crates of macaroni and canned beans. Ida turned to Fenia. "Go ahead. Say what you want to say."

Fenia tilted her head to the left, listening to something only she could hear, then pulled her knees together and leaned forward. "I was so beautiful." Fenia giggled, covering her mouth with a hand, gnarled clawlike in its age. "All the men, heading north to Nome or the whaling grounds, wanted me. I tried my best to love every one. They were handsome men, so tall and hopeful. Your mothers and I watched these men, for some of them became too entranced by our Aleut girls.

"It was your mother, Irene, who crushed their heads. She said it made her ill. But these were poor men, who didn't know how to love. I helped them find the way. They all died with a taste for what love could be like."

Fenia told the story, slightly changed as she remembered it. "When your mothers' mothers' mothers were young, they took something from the dead ones in order that their village would live." Fenia's words were unfiltered by emotion, dense and low like the clouds. "Your mothers and I, we knew when our grandmothers told us that we had been born for this. We were marked. And you are marked."

Ida remembered her mother speaking of a time forgotten, just after the first white men came. When the Destroyer had taken the food and weapons. When the men were gone and babies starved. Ida stilled inside. Her familiar ruffled interior flattened smooth like a cove sheltered from the wind. The story reflected in the still water with a clarity that merged the hearing with the doing. Ida knew this story was true.

She had always done her best. She had learned to cook and sew from her mother. She had found a hardworking, loving man, who could get along with white men and didn't need more than he had. They had saved enough to buy their own boat, and before the children came, Ida had gone with Marcus to the fishing grounds, stringing lines, knocking the life from flapping halibut, reckoning position through thick fog, scrutinizing the cannery scales. Later she had borne children and watched them well. Marcus worked hard in dangerous waters. Ida kept her house smelling of bleach and tea, stayed away from the lazy, the drunks, the gossips. The sweat of her labors leaked from her, mingling with the gray ocean and the bending grass. She thought it was enough—to keep her own family safe. But as she watched young men turn to sodden drunks, as she saw young women give themselves to the soldiers at the base with a despair that tore chunks from her heart, as she saw the ranks of those who could not feed themselves or their families swell and swell again, she wondered if she was wrong. If her family was larger than Marcus and her children. In moments when her work was done and she had no easy way to stop her thoughts, she could smell the decay deepening, eating away what was left of her people. And in those moments, came a fleeting, desperate longing to do more.

As Ida listened to Fenia now with this strange new calm, those thoughts settled deep. She felt their weight like a rock thrown into the sea that has no choice but to sink. It was true, those quick, desperate thoughts; she had been born into a purpose, as great as her people had been once.

Fenia's hand came down around Ida's knee. "You feel it, don't you?"

Ida nodded, the slightest assent.

"It was the same for me."

Fenia rocked slightly and stroked her own arm through her coat as she sketched out her plan. They would take Mr. Walton like their mothers had, alone on the beach. Fenia would hold him as he died.

The stories and the knowledge coming as they did all at once overpowered Ida. She couldn't begin to think, to plan. But murder. This was more concrete. She focused on it with a biting intensity.

"Killing Mr. Walton would do nothing," she said. "Another manager would be sent. Another manager bribed."

Irene nodded. "Best to stop the liquor runners."

Ida looked at her friend, dismissing Fenia with a turn of her shoulders. "How?"

The women were silent for a moment. An idea pulled itself together in Ida's mind. "They can't bring liquor if they don't have a boat."

"But they do have a boat."

"You and I know boats." Ida smiled, the idea a bolt of hot joy. If they sunk the boat, the bootleggers would be hard-pressed to find another. With the military commandeering half the tugs and trawlers, oceangoing boats were scarce and expensive. It could take months or longer.

Ida and Irene nearly forgot Fenia as they laid their plans. The old woman's desire to kill was lost in the strategies curling between their minds, which emerged a completed circle.

Ida heard the wind caress the sides of the storage shed, heard the creak of branches rubbing against one another. "How will we know when the boat is returning?"

They turned to Fenia, needing her strange mind at least for this.

"I will know," she said, and neither asked her how. "But your way is like a rudderless boat; no control. You think killing is a bad thing. But you will understand better someday. You were born to understand."

In the next days, Ida spent many hours in the tiny church, kneeling, eyes closed or gazing at the Virgin. She asked God to direct her, to tell her if what they were about to do was right. She heard the gathering of her own surety and sent her gratitude toward heaven.

Fenia told them after dinner, "The boat comes tonight."

Ida didn't try to sleep. She lay beside her husband, her mind alive with fear, excitement, hope. She did not think about the immediate consequences of what they would do. She knew only that this would be the last liquor coming into the camp for a time. The crew could find another boat, but it could take months. Dry months. Living months. And they could take care of other boats the same way. Perhaps a legend would arise. Boats that carried booze to the camps were cursed.

She and Fenia met Irene at the back of the bunkhouse. They carried no light as they followed the snow-spotted trails behind the camp until one branch cut to the right, back to the beach. They came out on a low bluff above the beach at high tide. They hopped down and moved quietly to the small skiff they had hidden in the brush.

Fenia pulled out the tobacco tin she always kept tied round her waist inside her dresses and opened the lid. She dug her finger into the thick grease, offering a scoop to each of the women. Fenia rubbed the dead-man's fat against her palms. When they were slick, she rubbed her palms across her forehead and cheeks. The last bit she placed on her tongue and closed her eyes.

Ida hadn't known if she'd be able to do this. A part of her thought it silly anyway. She did not believe in magic or mummy power. But here in the night with the ocean lying at her feet, the ancient ways flowed forward across time. And when she thought of what she would do in the coming hours, she decided perhaps she could believe.

She rubbed the fat into her hands and her face. Its stickiness surprised her. The taste she never knew. The fear in her body had dried her mouth and coated her taste. She placed the fat on her tongue, like communion bread, and swallowed.

They carried the skiff to the waterline. Fenia stepped over the side and settled near the stern. Irene and Ida pushed the stern into the waves and stepped in. Ida pulled the oars, wrapped with pieces of a worn skirt, from along the keel and slid them through the locks, also ringed with cloth. She pulled with the starboard oar until they were parallel with the beach then slowly and steadily rowed around the point of land to the south.

Within an hour they slid into the next cove. They rowed until they'd traveled half its length, then turned to shore. When the boat bumped the rocky bottom, Irene jumped out and pulled the bow onshore. They waited.

An hour passed before they heard the first steps and quiet voices. The shapes of five men moved across the beach. One of them smoked, and the women followed the glow of his cigarette as it marked the group's journey to the water's edge.

"The boat." Fenia pointed to the mouth of the cove.

Ida heard the engine and let her eyes rest there until the darker shape of the boat formed. A small tug, no more than forty feet long, moved slowly toward the beach. When it was only a hundred feet offshore, Ida heard the grinding anchor chain. The men onshore had launched their skiff, which Ida guessed they had hidden along the tree line.

Irene pushed the boat silently backward, lifting herself in as it slid into deep water. Ida rowed smoothly, keeping her hands level. Although the idling engine, the wind, and the water easily masked her oars, she didn't want to bang the boat's sides. Loud low noises would echo across the cove. Ida slowed. The men were unloading from the bow, which pointed toward the shore on an ebbing tide. She waited until the men's skiff was loaded for its first trip.

When it was halfway to shore, the women eased up to the tug's stern, where step rungs led from the waterline over the rail. Irene slipped a line over a cleat. She placed one foot on the ladder and lifted her weight slowly from the skiff to the boat. She climbed two steps until her head cleared the rail. A dark, deserted deck stretched in front of her. She swung her body over and dropped to the deck. Ida followed.

The women waited, listening to the voices coming from the port side of the bow. Three men, talking low. Ida crawled forward toward the cabin. She eased the door open a crack and listened again. The men remained outside, waiting for the skiff to unload and return. Ida crawled over the doorway lip and scanned the floorboards in front of her. Irene crawled beside her and pointed. Ida saw the handle. They crept toward it.

The hinged engine hatch creaked when Ida lifted it. She froze. Nothing. She hung a leg over the side, feeling for the ladder, found it, and descended seven rungs to the engine room floor. Irene closed the hatch above them.

The engine's staccato roared through the room, pressing out every other sound but the hard slaps of waves against the hull. In the dark, the smell of oil and grime lay like a hand across Ida's nose. Irene reached for the flashlight in her pocket. She scanned the compartment quickly. The women didn't know how long they had but hoped the men would need at least three trips to unload the liquor shipment with their small skiff. The first trip had taken fifteen minutes. They had at most thirty more to finish the job.

"Here," Irene whispered. She found the seawater cooling through-hull fitting along the starboard hull. She stepped over a pump and located the shut-off valve. Irene ran her light along the attached hose that disappeared behind a crate before running into the diesel engine. The pump sucked water from the ocean to cool the engine. Ida and Irene moved toward the crate. Ida slid it aside while Irene pulled a hacksaw from under her coat. She sat on her heels and lined the blade up with the hose. It took only a minute to saw halfway through the rubber. The water would gush into the engine room while the engine grew hotter.

Ida slid the crate back in place, and the women turned to hunt for the bilge pumps, which pumped engine room water back into the sea.

They traced the lines, pinpointed three places, obscured by food supplies in one spot, and spare engine parts in the others. Again Irene sliced.

As they finished, they heard the bump of the skiff against the bow. The second trip.

"Hey! Watch it," someone shouted. A splash.

"Dammit. You're paying for that."

Ida and Irene climbed out of the engine room.

"Not paying for anything we don't get."

"By God you will or you won't get nothing else."

Irene crawled back to the cabin door. Ida heard the skiff push off as she gingerly closed the engine hatch.

"Let's get off," one of the men said. "Roger, pull the anchor."

Ida didn't crawl; she ran for the cabin door. She followed Irene to the stern and nearly stepped on her fingers descending the ladder back to the skiff. Ida heard the men dragging the anchor chain up over the bow as she slipped her line off the stern cleat.

The rush of water spun the skiff backward as the engine was thrown into reverse. Ida plunged the oars into the water and worked her shoulders back and forth. The boat had turned to open ocean by the time they reached shore.

Ida shook as she swiveled the oars into the skiff. Her legs rattled like reeds. The women clamored out and watched the dark shape leave the bay.

The news did not take long to reach them. It came at lunch that afternoon. A boat had gone down not more than twenty miles from the island. The crew radioed for help. But they'd waited too long. By the time rescue boats reached the last known location, the radio had gone silent. None of the three crew members were found.

Ida knelt under her precious icons often in the next weeks. She thought about what those last hours on the boat would have been like. The skipper feels the boat grow heavy. Feels how its bow refuses to rise over each wave. He tells the engineer to check below. The engineer finds water, maybe knee-high, sloshing with the rolling boat. He turns on the bilge pumps. But water flows through pierced lines to flood new sections. He searches for the leak, plunging his arms into the icy water again and again. Maybe he finds it. But not in time. The engine cuts off when the water tops its intake. Maybe the boat sinks then, or maybe the crew can't keep the bow into the waves, and the boat wallows helpless in the troughs until it rolls and never rights. It sinks slowly at first, then all at once.

At times images come to Ida through a new and unfamiliar awareness. The crew knows, in those last moments before they hit the icy water, that someone has cut the lines. Why? they scream. And in the water, as their legs grow too numb, their brains too slow to hold thoughts or images, they remember only the feel of a child's arms tight around them, a small face pressed into their neck, the smile of a woman they love.

Ida wondered if these are their final dying memories, or if something darker comes last. She searched the Virgin's face, looking for an answer.

When the liquor was gone a week later, she began to believe they'd done the right thing. There would be fewer deaths now. Wouldn't there?

She wasn't sure if Fenia had been right about the new awareness given them by the dead-man's fat. The familiar part of herself thought not. But sometimes she did know things she shouldn't. And people looked at her differently. Mr. Walton wouldn't meet her gaze when she complained about the overflowing toilet or the iron-colored water. He didn't argue with her or remind her how grateful she should be that the government was protecting her from the Japs.

Fenia died in the spring. She came down with the flu, then pneumonia. The morning of her death, she called Ida and Irene to her.

"I will tell your mothers of this beautiful thing you have done when I see them. And in time, you will tell your daughters."

Irene nodded.

"You must find Anna after the war. You must tell her. Make sure she comes back to the island and watches with you."

Ida took Fenia's hand, slight as a bird's wing. Fenia's only daughter had gone off to college just the year before. Ida knew that Anna had been desperate to escape her mother, that her dreams of Seattle and college were nothing more than the most comfortable way to untangle herself from her mother's delusions. She would have done the same.

"I will find her and tell her," Ida said, imagining that day when she would sit Anna down and give her the missing pieces of her mother's mind. For the first time in all her years of knowing Fenia, Ida loved her. Slivered tears came, one at a time. Ida saw both Fenia's madness and her heroism at that moment. She did not know which scared her more. "We will watch. Always."

Fenia held a long breath, then exhaled. "I want you to take my body home with you. I want to lie in the cave with the Dry Ones, with your mothers."

Fenia is confused, Ida thought. She spoke her next words slowly. "My mother was buried in the cemetery. You know that, Fenia. You were there."

Fenia smiled. "She never wanted to stay there. Too dark underground. Patricia and I took her. And I took Patricia."

Irene gasped.

Ida remembered all the afternoons she'd sat by her mother's headstone, talking to an empty grave. She saw the blackened corpse Fenia would soon become. She imagined loading it on the boat. She imagined laying it down like a sleeping child in the dark warmth next to her mother and Patricia. Three mummies, in a cave she had not yet seen, waiting and watching.

looking at herself

Thad came back. I didn't meet him at the dock because I
didn't expect him.

I'd been cleaning rat shit out of the kitchen and thinking. About the
Aleuts. About conquest.

There are those who will wish to think of these Aleuts as pure of
heart and deed, living in pristine nature, at one, and all that. We have
that tendency, those of us from recent conquering cultures. After a
few generations the guilt sets in, and we nurse that guilt, making our
once-and-former enemies into phantoms of some imagined time when
humans were innocents.

None of this is true. People have been nasty to one another from the
get-go, and those cultures that lost the conquest game did not lose because they were any less bloodthirsty than the winners, but because
they hadn't figured out how to make a spear, or a bow, or a sword, or a
musket, or a Gatling gun, or a bomb. The victims are only victimizers
without the equipment for the job.

The Aleuts had been fighting other Aleuts, taking slaves, who could
be killed at the whim of the *toion*. They'd gathered hundreds of warriors together for stealth raids on the Koniag of the mainland, taking
supplies, women, lives. These peaceful people were set upon by the
Russians, many of whom were themselves recently conquered. Most

of them had been scattered bands of Siberians up until 1639, when the Russians pushed to the east and called the land they'd taken Russia. These Siberians were still getting the feel for this new nationality of theirs when they fell upon the Aleuts. "Ah-ha," they may have said, "here's a new people who are even more savagely backward than we were before those Russians got to us."

And so it goes.

Those Russians who took Siberia were the descendants of a people who had been, in turn, conquered by the Mongol hordes in the thirteenth century, many of whom had conquered western China, only to become Chinese despite their victory. Rome conquered the Germanic tribes, only to be undone by their descendants. The British fell under Roman conquest, learned well, and emerged hundreds of years later to conquer India, parts of Africa and North America, half of which got rebellious and set off to conquer the land to the west, including the pieces of Alaska the Russians had not subdued.

And so it goes. The circling winds of history and all that. What I didn't get then and understand oh so well now, is that this same cycle circles for individuals too. That all you have to do to turn a victim into a victimizer is give her a baseball bat.

And so it goes. The circling winds of my history and all that.

I had a cigarette in my mouth and Madonna on and was crawling along the wall trying to see where the rats were getting in when I heard bootsteps on the porch. I stood, shook out my legs, and opened the inner door just as he entered the outer one.

"It's you," I said.

"It's me."

The sun was low behind him, and I was struck again by how handsome he was. I felt overwhelmed by his sudden presence—both rescued and doomed. "I hadn't heard you were coming in."

"I know. I wanted to surprise you."

He followed me into the cabana and set his duffel by the door. "You look different," he said.

I let my hair down from its ponytail. "I wasn't expecting you." I moved into his arms and felt the solid quality of him. I could smell the fish and the work and the water. His hand followed my arm as it rose to his neck and stopped me before I could pull myself up for a kiss.

"I've been thinking a lot while we were out. I've been thinking about what happened last time. I figured some stuff out."

I saw it in his eyes. The look that says, I've planned this, studied this, I will be heard, I will make myself understood. I did what any girl would do. I crossed my arms, grasped the bottom of my T-shirt, and slid it up and over my head. I walked backward, dropping my pants and undies, and scrambled up the ladder. "Come on up," I called, "and tell me all about it." He was there before I finished the sentence.

We fumbled in the low dark space while he lit one of the candles. I thought I could waylay his intentions by simply stretching out there on the comforter. I was naked in candlelight with a man who hadn't seen a woman in two weeks; it should have been a breeze.

His hand began to trace circles around my breasts, slow and deliberate. "I've been thinking while we were out," he said again. "You know I've never really had my own place. Not since I've been fishing anyway. I've been thinking we should look for a place to buy, a real house. You know?"

I laughed. "You've been bunking with Steve too long. That's what I think."

I needed him to laugh with me; he didn't even chuckle.

"Maybe, but Brandy, I want to have things. I want a house, maybe some land; I want a family, kids, regular things. I've been thinking about it. We could buy something near Seattle or even here. Do you like it here? I don't care where really."

His fingers stopped. He seemed to have forgotten his hand lying there between my tits. He wasn't really seeing me; he was seeing his fantasy. I slithered under him so he could feel me against his chest. "Let's talk about it later," I said and gripped his ass against me.

We were in the midst of a long tonguey kind of kiss, our hands between each other's legs, and I was so ready, when he pulled back and propped himself on his side with his elbow. "I saw this place last year a couple hours north of Seattle. It looked like it had been built in the trees. I mean right up in them. Like a tree house. I was thinking about what happened between us last time. I think you've never really had someplace you could count on. Your own place, something we could make into our own home. And I think you haven't had someone you could count on." He brushed a lock of hair away from my mouth, his eyes on mine.

I was finding it hard to breathe. I didn't want to hear shit like this. Something clunked in my chest and sent slivers toward my nose, which got all tingly. "Shit, Thad, can't you shut up for a minute and fuck me."

"Not until you tell me your dreams. We never talk about the future. I think that's what we need, to see a future, you know? Besides, we have all night." He was getting giddy now, flush with faith in his diagnosis and treatment plan. "Tell me, what kind of house is your dream house. Not that we could get that right away. But I got about thirty grand saved up. Enough for a down payment on something. Steve says his place wasn't much more down than that." He kissed my abdomen. "Tell me, where do you dream of living?"

In the awkward silence he looked at my face and saw the tears running down to the pillow. I could feel him staring down at me while I stared up at the ceiling, tears soaking up each side of my pillow.

"What? What did I say?"

I pushed his hands away from my face and sat up. "What do you think? Do I look like the kind of girl who carries a fuckin' picture of her dream house in her purse?"

"I'm pushing, aren't I." He turned my face to his. "If that's what it takes, more time, I can wait. I love you. I don't care where we live."

"You don't care?" His capitulation snapped something in me. Couldn't he see how weak it made him look? To be the one who gave up the power? I could see the weakness on his face, and all of a sudden I hated him for it. "You're just going to tag along with me. Yes, Brandy. Sure, Brandy. I love you, Brandy." I was screaming at him now, and he just sat there, mute. "You spineless prick."

I think I threw something at him—maybe it was an ashtray. He turned his shoulder into it. "How the fuck do you think it feels when I'm lying here naked and all you want to do is go the fuck on about some tree house? Fuck. Don't you have a fuckin' clue?"

I sat there in the bed, crying hard now, my body betraying me, shaking with it, breathing ragged. Tears had smeared up everything. I could feel him a couple of feet away; I could feel the weight of his growing awareness and then the judgment.

"You don't love me, do you?" His voice was so calm, so unaffected. He'd already decided. "You never even wanted to get to know me. I was just some guy." He watched my crying ease and listened to my breathing steady.

"Why did you have to go and ruin it?" I whispered the words. And as I did, I knew that even now I could salvage it. I knew that I could nestle against him and tell him lies—that I did love him but was afraid of the strength of it, that I'd never been with a man like him. These were lies I'd used before with no remorse. Or I could tell him the truth. That I was scared shitless. That in Thad's love I saw my father's helplessness and in myself my mother's cruelty. It would have worked; he would have been willing to work through this with me, take the risk for me. But even then I knew there was a different kind of sickness in that. In asking him to take responsibility for all my crap. And maybe I could see that having a partner in whatever change was growing in me would too easily dilute it, and that I'd never know what could have been. So I was silent. Everything was changing, and as much as I wanted it back, I wanted what came next even more.

"I didn't ruin it, Brandy. I hope you figure that out someday."

As he climbed down the ladder, I wanted to tell him that I already knew. And that because I knew I'd only continue to screw things up, I was letting him go now, before it got worse for him, and because there were no guarantees it would get better. But all that would have sounded too noble for what I had done.

I listened to him packing, just a few clothes and little things. I heard him scratching a pen against paper. I heard the door open. "Do you need anything?" he asked, and I could hear the measured effort in his words. "I can get you a plane ticket out. Or pay Darlene up for another couple months."

"No, I'm fine."

His chivalry in defeat washed great slabs of tears down my cheeks. And I was afraid. Afraid that if I opened my mouth again it would only be to beg him to stay.

He opened the door. "This isn't what I wanted," he said. He left the door open, and I felt a reckless wind blow through, shifting for something to pry loose.

I gave him five minutes, then climbed down to look for the note. I couldn't find it. Maybe there wasn't one.

And so began the first night of my life that I was alone by choice. I cried through all of it. When I awoke, something felt different. As I drank my morning coffee on the deck, I knew what it was. I wasn't crumbling anymore. I had grown older, and my skin had worn to a patina of sadness. And the weird thing was, it felt overdue. It felt like I should have been feeling it for a long time now.

what to tell

parked my bike in the lot between the Elbow and the Old
Voyagers. I needed to know more. Especially now. He'd
been gone three days. In Thad's wake, those old women became an
obsession. Not much was different. I'd been alone most of the time
before he left. The truth was that Thad's leaving didn't create the obsession as much as the obsession allowed me to let Thad leave. I just
felt I was on to something, and I was willing to go manless for a while
to track it down.

I'd finished or skimmed all the books by now, at least the parts about
the mummies. But none of them had mentioned any current mummy
use or anything about why old women would still be visiting the caves.
In fact, according to the books, only men had used the corpses. Apparently mummies along with hunting weapons had been taboo for Aleut
women. Few of the books mentioned women at all, except under the
headings of kinship relations and labor divisions.

The wind was a hand holding the door shut, and I had to yank twice
before I won.

Anna didn't look up. "Why are you here?" She sliced the blade of an
X-Acto knife through a strip of tape on a shipping box.

"I finished the books," I lied again. "Thought I'd get more."

"Over there." She gestured with the knife toward a book-heaped table.

I perused the books, carefully keeping the piles the way she'd organized them. I didn't see what I was looking for. I glanced back at Anna, slicing tape from another box. I took a deep breath.

"Do you have anything, any books that. . . ." I paused, looked up at my Aleut Mona Lisa, hovering over a shelf of patterned baskets. "Anything about the women?"

"It's all in the books I gave you. The menstrual customs, the birthing customs. What they ate, wore. It's all there."

"I know. I've read all that. I want to know what she knows," I said, nodding toward the sketch.

She followed my gaze. Then she laughed.

"That," Anna said, "is not in the books." She lay the X-Acto on the counter and walked toward the picture. "Look at her eyes. What do you see?"

I stepped closer, blocked the lower half of her face with my hand. "They don't focus," I said. "She's looking right at me but not seeing me."

Anna nodded. "Yes. She's disassociated part of herself. At least from the artist. Tell me about her mouth."

I'd done this before, stared at that mouth, trying to figure out its secret. "I don't know." I kept looking, shielding the top of her face now. "It's too perfect. Sensual. It doesn't belong to the same face."

"Yes." Anna nodded again.

We both stared, heads tipped back, transfixed.

"The eyes of a victim. The mouth of a victor. It's her little secret. The artist didn't even see it."

"What? What secret?"

"She's won. Or she knows she will win. She knows her power is deeper and older than his."

"That's it." I squeezed Anna's arm. And she let me. Suddenly I got that twisted smile, and the knowledge sent a jolt of what could only be hope through me. She wasn't a victim. The men are gone, people are dying, and still she's not a victim. "She's mocking him."

She flashed her eyebrows up and grinned. "Um-hmm," she said with a single slow nod. "They'll never tell you that in the books or in the schools. They tell you conquest is a man's game and women are the innocent victims. But they forget what it means to be a mother. They forget that whatever merged culture comes next is hers."

A wad of saliva collected in my mouth. I swallowed. "She's in control, isn't she. And she knows it."

"Yes. No conqueror, no army, no force can stand against her. She is a mother. And her power will outlast them all."

They weren't victims. Shit, I'd had it all wrong. They knew how to pretend, but that's all it was—a pretense. They had these warriors, conquerors all around them day and night, and they played the part. This girl wanted us, so many years in the future, to know. They weren't victims, at least not for long. In contradiction to all the histories and firsthand accounts, she fixed an expression on her face that would outlast them all. That would tell us she had taken back the night.

With our heads tipped back and our fingers steepled in front of our mouths, Anna and I grinned at each other, wide and open. I cannot tell you how welcomed I felt then, how accepted. Anna was actually guiding me toward this revelation, speaking to me like I could understand, like I deserved to understand. I felt like we were on the same side. So I let my guard down, and I made a mistake.

"What about the mummies? Do you have any books about them?"

Her head shot up. The spell broke. "We're closing now," she said, marching back to the counter and starting in on the boxes again with the X-Acto.

"Oh." I grabbed a couple of books on the table, one on kayak designs, another on edible plants. "Okay, I'll just take these."

"Time to go," she said, and she sliced the X-Acto along the edge of her finger. I saw drops of blood splattered on the cardboard. When I didn't move, she came from behind the counter, the X-Acto still in her hand, the blood dripping down her wrist. The blade scraped against the wooden door as she pushed it and held it against the wind. She fixed me with another of those pinned and wriggling stares.

I set the books down, suddenly aware that I'd failed before I'd begun. I eased by her out the door, keeping my eye on the knife. She pulled it shut as I stood on the tiny plank porch. I heard the lock slide shut. I felt for the edge of the step and backed away from the door.

*　*　*

Have you ever really felt the wind? I mean stood in it, let it beat against you, let it come inside you? The first week of September came like that. It blew from the hills, from the sea, never stooping to a breeze. It brought an eerie solitude to the cabana, where now I was alone for good. I'd heard he was in Anchorage. The skipper was moving the boat down to Seattle, and Thad would have some time off. Fall lurched into town. Patterns changed. The sun grew more cautious, hunkering lower every day. People stayed indoors. The Elbow Room's usually thin afternoon crowd grew.

I pulled up a stool next to Carl.

"Look," Marge said, holding a lopsided but somewhat charming and dainty grass basket on her open palm. "I finished it." Marge's red, red lips protruded ever so slightly, daring me.

I managed a neutral, "Nice."

She set it carefully back on a shelf behind the bar, where it listed to the left over a slight concavity in its side. Marge admired it there for a moment then turned back to me. "Got a letter for you," she said, sliding an envelope toward me. "Where's Thad? I heard the boat's moving down south for the winter," she said as I ripped open the envelope.

"I don't know," I said, opening the letter. "Gone, I guess."

"Gone?" She stopped when she saw my face.

The letter was from my mom.

Dear Brandy,

Bad news first. Your dad died. Granny Jane called yesterday to tell me. We didn't have a number for you so I'm sending this general delivery. I hope it reaches you. Granny Jane told me he died peacefully in his car. The couple he was staying with sent news to Granny Jane, and she took care of his body. He'll be cremated. So all that's wrapped up.

Now the good news. I'm thinking about coming up there to visit you. I want you to call me as soon as you get this. Things here aren't working out too well. Russell died a few months ago. I'm going a little crazy here. When Granny Jane told me where you were, I knew I just had to see you soon. I saw that Oprah show on Alaskan men. Are there really eight men for every woman? They say Alaskan men are rugged and rich.

What was that saying? The goods are odd but the odds are good. So I was thinking, now that I'm a widow, maybe I should travel some. You could show me around, introduce me to some of those rich love-starved Alaskan men.

Give me a call as soon as you read this. I'm at the same number.

Miss you, hon.

My stomach lurched. I checked the post date. The letter had taken two weeks to find me. He'd been dead two weeks. And Mom, she'd been waiting for me to call. She'd wait for me to call, wouldn't she? She wouldn't just hop a plane?

Marge hunkered over the bar toward me. "What?" she asked.

I looked up at her. "My dad died."

She stood back and stared at me for a minute. "Hey," she yelled, and all conversation halted. "Brandy's dad died. We're gonna remember him with a round of drinks."

I hardly heard her. Something was shouting in my head. The men are gone. The men are gone. Then in a whisper—you are alone.

I don't know how long I sat there, closing my eyes to the sound inside. When I looked up I saw about twenty guys, some I knew, some strangers, crowding around the bar. Liz was there, sitting at her post. Marge poured each a new drink. When they were all served, she turned to me. "Tell us about him."

I looked around the room. Was this all I had, a group of strangers and half-strangers, willing to listen because a free drink had been poured? Was this the way I would see my dad, the last man standing in my life, gone? I bit my lower lip.

"His name was Henry. He died in a car he lived in. He was a drunk." I didn't want to tell them anything else. How he'd been when I was little. The way his mind could take apart an argument, diagnose its flaw, and rebuild a towering scaffold of an idea. How listening to him do it made me dizzy with the freedom of it, the freedom to think anew and form fresh concepts out of flawed ones. The careful way he read, putting ideas into a spare parts box that would, on another day, be used to create something unspoiled. The way I knew our minds worked in the same way, and the anticipation I felt at knowing I would be able to do it too someday. That we were alike and all I needed was time and to keep watching him and to keep protecting his fragile gift from her.

"Can't you think of something good to say?" Marge shot at me.

I thought for a moment.

"He dreamed, I guess."

Marge raised her glass. "To Henry, the dreamer," she shouted and tipped her drink back.

"To Henry, the dreamer," the crowd repeated and drank.

I tipped back my own shot.

I eyed the telephone behind the bar. I wasn't going to call. There was no fucking way I'd call her. Let her stick to her marina, California, polo-shirt-wearing men.

I drank too much. Everyone had to buy me a drink.

And I drank. My eyes kept traveling to the phone. I knew I should leave and was going through the steps necessary to get myself up, using visualization techniques to improve my odds of getting home safe, when Liz appeared by my side. I hadn't seen her make the trip from the other side of the bar.

"He die alone?" She looked up at me with her half-tooth grin.

The entire bar hushed. Liz so rarely spoke, it was as if royalty had stepped into our dim, liquid world and silenced it.

"No. There was a dog."

She nodded. "A dog." Then she began to laugh. She cackled all the way to the bathroom door, stumbled, and groped for the light switch. Then she stopped, turned back to me. "A woman's courage," she said, "is often mistaken for insanity."

Spotty chuckles skipped along the bar. People didn't know quite how to take the exchange, and the snickers helped push it toward lightness.

I was just pissed. I hated that woman.

I hated her like I hated my mother. No way was I going to call her.

like a movie

One image returned to me those next few days. I couldn't say I was mourning. I'd lost Dad years before. I just had this picture in idle moments, a memory. Dad and I are at the lake. He's given me this six-foot-tall inflatable Wild Turkey bottle, the kind liquor companies hand out to bars as decorative advertisements. He holds me onto the thing as it rolls in the water under me. The other kids are floating around on pink air mattresses and sea horse–heads rings. I remember thinking I am special. My dad has given me a floaty a whole lot bigger and a whole lot better. I am the only kid trying to float on a bottle of whiskey. We laugh, Dad and I, as the bottle rolls and bobs. I am six years old and riding the waves on a whiskey bottle.

The next day I fucked up twice. The first time, I screwed Tom and promised myself never to do it again. The second time, I screwed Tom and told him I'd think about coming with him to San Luis Obispo.

He showed up at the cabana about ten in the morning, all loaded with money and eager to get home. I knew the moment I opened the door where this was headed. I let him in anyway. Maybe I just didn't want to think about Dad and the way he had died. Maybe I just welcomed anyone who would keep me from being alone. I made another pot of coffee and shared Tom's offered joint. He talked about waves and California, bonfires and boards. The sex was better this time, without the booze. He left with a smile three hours later to catch a flight back to Anchorage, then San Francisco.

I sat on my porch afterward and watched the clouds roll in from the ocean. This storm came with forthright intentions, the line between blue, sun-happy sky and blackness clear and brazen. It wanted you to expect it, to think about its approach. By the time it hit, I knew I'd fucked up. I'd screwed Tom out of boredom and habit and my instinct to hunt a new man. Not much different from a chick who screws a guy for his coke—instinct, boredom, habit. If I replaced Thad with Tom, I'd fall behind. I'd be just doing the same thing over again. That's what I kept telling myself, although I couldn't fill in the blank—behind what? I promised myself it wouldn't happen again. And because I knew keeping promises was not my forte, I stayed when the rain and wind hit. I made myself say it out loud over and over. "I will not fuck around. I will not fuck around."

And I really meant it. I did.

By six that evening the storm had eased into a lazy mist. I'd been practicing my alone skills, which meant I watched myself meander around the place, seeing what I'd do. I'd decided the only way to deal with it was to create a kind of alternate me, who could watch in a detached way and provide its own feedback. Baby steps. So far all I had done was play a tape, fold some laundry, smoke, make orange juice, and experiment with various hairstyles. The observer-me had been able to ascertain only that I was still pathetic, but there didn't seem to be any more flakes on the floor.

I was riffling through the bookshelves, looking for something that had nothing to do with them and their past, when I found it. A card, tucked inside a pink envelope. At the bottom of the envelope a silver chain slithered from side to side when I tilted it. I was afraid to read the card and pulled it out slowly. Spires of monkshood, purple clusters reaching for the sky on the front, and Thad's words inside—Think of me. I tipped the envelope up and the necklace slid out. A heart-shaped locket fell into my palm.

I stared at it, my mother's warning tumbled from some locked space. "Who gave you this?" she says, ripping a tiny heart locket from my neck. I am eleven and Nicky Robins gave it to me that afternoon at school. He shoved it into my hand and ran off with his friends. I'd been mesmerized. It was the most beautiful thing I'd ever seen. I slipped the smooth chain over my head. Nicky. Nicky. Nicky. I'd said it as my fingers traced the shape.

"A boy at school," I say, the tears heading for their ducts.

"Shit, Brandy." Her tone softens, and she touches my cheek. "Didn't I tell you, Never, ever, ever wear a locket like that, honey. It just sends the wrong message."

"What message?"

"Just the wrong message. Remember that."

I held Thad's gift and brushed the heart's face with my thumb, feeling the silver slip under my skin. I raised my palm above the envelope and let the locket fall, then tucked the card back inside and replaced it in the bookshelves.

No heart lockets. No heart lockets.

I heard her laugh again, soft at first, then spiraling upward until it filled the cabana.

I mistook it for my mother, at first.

"Shut the fuck up," I yelled. "You were wrong, weren't you? All wrong." But as soon as I'd let the words out, I realized my mistake. It was Liz.

"Shut up," I whispered.

The cackling sunk lower, eased into the floorboards, and left me in silence again.

I was still standing there, for how long I don't know, when I heard the knock. I really didn't expect it to be Tom. I suppose I should have known that his plane hadn't been able to land, but I'd been so busy imagining my virtuous self and teetering near the insanity precipice, I didn't prepare.

"Hey," he said, all sheepish and wet.

He looked like one of those unkempt Eurail traveling guys you see crashed on airport seats, hair too long, bulky sweater, always alone, always drawing you toward them with the question "What did you find?"

Boredom, instinct, habit. "Why not," I said and let him in.

We settled into the living room, cups of warm Baileys and coffee in hand. "I've spent the last several hours promising myself I wouldn't screw guys like you anymore," I told Tom. I held my cup near my face, letting the steam drift over my skin.

"Are you shitting me?"

"No."

He smiled. "That's heavy. I can respect that, but you've got to ask yourself why."

"Why not?" I realized then that by bringing up my promise, I'd offered him the role of adversary. I'd laid out the debate and given him a side to argue. He did it well. Of course, I hadn't had much practice at refusing to be easy.

"No reason. Just, it doesn't get you anywhere. What's your destination? You gotta ask yourself that."

"Somewhere else."

"You're stuck."

I sipped my Baileys and thought about the way his hemp pullover pulled tight across his biceps when he gestured.

Then he laid the Zen-and-the-art crap on me. Seduction à la Robert Pirsig.

"Maybe your thinking's too narrow. You ever read *Zen and the Art*?"

"Yeah."

"This guy says you should just be okay with being stuck. He calls it the 'psychic predecessor of all real understanding.' You're like stoked for something."

"And what psychic gem am I stoked to understand?"

"Yourself."

"Of course." I actually hadn't read all of the book. That quality section had done me in. "He also said motorcycles are rational machines. He's full of crap."

"Naw, you just aren't letting yourself get into it. His stuff is major." He pulled a copy of the book from his pack and flipped through pages. I'd seen this before, even done it a bit with *Atlas Shrugged*. You read some book at the right time in your life and start thinking that if everyone else read it too, the world would remake itself. You carry it around, underline parts, read it to friends, who say things like, "That's deep, man."

Tom knelt on the floor in front of me. "Listen to this." He read from an underlined section. " 'We take a handful of sand from the endless landscape of awareness around us and call that handful of sand the world.'" He closed the book. "You got to open yourself up to it."

"What you mean is I've got to open myself up to boinking you again."

"Yeah, but to everything, to living radical. Come with me. Tomorrow morning, get on the plane with me. I need someone like you—you're free. You're like me. I can feel it. We'll get an apartment on the beach. I'll teach you to surf. It'll be awesome."

He pushed my legs apart and leaned in to me. I imagined myself on a beach, watching the surf, smoking a joint, the sun a poultice of heat. Trading men; trading lives. "'We keep passing unseen through little moments of other people's lives.' Don't pass unseen through mine." His breath brushed my ears, and when he kissed me, I wanted him badly. Not because his sloppy philosophy had convinced me of anything but his irrelevant optimism, but because he was a man, and I had a habit of needing one.

As my shirt came off, he whispered, "The past exists only in our memories, the future only in our plans." As my pants came off, he whispered, "'The present is our only reality.'"

I wondered if I'd have to listen to this Zen shit through the whole thing, or if he'd shut up once my panties came off.

I didn't go with him. Sun-drenched beach living seemed too bright, too hopeful. Besides, he'd be just one more, and I'd be just as stuck in the sunshine as I was here in the fog. He handed me his dog-eared copy of *Zen and the Art of Motorcycle Maintenance* at the door. "Read page one thirty-four, the underlined part," he said and left me with a kiss and a couple of joints.

I sat down and flipped to the page.

You are never dedicated to something you have complete confidence in. (No one is fanatically shouting that the sun is going to rise tomorrow. They know it's going to rise tomorrow.) When people are fanatically dedicated to political or religious faiths or any other kinds of dogmas or goals, it's always because those dogmas or goals are in doubt.

So he'd known my frantic promise to myself was crap. The very words "I promise myself" convey the predicament. They set you against you—the advocate and the adversary. If you have to promise yourself, you're doomed. Tom had known this.

Now I knew it too.

Forgiveness

Unalaska hadn't even made the National Marine Fisheries list of top U.S. fishing ports a decade before, but now it was number one. Crabbing, halibut, bottom fishing brought billions of dollars and thousands of people. With no landfill, sewer system, or extra housing, the town staggered under the onslaught.

Congress had at first denied Aleuts eligibility in the statewide Native Lands Claims suit because of their high percentage of Russian blood. But the Aleuts protested and eventually won. The fully chartered Aleut Corporation was awarded 38.2 million acres and about $12 million in congressional settlements to find and rebuild a future. Suddenly there was a new pride in being Aleut.

Although by the mid-1980s only 10 percent of the population was Aleut, this remnant had begun to reclaim its past. They had taken control of their lands, reached back into memories for pieces of their culture. Old women taught the young to form grasses into famously delicate baskets. Those who could still speak their language taught those who knew only English. The old ways were taught by modern means, in night classes at the public school. Money for an Aleutian museum was gathered, repairs for the church planned. An Aleut renaissance had begun.

* * *

Liz shook her head when Les placed the usual rum-and-Coke in front of her. "Only Coke," she said, staring at the drink. He poured it out and refilled the glass with straight soda. She pushed her lower back forward, hardening her resolve with her posture. She sipped. Too sweet, without the rum.

She watched the berdache work, his face still telling the story she had heard of the beating. She had been told of how berdache lived before the Russians came. Sometimes a baby boy was born, especially pretty and showing feminine ways. These boys were not trained as men, but to skin hides, sew, prepare meals. Trained to be wives. Liz watched him washing glasses in the sink with efficient twisting wrists. She cackled behind the cloud of her smoke.

"What are you laughing at?" Les glanced up, his earring catching light.

"You will make a fine wife someday."

Les grinned and turned to take an order. Liz watched him reach for a bottle of rum, her eyes an eagle's talon on the glass. She turned her head. She was not here to drink.

Not this time. Liz had a job to do. She waited for Blondie to show.

She feared for the white girl, who had no way of knowing what she was messing with. Liz thought of the first time she'd entered the cave, touched the Dry Ones. She swallowed, eyes darting to the glass rows behind the bar. If she'd known how they would curse her, layer her future in guilt and degradation, would she still have touched, have eaten? It was a question Liz had never been able to answer.

Blondie came in just behind a group of outsiders, her hair pulled into a pony's tail. Liz felt it immediately. Like a birth cord, unsevered and pulled tight, their connection stretched across the bar. She yanked, and Blondie's eyes jerked to hers then fell away.

The ache from her center, the point of attachment, bled into her. Drowned her resolve. She signaled for a rum and Coke with a nod. This would be the last, she told herself as Les slid the drink before her. She set the glass down between sips. Slow. She focused on what she'd been sent to do.

* * *

"She's been to the cave," Anna had said that afternoon when they met with Ida and Bellie at the bookstore. "She came in to ask for books on the Dry Ones. I sent her away."

"What could she know?" Bellie said. "She's been to the caves. So?"

"She knows Nicholas is dead; she knows we wanted him dead," Ida said. "If she's not suspicious, she is as dumb as she looks."

"She's not dumb," Bellie said.

Ida nodded. "We agree."

Liz scanned the walls. Anna had moved her favorite sketch, but Liz found it on the wall behind the counter. She pulled in the image again, the young woman, striped with black marks, studded with bone, the sharp cut of her bangs high on her forehead, those eyes, hard and lost, the secret in her half-smile. Liz imagined her as the first, this woman-girl, looking past whoever sketched her. She believed she could see the memory of the first act in those eyes, see the lingering taste of the fat in the way the girl held her mouth, so tight, yet drifting at the edges with a hint of sweetness. Two hundred fifty years, and no one had known but them.

Liz had watched the blond woman from the start. She'd seen the bead lying flat on her white skin. She'd seen her eyes change. Now when Blondie helped her to a cab at night, Liz sensed knowledge in her hands. They all thought she was too drunk to feel anything, know anything. But she did.

Liz turned away from the picture, back to Ida and Anna.

"She can't stay," Ida said. "What is suspicion will grow. She doesn't belong here."

"She doesn't know where she belongs," Liz replied.

Bellie pushed herself from the wall she'd been leaning against, and Liz smiled, remembering her own first months after being told. The excitement, the hope, the fears all tossing about inside. She could feel the same fresh power and confusion in the girl.

"Then we have to tell her," Bellie said.

"What is it you want to tell her, girl?" Ida's words came flying with spittle, stinging. "What would you have her know?"

"We have to tell her something," Bellie shot back. "She's got to have a reason to stay away from the caves. Go back where she belongs."

Liz felt the snarl of loyalties in Bellie. She admired the girl, foolish as she was. Few people would have dared oppose Ida.

Liz watched Ida's thoughts pulling upon one another. Ida shook her head. "You have become too friendly with her. What did I tell you about this?" Ida stared Bellie down. "Sure, tell her about all the others. Do you keep count? Five. Six. Then the others on the boat for me. Ten, for me."

Auburn hair. Curled on the floor at Liz's feet in the candle's dancing shadow. The image, remembered, absorbed the room. Even after all the others, this was the death her guilt had woven itself through until it became the warp that shaped everything else. If she could just warn Blondie away from this destruction, she could redeem some small part of herself. The sacrifice that brings reprieve. "We have to tell her enough, enough to warn her what will happen if she uses the Dry Ones."

"Nothing happens," Anna said. "There is no curse. You are just a drunk." Anna spoke with the venom of denial. Liz could have told her what she saw, that the curse had claimed Anna in a different way. She'd been cut in half. The part that had gone away to college and returned, hoping to teach the white people who her people had been, their skill, tenderness, courage, and how they had been destroyed with guns, disease, rape, contempt. The other part despising these same people whose ancestors had changed everything and despising herself for mingling with them, for desiring them. Her hate clung to the room, and even the curious outsiders often felt it when they stopped by for a book or a basket. But Liz didn't say any of this. Anna's two halves joined at a fresh scab, and Liz did not want to expose her wounds.

She wanted a drink.

"I want her off the island," Anna said. "I don't care how."

Liz watched Ida's face, so different from the face she had known as a child. That face had been trustworthy, flexible. This face was dangerous, immutable. Even after all these years, she still made the difficult decisions. Ida gazed out the window facing the bay. A weeping fog swirled, wind driven like curls over the water.

When she turned back around, Liz saw the decision in her face. "You will watch her tonight. See how far she has gone. From this we will know how much to tell her." Ida's wrinkled face tightened like a cat's cradle stretched between fingers. "Then we will make sure she leaves."

Liz nodded, already feeling the comfort of her stool and a full glass under her hand.

"Don't drink. This will not be easy." At Ida's last words, the imagined glass broke in her hand.

"And if she won't go?" Anna asked.

"She will," Bellie said.

"And if you are wrong?"

No one answered.

It did not matter now. Liz drank another and another. The eyes with which she watched Blondie grew heavy, twisting her vision. Already, the white girl didn't laugh as much, didn't brag through her body the way she had. And Liz felt the eyes watching her. She had taken the fat.

Liz was as sure of this as of anything.

She shoved the bathroom door open. She slid the metal tube from the toilet paper holder and wrote. Just one word: *Beware*.

When she came to, the smell of piss made her smile with the comfort of routine.

"Liz, time to go." She heard Blondie's voice and felt her bend near. She opened her eyes as Blondie trapped her hands before lifting her sagging body. Liz felt the cord, shortened now with their nearness, and held it tight with her mind. Just one thought, that's all she needed. She pulled the cord to stop the spinning in her head.

"You been somewhere you don't belong, Blondie." Then the cord went slack as the bathroom swirled again. Dizzy. She felt the laugh rising, not wanting it to, but it came and choked with the vomit that followed. The hands that lifted and guided her outside were tender in some way Liz could feel through the pain.

It was this tenderness that perverted her vision. She touched the white girl's auburn hair. "Forgive me?"

a pleasant elevation

'd been riding the old war roads back into the hills, not expecting or looking for anything. My hands were so pink and scoured from the wind, I stopped into the Elbow Room before riding back home.

Something was off.

A crowd of men pressed to the bar, their conversation thick and fast.

"Shhhhh!" Marge is one of the few people who can shout this phoneme. "It's on."

She turned up the volume on the radio.

"The Coast Guard has issued a tsunami warning for the following islands: Attu, Adak, Atka, Umnak, Unalaska, Akutan, Unimak, and along Bristol Bay. An eight-point-five quake struck the north Kamchatka Peninsula at four P.M. The wave, believed to be traveling at up to four hundred knots per hour, could reach Attu by five P.M., Adak by five-thirty P.M., Unalaska by six P.M., and the mainland by seven P.M. All residents of communities on the north and west sides of the Aleutians and Bristol Bay must move to high ground immediately until the Coast Guard issues an expiration. Again all communities including Atka, Nikolski, Unalaska, Akutan, False Pass—"

Marge twisted off the radio.

We had just under two hours. Immediately the room was buzzing.

Carl headed for the door without a word. Two guys left together talking about getting to the boat. Marge ordered someone to stop by her house and pick up something. She yelled at another guy to stop by the store. A man was counting out something on his fingers. Another left to find his wife and son, who were out clam digging.

I would have started to panic, but none of the hubbub felt like the first waves of hysteria. I tried to catch Marge's eye to ask her what was going on, but she'd picked up the phone and started giving orders. I caught only bits and pieces. "Get someone to drive over to. . . . Find out who's got. . . . Call Leslie and see if. . . . Fuck, who had the . . . last time. . . ."

I decided to sit back and finish my whiskey sour and try to pick up what I could. Two of the dogs, which had followed their owners into the bar, started to fight. They went at each other the husky way, darting in, dancing back, then coming together in a snarl, intent on getting at each other's throats. When they got too loud, someone kicked one in the ribs. The dog yelped and slunk to the corner while the other dog stalked about, every inch the victor.

I visited the head just to see if Ida had gotten around to cleaning up Liz's last message. It was still there. Suddenly that single word—*Beware*—took on greater significance. Had Liz know about the tsunami? Had she been warning someone? Me? The way she'd looked at me last night and what she'd said. Forgive me. I stroked my fingertips over her words. And I felt that same flood of tenderness toward her I had last night. I did not want these feelings, and I could not forgive her.

I should have gone with Tom. That's what I kept thinking, feeling. I didn't have to be here, deserted, facing a tidal wave, powerless. I could be on a wholly different kind of beach, tucked into a wholly different kind of life. Instead of here, caressing graffiti in a shabby bathroom, in a feral bar, on an unsheltered island.

I washed my hands, more to slough off those feelings of regret than to rid myself of Elbow Room toilet germs, and headed back to my bar stool.

Marge hung up the phone and opened the back door. Two pickups had backed up to it, and as soon as the door swung open, three guys began loading the bar's cases of liquor and beer. I looked out the big window. Several boats had untied from the docks and were headed full steam out of the bay.

About twenty minutes after the warning, the Elbow Room was empty. Marge was counting out the till.

"What's going on?"

Marge looked at me like I'd asked her what color panties she had on. She lit a cigarette. "Tsunami party," she said and stuffed the money into a cash box. "You haven't been here for one yet, have ya?"

I shook my head.

"You're in for some fun." She flicked off the lights. "Come on. You can follow me up."

We walked outside, and she locked the back door.

"We get these every so often, and used to be everybody got shit scared, ran around, talking shit." Marge climbed in her truck and leaned out the window. "So 'bout ten years ago, someone up on Tsunami Hill, 'course it wasn't called that before, decides, 'Fuck it. Let's make a party.' So everyone heads up the hill, brings whatever's in the freezer. We cook a shitload of stuff, clean out the bar's storeroom, and watch for the wave."

I started my bike and followed Marge, who was following a gray van. We crossed the channel and turned off to the left up a gentle hill. The incline under my wheels felt good, safe. Until I realized that this hill was *the* hill, Tsunami Hill. Now Unalaska has hills and mountains, and a lot of them have roads right up to the tops, thanks to the military. But this was the barest of hills. A mound really.

Three houses sat atop. Trucks and vans had filled all the driveways and were lining up along the road. Several dogs barked back and forth between truck beds. Marge threaded through and pulled right up on the tufts of wild grass that served as lawn. I parked behind her. She slammed the door, yelling at a woman walking by as she got out, "Where's the boys with the bar load?"

The woman pointed toward a group of people standing over a just-smoking fire pit. I'd say there were probably fifty people milling about, some busy with food or firewood. And more were coming every minute. I ran straight to the edge of the mound overlooking the bay. It was steep here, sliced into cliff eons ago when the ocean had been braver. I peered over the side. We must have been all of six stories up. The water lay a quarter mile away. On the other side, I could see the airport runway, which ran between the water and a cliff. The ocean here was farther away, maybe half a mile, but still only sixty feet lower.

Did the radio report mention how big the wave might be? I tried to remember everything I knew about tsunamis. How high did they get? Can you see them coming? What happens when they hit shore? After several minutes of brain wracking, I realized I knew nothing more than that a tsunami was a big wave.

"Hey." Bellie walked toward me on those boots with the wayward heel. She had a beer in one hand and a joint in the other. She handed me the joint.

I took two long tokes. That's when I noticed the absence of wind. The smoke I exhaled just clouded around my face. I stepped to the side to evade it.

"This doesn't seem like the best place to have a tsunami party," I said, handing the joint back to her.

"Why not?"

"Well, look," I said, gesturing at the beach not far below. "It's got to be one of the lowest hills in town."

She looked at me funny. "You can see way out both bays. You can see the wave coming for like two miles. If it comes, it won't get more than twenty feet high."

"How do you know?"

She shrugged.

"So this whole find-high-ground stuff is about getting a good view of the destruction."

She shrugged.

I looked around. Half the island was up here. Sure it was the hanging-out-in-bars, who-the-fuck-cares crowd. But some of them had reached middle age alive. I decided to try not to worry.

"Follow me." Bellie started toward the trucks lining the road. We stopped at a gray, newish truck with a HIGHLINER, INC. sign painted on the side panels. Bellie opened the passenger door and we squeezed in. She pulled out a Ziploc of powder from the glove compartment, then rummaged around for a tape. She found a new Talking Heads and shoved it into the player. A mirror materialized, and Bellie had four lines laid out in a minute. We snorted two lines each.

I leaned back in the seat, closed my eyes, and listened to David

Byrne sing. Bellie and I joined him in the chorus. "'The world was moving and she was right there with it and she was. The world was moving she was floating above it and she was.'"

We both knew scattered phrases of the rest and sang along until the end. Bellie shut off the player. "Know what that song's about?"

I shook my head.

"A dead girl. That's what they never say, 'And she was—dead.'"

I thought about this for a minute, replaying various lines and decided it could be true. This was not a song I wanted playing through my head. Now I couldn't get it out.

"Why the fuck are you playing me a song about dead girls? Right now, of all times."

Bellie turned her whole body toward me on the seat. "I just want you to think more. Think about what you're doing here."

Her fingers were fiddling with her birthmark again, and I suddenly realized that that scared the shit out of me more than the approaching tidal wave.

A van eked its way between the truck and the line of vehicles on the other side of the road. Mary was driving. She waved. I saw Ida, Anna, and Mary's sister along with several kids, noses pressed to the glass, inside.

Bellie waved her Baggie of coke in front of me. "You want to take some?"

"I want to know what the fuck you're talking about," I said, rummaging through my purse for the silver vial I'd found but not yet used.

She took it. "Nice."

"I found it on the floor at the bar."

Bellie filled it half full. One can't be too generous, even with some temporary guy's coke. "We'll talk about it later, okay. I need a drink."

I stuffed the vial in my pocket and followed Bellie over to the fire. It was huge now, bonfire size, the smoke rising straight into a light gray sky.

"What time is it?" a woman asked.

"Going on five."

A rowdy whoop erupted, followed by a chant. "One hour to go. One hour to go."

Someone asked if anyone had heard from the weather station at Attu. The wave would have passed by there already.

"I heard the Attu weather station wasn't responding."

It got quiet for a moment.

"You don't know what the fuck you're talking about," another man said.

"No wind," a woman said, and everyone turned to feel for moving air. "It's not good," she added.

Just then I heard the tires of a truck skittering rocks and stopping in a spray of gravel. The driver parked dead center in the narrow road, blocking everyone. The four HiTide babes nearly fell out the doors. They headed for the fire, doing that tiptoeing walk that drunken women in heeled boots, holding drinks, have to master.

Honey reached the group first. "Hey," she yelled. "What's goin' on?"

Jill and the other two came up beside her. One yelled something about "party" and "fuckin'." The others hollered in agreement.

The arrival of the fake blondes set me on edge even more. That song kept playing in my head—flickering the image of a dead girl "joining the world of missing persons." I pictured the scene if a big wave did obliterate Tsunami Hill. They'd find the bodies all rolled together at the base, bottles of beer wedged under an arm here, an angled neck there. I'd end up heaped with Honey, Jill, and the others, tossed in with the fake blondes in death. My gray face would be pressed into Honey's gray-green neck, our hair having spun together in the pools of water left behind. And no one would know the difference. The vision's clarity, layered with death colors and smells, startled me. I decided to try to keep space between us to lower the odds.

I headed toward one of the three houses, from which people kept coming and going, stopping by the stack of booze boxes to fill a paper cup with tequila.

Inside several women were buzzing around the kitchen. Little Liz sat heavy on a stuffed rocking chair in the living room, drinking from a Rainier can. Seeing her there froze me for a moment. I could still feel her hand stroking my hair and hear her broken voice asking for forgiveness. I shivered. They were all three here. I hadn't seen them together since the funeral. The memory of the cave stuck in my head like wet hands on frozen steel, an attachment that would only be broken by peeling skin.

Her eyes tracked me as I walked by. I pretended to focus on not spilling any tequila. Les was cutting potatoes at the kitchen island. I set my cup on the counter across from him and leaned against it.

"You made it," he said.

"I followed Marge."

"So what do you think?" He grinned and threw a handful of potato quarters in a pot.

"I think this is the absolute worst place to wait for a tidal wave on the whole island."

"The view is great."

"So I've heard."

He laughed.

"What happens to the boats that are out?"

"Nothing. Usually they don't even feel it. Wave isn't dangerous until it hits shallow water. The ferry was supposed to come in tonight. It'll wait out in the open." Les stopped cutting. "You worried about our pretty boy? He's probably already in Seattle by now. Mighty white of you, cutting him loose for me, by the way."

"He cut me loose."

Les looked at me. "Hey." He knocked me sideways with a hip shot. "Men come and go. Couple of veterans like us know that."

I nodded.

Les picked up my cup and downed the rest of the tequila. "Refill."

I rolled my eyes and went back outside to the liquor stack. I brought two cups back, set one down for Les, and headed to the cliff side again. As I passed Liz, I thought I heard her whisper something, but when I turned she was gazing at her beer can.

The air was heavy in its stillness. The sun was sinking, the land cooling faster than the water, and still no wind. I shivered and stared out at the bay. Only half an hour to go.

I stayed there alone, my hair hanging straight in the calm. About fifteen minutes later, people started coming over. By ten to six, everyone was standing along the edge of the hill, gazing toward the mouth of the bay. In every hand was a beer or a cup. Most of the other hands held cigarettes or joints.

Something ominous gathered in my chest, and I fumbled a cigarette out with shaky fingers. I sucked in big gobs of nicotine, but the thing wouldn't stop. It grew until I could feel it in my mouth. The people lining the hill looked like Indians in those western movies, suddenly appearing at the rims of canyons, all rigid and ordered. We waited.

At 6:05 someone said, "It ain't coming." A few people dropped back to the fire, passed around food. I stayed, eyes fixed on the horizon. The thing in me was too heavy to move. I wasn't going to die. By 6:30 it was dark, and I was the only Indian left on the cliffs.

Bellie came up beside me. "The Coast Guard canceled the warning," she said quietly. "Nothing's going to happen."

"Why?"

"If the wave doesn't come straight at the opening of the bay, it passes right by. Can't get in. Most of the warnings are like that."

"And nobody could tell me that before?"

Bellie started back toward the fire.

When I didn't follow, Bellie came back. She took my hand and pulled me. "Come and eat."

I piled my plate high with macaroni salad, salmon steaks, *alodiks* bread, and roast corn like everyone else and found an unoccupied folding chair. The talk was all tsunami.

"I was in Anchorage when the '64 earthquake hit," a man I didn't know was saying. "Quake didn't get but ten of them, the other hundred-plus got taken by the wave."

"I seen the suck before a wave once out at Cold Bay," a woman said. "The way the water just backs out of the bay gives you the creeps."

I'd just bitten into an ear of not-quite-done corn when he came over. His red hair was tied in a long ponytail, frayed like rope ends. He was big and young, probably midtwenties. He had on karate gi pants, stained with yellow blotches and worn thin. I didn't like him at first. Never trust a man who wears karate pants to social events. I'm not sure what message he's trying to send, but it isn't good.

"Hey, babe," he said, crouching on the ground beside my chair. His hand slid across my thigh, nearly upsetting my paper plate.

I looked at his hand. "Hey, babe?"

He smiled, eyes half closed in that oblivious, basking stage of inebriation. "You look too good to be all alone."

I smiled. He wasn't bad looking. With a shower and jeans, he might even reach the handsome range. And he was right—I shouldn't be alone. It brought up too many uncertainties. I had no idea what I was going to do next, where to go, who to be. I was alone with no glimmer of companionship on the horizon. Except him. He was not a sparkling glimmer but was smack in front of me with a hand on my thigh. "Maybe you're right," I said.

And when he grinned and his hand traced a line along my thigh I felt the power rush. He desired me. I'd missed this—this sense of mastery and control. Now it expanded in me, squeezing out silly promises. I noticed his broad shoulders and the firm muscles squaring his jaw. He wanted me, and it made him look good.

"Sure I am." He leaned a bit too far back on his heels and nearly toppled my chair righting himself. "So what're you doing anyway?"

"Just hanging out with the rest of the tsunami party crowd."

"Tsuwhat?"

"The tidal wave? The reason we're all up here?" He was even more wasted than he appeared, which was tough.

"Don't know about that. I was partying with them," he said, rolling his head toward the clump of HiTide chicks across the fire. "I was just coming along, you know."

I glanced at them, watching our interaction and giggling. Jill raised her glass in my direction with a catty smile.

Shit. I looked back at gi boy. They'd turned him on to me. Tossed him my way. Here's one for you, Elbow Room bitch. Here's where you're headed. Take that. Suddenly I missed being alone. Whatever nasty familiar little trip I'd been about to take, collapsed. I was done. With him. With them. All of them.

I picked up his hand, which had crawled to my inner thigh, and replaced it on his own leg. "You know I'm not that lonely after all. Tell your friends I said 'fuck you.'" I smiled as I said it.

"Naw," he said in that male crooning way. "I already talked to them. They told me about you."

That's when I knew something more was going on here than a pickup attempt spurred by vengeful coke-whores. His approach wasn't tinged with the possibility of failure.

This guy was sure.

I smiled at him. "I know I'll regret it the rest of my life, but I'm gonna pass."

By this time, he was leaning into me, hand on my thigh again. I pressed him away. He reached out to keep from falling, spilling his drink.

When he'd righted himself, he was disoriented. "Shit. What do you want? I got the blow right here."

My eyes shot to the HiTide chicks. Sure enough Jill was whispering to Honey and giggling.

I'd crossed some line with them, and now they were paying me back. It could have been anything—bringing Les to the beach party, failing to console Jill at the HiTide when she'd broken down, or maybe they just hate me on principle like I hated them.

I'd never know for sure, and right now I had a large, drunk fisherman draped over me, certain I was a coke-whore in need.

"Listen, I don't know what they told you, but I don't put out for coke. I've got a boyfriend."

I ached when I said it. Because I missed him. Thad had been too good for me, and staring at this asshole reminded me how undeserving I'd been. And how lucky. I realized that I detested the HiTide whores because they had something I didn't—clarity. Sure, they were sluts, but honest sluts. I wasn't trading sex for blow; I traded sex for a direction. A man with a plan. And I never let them know it was only temporary and only based on need.

I hate using the boyfriend line, but it often works, and I felt cornered. Of course, he didn't hear a word.

He leaned on me, wrapping his arm across my hips. A hand slid under my ass.

He half-fell, half-collapsed on the chair when I wiggled out from under him and stood up. "You just sit here and relax," I said. "I've got to use the bathroom." Usually I would have handled this a little better. But my reserves had run out. I'd half believed I was going to die, and half feared I was going to continue living broken promise to broken promise. I stepped over him and went straight toward the house, thinking if he couldn't see me, he'd forget me.

Inside, the lights were on but nobody was there. The place felt odd after all the bustle before. So quiet without people, without the muted rush of wind at the roof and windows. I sat down on the recliner Liz had occupied and lit a cigarette. I was thinking about Thad and realizing what it would really mean to be alone, not just temporarily but for a good long time, when I heard the door bang open.

"There you are," he said, all friendly and seductive. He came clomping toward me, the door banging shut behind him. He leaned over the recliner, a hand on each armrest, and started bragging about how good he was at giving head as he eyed my crotch.

I was just too tired to talk my way out of this. Besides he was drunk, and all I needed was to get to the door. I ducked under his arm and took two steps before I felt him wrap me from behind.

"Hey, hey, not so fast," he said, chuckling. He held me in a grotesque slow dance step for a couple beats, then turned me around.

His body draped me, no eye contact, just grabby, heaviness. I could feel it through my clothes, through my skin. Fear banged down my back and legs. By the time it rebounded to my brain it was something else entirely. It was anger. I didn't want to do this. I didn't want to have to ease out of it. I was quite simply and purely pissed.

I tried to knee him in the groin but missed and got his thigh. We swayed briefly then crashed back against a wall. His lips and tongue were slathering my neck while one hand groped my nether regions.

I backed my fist up the few inches I could and hit him in the trachea with a jab.

It wasn't hard enough.

He stepped back. His brow crunched. "You don't gotta to be like that. What're you doing that for?"

He grabbed a fistful of my hair and banged me back against the wall. It didn't hurt really, but it jarred me.

I breathed deep, gathered concentration while he fumbled his hand up my T-shirt. I could feel the ridged cracks on his fingers from the cold water and rough work. He was drunk, and a break was all I needed. I shuffled through my options—something that would back him off.

I nailed him in the jaw with an elbow uppercut at the same time my boot dug into his shin.

He bent to grab hold of his leg and I tried to step by. Too slow. He caught my leg and I went down on my ass.

I had escalated. This should have been an easy one. Talk. Talk. Nice. Nice. Kiss. Kiss. Just a minute. Wait for me. And I'm gone. But, no. I'd had to go and prove something. Make it a battle I could well lose. It wasn't just him. It was all the guys who'd groped. It was all the men I'd fucked, willingly enough, but only because I had nothing better in mind. I was sick of taking it, sick of needing it. I wanted to scream. I wanted to hurt someone. I wanted to be free of the consequence of being rational.

"Fuckin' bitch." He landed on me, a knee on each side of my hips as his fist drove toward my face.

I twisted my neck to take it on the side of my head. His fist hit just above my left cheek, and I felt the thud of it in my brain. The edges of my vision went brown, but I saw the door open and Carl step in.

Carl and I looked at each other—me on the dirty carpet, Carl by the open door.

He didn't say anything. No warning. He was just on the guy. Carl pulled him up, then sank a fist into his stomach. I scrambled up, slightly unsteady.

"Get out," Carl said.

I hesitated. Thoughts flickered quick as a strobe light. Would Carl stop if I asked? Did I want him to? All my yelling and screaming hadn't made a difference before. I had been shaking with fear, revulsion that time. This time I was afraid too, but a sweet fear, the kind that makes your mouth water. A fear cool with intention.

Was it any different? My hands or Carl's? Wouldn't it feel just as good?

I turned toward the door. With each thud of Carl's fists, my ears tightened, but I didn't look back. I stepped onto the porch to see a group of men rush toward me. They'd heard the fight sounds, this posse coming to see blood, coming to the rescue. The enemy this time.

I felt the pinched knot of the lock between my fingers as I twisted it and the hollow weight of the door as I pulled it shut behind me and heard the lock click.

There. Take that.

They swore and pounded on the wood as I lit a cigarette and walked away from the house, back to the side of the cliff, where I'd watched for a killer wave. The still air pooled the smoke around my face, and I exhaled the next puff out the corner of my mouth. I heard an eagle scream below me, over the water. A predator, a hunter. I smiled and hid behind closed eyes, letting the air weight my lids. My fingers close over the bead around my neck.

I felt vindicated, alive, and powerful. I touched my cheek, where I could feel the swell rising—a validation of my righteous anger, the Warrior Me. I'd finally said, no. To him yes, but more importantly, to myself. I'd said I wasn't going to keep on following, and I'd carried through. I was alone, and other than a swollen cheek and a bump on the back of my head, I was okay. I was good. I had taken back the night.

The feeling lasted all of half a minute. That victorious, break-out-the-grog, beat-my-chest feeling coasted to a stop inside me. And before I could prepare or rationalize, it was gone.

In its place lay a field of anger and of blame. I covered my face with my hands, fingertips digging into the line where hair gives way to naked flesh. My anger was an anger infected by shame. The anger of a bully who's just been beaten. The anger of a whore who's just been raped. They tell us and then we tell ourselves that it's never our fault, and we know it's a lie as we repeat it like a mantra. The victim is never to blame. Never. It's always his fault. You didn't do anything wrong. You go, girl. Wear that tube top, hang with the wrong crowd. Drink ten Everclear shots at a frat party. You go, girl. Take back the night.

As I stood above that ocean on that insubstantial cliff, I stopped believing. I felt the weight of my choices, both a few moments ago and for years; I felt the wide expanse of right and wrong and the shades between. The illusion of pure and righteous victimhood slipped out of my grasp. I'd used it in all the wrong ways—my sexual power, with my tight jeans and the thrill when I knew I was wanted. But it's an amoral power—it can go either way. It had brought me down.

I'd just set up the severe beating of a man. Sure, he was an irritating, possibly even dangerous man, but just a man, who'd been misinformed, needy, drunk. I couldn't pretend shreds of culpability hadn't stuck in my hair, in the treads of my shoes. When I recognized this, it felt like drowning, all reference points submerged in gray-green, all confidence gone soggy.

And then.

It felt like freedom.

In saying I did this and this and this wrong and it got bad, enough of the fault lies with me. And so does enough of the power to do it better next time. And this power isn't shared. This one is all mine. It's all I've got. It may not always be enough, but at least it's not on loan from someone else. I felt like her in that moment, like my Aleut Mona Lisa. Like I was in charge of the future, no matter how bad the past had been and how bleak the present.

I was just feeling this possibility, this murky oozing potential that I could do everything differently, better, when I uncovered my face and opened my eyes to Liz. She stood beside me, her dark eyes turned up to mine. Beside her stood Ida and Anna.

And Bellie. Like a foretold fortune, when I saw them, I realized I had expected this. Except Bellie. I'd never expected her. All my new-born freedom turned on me, caved in to shame.

Then fear.

They were so close, too close. I could feel their breath, cutting separate paths in the stillness.

"Give me a cigarette," Liz demanded. I could still see something in her of the woman who came to my cabana at night, something of the clear-eyed guardian, the vigilant watchwoman. I handed her a cigarette, then the lighter, feeling as if each incremental movement to accomplish the exchange had been scripted, practiced many times.

I kept my eyes on the other two, on Bellie. We were too near the edge of the cliff. This cliff, so inadequate such a short time ago, now rose under my boots.

Liz lit the cigarette, exhaled, handing the lighter back to me. She smoked and looked over the dark bay for a few moments, the others beside us. The silence felt like the waiting moments before throwing yourself from a high dive, that exhilaration mixed with panic, all wrapped in knowledge that you would jump, and once you did, the descent would be uncontrollable.

It was Ida who spoke for them.

"Why do you hide your face?"

I slid my teeth against one another to keep tears back, feeling the peaks and valleys bumping along my jaw. I couldn't answer. Couldn't tell them I was ashamed of my face, my life, myself. "Fuck." It was all I could get out.

And then Ida touched me. Just the gentle laying of a hand on my arm. "Who told you to feel this shame? You have been to the cave, taken something you shouldn't."

It was a statement, but I needed to treat it as a question, something with room for explanation. "I was just following you."

"We know." The sorrow in her voice broke something, and the tears came despite my jaw-grinding resolve. "What is this you have done?"

"I was curious," I said, tasting tears at the corners of my mouth. "I wanted to know."

"So now you do," Ida said. "You have become like us."

I lifted my face to tell her she was wrong. I was nothing like her, like Liz. She put her old hand to my mouth.

"Nothing will be easy again."

The sky darkened as clouds moved in low, and a puff of air roused the grass around us for a moment, then dissipated back into the strange calm. And she told me a story. It reached back 250 years, leaped from woman to woman, and ended in the four faces before me. The faces of killers, tortured and courageous.

Five cigarettes lay on the ground between us, a measure of the time it takes to move from ignorance to understanding.

Bellie stepped closer. "You have to leave now, Brandy."

I moved back, feeling the thrust of her betrayal. "What, you're kicking me off the island? I thought we were friends."

"We are."

I stepped back again, looking at all of them as one. "Who the fuck do you think you are?"

But I knew who they were. They were the island's bouncers, and I'd just been kicked out. They were the island's executioners, and I'd just been spared.

Anna stepped forward. "You wanted to know more, and now you know more than enough."

Liz tossed her last cigarette, still burning, on the ground. "You use someone else's hands. You hold nothing in your own." She snatched my hand and held it palm up. "See? Empty."

I yanked my hand away.

"The wind is not a river. Someday it will stop." She grinned up at me with her rotting smile. "Go while it breathes."

Her last words had an edge, angry, full of meaning I unexpectedly understood. They were angry that they'd had to admit so much to set me free. Angry at the risk.

Ida, Anna, and Liz turned away and started back to the fire.

"Liz," I shouted.

She turned slowly back toward me.

"I forgive you," I said. She simply stared at me, but I saw her face drop its ugly mask. Her eyelids lowered, squeezing forth a tear, then she was gone.

Bellie remained beside me for a moment. "Maybe I was wrong, what I said when you first came. Maybe you did belong here for a while." She turned and left me too.

The wind blew up into her place, hitting my face in a sudden gust. It came on hard, flipping paper plates out of hands, sending the fire low then high. People yelled and ran inside. The cigarette blew out of my hand.

Fists clenched, hair blown straight back, I stood and opened my mouth to yell, to force them to hear how wrong they were about me, how right they were about me, how I hated them, how my gratitude felt like gravel tearing across bare knees. "You didn't banish me. You know that? I knew it before. I knew your fucking weird island wasn't mine. You know that? Do you hear me?" These thoughts formed into words, but these words never formed into sounds because I had swallowed the wind.

Diaspora

D utch Harbor in the late 1960s was a world in waiting. It had been the center of the fur trade, a gold rush supply route, a military outpost. Now it was all but forgotten. But even a forgotten place has its purpose. The Department of Defense had noticed this remote outpost. On October 18, 1965, it tested an underground eighty-kiloton hydrogen bomb, four times more powerful than those dropped on Japan, off the coast of Amchitka Island at the western end of the Chain. Two larger bombs would be tested in the next six years, despite Alaskan protests. As an Atomic Energy Commission spokesman put it, "No realistic alternative is believed to exist anywhere else on American soil."

Meanwhile most of the military installments—the submarine installations, the airfields, the bases, the radio and weather stations—along the Chain had been closed, leaving polluted bays and salmon streams, and hundreds of abandoned warehouses, barracks, cabanas, and Quonset huts along the beaches and into the hills. With this exodus of jobs and the decline in subsistence sea mammals and fish, an economic depression settled among the islands. After their internment, many Aleuts had not returned, and those that did abandoned their small villages for the comparatively bustling town of Unalaska. About 350 people lived in homes scattered among the debris of war.

Poverty and alcohol reigned in many families. Few were strong enough

to fight the forces consuming what was left of a people. Children were
born with fetal alcohol syndrome, many were neglected, some abused.
One small group of women tried to keep the promise of a future alive for
yet another generation. The Sisterhood of the Russian Orthodox Church
dedicated themselves to delivering aid to the remnants.

Liz let the door swing shut behind her. She counted the loaves of
bread, jars of peanut butter, cans of beans and vegetables the family
would need. Four children under ten, the grandmother, the mother.
She added these needs to the list she kept in her head. Tomorrow she
would collect what she could from those who had enough and see how
far the supplies would stretch.

She was thirty that year and one of the most prominent women in
Unalaska Village. She and her mother's friend Ida belonged to the Sisterhood of the Orthodox Church of the Holy Ascension of Christ. She
and the six other most active members of the Sisters held this town together, begging from the poor and giving to the poorer. It's an old
story—upon the often stooped shoulders of old women falls the burden of a crumbling culture. The anthropologists and sociologists say
it's because the men lose their protector roles in the first clashes and
their provider roles in the invasion. They are no longer equipped to rescue anyone. But the women remain caretakers, they remain mothers.
With their roles intact, they retain their strength. Liz knew nothing of
the theories, but she believed that everything, the future and how the
past would be remembered, depended on the Sisters and on her.

Walking the four muddy blocks to Ida's house, Liz calculated supplies, counted needs. She bent to pick up a candy wrapper that stuck
in the mud along the road. The wind had not blown for two days now.
In the strange calm, Liz had grown more uneasy. "It is unhealthy
weather," men muttered to one another at the post office when they
picked up the weekly mail delivery. "It is unhealthy weather," women
whispered as they passed each other in the narrow aisles of canned
sardines and pilot bread at the store. "It is unhealthy weather," they
said as they sat with a bottle on the beach at low tide. "It is unhealthy
weather," Liz said now as she knocked on Ida's door.

Ida was waiting in the kitchen, her hair tucked under the handkerchief married women always wore, a teapot warming on the stove, her great-granddaughter playing with pot lids. Liz sat down at the table and drew in the spices as Ida poured hot water over dark leaves in a strainer. She waited.

Ida asked about the families Liz had visited that day. She asked about supplies. They discussed the charity dance they were planning when the next Coast Guard vessel docked. When all the small things had been discussed, Ida paused to stir another lump of sugar into her tea. "Belinda, go see what Grandma has for you in her sewing basket," Ida said. The six-year-old jumped up, scattering pot lids from her lap, and skipped into the back room.

"Four more," Ida said, when the girl was gone.

Liz closed her eyes. "Who?"

"Prokopeuff's three children. And Kathy's new baby."

"Do we have anyone left?"

Ida shook her head. "Busy Mouth rejected the Malkins. Said their place was too small and dirty. Said the oil stove sent too much grease smoke through the house."

In the last year, sixteen children had been taken from their homes by Miss Holton, a state social worker flown out from Juneau to see what could be done about "the Aleut problem." The Sisters had found a home for only one. Fifteen children had been sent to foster care on the mainland. White homes among trees, far from the ocean. Liz knew in her soul these children would never return. She felt the losses like they were her own. So few remained. Their disappearance was like the water sucked offshore before a tidal wave. The wave that would follow in the next generation, shrunken and misshapen by alcohol and poverty and loss, would take them all.

"This storm cannot be weathered," Liz said, setting her tea down.

Liz was not given to easy despair. She had never let such words into the open before. Yes, she had thought them—that no solution existed, that she and the other women were patching holes in a boat with no bottom. But she had not said them before.

It marked the turning of her heart.

Ida waited. "We meet with Busy Mouth this evening. We'll see."

As Liz was leaving a few minutes later, Ida stopped her at the door with a brief touch. Liz knew her mother's old friend wanted to give her hope, something to hold. Ida looked into Liz's eyes, an uncommon gesture. "The wind is not a river," she said. "This too will stop someday." It was a common proverb that Liz had heard others say in these bitter times. But Ida's next words were not. "There are other ways," she said, "if these do not work."

A sudden heat warmed Liz's chest. A flare that reached into the shadowed part of her brain, the part that held vague suspicion, an old knowledge her mother had almost spoken of the day she died. Irene had held her daughter's hand. "Lizzy, I must tell you something heavier than the rocks and sands." Liz, just twenty, and not yet willing to lose again, had shushed her mother. "You are too weak. Rest now. We will have time when you are better." But they hadn't. Liz wondered if she had stopped her mother's words as much out of concern for her weakness as out of fear of what those words would be, for she had known for many years that her mother held a secret.

Then the flare was gone. Ida's eyes fell to the floor and her hand left Liz's arm. The door closed.

The village was dark and quiet as the women walked to Anna's. Without wind, the town felt like it was waiting for something, Liz thought. She noticed that Ida kept looking behind her at the stretch of gray-framed buildings between the beach and the river. Anna lived in a two-house home. The war had left Unalaska one resource—wood in the form of hundreds of former military buildings. People had dragged many of them together, cutting passages between them to make for livable homes. Anna's was right along the beach road, and Liz glanced back at the flat ocean before she entered. She and Ida drew chairs around Anna's metal and Formica table, strewn with tea and *alodiks*. Miss Holton was already there, her binder opened on the pink and yellow mottled tabletop. She picked up a pencil and tapped its tip on a lined page.

"I must tell you, I don't believe I have any options right now." She sucked on the eraser end of her pencil. She looked at the three women seated around her, then quickly withdrew the fleshy eraser from her mouth and set the pencil down. Her fingernails, trimmed and bare, tapped at the thin handle of her teacup. Her auburn hair, curled in waves, slid across the shoulders of her pressed navy dress. A row of white rickrack edged her collarbone in tiny teeth. Even sitting, she rose above the small Aleut women. Liz wondered if she had any awareness of how awkward she was, how ugly, how out of place.

She had answered a newspaper ad for social workers in bush Alaska. Fresh out of Biola College in Southern California, she had been eager for the job. For the adventure, certainly, but it was more than that. She wanted to make a difference. She wanted every child to have what she had taken for granted—a working father, doting mother, grass in the backyard, a swing set, twelve years of public education. She'd been appalled to learn that Unalaska had only four teachers, most of whom fled after putting in a year on this forlorn island. She'd been appalled that any student who wanted more than an eighth grade education had to travel to boarding schools in Sitka or Oregon. She'd been appalled that so few teens chose to continue their education and that so few parents forced them to.

As she looked at the women around her, she was again appalled that they could not understand what was happening to their children. Many ran about in dirty clothes and weren't fed with any regularity. The Aleut custom of extended relatives watching one another's children often meant that nobody was watching them. Meanwhile husbands and wives were drinking and fighting, and grandparents were trying to feed their grandchildren when they hardly had enough for themselves. The "Aleut Problem," she had decided, could only be fixed by creating a new generation, educated and acclimated to a better way of life.

"I know you have tried," she told the women, "but really it's better this way. You'll see."

Anna shook her head. "We will find the homes you require. There are others who will come forward." Anna set her teacup carefully in its saucer. "I have written to Juneau. I've told them we can care for our own children. That the rules can be changed so we can keep our children. We need to wait for their response."

Miss Holton winced. She pursed her lips just so for a soundless drink from her cup. She reached for Anna's forearm and patted it three quick times. "Now, Anna, we've discussed this all before. The state is not going to further endanger children to allow for native customs. Just because you've been to college outside doesn't mean you understand what is best for the children."

"Several good families have offered," Ida cut in.

"You know these people won't do." Miss Holton sighed. She flipped through her notebook, unlatching its rings to pull out a sheet of paper. She handed it to Ida. "I've shown you the guidelines before. I don't know why you persist in bringing me families that don't even begin to meet these requirements."

The faces of the three women remained blank. Miss Holton sighed again. "Look here," she said, pointing to a line of text. "Right here. It says, 'Prospective families must be able to provide each child with a safe and stable home.' The last family you gave me all slept in one room. That simply isn't a stable home. Where did you think they were going to put the two foster children?"

Again silence. At last Liz said, "The Malkins are a good family. Their little ones go to school, eat, wash. They sleep in one room. Our homes are small. The children like sleeping together."

"Now, Lizzy, I know you people are used to living in small spaces and sharing rooms, but times have changed. Alaska has been a real state for more than ten years. Your people have to start behaving like American citizens. You can't keep doing things like you've done them in the past."

"Two more families will be found," Liz said, "with big houses." Her mouth twisted at the edges. "A week is needed."

"I'm sorry, but no. I don't have a week. I've made arrangements for the four children to fly out on Friday. We've identified a home in Seattle."

Even Miss Holton felt the dark rage around the table. It poured from the three women who did not speak but could not hold it back from their eyes and the flare of their nostrils.

"I know this is hard for you," she said, her voice warm with her conviction and sympathy. "But you have to see that this is for the best. These children will be better off on the mainland. What schooling do they get here? What future do they have? You have to put the children first. When will you learn that?"

She looked at Liz the longest. The two women were not far apart in age, and Miss Holton believed if any of them could be made to understand, it would be Liz.

But Liz refused to look up from her tea. Her hands remained still in a circle around the cup. It was not the first time she had heard such talk, and she felt the expectation Big Mouth placed upon her. It baffled her. Liz did not understand the way these white people thought. How could sending children away from home, from their people, ever be best? How could they not see to the next generation when so few would remain? How could a bedroom help a child whose people were drowning? Did one child mean more than the people to whom that child was born?

She did not ask Busy Mouth these questions. Nor did Anna or Ida. The answers never made sense.

A day later Liz sat near the stove in Rita Katovich's kitchen. She had been there two hours already. Rita had lost her husband last fall in a fishing accident. Her children were nearly grown and only two remained at home. The Sisters had not asked Rita before because they knew she was barely holding on. But with the promise of double food deliveries, Rita had lowered her eyes and said yes. She would move Nicholas to the couch; he was rarely home anyway, fishing, staying with friends at Nilkolski for weeks at a time. Timothy would move into her bedroom, a sheet hung for privacy. With a bedroom freed, she could take one child.

"This is temporary?" she asked again when Liz rose to take her teacup to the counter.

Liz nodded. She felt Rita's fear of being alone, of empty cupboards, of sons moving off under an overcast sky. "A couple of men will come to patch that roof and fix the door tomorrow. Busy Mouth can be expected within a couple of days."

"What will she do?"

"The house will be inspected. Make sure everything is scrubbed. She'll ask questions. Say what she wants to hear."

The door burst open as Liz reached for her sweater. Nicholas, urine stains around his crotch, red eyes, purple swollen cheek and blood-tinged nostrils, lurched through. Liz stepped quickly out of his way. She smelled the booze seeping from his mouth and pores. It mingled with the smell of dried blood. A shot of fear raced down her legs and rose again to burrow into her belly. He made it to the couch and flopped down, boots laying curls of mud on a bright yellow throw pillow. Liz and Rita watched as his eyes rolled back and he fell asleep.

"Can he be sent off for a while?" Liz asked.

Rita watched her son, only nineteen, already falling. "He's not a bad boy," she said, softly, slowly. "No place has been left for him, nothing to give."

Again Liz felt the looming helplessness. Everywhere she went, every home, every family, she heard the sucking noise, saw the stench uncovered as hope pulled away. So many of this generation were lost; but the children could be saved, the six-year-olds, the two-year-olds. She tried to remember what her mother had said, what she had passed down from her mother before. Her people carried the strength and courage of thousands of years in their blood and hands. It could not be easily destroyed, only polluted. If they only held on until times changed, until they could clean themselves, the old power would endure.

She watched Nicholas, sleeping like death.

"Try to get him out for the next few days."

Rita said nothing.

Would it have mattered if Rita had found Nicholas another couch on which to pass out the day Miss Holton came? Would it have mattered if Nicholas had left the bar only two hours, one hour later? Liz didn't think so. Busy Mouth would not stop until she had emptied the village of children. She would have found something else. Nicholas was convenient.

The day the four children left, Liz escaped to the church. Tears blurred her vision when she looked up at the onion-domed bell tower, the highest point in town. The perennial eagle perched there stared down at her with sharp, accusing eyes. She pushed open the double doors and waited to absorb the peace she was accustomed to feeling here. She turned to face the icon paintings stretching across the east wall. She focused on the painting of Christ ascending from the cross. The children would be on the plane by now. She thought of their small feet making big steps up the plane's stairs, their faces blank, their knees weak. Her eyes traveled along the wall. She gazed at each saint, willing them to speak to her, tell her why. She heard nothing.

She didn't cry. She screamed. She pulled at her hair and fell to her knees, rocking. Nineteen. Nineteen. The number broke against her forehead. She felt as if her skull would splinter. She thought of the others who would follow. Because there would be more. Babies born, fathers lost. More and more. She walked to the platform from which she read the Holy Scriptures each week and stood in the familiar spot, looking out at an empty room, so rich in color and the images of faith. Her eyes dried. She looked again; the room had changed. The icons, so alive, so meaningful, had flattened, losing themselves against the walls.

How long she stayed alone in the church, Liz didn't know. It was dark as she made her way to Ida's house. Ida had asked her to come. "There are things I must tell you," she had said. As she walked the dim road, Liz felt longing and fear. Even as she opened the door, a part of her knew that whatever Ida meant to speak of would change everything.

"Come and sit." Ida lit a candle on the table before her. Liz blinked at the point of light. She saw Ida and Anna watching her. Liz obeyed her mother's old friend. Two more candles were lit. They sat in silence several minutes.

"Busy Mouth will return in less than a week. We don't have much time to plan," Ida said.

Another silence followed. Liz waited. Just the word—*plan*—brought back the warmth.

Plan.

"A long story must be told," Ida said, folding her hands in her lap. "It's a story our grandmothers told our mothers, back generations. It's a story not easy to hear. Maybe you feel you already know a part."

And like generations of young women about to be brought into the circle in which they were born, Liz felt a tension growing in her body, rising from her abdomen to her heart, her throat, her mouth. The taste almost familiar, a sense she was about to remember something she once knew. She pressed the muscles of her shoulders flat where they had crept close to her ears.

"Our mothers' mothers' mothers were starving long ago and decided to step in the way of fate."

As Ida told the story, the taste grew in Liz's mouth. She found herself easing it about with her tongue, testing it in different spots until she recognized the flavor of hope. It was not a light taste, a promising taste, as hope is expected to taste. But dark and dense and powerful. This taste didn't come naturally but had been scraped raw from the living. She swallowed hard as it grew sharper against her cheeks.

That Anna didn't balk, didn't even question Ida's direction, felt at once eerie and expected. Talk never approached right and wrong, a failure that would plague Liz in the years ahead. But that night, sitting around her candlelit table, she did not notice the skips their minds made. The plan, dark with hope, rose without hindrance, a reef exposed by low tide.

As she walked up the long road to her cabana, Liz felt something brush her cheek. She smiled and looked up into the hills. The wind had found its path again.

When Busy Mouth returned, Liz was the one who invited herself and the others to her cabana. "We are coming to tea at seven. We have items to discuss." She turned away before Busy Mouth could respond, the invitation firmed by avoidance.

That evening the women journeyed to the caves and ate what they took from the Dry Ones. They did so on the shore as their grandmothers' grandmothers had, mixing the mummy flesh with oil bit by bit until it felt like lard under their fingers. Liz took the fat willingly, eagerly even. As she held the glistening dollop between her fingers, ready to place it on her tongue, she felt that in a moment all would be well, the future secured, a solution hoisted high. She could see the wall of water faltering, breaking on outer reefs, where it could do little harm. She tasted the fat, closed her eyes, and sighed.

Liz made the tea, adding the monkshood juice Ida had gathered and boiled down. Liz placed three lumps of sugar in the cup to cover the bitter taste and set it before Busy Mouth. She tried not to watch her drink but couldn't keep her eyes from flicking upward into that pink face, watching those colored lips pursing to drain dainty sips.

Miss Holton spoke of the nice family kind enough to take in the children. The big backyard with a swing and a tree house, the lovely casseroles the woman made, the school nearby with courses in almost everything.

"Lizzy," she said, leaning close, "I think it's going to get better." She reached for Liz's hand. "We're saving the children."

Liz let her hand rest under Busy Mouth's, afraid to slide away, afraid even to flinch. Bile rose in her throat, and she swallowed hard. She stared at Busy Mouth's hair because she could not look at those round, hopeful eyes.

Miss Holton touched the side of her head and said, "I don't feel well."

Then she fell off her chair and hit the vinyl floor with a saggy thump. Her left shoe popped off with the angle of her fall. *The children.* Liz felt Miss Holton's last thought seep from her brain into the floor. *The children.*

Anna washed their cups, wiped the table. Liz stepped over Miss Holton, opened the service compartment to the stove, blew out the pilot light, and turned the propane release to full-on. She returned to the table and lit one small candle. Ida and Anna exited first. Liz turned back at the door. She saw curls of auburn hair soft against the orange-yellow floor. She saw the candle flame rise and fall in the slight breeze. She shut the door and followed the short path toward the road.

Half an hour later, Miss Holton's cabana exploded. Liz heard the initial roar, then the splintering pops. She had stayed at Anna's, too tired to journey up the hillside to her cabana. When the villagers ran to the house, forming a futile bucket brigade to the beach, Liz and Anna stayed near the back. Ida didn't come. Liz listened with her new ears for hints of suspicion and heard none. Her first ears heard the simple words.

"The propane got left on, is my guess," an older man said.

"Dangerous if you don't know what you're doing."

"These white girls shouldn't be allowed to live alone out here. They get themselves in trouble."

Liz and Anna looked at each other only once as dawn slipped across the water and through the ryegrass. They were safe. The children were safe; no more would be taken.

Liz tried not to think of Busy Mouth in the weeks that followed.

When the image of her auburn hair coiled on the floor came, Liz shut her eyes tight. She thought about the chores she had that day, about the food deliveries, or the meeting with Father Ivan. When night came and she had no easy diversions, she poured herself a drink of whiskey and pulled an afghan around her shoulders. She did not talk to Ida or Anna about that night. To do so would betray something pure and old. To admit guilt would admit doubt, and not just about what she had done but about what her ancestors had started, back to the very beginnings.

Eleven weeks later, the new social worker arrived. For eleven weeks no complaints were made, no homes inspected, no children taken. Father Ivan asked the Sisters to greet the new woman Friday afternoon when her plane flew in. Anna agreed. Liz agreed. Ida refused.

Did Liz imagine a different sort of woman? A woman who gulped her tea, occasionally slopping on the saucer. A woman whose eyes didn't linger on forgotten bits of food peeking from beneath the stove. More normal in size, darker of skin. More able to see past things and into them.

The answer was yes. It was the only answer, after one has killed to make it so.

Miss Sandra Kartuse stepped off the plane and onto the gravel runway in a yellow dress with yellow sandals on a bright spring day. Her light brown hair swept back in a loose knot. Father Ivan stepped forward; introductions were made. Liz felt the first tinge of doubt as she watched Miss Kartuse let Father Ivan lead her up the gravel airstrip. She watched the long legs and big feet, the small steps.

When the Sisters met for the first time with the new social worker in the church, Ida refused to come. Miss Kartuse was less sure of herself, more tentative in her questions. Liz, sitting beside her, held on to this difference, sure it would mean everything.

Liz saw Ida enter. Saw her stride toward them. When Ida stopped in front of the new social worker, Liz felt fear ripple through her. She longed to stop Ida, whatever the old woman intended.

"Does this one mean to take our children too?" Ida stood five feet from Miss Kartuse. Ida did not look into her eyes, but above her head.

"What do you mean?" Miss Kartuse asked.

Ida did not answer. Liz felt the weight of response shift to her. After a full minute of silence, Liz spoke. "She means, will you search through our homes for unfed children and through our garbage heaps for empty bottles so that you can rip our children from us."

Miss Kartuse looked uncertain, startled, and fearful for a moment, then she smiled. A wisp of light hair fell across her cheek as she reached for Liz. She patted Liz's arm three quick times.

"Now, Lizzy," she said, soothing and sure. "You know I'm not here to take anything from your people. I'm here to help."

Ida spun and headed for the door. Liz and Anna scraped back their metal chairs and followed her wordlessly outside.

They never returned. Liz would never enter the church again. Without these three women, the Orthodox Sisterhood floundered, then collapsed.

Most people believed it was the loss of nineteen children in fifteen months that broke the Sisterhood's heart. It was this story that achieved dominance and was passed down as truth. Liz nodded from her bar stool and let them believe it was a void of sorrow that brought her there, not the unforgettable knowledge of her own evil hand. And at times, when that knowledge became too much, she would take a marker to the walls.

It was the same instinct that had led her to mark the walls in the scruffy outhouse at the Duration Village twenty years before—to confess her pain, her horror, and her anger. When she moved the marker against a paint-slick wall, for a few moments, the hidden things shifted their weight to her hands, to the ink, to the building, to the land itself, and she felt the burden lift.

For years she wrote about Busy Mouth's death. Little things that amounted to nothing. *Auburn hair. Gas-lit candles.* Ida checked the bathroom regularly and washed them off. She let Liz have her words, now as she had then, but never too many, never enough to raise questions. In the years to come, Liz would have other deaths to write about. But always they were blurred images of the first one, the one that took her innocence. And her words would become more bitter, more cryptic. *Dry flesh. Poison hands. We watch. Wasted.*

In her outhouse skirted round with ryegrass, she wrote only once,

but the words remained part of the gray wood and sweeping moun-
tainside. A year after Miss Holton's murder she sat on the edge of the
seat planks and wrote the story. She had been mostly drunk, and words
came crooked and loose. But it was all there.

*She took 19. Sent them away to white, bleached kitchens and tree
houses. She would have taken more. We did it like our mothers' mothers
said, with dead-man's fat and a plan. No one knew I let the gas on and lit
the candle. I saw her auburn hair on the floor before I shut the door. I
thought we would save some. 1968—one year past.*

in all directions

There's something unsettling about the wind. Something that lets you know things are not so described and organized. People attach words like *clean, refreshing* to the wind, but those are words striving to tame something that scares us at the edges. Try not to be so banal, so condemned. It's more like *purify, scour.* The wind doesn't fuck around.

You're standing somewhere, firmly you, with all the thoughts, feelings, markings of who you've always been. A wind rustles over your ears, pulses against skin. And suddenly everything's different, everything's possible. Each gust brings a trace of things far away and unseen, pushing over you, through you. You're powerful. You can do anything. Change smashes through an instant until nothing looks the same.

Think I'm exaggerating? Then why do we stop what we're doing when that first breath of wind brushes the path? Why do we look up, out, meeting it full in the face? Why do we stay until our cheeks feel like the surfaces of glass? A biting wind, a warm breeze, wind slung with ice, or flying leaves, or tossed-out paper plates. They whisper, they shout—"move with us, unlash, fly."

I turned from the view and walked toward the bike with the wind slamming my back.

I still won't admit that I knew where I was going. I did know I wanted off this island as much as they wanted me off. Like a pebble in my shoe, this strange quality of wanting something poked at me, an uncomfortable, unfamiliar feeling. But it made me aware of my foot, my step, my destination like I'd never been before. The old women were right—I had to leave. There was nothing here for me, nothing real to fill my hands. I balled them into fists and wondered what it would feel like to hold my own future.

The hilltop was deserted now, everyone inside. Whatever Carl had done, I had done, would be in the hands of others now. I threw my leg across the seat of my bike and gave the starter a kick.

But the old women had been wrong about one thing—they thought I'd taken from their precious mummies, eaten dead-man's fat. The thought sickened me. Not simply the idea of eating long-dead human flesh, but the awareness that I believed in it. That I believed their story from beginning to end. That I believed they had stolen lives from fate and paid with their innocence.

I still wasn't much of a rider. I had a crosswind to deal with and wasn't at all sure how best to handle it. I rode at a steady speed and tucked my head down. Occasionally a clump of dead grass or trash blew across my path. An empty beer can hit my shoulder. The plastic front fender had twisted even farther and now seemed to be directing a constant splatter of mud right at my neck. I crossed town and went east. The headlight illuminated only the strip of road right in front of me in the darker night brought by thick clouds. So I really didn't have the chance to avoid many of the potholes. I took them in with my shoulders and legs until a rattled numbness encased my body.

When the rain hit, I was nearly at the path that cut away from the ocean, cleaving between the mountains. I shut down the bike and started walking. The grass bent with wind and water, wiping itself on my jeans. My suede jacket turned dark and grew heavy. My hair turned dark too. It took in the rain and let it go again in the wind. It whipped in drenched strands across my face.

I reached the cliff face an hour later, nothing but a sodden mass of clothes and hair. I could not hesitate this time. I edged along the first narrow spot. The rock shelf was slippery, but the wind pushed me against the wall like a hand holding me safe.

When I reached the cave, I ducked right in. I suppose there was fear, but not the creepy kind, the eeekkk kind. More of the fear of possibility. I was pulling on a thread that became a string, then a rope, growing thicker until it could support nearly anything.

I fished out the silver vial from my pocket, rolling it between my fingers. I flipped the lid up in the dark and poured the teaspoon of coke on my palm. I ran my wet finger through the powder, quickly turning to paste, and rubbed it across my gums. I held the rest out to the wind, then wiped my hand on my jeans. My lighter wouldn't work at first. Rain had seeped even into my pockets.

Several flicks later, the orange glow spread from my fist. The light sprang up, casting shadows against the low ceiling. I breathed in air so sauna-hot and dry it baked my nostrils. I moved left—toward the three bodies resting just inside the entrance. The ones I'd tripped over before. The ones I knew.

I realized this was my moment of truth. This was the first and last great choice from which all others would flow. Would I do this? Would I defy the old women? They had done this terrible thing to gain the power to live, to see their people live. What power did I seek?

I knelt beside the body closest to the entrance, the one I imagined was Fenia. Skin still clung to bone around her forehead, between her eyes, and in swaths over her cheeks. I sought the power to choose, to control my own fate. The power to be fully human. And then I understood all at once the change that had replaced the woman I was with the woman I was becoming. Some part of myself mourned for that lost woman, the parties, the men, the sweet ignorance, the dizzy oblivion. But the larger part looked into the future, saw a woman who would never forget Liz's contorted face, or the pulse of Ida's low moan, or Bellie's legend, or the feel of mummy flesh in my fingers.

I reached for Fenia's exposed hand, lying on her black thigh. This hand had been tasted before. Only one finger remained. Fenia had saved this for me. It broke as easily as dry bread crusts, the bones falling like ash into my vial.

I felt elated, infused with knowledge and curiosity, and afraid, casting quick glances into shadows. I stepped out of the cave and onto the ledge. A strange sensation crept down my right arm until it formed a heat in my palm. I opened my fingers to see the now full vial. Full hands. I held them up to the storm. And, some part of me believed, to Ida, Anna, Liz, and Bellie.

"See," I shouted. "Full hands."

Sitting on a worn brown couch at the marina rec room, I kept my eyes on the ocean. I could see the white, red, and green lights of the ferry slowly churning up the bay. I lit another cigarette and waited. I had that antsy, night-before-school-starts feeling—all calm on the outside, but inside a zillion neurons firing with a million suggestions.

I had stopped by the cabana, grabbed my Crown Royal bag of money, latrinealia notebook, packed a bag of clothes, and pulled my Aleut Mona Lisa from its nail. I pried the back off the frame, rolled her up, and tucked her among soft sweaters. The books I crammed into a backpack. I tried not to think about much as I stuffed it all into my saddlebags. If I'd stopped to think, I would have lost momentum. And that's all I had going for me.

I watched the lights get closer, reach the dock. A few people walked down the gangplank. It was midnight. The rain had stopped and left itself in pools on the dock. The wind had slowed, only bothering with looser things. A Snickers wrapper dashed itself against my boot. I picked it up and threw it in a trash can.

I walked to the boat. The woman running the ticket desk was on the dock having a cigarette.

"You going?" she asked.

"Yeah. Me and a bike."

She crushed her cigarette under a shoe. I reached in my pocket and pulled out several wet twenties. She shoved a ticket at me.

I rode my bike up a metal ramp into the ferry, parked alongside a concrete wall, and walked up three flights of stairs. On the top deck the familiar sprawling lounge, upholstered in burgundy, sat behind glass. The engines rumble under my feet, and I turned to look out. The boat eased away from the dock, leaving the gangplank a broken arm jutting over blackness.

I stepped through doors and onto the back deck. The rail hit my sternum, and I leaned against it. The wind brushed its drying fingers through my hair, lightening its weight.

My fingers found the slim silver vial, crusted with turquoise, inside my pocket. Without taking it out, I flicked open the lid with my thumb and slid my pinkie inside. I circled the pad of my fingertip slowly across the top, feeling the dry flakes crumble to powder. I withdrew my finger, felt a greasy residue, and snapped the lid shut.

I thought of Liz and Ida and Bellie, of all the women who had lived and loved and died and left something of themselves on this island vanishing before me. I thought of the taboos they had broken, the price they had paid. The knowledge of their lives and the lives of their mothers and grandmothers felt as heavy as the weight of that full vial in my pocket. It's rare to feel the import of a moment as it passes. But I did then, in those moments as the dark ocean widened between me and the land. That island had been mine for only two months, but it had changed everything. They had changed everything. I was breaking my own taboo. I was going for the first time without anyone leading the way. The price, however, would not be mine to decide.

The heft of this awareness ground my boots firmly on the deck. I walked inside the lounge and ordered a whiskey sour. Did I feel different? I suppose I did. I felt a sense of my future. Not a small future like what I'm going to wear tomorrow. And nothing certain or planned. No goals materialized. I just knew they would come and they would be my own. I had only one destination. Ever-New. I would get the dog. I imagined that Cowboy had laid his big head on Dad's thigh as he died in that hot car. Dad had needed him. And now he needed me. I'd watch out for him like he'd watched out for Dad. Together we'd hunt down a future. For the first time, I knew I'd chosen something simply because it was right.

Of course, it would be dangerous. Moving with full hands always is. Like an egg race. Careful. Delicate and fragile steps. A lot of damage can be done with full hands. Shells crack, break. But nothing is wasted, even if it goes all wrong, painfully wrong. That much I was sure of. The wasting was over.

I turned from the bar and scanned the lounge. An expanse of emptiness. A place designed to hold so many people, so many conversations, plans, stories. It stretched the width of the ferry, dark windows on each side, glowing with the reflection of pushed-in chairs, clean tables. The bartender had gone in the back, leaving only the hum of the engine, fading in constancy. The emptiness welcomed the way a blank canvas or deserted stage does, calling you to come create something. I thought about the song Bellie had sung with me. She'd been wrong. It was never intended to be filled in with a word. The last word had not been left out, an intentional trick to convince some they were in the know. There was no last word. It was the blank line at the end of a test sentence. It was the question waiting for an answer. And I could pick anything. No one was watching.

I laughed and twirled around, just once, just spilling a sip's worth on the burgundy carpet.

> And she was ———
>   lying in the grass
> And she was spinning in a barroom
>   drifting through the backyard
> And she was all alone
>   taking off her dress
> And she was moving with intention
>   moving out in all directions
>   glad about it. No doubt about it
> And she was taking something with her
>   joining the world of missing persons
>   missing enough to feel all right
> Missing enough to feel ———.

I made my way, drink balanced in my right hand, to the head behind the bar. It was empty, touched only with the glare of commercial light. I didn't mean to look in the mirror, but some part of me must have caught sight of my reflection and been startled. I turned to face myself. My hair—all that blond fluff and flow—clung to my scalp in a dark straight sheath. My face was so vulnerable, so obvious without all that hair. I touched it tenderly, like a newborn baby. I looked in my own eyes and saw someone for the first time.

I pushed open the pinkish tan stall door. My glass clinked on the cool white toilet tank, ice bobbing in golden liquid.

I fished a thick black marker from my purse. Did I know what I would write as my pen touched the solid tile? Not that I could tell. I watched my hand move over inch-high letters, breath held.

Non sum ego quod fueran, my fingers finished. *I am not what I was.* And in sheer inspiration, and with my conscious mind, I added the flourish of an exclamation point, thick and bold.

missing enough

Bellie watched Nicholas flick off the boat's floodlights, his last act of a long trip. She'd seen him send the crew home, seen them walking eagerly back to their families. But he lingered, she believed, because he could not face Mary. Could not face the house so empty without the kids. Bellie had come for the children. As Ida reminded her, Nicholas was the obstacle to their return. Even childless, Bellie understood. They had always killed for the children. They were mothers first.

When the women had told her the story, her place in this chain, she felt as if she had joined hands with some power she had always sensed, just offshore, just out of reach. And now the hands of her ancestors held her ready for what would come next.

Strange, she couldn't feel Nicholas's anger any longer as he leaned against the boat rail and watched the shadows swaying across the deck. He had entered an in-between place where he was free from rage. Bellie remembered what Liz had said about him. That she had blamed him for the loss of a child to foster care many years ago, and the guilt she had felt later, knowing he was just another lost child himself. That his mother had cried for him as he sunk into drinking and fighting even as a teen. Bellie watched him light a cigarette and turn to the black water rolling between him and the bleak lights of town.

He did not hear her feet move down the dock, down the ladder, but she sensed that he felt them as she and the others descended to the boat. Bellie felt the boat whisper to him—intruder. Still it was too late. Liz drove the iron net hook across his neck just as he turned, just as he saw her. He went to his knees, pressing the blood back into his artery. It didn't come fast at first and he had time. Time to see them in the leftover dock light that swept across the deck with each swell. Time to recognize each of them.

"Bellie?" His eyes fastened on her, and she felt his hope pool in her. Everything inside her screamed stop, but her lips never moved.

The iron thudded against the side of his head, and he couldn't see her anymore. He is thinking of a dying promise, the one he has made every time. To be controlled, gentle, loving, to escape himself and become what he wishes he were.

"Bellie?" She never knew if this, his last word, had actually been spoken, or if she just felt it leaking from his mind along with the promises he has failed to keep. Nicholas died with the third blow, against his forehead.

Bellie and Anna heaved his body to the rail then rolled it overboard. It clung to the boat's wooden hull at the waterline, pressed by the waves and familiarity.

When Bellie began to shake, when she could not climb the ladder back to the dock, Liz folded the girl into her arms. She smoothed the hair back from Bellie's face, where it had stuck in the grease. "It never gets easier," she said. "Never."

The four women climbed to the dock, walked back to land, back to uncertain lives. One died six months later in her own home, wearing a housecoat and beaded slippers. One stayed sober for three months after the funeral until the body could be discreetly moved, and years later froze to death when she collapsed in the snow on her way home from the bar. One added a workshop to her store, a larger space to teach Aleut girls, and the occasional white woman, to split ryegrass and twirl it into baskets. And one found a white man to love and had two wise little girls.

And all of them watch and wait near tide pools and bar stools, in long waving grasses and a neighbor's open window, on round-weathered hills and the docks that bring newcomers. They pass from one woman to the next, always watching, always willing.

It doesn't get easier. Never easy enough to see through the fathomless gray. To live with intention, in the full force of our own will, is the most essential and the most dangerous thing we will ever do. It is the act that makes us fully human.

I suppose you want me to tell you they were heroes nonetheless; even dark or fallen heroes we can still put our hopes in. Still look to. And I don't know, all these years later, what they were, are. Monsters? Martyrs? Heroes? But I do know that their story, reaching back so long and stretching forward into uncertainty, has filled my hands.

I suppose you want me to tell you that I found Thad, after I finished college and found myself, that we married, had children. We want to believe in second chances. You would not want me to tell you they are rare. That I'm a cocktail waitress, still working between the tables. But a list of the whos, wheres, and whats would be illusions. And if I've learned one thing, it's not to trust in those. And who am I to tell you about second chances anyway.

I will tell you this much, that I found a man to love, had children, and cultivated friends. I have people around me for whom I would die or kill. I'm vigilant in watching out for them.

I will tell you I write to Bellie now and then. Our children are pen pals and send pictures to each other as if they were from distant countries. I will tell you that Liz wrote me once—a letter that stretched for pages and covered centuries. And I will tell you that in the back of a drawer in my desk I keep a turquoise-studded vial, but I have never looked inside, haven't touched it for years. And I will tell you that I have settled someplace inland, someplace where the wind sweeps across the grasses, where I stand and cleave its current like a rock.

Cowboy died four years ago. He rested his massive head on my thigh one night, a last good-bye. I still cry when I think of those early years with him, when looking at the ugly dignity of his face taught me to hope and to trust. I buried him under the rosebush by the back fence. Then I shook my son and daughter awake and led them to the yard. I kneel by the swing set on too-long grass and press my face into their hair. I take their hands in mine. "Say you will remember what I am going to tell you."

"Yes, Mom," they say.

I turn their palms up. "You hold your fate, your future right here in these hands. They are full. Do you feel it? Do you feel the weight?"

They nod, understanding only the strange urgency in my voice.

"Yes, Mom."

I look into their faces and see innocence and trust. They do not understand. But they will. And if I fail, if life and God conspire to bring them, someday, to the edges of their worlds, empty and wandering, I will tell them it is here they can be remade. I will tell them to open their hands.

I will tell them.

F or many readers the history of the Aleutians and the Aleuts portrayed in this book seems fantastical, unbelievable. I want to clarify what is fact and what developed from my imagination.

Each of the chapters focusing on the intergenerational groups of Aleut women is built upon historic events.

The conquest of the Aleutians by Russia was brutal, decimating as much as 90 percent of the Aleut population within a few decades. Many Aleut groups did become virtual slaves to Russian fur trading companies. We don't know if any groups of women broke taboos to hunt sea mammals during the Russian-Aleut War. We do know that many starved. As a mother myself, I imagined what a group of women with starving children would be willing to risk to protect their children, inventing a group of women who did venture into the male role as sea hunter.

The Aleuts did mummify their dead, often placing them in seaside caves. Archeological evidence and legends suggest some groups only mummified revered community members while other groups mummified most of their dead, even children. We do know that substances concocted from these mummies were considered to have protective and magical powers, used in sea-mammal hunting, perhaps as part of a mixture that included plant poisons. Some legends suggest the concoction was sometimes rubbed into the face and hands. A few documents suggest these concoctions were ceremonially eaten, although this evidence is debated in anthropology circles.

The journey of Hieromonk Makary is entirely true. This tragic hero, along with six Aleut leaders, traveled for years across the Bering Sea, across Siberia and back, to protest the brutal treatment of Aleuts by the Russian Emperor. They drowned within miles of their home.

The Aleut Mona Lisa is a real sketch, titled The Woman of Ounalashka. The original now hangs in the Museum of the Aleutians in Dutch Harbor.

A small pox epidemic did sweep the Aleutians in the 1830s. Although the major port communities were largely vaccinated by Russian Orthodox priests, some small villages were destroyed during the epidemic.

During the Nome Gold Rush, Dutch Harbor was a stop over for hundreds of ships waiting for the Bering ice pack to break. By all accounts, the town became a rough place each spring as hordes of would-be miners flooded in. Although there were certainly prostitutes working these visitors, the murders were entirely from my imagination.

During World War II, Japan did bomb Dutch Harbor, killing soldiers and disabling ships. The Japanese also captured and occupied two Aleutian Islands. Aleuts all over the Chain were forcibly relocated to camps in Southeast Alaska, which were notoriously unsanitary, ill equipped, and poorly managed. In writing about the Etolin Island camp, I combined the documented stories from several camps, some of which were plagued by liquor problems. The sinking of a bootlegging boat is entirely imagined. The plight of these interned Aleuts is not. Death rates at many of the camps increased by three fold, and half of the Aleuts interned never returned to the Aleutians.

The plight of the Attu Aleuts is entirely true. They were taken to Japan as prisoners of war, where half died of disease and starvation. When they returned, they found their village had been destroyed by U.S. forces.

The 1960s removal of Aleut children from Unalaska is true. A social worker removed nineteen children in eighteen months, nearly emptying the village of children. The Sisterhood was a real group of women who tried to stop the exodus, failed, and disbanded shortly thereafter. The murder of this social worker is entirely from my imagination.

The Aleutians and the Aleut people are fascinating. I invite you to read more from some of my favorite nonfiction resources.

Prehistory
Lost World by Tom Koppel
Constant Battles: Why We Fight by Steven A. LeBlanc
Ancient Men of the Arctic by Louis Giddings

Conquest
Russian America: The Great Alaskan Venture 1741–1867 by Hector Chevigny

World War II and Evacuation
When the Wind Was a River: Aleut Evacuation in World War II by Dean Kohlhoff
The Thousand Mile War: World War II in Alaska and the Aleutians by Brian Garfield
Koga's Zero: The Fighter That Changed World War II by Jim Rearden
Tatiana (fiction) by Dorothy M. Jones

Other
Moments Rightly Placed: An Aleutian Memoir by Ray Hudson
Seven Words for Wind: Essays and Field Notes from Alaska's Pribilof Islands by Sumner MacLeish